BETWEEN
TWO FIRES

······································

Pamela Edgar

ORION

An Orion paperback
First published in Great Britain by Orion in 1994
This paperback edition published in 1994 by Orion Books Ltd,
Orion House, 5 Upper St Martin's Lane, London WC2H 9EA

A CIP catalogue record for this book is available from the
British Library.

ISBN: 1 85797 400 X

Printed in England by Clays Ltd, St Ives plc

To my husband, Michael,
my sons, David, Peter and Chris,
my in-laws, Dorothy and Bill,
and in memory of my beloved father,
Ferdy

PART ONE

1899–1902

I

Arabella braced herself against the damp rail of the *Sandringham Castle*. The polished brass barrel of the telescope in her hands was directed towards the heavy mist that rose like ghostly shapes from the waters of the Indian Ocean, still some way off Durban. She could see nothing as the grey-white blanket swirled around the smokestacks rising high above the deserted decks; the ship seemed to steam slowly in a dead world full of eerie stillness.

The silence was unexpectedly broken by a figure that suddenly deposited itself beside her at the rail.

'A very good morning to you, Miss Allen,' a cheerful Australian voice drawled. 'You're up bright and early.'

After a moment's surprise, Arabella lowered the telescope as Archie Mungo, a lanky young man, joined her. She shivered, drawing the long dark travelling cloak tighter around her. 'I couldn't stay below in steerage a minute longer,' she told him. She tried again to make out shapes but the enveloping grey-whiteness was almost total. 'I do wish the fog would lift.'

'These mists disappear very quickly when the sun gets up.' Archie looked at her, his slate-coloured eyes alive with interest in a prematurely lined face. 'London seems so far away here, where out there war clouds gather fast across the border between Natal and the Transvaal.'

Arabella lifted her small determined chin. 'I cannot see the Boer farmers being foolish enough to wage war against the mightiest Empire in the world, Mr Mungo, and one with almost inexhaustible resources.' She gave him a sudden penetrating look from her luminous green eyes, and he cleared his throat.

'Not bloody likely, if you'll excuse the expression, Miss Allen. It's my view that if the British Government has made up its mind to force the issue against its Liberal Opposition, the Transvaalers are also spoiling for a fight. There's plenty of evidence that the young bloods up there are more than ready to go to war.'

The ship suddenly lurched, heaving to on the invisible waves and almost making Arabella lose her balance. Archie put out a hand to steady her. In the muffled quietness, she stiffly drew away from him.

'I still believe there won't be war, Mr Mungo,' she said loftily.

Archie looked thoughtful for a second, flicking back a lock of sandy hair from his furrowed forehead. 'That country over there is no place for a lady alone, Miss Allen. It could get very nasty.'

'You know very well, Mr Mungo, that I have given up my nursing post in England for an indefinite period, and that I'm on a long overdue holiday to visit my cousin Rosamunde and her husband, Lord Stradcombe.' She bit her lip in annoyance as Archie Mungo's mouth curled in a slight smile, then turned her face away to stare once more into the mist.

It was a strikingly proud face. Though her features clashed with the prevailing ideal of a rosebud pout and dimples, her real beauty lay beneath the surface. Sweetness and determination shone through her eyes, and the fact that she was one of those delightful people who can laugh at themselves was not lost on Archie Mungo, although Arabella could also be stubborn and unrelenting if she thought she was right about something.

He had tried to become more intimately friendly with her, but she had cleverly deflected all his amorous advances. His lively eyes took in the dark travelling cloak moulding her small body, and the grey toque hiding most of her light-brown hair, then, biting back his disappointment at not breaking down her defences, he leaned against the rail with his back to the sea.

'I had hoped that I may call on you at your cousin's farm. It would be interesting to talk with Lord Stradcombe, especially as he's friends with all the big nobs involved in the Jameson Raid some years back – Mr Cecil Rhodes and Sir Alfred Milner for starters. I believe he served in the Eastern Sudan under Sir Kitchener when he was Governor-General there.' Archie screwed up his eyes, trying to see through the mist. 'I met him once – Kitchener. The coldest bastard I've ever set eyes on.'

Arabella's eyes appraised him, then she lowered her lashes, faintly blushing under his close scrutiny. 'You've done your homework well, Mr Mungo, but I don't think that either Lord Stradcombe or my cousin will be willing to expose themselves to a reporter.'

A faint grin curved his lips, then it vanished. 'I suppose not, after their scandalous elopement seven years ago, eh? My paper ran a full story at the time – only daughter and heiress of well-known bill-broker and Member of Parliament runs away with Viscount and ex-cavalry officer after his father commits suicide and leaves his only son a heap of mounting debts. Many believe he married your cousin for her inheritance and she for his title –'

'That's not true!' Arabella swung around. 'Ben loved my cousin and as for Rosamunde, I've never seen anyone so in love as she was with him. Money and a title had nothing to do with it!' A strange look came over her face, and her lips tightened until the lovely softness of her mouth was a grim line. 'It was newspapers such as yours which spread those ugly, cruel rumours and I don't want to talk about it any more.' Her cheeks were flaming and there was a brightness in her eyes that spoke of a certain defiant anger.

'I don't make the news, Miss Allen, I only write about it.' Archie sighed, cursing himself for his clumsiness.

Just then, the eerie cries of gulls shot through the air, as they dived around the smokestacks high above, and with relief, Arabella knew that land was fast approaching.

Her thoughts turned to Rosamunde's last letter. There was nothing in it she could put her finger on exactly, but it was there all the same ... a desperate plea, somewhere in those pages about Suncrest Farm and her two small children, Luke and Cynthia. And finally, in the last paragraph, Rosamunde had practically begged Arabella to visit them. Thus had events in South Africa touched Arabella's well-ordered days, dedicated to nursing at St Albans Hospital, and reached out to her – events she knew were going to change the course of her life.

There was a heavy swell, and as the ship heaved to, the waves parted by the bows rushed past in a flurry of foam. Arabella could discern the faint high shape of the blue bluffs to the south of Durban entrance looming up out of the thick grey haze, and then a tongue of land jutting into the sea like a bloated whale. A moment later, it vanished; passing vaporous clouds obscured everything, and she felt the rail under her fingers wet and slimy. She was conscious of Archie Mungo at her side, but he no longer mattered as her excitement at seeing Rosamunde and Ben after seven long years began to grow.

A tall lighthouse on the topmost point, at first half-concealed, loomed like some sinister ghostly shape, until the whole towering bulk lifted itself into the lightening sky. A small craft moved out from the port, a yellow light bobbing above it. It was a lighter, making for the ship surrounded by shrieking and wheeling seagulls.

Another low-humped bluff, once the home of black-green mangrove forests and herds of elephant, made a limpid backdrop, glowing luminously pale as the last of the mist vanished with startling rapidity, and now the smoke from the funnel, black against the grey sky, was blown ahead over the bows.

Arabella put up the telescope again, and scanned the approaching coastline. Her heart raced as the sun pushed through a welter of fiery clouds and the sea caught its glow on its wide, heaving expanse. The

5

outline of the pretty subtropical port took on a vivid texture, and further down the coast, a row of palm trees and lush vegetation made a glorious arch along the skyline. So near and yet so far. Intense excitement, tempered with growing impatience, surged through her as she lowered the telescope.

2

Under the bright September sky, filled with billowing cumulus clouds, Arabella stood erect and alone on the quayside, her luggage piled up around her. She was bitterly disappointed that neither Rosamunde nor Ben were there to meet her. She did not like crowds, and had forced her way back from the edge of the wharf as people swarmed, pushing past her. The ringing of the *Sandringham Castle*'s bells had long since ceased, and the ship's prow was motionless as she stood at anchor in the roadstead. Now, surrounded by the sweet-sourness of tarred ropes, salt-steeped timbers and the canvas of many different cargoes, Arabella wondered if she should have dissuaded a disappointed Archie from staying with her.

She looked about anxiously. To her right, a railway line ran past warehouses where bush and sandhills had once been, and horse-drawn trams were lined up, operating via several routes into the town. A row of whitewashed houses snaked away, not far from a cluster of dilapidated hovels, where swarthy Indian and black children played in the dust.

It was a bustling, oriental-looking scene, filled with the scent and stink of Africa. The wharves were thronged with people – white colonials, turbanned Indians carrying baskets of fruit and vegetables, wizened black men offering monkeys' paws and pots of hippopotamus fat, beggars, Indian priests, and lined up further back, rickshaws – two-wheeled vehicles with upholstered seats and movable hoods drawn by large Zulu men who had possibly fought the British themselves some years back. Small grey vervet monkeys ran along the ground looking for food, as gulls dived for fish in the blue sea flecked with the white sparkle of dancing spraylets.

And yet, beneath all this surface bustle and normality, there loomed the sinister presence of war. Gangs of Zulu men scurried about, in the midst of the roar of soldiers' voices crossing one another in commands and oaths, and the gun-thunder of the wheels of a long string of carts and wagons assembling along the quayside. A guard was drawn up in review order not far away, and a military band played in the shade of

7

a warehouse. Several men-of-war were anchored in the roadstead, obscenely riding the sparkling swells, transforming its life and beauty into something ominous. Troops were pouring into an armoured train somewhere down the tracks, and from a transport ship, slings from derrick arms were lowering nets filled with soldiers' kitbags, boxes and bales of supplies, and bundles of military gear.

Wondering what to do next, Arabella sat down on the worn portmanteau with its tarnished, brass-headed nails, that had once belonged to her late father. It was well past noon and beside her, the very familiarity of her belongings seemed to accentuate the strangeness of this new environment. The umbrella, the bandbox with its London label, the floral carpetbag ... all were reminders of that world she had left behind. Her thoughts turned nostalgically to the ten years she had lived with Rosamunde and her uncle and aunt in Allenbury Manor, a majestic old Georgian house set in its own grounds, overlooking Somerton village in Suffolk. A small part of a lifetime, but a memory much alive to her as she watched the crowds come and go.

Restlessly she rose and paced up and down not far from her luggage. Could they have been taken ill? Had they had an accident? For a split second her courage failed her and she wanted to leave on the first ship returning to England, back to the comforting presence of her Aunt Matty in the cosy cottage in Heather Lane on the outskirts of London.

Just then, a ragged, dirty black child darted across the track close by, chasing a small grey monkey and headed straight into the path of a stationery horse and cart. Arabella did not see what happened, but the movement must have frightened the stallion, for it reared up on its hind legs and blew down its nose, whinnying furiously. There was a clatter as the animal, with a great surge of energy, plunged across the track, breaking its tether in one violent, jerking bound. It reared before the frightened child, then changed direction, plunging right into Arabella's path, who was caught off-guard. White-faced, she came to life and jerked away from the dangerous hooves just in time, but could not save herself from falling to the ground, her luggage spilling all around her.

There was a swirling of noise, the heat seemed suddenly intense and she heard a shout lash the air. There were loud cries and the animal swerved violently. She thought she caught a glimpse of a familiar face, but could not be sure. When she looked again, someone had stepped forward and grabbed the horse's reins, skilfully pulling it to a halt.

Arabella's view was blocked by a very tall lean man wearing the black cassock and cincture of a priest, who helped her to her feet. The spotless white collar around his neck shone in the bright sunlight, hurting her eyes.

'Are you all right, my child? You look so pale.' The soft Irish voice was concerned. She looked up into a long, angular face capped with a head of shining, prematurely silver hair, for he was still quite a young man. There were glasses on the tip of his nose which he pushed back into position as he straightened up. 'How do you feel? You could have had a nasty accident.'

Arabella smiled tremulously. 'I'm all right, Father, just a little shaken.' Her voice wobbled ever so slightly, but before she could say any more, the priest had led her back to her overturned luggage, which two men were stacking neatly.

'Will someone be fetching you, child? You should not be here without an escort.' He took off his glasses to clean them for a second before replacing them on his nose, and she saw that his eyes were a penetrating, pale blue. 'I am Father Sebastian, soon to leave my duties here in Durban for those in Ladysmith. Can I take you into town where we can make arrangements to have you fetched?'

Her gaze flew about the wharves in desperate pursuit of someone familiar. 'I am Arabella Allen, Father. I travelled in the *Sandringham Castle* from London to visit my cousin and her husband, Lord and Lady Stradcombe, who live near Ladysmith at Suncrest Farm. Please don't put yourself out on my account. I feel sure they will come for me.'

Father Sebastian studied her closely. 'Lord Stradcombe was here only a moment ago, my dear – we must find him in this crush. I am acquainted with him and his wife. He's well-known in the racing world, with one of the finest stud farms in the whole of Natal, and being an Irishman, I appreciate his knowledge of good horseflesh.' A faint smile crossed his lips, then disappeared. 'I shall wait with you until Lord Stradcombe appears, Miss Allen. You must not be left alone, especially when a war with the Boers is closing in on us every day, and spies are everywhere in town.'

Arabella looked up at him, her back straight and determined, compensating for her lack of inches. 'I have been told nothing else since I boarded the ship. Surely it can't be that serious?'

'My dear Miss Allen – have you not heard? British troops are moving up to the western borders of the Boer-ruled Transvaal and the Orange Free State, and others are on their way from Britain, while large Boer forces are mobilising on the various frontiers. Every week there has been news that committees and deputations from the Cape Colony have travelled up to make last attempts to avert the catastrophe of war, but so far, they have not succeeded.'

9

Before she could reply, someone was addressing Father Sebastian in a lazy, cultured voice that set her heart racing. Memories from the past rose sharply, memories that had brought colour and excitement into a lonely and cheerless young life . . .

'Arabella, is it really you? Arabella Allen, the little waif who stayed at Allenbury Manor on the cold charity of wicked old Mildred Allen?'

Benjamin Saville was standing quite still before her, looking incredibly dashing in the khaki-green uniform of a Captain. He doffed a brown slouch hat, swept up at one side, which emphasised his tan and his dark, almost gypsy-black hair. 'Captain Saville of the newly formed Imperial Light Horse at your service, ma'am.'

All anxiety dissipated as she looked into the fine-featured face revealing strong white teeth below a close-clipped black moustache.

'You shouldn't be here, you know,' he reproved her gently. 'I sent you a letter some weeks ago, explaining about the explosive situation and suggesting you delay your trip until matters are resolved – which they should be by Christmas, all going well – but as we never heard from you, I took the chance and came to meet the ship. I see you have already made the acquaintance of Father Sebastian – the very devil at the races.' He chuckled with the priest, whose pale eyes twinkled with amusement.

Arabella cleared her throat, looking from one to the other. 'I had to come, Ben. I had no idea that things were so bad. Thank you for saving my life! It was you who handled that horse so well, wasn't it? I remember—' She stopped abruptly as he smiled in a faintly teasing manner, and tried to stop the sudden racing of her heart.

The sun threaded flecks of light through his dark hair and it glinted on the gold buttons on his jacket as he moved. His face was more lined, and there were now faint creases at the sides of his deep-seated grey eyes as he screwed them up against the light, but he still emanated that romantic, masculine appeal she remembered so well as a skinny, gauche fifteen-year-old when Rosamunde had first drawn Ben into their lives, after her 'Coming Out' season in London.

Father Sebastian excused himself, and disappeared as she heard Ben say, 'How you have changed, Arabella. Do you know, I had quite forgotten just how *petite* you are.' Aware suddenly of the way he was staring at her under arched black brows, she blushed. 'But Ben, why are you back in uniform? You left the army years ago,' she managed to ask, frowning as other soldiers shouldered their way past.

He pursed his lips. 'I've recently joined a colonial mounted corps to knock the hell out of the Boers, dear girl, financed by the gold magnates Jacob Brandauer and Wernher Beit.' His white teeth gleamed as his grey eyes laughed down at her. 'We are led, I hasten to add, by the same men who have been the political leaders of the Witwatersrand ever since the Jameson Raid.'

Clammy perspiration, starting under her armpits, began to creep down her ribs. It could not be true! Surely there would not be a war, not for years – never, if the Liberal Opposition in London had its way.

Ben turned to a stocky, middle-aged man dressed in loud tweeds and a jaunty dark coat embellished with a bright red bow tie. 'Let me introduce Mr Robbie MacPherson, our farm manager. Robbie and I go back a long way – to Kitchener and the Sudan. Robbie, may I introduce Miss Arabella Allen?'

Robbie drew off his bowler hat. 'How do you do, Miss Allen. So you're the wee lass I've been hearing so much about for weeks.' His voice boomed out in a full-bodied Scots accent which filled her with pleasant nostalgia for home. 'I must apologise for us being a bit on the late side, but we had a spot of bother with the brougham.' He glanced quickly at Ben, and for a moment Arabella suspected a conspiracy between the two men, but dismissed this thought as utterly ridiculous.

'May I ask why you are not also in uniform, Mr MacPherson?'

'Ach, lassie, I've really no time for such goings-on as war. The Sudan campaigns finished me completely. What is the point, I ask you? And if there is a war, it will be an unjust one – to crush Boer independence. Sorry, Ben, I know what you think of that!' He grinned and patted Ben on the shoulder in a comradely fashion.

Ben smiled ironically, replacing his hat on his head. 'Robbie is guilty of being a confounded Liberal, Arabella. He's hoping they'll prevail upon good old Queen Vic and the Tories not to go to war, even at the last minute. But Robbie and his lot are quite unrealistic. The Boers are trying to stem the tide of industrial progress, and it won't work. Well, come on, let's be off from this stinkingly hot place, and go to the Ocean Tea Rooms for light refreshment. The train to Ladysmith doesn't leave for another three hours.' Ben held out his arm to her, and Arabella took it, as if it was the most natural thing in the world.

Robbie vanished, moving through the crowds to find Sinjan, their Zulu servant, who would collect her baggage. Arabella found her thoughts wandering uncomfortably, partly because her heart was beating as painfully as a schoolgirl's, and partly because she was increasingly aware of the military personnel and equipment along the quayside.

Ben smiled as they slowly made their way towards the carriages. He stopped as someone bumped against them. 'I still can't believe the transformation,' he complimented her.

There was an awkward pause, and they started walking again. As always in the past, she was aware of an intriguing enigma behind the masculine personality confronting her. Ben brought back so many heroic and dashing memories – of the brave young cavalry officer riding against the enemy in glorious charges in the desert, the elegant hero in evening dress trying to teach her to dance in the schoolroom at Allenbury Manor while he waited for Rosamunde before a supper-dance at some wealthy mansion . . .

'How is Rosamunde, Ben? I expected her to come with you.'

He hesitated for a moment. 'Rosamunde sends her apologies for not being here, Arabella. Young Cynthia has a fever – it's nothing serious, but your cousin tends to get over-emotional about such matters. She sends her love and waits for you at the farm.' His tone was casual, but his fingers were tightly curled round the ebony-topped cane which he carried in one hand. The alertness had gone from his eyes, as if a veil had been pulled over his thoughts.

'At the farm?' Arabella repeated. 'You came all the way here with Robbie to meet me?'

He smiled wryly. 'Afraid so, dear girl. Now you're stuck with just the two of us all the long miles back. But don't worry, we had a spot of business to attend to in Durban, so we killed two birds with one stone, so to speak.'

She was concerned about his daughter. 'I hope little Cynthia is not too ill? Fevers can be dangerous . . .'

'It's only a slight fever, but Rosamunde behaves as if it's a terminal disease. Ah, here is Robbie with Sinjan and the bags, and there's the brougham.'

The crowd milling about in the hot sunshine was still so large that it required a certain amount of manoeuvring from Ben and Robbie, and Sinjan, a strong young Zulu, to escort her through with the baggage. Arabella heard Ben's name spoken and greetings followed as he acknowledged first one person, and then another. He did not pause as his acquaintances evidently expected, but swiftly piloted her out of the quayside area where they stood while the tramcars pulled away, and wagons rolled forward slowly, ready to be loaded with military gear. The band was still playing, as Zulus swarmed all over the army piles under orders from a ruddy-complexioned Ordnance sergeant. Several British officers were standing to one side, watching the proceedings, and Arabella was aware of speculative eyes following Ben's figure. She caught the glances directed at him – glances that curiously included her. One woman turned to her, her eye holding such a glint of malice and amusement that Arabella instinctively drew herself up. Somehow, her presence with her cousin's husband had been distorted into something distinctly unsavoury.

And then she felt a hot rush of blood creeping into her cheeks at the way two men nearby stared at her in cool appraisal. But it was the younger one who caught her full attention. She had to admit that he had a certain arrogant handsomeness, but she found no difficulty in disliking his whole bearing. He had a look of bombastic self-confidence; his eyes, staring at her beneath heavy lids, were brazen and crafty. His mouth was thin-lipped, and to her, it sneered.

The eyes, in a face distorted suddenly with lust, swept over her motionless body, and she was immediately made aware of the neat austerity of her dress, and the genteel modesty of her luggage. She froze for an instant, as the man's dark eyes locked on to hers and forced her gaze away. As she moved on, there was a light tap on her shoulder and, annoyed, she turned to stare right into his repulsively sensual face.

'I don't believe we have met,' he said, in a deceptively soft Irish voice. He gave her a lewd glance from the corner of his eyes. 'Sean O'Shea from Dublin. You and I must get t' know each other – I think we'd go well together.'

Arabella, unable to bear the insulting boldness of his attitude, said with fierce defiance: 'I have no desire to get to know you. Now please go away.' His lustful face, became smooth again, his eyes now cold and hostile. ''Tis time you bloody Saxons learned good manners. In this coming war we'll help the Boers to grind you into the dust where you belong so you'll never rise again.'

As he turned his back on her, Ben sprang forward and grabbed his shoulder. 'Oh no you don't, my lad! You don't talk to a lady in that manner. Who do you think you are?'

'*Lady!* You don't say ...' The Irishman caught the meaning in Ben's eyes, his own narrowing as they swiftly travelled over the khaki uniform.

Ben's hand swung back and then stopped, his gaze not moving from Sean O'Shea's face. 'If you want a fight, we'll get it over with right here and now.'

Sean O'Shea's fingers bunched momentarily into fists, then he raised a taunting arm above his head in salute. 'No, we'll have that fight on the battlefield – *sir*.'

Ben moved forward angrily, but Robbie stepped between them and firmly pulled him back. 'Ben, he's not worth the trouble. Come away, man – let the silly ass be.'

Hearing the voice, the Irishman pulled a disgusted face. 'Go away, you gutless Scots dung-fly! You're as bad as the worst Saxon bastard.'

Arabella watched motionless, her whole body trembling with alarm. 'Ben, Robbie's right. Let's go!'

A small crowd now shoved and heaved around them, jostling closer. Ben looked up, a film of hate across his eyes, then he turned and walked towards her, slipping his arm protectively through hers again.

'I hate those cocky bastards, Arabella,' he murmured furiously under his breath, 'always causing trouble. But soon their arrogance will be a memory! If that's the kind of support Kruger has on his side, God help him!'

Arabella watched his face, her eyes puckered with acute anxiety. She had never known him like this, so full of hate and bitterness. She thought dismally of Rosamunde. What had happened to change him so much?

3

Arabella braced herself for the moment of departure, settling herself on the hard, narrow bench of the carriage. Ben had booked a fairly comfortable compartment in which the seats could be converted into beds by the addition of a rug and pillow.

The train was crowded with soldiers travelling north, and amidst the clash of couplings and hiss of steam, Arabella watched the latecomers pushing past each other, heaving haversacks on their backs. With a thunderous chugging, the train slowly steamed out into the light of the dying day. Even the dirty pane of glass could not hide the luxuriant, lazy ambience of Durban, which had started as an ivory trading post and had finally, and grudgingly, been wrested from both the Zulus and the Voortrekkers to become a British colony.

The strong scent of old Murray pine permeated the air; in the distance, Muslim mosques and Hindu temples rose into the bloody glory of the African sunset. Great showers of brightly coloured flowers tumbled from white pillars surrounding gleaming double-storeyed residences set amidst sweeping emerald lawns, flamboyant trees and ilala palms. The ochre-red earth pushed up lush vegetation alongside the narrow-gauge line, where tiny monkeys darted through the low-hanging trees on either side. The train chugged along the sharp curves of ancient shadowy hills covered with broad, wind-frayed fronds of miles of bananas, broken by occasional patches of mealies, pineapples and pawpaws; it steamed around the weird and fantastical shapes of more hills convoluting their way inland. Looking out of the window as they rounded a long curve, Arabella could see the two lines winding ahead with a sense of sinuous movement like a couple of grass snakes side by side.

All this would have filled her with a dreamy pleasure, but for the presence of the military, which kept her mind focused on the fact that they were travelling ever closer to an ominous climax, one that seemed to be rumbling nearer with every new mile of track.

Ben had still not referred to Rosamunde, and every time Arabella mentioned her cousin's name, she could feel an intangible withdrawal on his part. Finally, she joined him and Robbie and a young lieutenant in the new type of whist called bridge, which, under Ben's instruction, she quickly began to enjoy.

The sky rapidly darkened as the train crossed the ridge of hills guarding the interior from the sea. The darkening shapes of smaller hills wound gently into long, sweeping valleys as they made their way towards the capital city of the colony, Pietermaritzburg. Sounds of loud revelry floated down the corridor, and Arabella dozed fitfully, time and again awakened by a burst of hoarse laughter from other compartments, male voices in the corridor outside, and the sound of heavy boots continually tramping up and down. She shivered suddenly and pulled her cloak tightly across her chest, watching the moon rising and a silver haze spread over the land, where each bush stood in a thin shadow. The chugging of the train and rattle of the windows drowned all other sounds for a while, as Ben and Robbie played cards under the light of a storm lantern that swayed precariously above their heads. As she shivered again, she caught Ben's eye.

With instant concern, he said, 'Do you want my rug, Arabella? It'll keep out the chill.'

She shook her head, thinking how fortunate Rosamunde was to have such a charming and gallant husband. She remembered how he had sprung to her defence against that odious Irishman, Sean O'Shea. Men like Ben were so rare.

He was smiling at her now, as he took his briar pipe from his pocket. 'Do you mind if I smoke?'

She shook her head again, not realising how remarkably arresting her face was, as he cocked an eyebrow at her.

'I remember those maths and science books you secretly pored over back at Allenbury Manor, dear girl. You hid them well from your Aunt Mildred, eh? Wherever did you get them?'

Arabella smiled at the memory of the hours spent learning those subjects, forbidden to girls because they were unfeminine. She thought of how much she had loved their pure objectivity and logic, and of how she had hungered to learn more. 'From that boy we called Porky Pig,' she giggled, 'in the village. They were his father's. Aunt Mildred would've been furious if she'd ever found out!'

'But I did.' He gazed at her as she sat propped up near the window, her straight hair brushed back and upwards into a gentle knot. The plain, awkward girl he had teased so long ago was gone. She now had a radiance, a kind of aura which was difficult to dismiss.

She laughed. 'And so did Rosamunde, though she swore never to tell. I remember that day in the schoolroom when you two burst in on me, and you took the books away and held them, high above your head, and swore you would tell Aunt Mildred unless –' She stopped in sudden confusion, and quickly lowered her lashes.

'Unless what?' A long moment passed as his gaze probed the green translucent depths of her eyes; then he gave a faint smile. 'It can't be all that terrible.'

She cursed herself for being so childish. 'Unless I let you kiss me – which you did, there and then,' she said with a deliberate lightness that belied the sudden racing of her heart.

He threw back his dark head and laughed. 'Was that all? Oh Arabella, I had quite forgotten. What an opportunistic scoundrel you must have thought me!'

But she had not forgotten. She would never forget that first cousinly kiss, and the touch of his lips against hers, nor how she had tried to conceal her embarrassment and pleasure before him and her giggling cousin afterwards. She had stored away that memory in the deep recesses of her mind, alongside the fragments of love that had come her way, and which she had pieced together to make a satisfactory life around herself, cocooned by her dreams.

She watched him surreptitiously as he became immersed once more in the game with Robbie, and noted how his face appeared to have fallen into heavy, listless lines. All about him there hovered some indefinable tension. The light from the lantern made him seem unnaturally pale and strained beneath his dark tan. Suddenly she wondered what it would be like to be married – a thought she had discarded long ago, being neither beautiful nor wealthy, and not having a mother who would help her find a suitable husband. She wondered wistfully what it would be like, to be married to a man like Ben ...

After clattering through miles of wild green hills and deep valleys into more mountainous areas, then past one little town after another, in the land where the mighty Zulu warrior Shaka once strode and where, more recently, Chief Cetshwayo had bitterly watched the British massacre his army in the final battle of a war he had been forced to fight ... the train finally arrived at its destination.

Ladysmith was a scattered town of dusty streets lined with syringa trees and even taller Australian gums – streets wide enough so that the Boer wagon with its full team of oxen could turn round in them. Houses with corrugated-iron roofs and open verandahs supported by slender latticed pillars, spread out in the valley, enclosed by an amphitheatre of a double ring of hills, the inner ring whitened by herds of Angora goats.

Arabella stood, shielding her eyes from the brightness. She had been dismayed to see a large military camp outside Ladysmith, with troops exercising in straight lines, and now it was obvious that something was astir around the town. In the main street, an army mule wagon, in a team of ten, was being driven by shouting brown men, and there were groups of soldiers dotted here and there, and the buzz of hundreds of strange voices.

A gang of soldiers was swinging out one of the six-piece field guns which had arrived on the train, and there was a pile of ammunition building up beside it. Several lines of long-horned, scraggy black bullocks clogged the one macadamised main street with its attractive town hall and distinctive square-shaped clock tower, and on the edges of the sky, etched in deep blue, rose the inner ring of serrated hills, in varying heights above the town.

It had been all very well, back in England and even on the ship, Arabella thought, to speak glibly of the unlikelihood of war, but here, surrounded by its evidence, was a vastly different experience.

Ben seemed unmoved as he rode on a dappled grey stallion sent from his own stables, alongside the wagon which was surrounded by Zulus from Suncrest Farm. The party advanced over the rolling veld, where occasionally from a reedy watercourse a small brown buck bounded out and then disappeared, and small black widow birds with long streaming tails rose complaining from the trees, while underfoot, large brown dungbeetles energetically rolled small balls of earth. And Robbie nonchalantly whistled the English marching air, *The Lincolnshire Poacher*, sitting up on the driver's seat beside Arabella, without a care in the world. Arabella, however, had a sudden feeling of apprehension. She wondered briefly if it was a premonition ...

The wagon seemed to crawl for a long time through the blackness of the night, impenetrable in the feeble glimmer of its only lamp. Arabella could sense a new underlying urgency in Ben to get to the farm, and soon she became aware of the darkness becoming light, strengthening into brilliance which flooded the wagon. And there stood Rosamunde, a servant behind her, with lamps held high.

Her cousin's face was wreathed in smiles, and Arabella climbed down, hugging her as if she was the strongest anchor in a new bewildering world.

Rosamunde, with sisterly beneficence, loosened her embrace enough to examine her closely. 'Oh Bella, how you *have* changed! You'll never know just how much I've lived for this moment. Now come on in, I've had the best guestroom prepared for you.'

Arabella was very much aware of how tall her cousin was, how extraordinary her good looks, the golden hair taken back and worn

18

with the curly fringe made so fashionable by Princess Mary of Teck. She noticed that the slanting hazel eyes were still restless with the stubborn wilfulness and unspoken passion she remembered. She saw with pleasure the exquisite small enamelled watch she had given Rosamunde as a secret wedding gift before her elopement, which she now wore on a chain around the neck of her cream shantung silk blouse. Then she smiled widely, overwhelmed by Rosamunde's natural spontaneity, and the warmth of her welcome.

At once, the past anxieties as to what she might find, vanished into the darkness as her cousin led her out of the garden, full of shadows, and into the spacious, double-storeyed house. She was immediately taken upstairs to meet the children – five-year-old Luke and his three-year-old sister Cynthia. Their nursery was not far from the attractive guestroom set aside for her.

Wonderingly, two pairs of eyes scrutinised this new person. Luke, a mischievous, dark-haired little boy, leaned forward in his bed, earnestly focusing on her, as if he was not sure about this newcomer in his life, but after she had presented him and Cynthia with a box of Aunt Matty's homemade butter toffee, he thawed rapidly, and they soon became friends. Cynthia, apparently now fully recovered from the fever, possessed the deepest of dimples and wheat-blonde hair; she held out her chubby arms to Arabella with complete and simple acceptance.

Later, a Zulu maid brought a tray of cold chicken and a glass of claret to Arabella's room while other servants carried a galvanised hip bath into the kitchen downstairs. There was great activity as they brought water for the bath in an enormous four-gallon paraffin tin, and not long afterwards, Arabella was enjoying the first wonderfully warm bath in days, in the privacy of the closed, silent room, lit by a few flickering candles.

Rosamunde came and sat down in her room afterwards. She was wearing a pale-lilac peignoir that outlined her rounded breasts, which still appeared to be in good shape even after bearing four children, two stillborn, in quick succession. Animatedly, she asked about her cousin's trip.

Arabella smiled, and told her the more cheerful highlights, then she said, 'There were soldiers on the train, Rose – and the large military camp outside Ladysmith is bustling with activity.' She paused, biting her lip. 'Ben is sure that war will break soon.'

Rosamunde frowned, as if she was hearing something unwelcome. 'How can it? The Boers wouldn't dare to fight us, and besides, that camp outside Ladysmith has been there for a year already.'

'I know, Rose – I thought they wouldn't dare fight us only days ago, but now that I've seen the reality for myself, it seems that there's every possibility of it happening.'

'Well, it won't happen yet, and I've arranged the most special dinner party for you on Saturday night. I believe you've already met one of our guests – Father Sebastian. Benjamin tried to get me to change my mind, especially at such an uncertain time, but I just went ahead anyway. You'll love it, Belle, even though I know you were never a party person, always preferring your dull books.' Rosamunde grinned. 'You were the best pupil every year at that starchy old girls' school in Bury St Edmunds. God knows why Aunt Matty persuaded your father to send you there. It must have cost him a fortune, which he certainly never had! I think it's all so degrading for a girl.' She pulled such a comical face that Arabella was forced to laugh with her.

'Oh Bella, I'm so glad you didn't get to take that entrance examination to Oxford University to become a doctor, of all things! I thought you were mad then, and I still do. Fancy a woman wanting to be so unfeminine! In my opinion, Uncle Horace fell ill just in time, forcing you to leave Allenbury Manor and nurse him before he died. It was he who saved you from a dreadful life.'

Arabella hid the intense hurt that knifed through her chest at the mention of university, and the bursary she had been forced to give up. Rosamunde would never understand. She had always had everything – good looks, friends, money ... and now she was married with two lovely children. She had always been fussed and petted, and although she was two years older than herself, Arabella at twenty-two suddenly felt much older.

'How was Benjamin?' Rosamunde asked suddenly, a watchful expression on her beautiful face. 'He's always such a charmer, and I know how much you idolised him back in England before we eloped.'

Arabella became very still, disturbed by the unfamiliar look in Rosamunde's eyes. Then she replied mischievously. 'He was as courteous as ever, my dear Rose – and I think the days of devoted slave for me are long over. I'm not fifteen anymore, you know.'

A slight smile curled Rosamunde's lips. 'You really were the end, Bella – following him around like a small, skinny puppy as if he was a knight in shining armour.' She sighed. 'What I meant was, did Benjamin see anyone while you were in Durban? Any –'

'Whatever do you mean, Rose?' Arabella was surprised, and it showed on her face. 'Any – women?'

Rosamunde turned her slender, pale neck to peer into the small mirror on the dressing table, lit by an oil lamp with a fluted shade. 'Benjamin and I – well, we know a lot of people – women – in Durban.' She straightened up and gazed at Arabella in the mirror, an enigmatic expression on her face. 'Was there any mention of a Mrs Georgina Prendergast, by any chance?'

Arabella frowned. 'Not that I know of. Really, Rose, do you suspect Benjamin of ...'

'No, of course not! It's just that well, women such as Mrs Prendergast try to take advantage of him – especially if I'm not around.' She gave a small mirthless laugh. 'An attractive man on the loose without his wife is very tempting.'

Arabella went cold, thinking of her own feelings for Ben on the train ... She quickly changed the subject, telling Rosamunde about Aunt Matty, and rummaging in her carpetbag for the homemade gifts which the old lady had prepared for Rosamunde and the children.

'Aunt Matty was always a dear,' Rosamunde said, clasping the small package and peering down at her cousin. She wrinkled her fine aquiline nose. 'I used to think her such a bore at times – going on and on about my suitors. She never really approved of me, and especially not of Benjamin. She didn't ever say so, but I could tell. Papa always said she should have married. It wasn't fair on him to be responsible for a spinster sister – after all, she *was* the oldest in the family!'

Arabella's eyes darkened and her lips opened in protest, but Rosamunde hurried on: 'It's true, Belle, there's no use denying it. You were always her favourite, ever since you arrived as a shy six-year-old at our house for the first time. You were with Uncle Horace and wearing that dreadful travelling coat and woollen scarf.'

'And carrying one small suitcase full of treasures.' Arabella smiled at the memory, suppressing the pain she had felt on that fateful day when her father had trudged away to his lonely austere vicarage, only recently having buried his beloved young wife and a stillborn son.

Rosamunde sighed. 'Mother never wanted you to stay, but I begged her to let you. It was so wonderful having a ready-made sister.'

'You were my only friend in those days, Rose.'

Rosamunde brushed aside this statement, her face lighting up impulsively. 'But let's not think of those days any more. You're here now and that's all that matters.'

'You have a lovely place here, Rose.' Arabella started to unpack her clothes on the brightly patterned counterpane. 'This bedspread is exquisite! You were always superb with a needle, which is more than I can say for myself.'

'Let the maid unpack for you in the morning, Belle.'

'I'd rather do it myself. I'm so used to it.'

Rosamunde shook her head distastefully. 'Always independent – it's so very unfeminine, Bella. I used to despair of you sometimes.'

Arabella chuckled, holding a shawl in her hands. 'I was never the daughter of the manor, darling, waited on hand and foot like yourself. I was the lodger, there on sufferance. Then when Father died, I had to fend for myself – or go under.'

Leaning back in the small, wide-backed chair before the dressing table, Rosamunde toyed with Arabella's tortoiseshell hairbrush. 'I'm glad you came, Belle. It's quite a different way of life from England, but I hope you get used to it and stay longer than you planned.' Her eyes glittered with excitement as she rose and put her arms around her cousin.

Arabella frowned. 'But what if there is a war, Rose? Won't that disrupt your life here?'

Rosamunde moved away, making a gesture of disgust. 'There won't *be* a war, Bella! You'll see, someone will stop it, even at the last moment. I think it's all a big bluff, a storm in a teacup. Now tell me all about England. We've been away so long, and as you know I can't go back – not with Mother cutting me off after the elopement. Luckily Father had arranged in his will that I be given half my inheritance on the eve of my marriage, and nothing could change that. She's never forgiven me for marrying Benjamin, you know. Even though she wanted me to marry a title, she never trusted him. Thought he was after my money.'

The shuttered windows stood open to the still night air, and the chilly breeze bellied in the cream curtains of Madras cotton, with a sudden rattling of rings. Under the iron roof, the calico ceiling of the room had gathered the warmth of the day, and still retained part of it as Arabella sat on the bed, adjusting the long full sleeves of her white nightdress. Then Rosamunde joined her and they sat side by side on the bed and the years apart disappeared as they talked about old times. The past had returned and cocooned them, and for the next few hours they sheltered behind their memories.

But when they had exhausted the subject for one night, the present came back to haunt them. 'I'm so pleased that little Cynthia has recovered from the fever, Rose. You must have been very worried about her,' Arabella said, as Rosamunde rose and sat on the dressing-table chair again.

Brushing back the glistening gold locks that slipped with a hiss over her shoulder, Rosamunde's oval face emerged from the frame of falling hair. Her lovely hazel eyes looked suddenly strained and shadowed in the light of the lamp, where moths fluttered in clusters, hitting themselves against the white, frosty shade.

She held Arabella in her gaze through the mirror for a few seconds, then, with a final toss of her head, which threw the hair into a glossy golden shower, her eyes came to life.

'Fortunately it wasn't as serious as I thought.' She played with a strand of hair and dismissed the subject. 'It's very hot here in summer, Belle – you must bathe your face in cucumber juice and buttermilk every night.' There was the slightest intake of breath, then, 'I'm so looking forward to Saturday night. I've planned the most scrumptious menu, to show you off. Much of it had to be brought in from Durban, and no expense was spared. Ben would kill me if he knew just how much it cost!'

She giggled flirtatiously. 'I shall have to watch old Colonel Dickinson – he really has his eye on me, Belle, it's quite embarrassing at times. But then his long, scraggly daughter always makes such an obvious play for Benjamin, not that I have anything to fear from that quarter. She's so plain, and looks like her favourite horse – and Benjamin always falls for beautiful women.'

A clock in the passage was striking twelve. 'I'd be quite happy if you didn't go to such trouble on my account, Rose.' Arabella looked at her cousin curiously, wondering about the constant mention of other women, and the sudden change of subject from Cynthia's fever. 'I don't think I'm suitable company for your sophisticated friends.'

'Nonsense!' Rosamunde burst out. 'I'll see that you meet a nice respectable husband here, Belle, and then you can stay permanently – I'd like that. I've invited a solid young man called Sir Everard Retheringham to partner you at the table. He's so reliable, has such charming manners, and is so terribly rich. We must get you a decent wardrobe though, darling. No man would ever look at you in that dull grey outfit you wore when you arrived. And you must do something about your hair! You may not be beautiful, but there must be someone who will appreciate your – talents, darling.'

Arabella tried to hide the smile that lit her face at Rosamunde's tactless evaluation of her. She knew it was just the way her cousin saw things, and said what she thought, careless of hurt feelings, to which she never gave a moment's reflection.

'I always seat Benjamin next to plain Janes. A woman has to look after her own interests, you know. But then, you wouldn't know about such things.' Rosamunde sighed. 'I think a dinner party is just the thing, especially with all this endless war talk, and being a mother can sometimes be a rather trying occupation.'

Arabella tried to push the troubling doubts to the back of her mind as Rosamunde rose, and stood looking down at her. She suddenly smiled back with a flash of a dimple in her cheeks. 'Of course, Rose. Here I am after weeks of travelling and seeing new places, whilst you've been closeted here with the responsibilities of two young children. I'm sorry.' She began to pack away her clothes in the chest of drawers.

'Not really closeted. "Neglected" is perhaps a better word.' The sudden bitterness in Rosamunde's tone was anything but reassuring. Then, without warning, she exploded, not loudly, but her voice cut like a lash. 'Oh, I'm so glad you're here, Belle – someone I can talk to, who understands how things were ... There are times when being a wife and having endless babies is not such fun, and pregnancy really does no good to the figure.' She made a small *moue* of distaste. 'I seem to have such an ingrained hatred of bearing children!'

She reached out and touched one of the pendants suspended from a lamp close by. Dancing prisms of light suddenly chased each other across the raised scrolls and flowers forming the intricate pattern of the base as Arabella looked at her more closely.

'You mean there's another world out there that is barred to us because we're women?' Her green eyes glinting with devilment, Arabella smiled, a wicked dimple reappearing in her cheek. 'Yet you despise maths and science as subjects for our fair sex, or any jobs that are not bound up with the home, such as nursing. What did you once say – that it was a filthy and menial occupation, fit for no genteel lady?'

Rosamunde pursed her lips. 'I still think so, and please don't tell our guests on Saturday night that you're a nurse, Belle. Promise me – it's not accepted as a suitable occupation for ladies of our – *my* – standing.' She missed the flash of indignation in her cousin's eyes. 'Don't get me wrong, darling. I love the children dearly and this farm, but there are times when I get so sick and tired of it all.'

Arabella studied Rosamunde. If she had to be brutally honest, her cousin had been spoilt and pampered before her marriage. She had never had to make her own way in life, or earn a living, or worry about where the next meal was coming from. She had always been spirited and wilful, accustomed to being the centre of attention and allowed to have her own way. But even the merest shadow of that knowledge seemed somehow disloyal. The smile on Arabella's face faded, and she forced herself to ask an unwelcome question. 'Does Benjamin understand your feelings?'

Rosamunde looked at her, the lamplight casting a secretive expression over her features. 'Benjamin is a man – he can hardly be expected to understand a woman, and my problems would only be petty and trivial in his eyes.'

Arabella wondered what thoughts were busily turning in her cousin's brain. There was a new and unexpected core of secrecy about her, which threw up a subtle, intangible barrier between them.

'Oh Benjamin's been a good enough husband. He doesn't drink too

24

much or gamble outrageously or anything like that –' She broke off quickly, seeing the expression in Arabella's eyes, and realised she had said too much. 'If we want the dinner party to be a success, I shall have to get Rashida, the cook, to start preparing tomorrow.' There was again that defiant note in her voice.

What Arabella saw in her face alarmed her. There was an inner tension there which broke through to her and the only thing Arabella wanted to do was to help her. She knew she had been right to come out to this country; her cousin *did* need her.

'Is there something I can do to help you, Rose? You look so unhappy.' She stood, all concern, but Rosamunde turned abruptly away. 'That's what I came for – in answer to your letter.'

'There's nothing you can do, except be with me.' Rosamunde whirled around again, her eyes unnaturally bright. 'Oh dear, sweet Belle – always there when I need you. But as sweet and kind as you are, what do you know about men, darling? You're still so inexperienced.'

She smiled kindly as a strange feeling of hurt rose in Arabella which she tried to suppress. It was true, after all. What, indeed, did she know about men?

One o'clock. The clock struck and Arabella walked over to the window, deeply inhaling the fresh night air, the depression in her and in the room weighing on her spirit.

'I can't wait to see this place in daylight – it must be a paradise. You will show me around later, won't you?'

Rosamunde smiled in the old familiar way. 'I'd love to, Belle. Now we'd better get some sleep. I'll send one of the housemaids in with your breakfast at about ten – will that suit you?'

Arabella smiled back, but when Rosamunde had kissed her goodnight and left, her smile vanished with the closing of the door. She stood, looking out into the darkness. The moonlight gave an unearthly look to the dark bulk of the tree outside, its pale glimmer making web-like shadows of the branches. An owl hooted and the long, drawn-out call of the black-backed jackal could be heard from a great distance. A swarm of fireflies rose from the undergrowth, tiny points of light rising and falling like minute stars, and somewhere a nightjar shrieked.

Arabella shivered, feeling the loneliness and a certain brooding savagery in the land about her. Her mind was filled with disturbing and uncomfortable thoughts, and for a brief moment she wished she had not come. Rosamunde's marriage was not what it seemed. It was not the romantic love-match she had believed it to be. Quickly, she pulled down the long sash windows. She was thousands of miles from home, with growing feelings for a man who belonged to someone else. And the country was exploding with war fever – a war which seemed to draw nearer with every passing day.

4

The sun rose through the clearing in the trees outside her window like a flame shooting across the sky. Arabella sat up, stretched like a cat, then climbed out of bed and opened the window. She looked on to a serene and breathtakingly beautiful scene. Each fern, and every stem and branch was imprisoned in a filigree of clear light. Hurriedly, she drew on a dressing gown then walked out into the cold early morning air, the depressing thoughts of the night before forgotten.

Standing on the upstairs balcony, which extended the length of the front of the house, and feeling the splintery boards under her bare feet, she could see that the homestead was situated on a hill which, through the tall trees, had a magnificent view of the surrounding countryside.

Its graceful grey masonry looked over a fairly broad river and was set in the midst of a garden containing a Victorian decorative pool, a summerhouse, fountains, orchards and pergolas, all resounding to the singing of the birds. Lower down the slope, Arabella could see neatly laid out paddocks, with stables in long rows, from which Sinjan and another Zulu were leading horses to pasture – magnificent chestnuts, coal blacks, bays, and a sprinkling of greys.

She was enchanted with Suncrest Farm. It was lovelier than she had ever imagined. A calm distilled from years of solitude lay on the spacious lawns, filled with pale, shifting shadows that seemed to heighten the deep background silence shot through with the distant whinny of the horses, and the high-pitched *chick chick* of a small party of long-tailed speckled mousebirds, sitting at the tops of the bushes, sunning themselves in the early sunlight. Another bird scolded in an orchard, and the hens clucked busily around the yard at the back of the house.

Arabella walked downstairs, down the steps of the front verandah, and on to the grass, the delicious feel of dampness underfoot. Beyond the gardens lay a secret wilderness, and over the hills and the distant purple mountains the sun was aflame between the craggy peaks. A restless russet-coloured hoopoe with a large black-tipped crest was

27

walking busily about the garden, probing with its long bill, as another flew from one tree to the next. A bright green chameleon catching a fly caught her eye and she stood there, transfixed. She suddenly felt alive again, and deep down there was a starting of a new life, as her attention was drawn to the fleet-footed young Zulu, Pendulu, chasing one of the hens across the lawn to its pen round the back.

Her memory tried to recall London and Allenbury Manor, but they were diminished before this bright and vivid part of the world. She would remember all her life the long grass rippling in the sunshine, the great arch of sky above the hills, and the black men whom she could hear already singing at their work.

She turned the sharp corner of the verandah, and climbed the rear steps to the kitchen. Rashida, a tall graceful Indian woman, clad in a pale peach-coloured sari and wearing many thin silver bracelets on her arm, had just finished making a batch of bread baked in cabbage leaves in the Dutch oven across the yard, and the aroma of steaming coffee percolated through the room.

Arabella stared through a door opening into a well-stocked pantry where sacks of sugar, meal and flour stood along the wall, and limestone jars and bottles of dried ginger, apricots and candied peel, fine Cape crystallised fruit, jars of preserved peaches, plums, jams and chutneys were stored in neat rows on the shelves.

There was something Arabella liked about this room and the woman, who was a descendant of one of the first contract workers brought out from India to work in the cane-fields, who when the contract expired, had stayed on. Somehow, in this quiet and comforting domesticity, the threat of war seemed only an evil dream.

During that week, as Rosamunde spent most of her time with Rashida planning the coming dinner party, Arabella passed many hours with the children and their Indian nanny Zareena, in the nursery where she read to them, or told stories, or painted pictures. Every so often, Ben would call in and sit and listen in silence for a while, before getting up and going out.

She felt stimulated in his company; he was never anything but charming to her as they talked, away from the sense of strain and tension which was becoming obvious in Rosamunde's presence. Increasingly Arabella recoiled before her cousin's familiar temper tantrums and the veering of her moods from one extreme to another, and she looked forward to her brief conversations with Ben. She found herself storing up amusing little sayings of the children, and it was reward enough to hear his chuckle, or to see his face light up in pleased response.

When he had left the nursery, she tried to stop herself from listening for the tread of his foot on the threshold again, for the sound of his lazy, mocking voice speaking her name . . .

On Saturday night, the wood-panelled dining room was bathed in the glow of candles throwing into soft relief the twelve diners at the long mahogany table, which was decked with the finest linen, silver and crystal. As English china bowls of steaming onion soup were laid before them, Ben looked around at the guests. 'I hear that commandoes of Transvaal Boers are planning to swoop into Natal and seize the port of Durban, to stop our reinforcements from landing. You gentlemen will have to join up, you can't avoid it.'

These days, whenever there were men present, the talk always turned to war; all conversations on any subject led inevitably to it. There was a murmur of low voices around the table, and Major Horton-Jones, smoothing his enormous dark handlebar moustache, chuckled, lifting a highly polished silver spoon.

'Do you mean *bores* or Boers, Ben?'

'I say, what a lark if those farmers do reach northern Natal! But from what I've heard, there's still hope that the former President of the Free State and recently appointed Transvaal State Secretary, Sarel du Rand, and the new State Attorney, that young Cape advocate, Jan Smuts, are urging Kruger to give a five-year franchise to the Uitlanders.' Colonel Dickinson's blue eyes opened wide and their sleepiness disappeared in an unsuspected intensity, as he adjusted his tie. 'If that happens, your uniform will be of no use to you, old chap.'

Elegantly formal in his dark evening suit, Ben surveyed the guests. The clipped moustache emphasised the brevity of his words as he replied, 'It is more probability than possibility, now, Henry. The situation is reaching a climax, and there's no alternative but war if Kruger refuses to budge – it's a fact we have to face.'

'Och, Ben, it seems to me that the Tories will not rest until they have shed the blood of men to steal the liberty of the Boers and their gold,' Robbie said heavily, as Pendulu served him a second helping of soup from a large silver tureen.

There was a sudden swell of disapproval around the table. 'Mined by good British sweat, Robbie!' Major Horton-Jones leaned forward, wiping his mouth on a spotless white napkin, his dark hair smelling strongly of Macassar oil. 'The goldfields have to be opened up for the rest of the country – it's utter nonsense that the Boers should want to hang on to it for themselves, dear fellow. They have the most extraordinarily narrow attitude to the whole thing.'

The talk grew more heated. It seemed to Arabella that it quivered and twisted about her like flames, igniting them all as they listened or flung out questions and answers, with opinions leaping from every side.

Rosamunde jerked her head up suddenly, as mayonnaise of salmon and lobster salad were served on fine china platters. 'Do we have to talk about war at the table? It's such a morbid subject, especially as this party is to celebrate my Cousin Arabella's first visit to Africa.'

Ben looked at her, a tightly controlled expression on his face as he glanced at the blonde hair, artfully swept up to set off her wonderful good looks, and the low-cut oyster satin gown which revealed her fair and flawless skin. Then he smiled, and made a slightly deprecating gesture. 'Of course, my dear – we were forgetting Arabella. To you, dear girl. I hope your stay in South Africa is not too eventful.' He toasted an embarrassed Arabella with a glass of wine to his lips.

There was another chuckle of laughter around the table, and the atmosphere lightened somewhat.

Mrs Horton-Jones, an expensively dressed, dark-haired young matron gave Arabella a long, searching stare, as she became the centre of attention. 'Having just arrived from England, Miss Allen, you must tell us what the ladies of fashion are wearing this season. Is it lilac? I do adore lilac.'

'Yes, do tell. It takes so long to receive the newspapers,' Lady Mortimer remarked, between dainty mouthfuls of lobster salad. An attractive red-haired woman, she raised her eyes and for a moment gazed at Arabella enviously. 'We haven't been back to the old country for simply ages. I do miss it so much at times.'

Disconcerted, Arabella answered, 'I'm sorry, I have not kept up with the fashions.' She forced a small laugh. 'My work keeps me so busy.'

Delicate eyebrows were raised at once in the sharp silence that followed, and Arabella wished she could disappear to the privacy of her room.

'But you must have seen the Queen! Is she still in mourning? It must be nearly forty years now. Can you believe it? And still all the poor widows have to spend their lives wearing black! How I loathe mourning.' Mrs Horton-Jones shivered in disgust, her well-manicured fingers toying with the silver fork on her plate.

'The Diamond Jubilee two years ago must have been quite splendid, my dears – all that pomp and splendour that only the British know how to do so well.' Tall, thin Mrs Willoughby looked around at the others, deliberately but subtly ignoring Arabella.

'Did you see any of the Jubilee, Miss Allen?' Mrs Horton-Jones smiled appraisingly at her.

'Oh, yes. It was, as Lady Mortimer has said, really quite splendid – an occasion of great public celebrations.'

There were low murmurs among the women, as each in turn eyed Arabella with veiled hostility and envy.

'And the shows! Oh, those London shows. I dearly love the Season. There can be none like it in the whole world.' Mrs Horton-Jones sighed as she popped a piece of lobster salad into her mouth.

It was then that Miss Sarah Dickinson, who did not in the least resemble a horse, turned her head in Arabella's direction. She was a cool, thin-lipped woman, handsome in a hard, dashing way. Her eyes held such a glint of malice and amusement that Arabella immediately braced herself for what she was going to say.

'I believe you are a nursing sister, Miss Allen,' she remarked haughtily, emphasising the words so as to make them sound beneath her dignity.

'I am.' Arabella smiled, determined not to take offence. 'I am totally dedicated to the cause of alleviating the suffering of the sick.'

Sarah smiled pityingly across at Rosamunde, and Arabella could see that all the women present in their expensive gowns and sparkling jewelry thought her a social liability, one of those poor plain spinsters waiting wistfully for some kind gentleman to take pity on them. She could see it in their surreptitious smiles and condescending glances. And all of a sudden she felt a slow anger burn in her. She did not need the pity of these well-groomed and stylish women, with their graceful gestures and constant smiles. It was she who pitied them – with their empty lives circumscribed and dictated by their husbands. She wondered how far she could deliberately suppress her keen intelligence in order to accommodate the conventions of her generation by continually having to be sweet and submissive.

Ever since her girlhood she had been obsessed by the desire to grasp a 'freedom' which she felt was imprisoned beneath the surface of things. In solitude, through her own struggle, she had pursued, in her own way, her destiny, and none of the women present, including Rosamunde, would ever understand the loneliness, the hours sometimes, of hollow sadness, she had endured along the way. She knew that here, in this élite gathering, she was silently ridiculed as an 'intellectual woman'.

'How can you bear to be in contact with illness all the time, Miss Allen?' Mrs Horton-Jones asked reprovingly. 'It's such a *filthy* occupation, if I may say so.'

Rosamunde immediately summoned Pendulu to bring in the creamed chicken, the game pie, the mutton in onion sauce, and the roast veal with potatoes, while Ben raised an amused eyebrow.

'If we all thought as you did, Caroline, many of us would have ceased to exist long ago. Arabella is dedicated to work that we all need and should be most grateful for.'

Ben's words brought warmth to Arabella. Intentionally or not, he had again won her allegiance. Common sense warned her that it would be advisable not to show it, especially before Rosamunde, when relations between husband and wife were strained, yet she realised that in many things she would often find herself and Ben in complete accord. He had again, as at the quayside in Durban against Sean O'Shea, offered his support as simply as if he was a friend coming to her aid, and she found it increasingly pleasant and stimulating to be treated as a person of consequence before his critical, sophisticated friends.

'I hear the play *Salome*, written by that vile man Oscar Wilde, was performed in Paris by that scandalous Sarah Bernhardt.' Sarah Dickinson broke into the discussion once more in her high insistent voice. Everyone stopped eating and looked up from their plates. 'Of course, I suppose I should never have mentioned it here.' Arabella understood at once that Sarah, piqued when Ben's attention had been taken from her, was determined to regain it.

'No, you shouldn't have, my dear,' her grey-haired father said quickly. 'Let's talk about something more appropriate to our dear friends' dinner table.'

'But it was all so disgusting,' Sarah persisted, her voice trembling at a higher, more excited pitch, as she strove to gain Ben's attention. 'Clare's sister Bea says that Oscar Wilde writes the most depraved plays.' She sat back to enjoy the shocked silence she had caused.

Arabella could no longer stand her own hypocrisy. She opened her mouth and her clear voice suddenly rang out across the table. 'I disagree entirely. Oscar Wilde is a brilliant playwright and poet. I saw Sarah Bernhardt in *Salome* in London, and she was quite outstanding.'

There was another stunned silence. Everyone except Ben was staring at her with pained, horrified faces, while Sarah Dickinson was seething that again, Arabella had captured the attention she craved.

'You actually went to see that dreadful woman in that appalling play?' Everard Retheringham, the tall, thin young man at her side seemed both horrified and disgusted.

Arabella glanced at him mischievously. He had shown an obvious interest in her from the beginning of the meal, but was far too submissive and insipid to interest her, and she decided that he was a definite bore. Rosamunde had chosen him to partner her at the table, and she could have compromised because of her lonely state, but Arabella was determined not to.

'I did – and I enjoyed every minute of it,' she told him politely, but staunchly. 'There's much social commentary in Wilde's works which would give you food for thought. You should treat yourself and go and see it. I highly recommend it.'

'I wouldn't be seen dead at such decadent entertainment!' Everard turned flabbergasted, protruding eyes on her, and then sought refuge for his brightly flushed face behind his napkin.

'You have actually *read* some of the works of this man, Oscar Wilde, Arabella?' Rosamunde's voice was subdued, her cheeks pink with embarrassment as she signalled for the cherry tartlets in small glass dishes, and the Savoy cake, piled high with whipped cream. Ben directed a quick glance at her, and Arabella noticed that her cousin's hazel eyes flared for an instant, then grew cold.

'Yes, I have – several of them.'

A clamour of voices rose about her, indignant, outraged, then Major Horton-Jones, brows lowering, cleared his throat, trying to diffuse the explosive atmosphere that had unexpectedly built up. 'I wonder if you could enlighten us as to what this play *Salome* is about, Miss Allen?'

Before Arabella could open her mouth, Ben, whose grey eyes met the flash of hers, and who was trying hard to control the wicked mirth welling inside him, intervened. 'Obsessive passion, Charles, and the French actress Bernhardt is ideal in any interpretation of it.'

Another sharp silence fell, broken only by the genteel scrape of cutlery on plates. Most of the women lowered their lashes, blushing, as Ben silently toasted Arabella, his smoky eyes dancing with reckless amusement.

'How can you speak of that terrible perverted man at this table?' Mrs Willoughby burst out, her thin, elegantly-attired body stiff with indignation. 'And for anyone, especially a young woman of Miss Allen's standing, even if she is a nurse, to expose herself to such degradation, is quite appalling!'

'Wasn't it Wilde who wrote, "A cynic is a man who knows the price of everything and the value of nothing?"' Father Sebastian, who sat sedately at the other end of the table, suddenly asked, his gentle Irish voice rising in the room. All eyes turned to stare at him, and he smiled innocently, his white hair gleaming in the candlelight.

'He was, Father,' Ben replied blandly. 'I see you have read him too.'

'He also wrote that, "Experience is the name everyone gives to their mistakes", or do I stand corrected?'

This produced a grudging laugh and the matter was quickly dropped. Arabella had listened to the remarks and the horrified intakes of breath, but all the time her eyes were on the glass of wine in Ben's hands across the table, and the well-shaped hands that held it.

33

She was struck by their strength and beauty, in contrast with the rich red of the wine ... There was no one there so debonair or so dashing, she thought, observing how at ease was his negligent pose, and how the candlelight gleamed on his dark hair.

'Coffee will be served in the drawing room,' Rosamunde announced, leaning forward, her eyes strangely bright and luminous.

Looking at her cousin, Arabella suddenly regretted her outspoken remarks, realising uncomfortably that she had put Rosamunde at a disadvantage in front of her friends. For the first time she saw, with growing amazement, her cousin's feelings of inadequacy, and her sharp need for social approval. But before she could think any more about it, Ben was beside her.

'Arabella, won't you play the piano for us, dear girl? I haven't heard you do so in years.' His sudden warm words won her attention. A long moment passed as his gaze rested on the green eyes; then abruptly he grinned, and turned to his guests. 'Arabella plays exceedingly well, if my memory serves me correctly. Just this once, Cousin, to soothe the rather explosive nerves at the table.' He turned his head and gave his wife a long, meaningful look.

'Of course – if that's what everyone else wants.' Arabella waited for a moment, wondering if Rosamunde would object, but only the sharp rising and falling of the lace on the soft curves of her cousin's rounded breasts gave any evidence of emotion.

The guests moved out to the drawing room and arranged themselves in comfortable chairs. Arabella crossed the room to the upright piano, sat down on the stool and waited as coffee was brought in. Even though she had not played for many months, she hoped that she was not too much out of practice. Ben gave the fire an impatient kick to get it going once more, and sparks leapt up from the logs. Arabella was less aware of these than of the intangible sparks of human antagonism which filled the room, as her fingers stole over the black and white keys and she tried to recall the notes of a waltz she had once loved.

As she started to play, the melody came back to her, though at first she fumbled over the deeper chords. A silence descended on the room and as her confidence grew, she began *They All Take After Me*. The piano took on new life under her agile fingers, drawing everyone around the instrument, where they sang along, laughingly raising their voices in the chorus. At the end there was total silence, before a small energetic explosion of applause.

'What about something rousing, Cousin – something to send us on our way before the Boers pour in?' Ben asked, leaning nonchalantly against the piano.

'It's almost as if you want to go to war, Benjamin!' Rosamunde's voice resounded across the room, her eyes overbright as she gazed at her husband. 'It's almost as if you're wishing it on us!'

There was a muted ripple of response around the room, and Ben shrugged. 'It's a fact we all have to face.'

He was looking at Arabella as he sipped his coffee, taking in the simple cream gown Aunt Matty had made, which seemed to flow over her body, drawn up and puffed gently over the small bustle at the back, her hair soft and gleaming in the lamplight, and again he was aware of the aura about her, that uniqueness that was at once compelling, and disturbing. He smiled at her, completely disarming her, and pressing her small hands tightly together she took a deep breath, and broke into *The March of the Cameron Men*. This brought a warm twinkle to Robbie's eyes and everyone joined in, the tensions in the room forgotten.

Just then, a servant entered with a message for Rosamunde. She looked up surprised, and made her way towards the piano. 'There's a gentleman to see you, Arabella – he's waiting in the entrance hall. I didn't know you knew any gentlemen here. Whatever can he want at this time of night?'

Greatly astonished, Arabella looked up, meeting her eyes. 'A gentleman, Rose?'

'A Mr Mungo – Archie Mungo. He has a letter for you.'

Arabella felt her cheeks flush as everyone listened to this unexpected interruption, the women's eyes widening with curiosity and disapproval. With a smile she rose and excused herself.

Archie was standing in the lamplight of the entrance hall, clad in a khaki-green uniform and holding a slouch hat in his long bony fingers, a dispatch case at his feet. After her first shock at his call, she went forward, glad to have escaped the claustrophobic atmosphere of the drawing room.

'I hope you don't mind me calling, Miss Allen, but there was a letter for you in Ladysmith, and I offered to bring it.' Archie's cheerful Australian drawl filled the space between them as he inspected her with open admiration.

Uncertain whether to be annoyed or amused at his audacity in calling, Arabella felt that an appropriate response was called for, but for once, was at a loss for conversation. 'It's so late, and this is surely out of your way,' she began, 'for just one letter.'

He grinned suddenly and handed it over. 'Thought you'd want it as quickly as possible. It's from England.'

'From England?' Her eyes dropped to the envelope, on which she recognised Aunt Matty's spidery handwriting, and her hands shook with relief. 'It's from my dear Aunt Matty – thank you so much, Mr Mungo.'

'I said I'd like to visit you, if you remember. I just didn't realise it would be so soon.' His easy assurance that he would see her again suddenly amused and touched her. She had never met such frank determination in a man before.

'Won't you come in, Mr Mungo? At least have some coffee before you go.'

'I'll do that, thanks,' he said as he followed her back to the drawing-room door.

From the room beyond there was no reassuring buzz of conversation, and Arabella shivered involuntarily. She paused on the threshold to take stock of the situation, and as she did so, became aware of a distinct stir about her, an audible gasp from a simultaneous intaking of breath. The women stiffened in their chairs, and the hush that followed her entrance with Archie was more ominous than a thunderclap.

Rosamunde's eyes widened in annoyed surprise as Arabella introduced Archie to the company. Recovering from their discomfort, they eyed him with well-bred interest, as somehow Arabella found herself in one of the chairs that had been set around the room.

At first, as with any outsider, polite questions and answers were exchanged, until it was discovered that Archie was a reporter. Then the atmosphere changed instantly, and became charged with excitement.

He was plied with questions about the Boer intentions. Taking a sip of coffee, he frowned and said, 'The first contingent of Boers from Pretoria have arrived by train on the Natal border. Ten miles from the border the veld on both sides of the railway line is dotted with tents and wagons under the leadership of old General Piet Joubert, who is accompanied by his wife.'

'But that can't be true!' Rosamunde's voice rose in bewildered shock.

Archie inclined his sandy head towards her. ''Fraid it is, my lady. Fifteen thousand horsemen are collected there, ready to invade Natal. Between the two republics, they have mobilised almost seventy thousand horsemen, distributed east and west, and now this great force, armed with modern weapons, is ready to invade both the Cape Colony and Natal at a given word.'

'But we've had no word yet –' Robbie broke off, his voice failing him.

'I'm sorry to bring such news, but the papers will soon be full of it. I saw it all first-hand only yesterday. I've just returned from the border, and I have the first newspaper report in the *Ladysmith Express*, hot off the press, which will be on sale early tomorrow.' He pulled a folded newspaper from the dispatch case on his lap, and handed it to Arabella.

She took it and spread it on the low table before her with shaking hands. The headlines were large, and in fresh black ink that smudged her fingers. It was true. She read them out to the silent company with a sense of disbelief.

'That's it!' Ben declared from the centre of the room, and all eyes swivelled to face him. 'Thank you, Mr Mungo. Soon the entire colony and the whole world will know! We men will have to leave within the week for our regiments, and those who have made no arrangements yet, will be forced to do so. Here, Mr Mungo, join us in a toast to the power and might of Britain, and to her swift victory!'

Glasses of port had been handed out, and now the small glasses clinked. 'I'll drink to that,' Archie announced, looking around from one face to another. 'As a member of the Commonwealth, the Australian states will have to fight at Britain's side. It's only a matter of time, of that I'm certain.'

There was a deep buzz of agreement from the men, while the women stared at them with large, frightened eyes. Arabella's heart began to pound even before she caught sight of Rosamunde's face. She had never seen her look so stricken.

'It's all right, darling. It'll all be over in a matter of weeks.' She hurried to her, searching her face in alarm. 'The Boers cannot stand in the face of the mightiest Empire on this earth.'

'Oh, Arabella,' her cousin whispered. 'I never believed it possible. Whatever will we do now?'

Holding Rosamunde's clammy fingers in her own, Arabella listened to the men singing *Rule Brittania* with resounding, triumphant voices. Her heart felt like stone. It was war now. Nothing could prevent it. The colony only waited to hear the official proclamation.

5

Rosamunde flounced into Arabella's room after the last guest had retired to bed, in a flurry of satin. 'Arabella, what *are* we going to do? Perhaps Alfred Milner will call the whole thing off – he has to!' Her slender hands were twisted together, and the lace and ribbons of the elaborate bodice rose and fell with great agitation. 'Benjamin can't go to war! I won't have it! Oh, why must we all be involved in this whole ugly mess that has nothing to do with us?'

'It's logical that with our much larger, better-equipped and well-trained troops, we must defeat the Boers within days. All they have in the Transvaal, I believe, is one police unit, and a citizen force that is called up in emergencies,' Arabella said gently, as she stood before the dressing table, unpinning her hair. 'Then we'll all be back again living our usual lives.' She spoke with a confidence she was far from feeling.

Rosamunde nodded abruptly. 'I hope you're right. But how could you embarrass me so, Belle, in front of our friends at the dinner party. It was a complete fiasco,' she suddenly flared out, turning flashing eyes on her cousin's straight back.

Arabella turned and braced herself against the dressing table, the lamplight drawing strange shapes across her face. 'I'm sorry. I did not mean to embarrass you, dear Rose, but everyone should be allowed to voice their own opinion, and no one should pass judgements on matters they know nothing about. Most of your guests know very little about Mr Oscar Wilde, and I had a right to speak my mind, and defend the poor man in his absence.'

'You shamed me!' Rosamunde's voice broke in. 'And Benjamin supported you in a most disgraceful manner! He's made me a laughing stock. He did it to get at me – I know it! He *wanted* to embarrass me.'

Arabella's face was white and her eyes blazed like emeralds. 'I can't believe that, Rose. He supported you only because he believes, as I do, that Oscar Wilde is very much maligned,' she answered with a quietness of manner and clear conviction that calmed her cousin. 'Now sit down, my dear, and don't blow everything out of all proportion. I think that half your guests really enjoyed it all – and haughty Miss Dickinson was well and truly put in her place.' She smiled impishly for a second, and Rosamunde, seeing the devilment, sighed.

'For that one thing I *am* grateful. Sarah Dickinson is a spoilt brat!' Rosamunde paused to draw a long, gasping breath, and sat down on the bed, putting a trembling hand to her temple. 'I suppose you are right, Belle – it was just so embarrassing, that's all. And then that disreputable Mr Mungo arriving like that, in such bad taste, and bringing that terrible news. And now he's sleeping under this very roof! Belle – he must go as early as possible in the morning.'

Arabella flinched as she stared at the strained, beautiful face. 'Mr Mungo is certainly not disreputable, Rose. He's very clever, having left Melbourne to take up a scholarship at Oxford University before joining the staff of the *London Daily News*. However, I'll ask him to leave as politely as I can in the morning.'

Rosamunde seemed distracted. A little later, she blurted out, 'I really am so angry with Benjamin – taunting me, and to make it worse, being so downright cheerful about going to war. He wants to get at me, Bella, I know it!'

Arabella sat down on the chair beside the window, and clenched her hands so tightly that her nails cut into the flesh. 'He loves you, Rose – he's given you everything other women would envy. And he *is* a soldier deep down, you can't change that.'

'I know.' Rosamunde was grudgingly forced to grant that much. 'But he's so cruel sometimes. He –' she wheeled around on the bed, and Arabella was alarmed to see that her anger seemed almost visible under the heaving lace and satin draping her body. 'We must get you married, Belle,' she said, suddenly changing the subject. 'I think that Everard Retheringham was quite put off with your outspoken views – and he's from such a good family. There's a nice young curate we know. Now he'd make you a respectable husband.' She wrinkled her nose. 'He *is* a bit dull, but then beggars can't be choosers, can they, and you are getting rather old, aren't you?'

Arabella was about to retort sharply when she saw the humour of the situation. 'Too old for what, Rose – making you embarrassed?' She smiled, gazing at her cousin with clear, candid eyes. 'I know you want to marry me off, for then you think your troubles will be over and I'll be safely behind matrimonial bars. But I don't want a respectable, dull husband, and especially not a curate. I had quite enough religion thrust down my throat by my father, and I do think that I should be allowed to make up my own mind about that.'

Rosamunde looked at her, exasperated. 'Well, you'll have to settle for someone sooner or later, or die a withered and lonely old spinster like Aunt Matty.' There was a short silence, then Rosamunde said, pouting, 'I'm sorry, Belle. I shouldn't have said that about Aunt Matty – I know how you feel about her. It's just that Benjamin really infuriated me!'

Arabella felt weary. 'I really think you are taking it all far too seriously, Rose.'

The two women looked at each other for a long moment in silence, then Rosamunde lowered her eyes. 'I think I had better tell you the truth. After all, you'll find out sooner or later.' She paused. 'After Cynthia was born, I did not want to have any more children. I was afraid after the stillbirths, and hated losing my figure and being tied up with it all, so I locked my bedroom door and refused to let Benjamin near me.'

She looked up at the ceiling with a deep agonised expression in her eyes. 'I don't know if you'll understand, but it's such a relief to talk to someone about it at last. Benjamin was furious. He ... dallied with other women on his horse-racing trips to Durban, and then he started staying away longer and longer, and I found out he had a mistress there – Durban's leading society hostess, that old witch Georgina Prendergast. She had been having an affair with my husband behind my back!'

At her cousin's astonished stare, she gave a quick shrug of her bare shoulders. 'That's the truth, and now you know it all. I didn't meet you in Durban when you arrived because I couldn't bear the ridicule of that Prendergast woman – everyone knows about it, have done for months, long before I did. I am certain that Benjamin visited her there before he met you off the ship, and that is what angers me so!'

Arabella looked down at her intertwined hands, unable to meet her cousin's gaze. It was extremely shocking to hear what Rosamunde had said, but now everything made sense, and she understood the significance of the curious stares directed at her in Durban ... She realised how humiliating it must be for Rosamunde, and all because of her fear of having more children.

For the first time, Arabella no longer envied her cousin. She pitied her and all the other women in her position, who were forced to take such desperate measures to prevent further pregnancies ... while their husbands could have the stimulation of a mistress, or two.

In the passage, the grandfather clock struck the late hour. 'I understand, Rose, and thank you for confiding in me. It must have been so hard for you.' Arabella's face was touched with concern. 'I really don't know what to say.'

Rosamunde answered, somewhat stiffly, 'Nothing makes any sense any more. It all used to be so clear, but now –' She sighed and stood up, brushing down the skirts of her gown. 'I'd better go to bed – there's the guests to see to in the morning. I suppose we should give that reporter, Mr Mungo, some breakfast to send him on his way?'

Arabella forced a smile, and nodded. 'I think he'll be grateful for that.'

When Rosamunde left, she sighed. Where would it all end? What would happen to Rosamunde and Ben? How could she even face Ben, now that she knew the truth? And what ominous news from across the border would the new day bring?

In the darkness she lay fearful of her own crowding thoughts while the crickets outside chirped loudly and an owl called with maddening indifference in the branches of the tree. She had seen another disturbing side to Ben which completely conflicted with her romantic notions about him and, with a shock, she had also come to realise how far apart she and Rosamunde had grown in the seven years since they had last seen each other. Their views about life and a woman's role in it, were fundamentally different. Although she had a deep compassion for her cousin regarding Ben, somehow she knew that if it had been her in her cousin's place, she would never have tolerated the humiliating situation.

The clock downstairs struck eight when Arabella awoke, unable to sleep any longer. She slipped from bed, wrapped a shawl about her nightdress, and left the room. No one was astir in the house except the children, the servants and herself. Luke and Cynthia were prancing about with childish gurgles of glee in the nursery, with their young nanny, Zareena, and smiling to herself, Arabella heard the sounds of drawers being pulled open. Downstairs, the smell of freshly ground coffee came from the kitchen as she hurried to the front door.

The world beyond the verandah might look as it had done yesterday, but for all that it would never be the same again. Too much had happened in the short space of time since then. She opened the front door and started towards the broad circular gravel driveway when the sight of a man on horseback made her pause. No other figure moved in the quiet of that Sunday morning and there was something urgent about the way he rode, waving a piece of paper and gesticulating, as soon as he saw her. Too breathless by the time he arrived to speak, he flung himself out of the saddle, and tied the horse to a post beside the verandah.

If he was embarrassed by her state of undress he did not show it, and she rallied her forces into a semblance of dignity.

'Good morning, mejuffrou,' he said at last, in perfect English accented with Dutch. 'Please excuse my rudeness in disturbing you people so early on this day of rest, but I have urgent news for Lord Stradcombe. Johan Vermeulen.' He doffed his hat, and smiled through a well-cut and full brown beard. 'We are neighbours of Lord Stradcombe and his wife. You must be Lady Stradcombe's cousin from England.'

Arabella acknowledged this with a slight incline of her head, still very much aware that she was in her nightclothes and her hair hung down her back in two braids. 'I will see that Lord Stradcombe receives your message,' she said politely.

He nodded. 'We were just coming out of church in Ladysmith – we like to go to the early communion service once a month – when a chap I know who works in the telegraph office gave me this message. It came through late yesterday.'

Arabella took the paper he held out. Quite forgetting her state of undress, she scanned it quickly, her heart suddenly in her mouth. Neither of them spoke for the moment it took to read the words. But in another moment the quiet Sunday peace had been shattered.

'You understand that British troops are at Dundee, only fifty miles away from here, and fresh troops have arrived at Ladysmith. Many of my own people, burghers and farmers, are leaving to join the commandoes. Please tell Lord Stradcombe, *mejuffrou* – the matter is of the utmost urgency.'

Arabella looked up at the big man, hardly able to breathe. But before she could nod her head, Ben had come running down the verandah steps, his dressing gown hurriedly thrown about his shoulders.

Seeing Arabella, his eyes gave her a quick, practised appraisal, and a swift current of embarrassment ran through her as she remembered Mrs Prendergast. Then something like a disciplined mask came down over his face, before he said, 'I heard your horse, Jan – what is it? Bad news?'

Johan Vermeulen smacked his riding whip against his dust-covered boots. 'Depends on how you look at it, my lord. It's all in that telegraph message I've given to Miss Allen.'

When he had repeated the information, Ben said, 'What are you going to do, Jan? Join us or the commandoes?'

The man frowned savagely. 'Many Boers have left to join the commandoes, my lord, all equipped with horse, saddle and bridle, and an eight-day supply of biltong and boerebeskuit. There is nothing else for me to do. I have no real quarrel with your people, but I feel in my heart that I must help my brothers across the border. Do you understand?'

Ben's lips under the dark moustache curled down slightly, as he listened with an air of natural courtesy, and Arabella found it hard to believe that he had treated Rosamunde so badly. 'Then we shall be fighting on opposite sides of the fence, Jan.' His white teeth suddenly showed in a grin. 'I won't hold it against you, but you'd be better off fighting on our side. We'll lick those brothers of yours in a month.'

For a tense moment, there was silence. Ben removed a fine linen handkerchief from his dressing-gown pocket and flicked dust from his sleeve.

'My lord,' Johan Vermeulen said heavily, 'I have no other choice.'

Just then, Major Horton-Jones and Colonel Dickinson came hurrying down the verandah steps, also in hastily-thrown-on dressing gowns, their hair impossibly tousled. Arabella suppressed a grin, realising that she must appear equally ridiculous. Seeing Arabella, they both stopped and hurriedly apologised for their state of undress, then briskly joined in the discussion.

'You're mad to join those unruly devils up north, Vermeulen. Why don't you change your mind, old man? It's not too late, you know,' Major Horton-Jones asked, his handlebar moustache quivering with indignation. 'You know who's going to win – the die is already cast.'

Ben looked at him with polite but mocking eyes. 'Now Charles, they need a good man like Meneer Vermeulen on their side – make it last a bit longer. They're damned fortunate to get you, sir.'

'See you on the battlefield, gentlemen,' Vermeulen said, as he remounted his horse. He threw them a mocking salute and trotted away in the early morning quiet.

There was another silence, and then the buzzing of the men's voices broke out. 'We'll have to inform the others,' Colonel Dickinson said. 'What will you do with the farm, Ben? Your fine studs will be very tempting to those Boers, with their love of horseflesh.'

Arabella looked at her cousin's husband. He stood there nonchalantly, his hands shoved deep in his dressing-gown pockets. 'Evacuate, Henry. Take the horses to Durban and book the women and children into the Royal Hotel until it's all over.'

Arabella felt a chill pass down her spine. There was no doubt about it – tensions had worsened irreparably on both sides of the border, and large numbers of troops and equipment were moving in, both British and Boer. It was just a matter of time . . .

'Why not just leave your stock here?' Major Horton-Jones enquired. 'You'll be well out of the firing zone – they'll never get this far,' she heard him say. 'Too expensive, surely, and far too much trouble for a bunch of Dutch-speaking farmers.'

'I'm leaving nothing for any Boer bastard to get his hands on, Charles. If they do come up get this far, they'll take every horse I own. They all go, and that's that.'

An odd look came over the Colonel's face. He and the Major exchanged glances, and then he nodded as Ben strolled away, pressing Arabella's arm, as she tried to keep her shawl in place. She had lost sight of the other two men, but she saw them soon afterwards, almost scampering up the verandah steps like two excited schoolboys.

She suddenly plucked at Ben's sleeve. 'Ben, what will become of us when war is declared? You can't leave all this ...' In that moment, she could not have been more frightened.

Somehow she found that he was holding both her hands in his, in a hard grip. He was saying things – things that made no sense, then she heard him ask, 'And what are we to do with you, Miss Arabella Allen, until the war is over?' He stared down at her, a thoughtful and amused smile on his face.

'But what of Rosamunde and the children? They can't just go to Durban and leave everything.'

'Ah yes, Rosamunde, of course.' The sound of her cousin's name caught in her consciousness. She looked up into his crystal-grey eyes and saw in them the remoteness that had baffled her before the shock of Rosamunde's revelation.

'It may not be safe here when war is declared, Arabella. Everyone must go.' His warm hands hurt hers. 'My dear you must help me in this. Help me to persuade your cousin.'

Her embarrassment forgotten in the seriousness of the moment, she turned to look up at him, but for some reason, he was staring after Jan Vermeulen's receding horse; there was harshness in his face, and the trace of bitterness she had seen before.

Then he let her hands drop, and was gone before she could answer. She heard the muffled sound of his footsteps dying away through the open front door, and the complete enormity of the situation overcame her.

6

That night, after all the guests including Archie Mungo had left, Arabella was awakened from a deep sleep by angry shouting coming from Rosamunde's room.

Her door opened and Luke stood beside the bed. She lit the bedside table lamp, flooding the room with light, and saw the small tearful boy rubbing his eyes.

'My darling child,' she breathed, devastated at the tears streaking down his cheeks.

'Cousin Bella, Mama and Papa are fighting,' he sobbed. 'Papa's going to war, and Mama's angry. Will Papa kill Mama?'

Arabella pulled him gently to her. 'No, of course he won't, darling. They're just both very cross with this silly old war. It will pass, and then they'll be friends again, you'll see.'

'But will Papa go to fight, Aunt Bella? Mama says he can't leave us.'

'He has to go to fight for his country against the Boers, Luke – otherwise they'll take away our port of Durban. But your Papa will soon be home again – it won't take long.'

As she buried her face in his soft dark hair, and he clung to her, she wished Luke was her child. But beneath this sudden desire, a grim conflict surfaced in her mind. On the one hand, she knew she had to get away from the dreadful, unhappy situation in this house, and from this country on the brink of war, but on the other she felt an overwhelming love and compassion for Luke and his little sister, innocently caught up in these wretched circumstances. Only that afternoon, Rosamunde had begged her not to leave them, saying that she needed Arabella now as she had never needed anyone before. What was she to do?

All the next day, Rosamunde stayed in her bedroom, as Ben and Robbie – who had finally made up his mind to join the Imperial Light Horse – prepared to take the horses and stock to Durban. In vain, Ben argued that the women and children must accompany them to the seaport, so that he could settle them in before he left for the front, but Rosamunde was adamant that they stay and wait for his return.

45

Arabella's feelings towards Ben were in the utmost confusion. She was disenchanted by his clandestine affair with Georgina Prendergast, and the hostility between Rosamunde and himself, yet he was still as warm and kind to her as ever.

She thought of Ben's plea to persuade Rosamunde to leave for Durban. While Arabella could have coped with the hysteria of an emotional, pampered woman, whose overwrought nerves were giving way under the present strains, she was finding it increasingly difficult to deal with Rosamunde's moods and rages. Nor could she forget Luke's tearful face on the night of his parents' quarrel; she tried to put this memory from her, but failed.

And all the time, war clouds were gathering fast over the horizon. An ultimatum was sent to the British by the Boers, giving them twenty-four hours to withdraw their troops from the borders of the republics, failing which war was to be declared.

It was at the end of a hot, listless day, while the country waited breathlessly to hear the outcome of this ultimatum, that Ben and Robbie had their last dinner with the family before leaving to take the horses and livestock to Durban. It was a strangely quiet meal; the roast duck, bursting with apple stuffing, the vegetables and salads, raised meat pie and rich cream pudding were delicious ... but everyone, including the children, remained subdued. Even when Arabella opened another box of Aunt Matty's butter toffee, Luke's enthusiasm was perfunctory.

Afterwards, when the children were in bed and Rosamunde, pleading a headache, had gone to her room, Arabella seated herself in the sitting room with a pile of sheets that needed mending. Forcing the needle through the material, she tried not to think too much of the imminent departure of the men, but all the time she was listening for sounds outside the door.

Moths buzzed incessantly about the oil lamp and it was very hot in the room; she longed intensely for some English coolness. Her thoughts were busy trying to plot out her own future, when she heard a sudden piercing scream from upstairs. She was outside the room at once, and stood shaking in the hallway. She knew that the scream had come from Rosamunde's room, that Ben was there, and that she was an outsider to anything that had happened between them.

Quickly reassuring the two children, who had run down in terror to her as she waited at the sitting room door, she called to Zareena, who led them back up to bed. Returning to the mending, she was finding it hard to concentrate, when Ben entered, looking slightly dishevelled.

'I'm glad you're here,' he said. 'You heard Rosamunde scream a little while ago?'

She nodded, all pretence at normality gone. 'She's been upset all day.'

He sighed and brushed a moist lock of dark hair from his forehead. 'She tried to kill herself with one of my Gurkha kukris. When I made to wrest it from her, she turned on me. Fortunately I managed to get hold of it before she could do any damage.'

Arabella sat for a moment in shocked silence. 'Did she harm herself in anyway?'

'Luckily she only grazed the skin of her wrist. I have nightmares about leaving her, but I must go. The war is imminent, and the horses and livestock must be removed. As you know, she absolutely refuses to come with Robbie and me tomorrow, so I am forced to leave her here and try to return to escort you all to Durban.'

'Ben.' Arabella spoke with quiet directness. 'What's to be done?'

He gave a helpless gesture. 'I can only hope and pray she comes to her senses. That's why I want you to stay with her, Arabella, and if I cannot return, see that she and the children get to Durban safely. I've made all the arrangements.' His voice had the old authoritative note. 'I know it's a lot to ask of you.'

'Do you think there's a possibility you may not return before war is declared?' Her throat suddenly felt tight as she waited for him to go on, a new dread in her heart.

'The situation may flare up at any minute, dear girl, and then I'll have to join my regiment immediately. If that does happen, I want you to be in charge here –' He broke off, and she was wise enough to keep silent. But her mind caught at his words.

She knew that he, always the soldier beneath the surface, was restless – in his marriage, in his life, that he longed for the action in war, but she also knew that, for all his disagreements with Rosamunde, he must be very anxious about her and the children, and the farm.

'Ben,' she replied at last, 'I understand, but I feel sure you will be here to escort us yourself.'

'I want that, Arabella, believe me. I want to be able to take you all to Durban,' he came closer, 'but first, Rosamunde will have to become reconciled to living there.'

'Whatever do you mean?' Her voice was unnaturally sharp, and she bit her lip.

He stood before her, his grey eyes looking down at her. 'Come now, Arabella. You know very well what's going on between your cousin and myself. You know about my – Mrs Prendergast in Durban. That's why Rosamunde refuses to go there.'

'Ben, it's not my business. What goes on between you and Rosamunde is your affair entirely,' Arabella began, uncharacteristically flustered.

47

He made no immediate response, but settled back suddenly into a chair from which he stretched out his long legs in their polished boots and brown puttees to the fireplace.

He went on, after a long pause, 'I don't want to burden you with our domestic problems, but we have to deal with one of them which we can no longer hide from you. I'm not pretending to be above reproach – God knows I'm far from that – but I do not play the martyr either, and will not accept being shut out of my marriage bed. However, it seems to give Rosamunde some strange comfort to play the virtuous, injured wife.'

'What purpose will it serve, Ben, to tell me all this?'

'I want you to understand the situation, and why I'm asking you to be in charge of organising the family when I leave. You *must* see that she goes. Durban is the safest place, and the furthest from the border. Promise that one thing, Arabella.'

Arabella could not answer, for she was suddenly consumed by sadness. 'Rosamunde loves you, Ben, and when she reacts against you, it's her deep need of you and the terrible guilt she feels in not wanting more –' She broke off, worried lest she had gone too far.

Wearily, his eyes closed for an instant, his thick, dark lashes fanning his cheeks. Then he opened them, 'I'm in a trap of my own making, dear girl – at least, I have had a share in it – and the more I struggle to be free, the tighter it closes around me.' He stopped, and never had she seen so much misery on anyone's face.

She dared not trust herself to speak. He was no longer looking at her. The lamplight shone full on his face, and she could see his expression – hard, wild and defiant. In that moment, she realised that he was not the chivalrous knight he had always seemed, nor was he a cruel monster who had deserted his wife, humiliating her and making her life painful and lonely. She saw him for what he was – a sophisticated, unhappy man who was paying some terrible price.

Then she felt him eyeing her curiously. 'I hope I haven't shocked you, my dear, but you're the only person in the world I have ever admitted this to. Somehow I knew you'd understand. You may not approve, but you'll understand. And Rosamunde needs careful watching, especially after this attempt to take her own life.'

'Ben, please don't go on.'

But he brushed her words aside. 'Just get Rosamunde and the children to Durban – that's all I ask.'

He rose and paced the room, while Arabella sat and stared at him, her face frozen. His words terrified her. He turned, and stood staring down at her.

'I've always been an arrogant fool, Arabella, and Georgina

Prendergast means nothing to me, nothing at all. Having last seen you as an untidy, shy young waif, it never occurred to me that the next time we met, you and I would both have changed so much.'

There was a bitterness in his voice that cried out to her. A long, haunted silence followed. Though he did not touch her, the intimacy in his words made her heart set up a wild beating. If only she felt nothing for him – if only she could forget him ... but they were drawn together by some invisible bond of spirit, by something far stronger than both of them, she knew that now. He had brought her face to face with a new aspect of herself.

As the clock on the mantelpiece struck ten, the silence deepened. His eyes met hers, which were bright with unshed tears. 'Have I upset you, Arabella? That is the last thing I intended.'

'No.' She shook her head vigorously. 'It's just the thought of you going to war – and Robbie, in his new uniform. He doesn't really want to go, not in his heart,' she lied, looking directly at his face.

'The young woman who went to see Sarah Bernhardt in *Salome* has admitted to a sentimental heart.' He allowed himself a faint smile, but the emotion in her words had moved him. He went to Arabella and took her hand, looking thoughtful, and she felt the hard pressure of his fingers.

'You really are an intriguing enigma, dear girl – on the one hand so passionately emancipated and independent, and on the other so deeply emotional. You have many qualities, my dear, but none that I admire more than your courage to face issues.' His fingers were warm and very much alive as they curled about her own. 'Will you promise to do as I ask you?'

There was a snap of silence, and she felt the atmosphere charged with sudden tension. Quickly she rose, firmly taking her hand from his. She turned away to hide the sudden rush of tears, and lifted her chin a fraction higher.

'I'll do as you ask, Ben. You can depend on it,' she said with sudden conviction.

'Good girl. I knew I could rely on you.' He smiled then, as she walked away quickly and out of the room. She went up to her bedroom and closed the door, leaning her back against it. Brushing a stray lock of hair from her forehead, she tried to think clearly.

She did not want to acknowledge what had been revealed so clearly between Ben and herself. She had felt the clash of temperaments, a suppressed tension, between him and Rosamunde ever since she had arrived at Suncrest Farm. And now it had been crystallised by Ben's own admission this evening, that they had both changed. He had not said in so many words that he no longer loved her cousin, but the implication was there, in all its horrific reality.

49

Rosamunde must have felt for months that he no longer loved her. She must have sensed her world slipping away between her fingers, and that was why she had written and begged Arabella to come out to Natal . . .

And now she had promised to see that Rosamunde went to the very place where her husband's mistress lived . . . Arabella was suddenly afraid of her own heart. Why, she wondered, was she so full of confusion, like a frightened child? But in the silence that had descended around her she found no answer.

Ever since the night of Rosamunde's attempted suicide, something changed in Arabella towards her cousin. Now when Rosamunde flashed her eyes and wrung her pale, ring-laden hands, she remained unmoved, thinking that if her cousin was half out of her mind with jealousy of the other woman in Ben's life, it was because she was afraid to blame herself for losing him. For the first time in her life, her cousin's problems were no longer hers.

As soon as Ben and Robbie had departed the following day, she tactfully broached the subject of leaving the farm, but Rosamunde was difficult. She refused to travel by train, insisting that the soot made her ill and that she would collapse before reaching the seaport. The house reverberated with her rage as she cursed Ben for leaving them to unknown dangers, and for his insensitivity to her feelings.

There was nothing for it but to put off their journey for another few days. To while away the tiresome delay, Arabella took the restless children for short walks, or painted pictures with them. And then the blow fell.

On 11 October 1899, England accepted the Boer challenge, and war was declared.

The Colony of Natal was intoxicated with excitement. Thinking that one battle would end the war, the young men hastened to join up, and more and more trainloads of troops travelled north. Panic-stricken women and children crowded into stations along the line to Durban, fleeing from their homes and farms, while the plains across the border were coming alive with enemy horsemen, guns and cattle, moving inexorably towards the frontier.

In the midst of this turmoil, a telegram arrived at Suncrest Farm from Ben, urging them to leave immediately. He had been called up and was no longer able to escort them. It was then that Arabella finally managed to persuade Rosamunde to agree.

Their plans were straightforward. Old Mr Squires, a retired coachbuilder who lived in a makeshift hut on the farm, making iron-rimmed wagon wheels for Ben, had agreed to drive them in the mule wagon as far as Pietermaritzburg, which was only a short distance from Durban. Afterwards, he would return to the farm and oversee it with the remaining servants in Ben and Robbie's absence.

Arabella and the children had breakfasted early, and were ready, dressed in their travelling clothes. Rashida had prepared food for the journey, and was waiting in the entrance hall, with Zareena and the children. Arabella was glad that the other women would be with them, for the weather was very hot, and it would be uncomfortable. She had her hands full with supervising everything as Rosamunde had refused to cooperate. Her cousin, she thought, could be very trying on such occasions. The trains at Pietermaritzburg would be overcrowded with refugees, and small children became easily fractious.

Pulling on her gloves, Arabella, listened to the rumble of the wagon wheels outside on the driveway. It was already nine o'clock, and still there was no sign of Rosamunde. With a frantically beating heart, she picked up the long, pleated skirt of her grey suit, and ran down the passage to her cousin's room.

She found Rosamunde still in her nightdress, seated at her writing desk by the window, fumbling through a mass of papers with unsteady hands. She's upset, Arabella decided. I must be careful. Perhaps I can still persuade her to dress in time. But when Rosamunde's lids were raised at last and the slanting hazel eyes met hers, she was not reassured.

'We are ready, Rose. Mr Squires has brought the wagon to the front door. Shall I help you to dress?' she asked gently, sensing the enormous strain in her cousin.

Rosamunde's eyes narrowed under the sweep of blonde hair. 'I'm not leaving, Belle, I won't be in the same town as that ghastly Prendergast woman. I warned Benjamin that Durban is too small for both of us, but he refused to listen.' She pressed a hand to her throat and sagged back against the chair.

'Rose, please listen to me. We won't have to see that woman, or have anything to do with her. Durban will be crowded with refugees. We won't even cross her path.'

Rosamunde appeared momentarily confused. She half-turned to regard the neatly packed valise on the bed, then clearing her throat, she said, 'Don't argue with me, Belle. I'm staying here until Benjamin returns to escort us somewhere else.'

Rosamunde's words fell like leaden weights into Arabella's consciousness. 'Rose, Benjamin has been called up – He *cannot* return. He has made all the plans for our safety, and now we must follow them through. Please dress – we must leave as soon as possible.'

But still Rosamunde remained seated, her pale, elegant hands buttoning and unbuttoning the fastenings of her nightdress. As Arabella watched those hands twisting buttons on a garment which she knew cost more than all of her own simple dresses put together, for a brief moment she knew a wave of resentment. Then, feeling unkind, her heart reached out to her cousin. She wanted to reassure her, but no words came.

In the silence that followed, they could hear the heavy tread of Mr Squires' boots in the passage and the thumping of valises. She knew there was no way she could force Rosamunde to leave, and no longer knew if she had the right to do so.

'You don't understand!' Rosamunde's pent-up feelings were suddenly loosened in torrents of rage. 'I'll not leave this place, do you hear me? Not until Benjamin comes to escort us. I'll not go to Durban without him! When I face that woman, he'll stand beside me, and show the world that I'm the one he loves above all others.'

She paused to draw a long, gasping breath, and Arabella thought of Ben's words before he had left. She experienced the guilt of her own feelings for her cousin's husband, and the painful knowledge that he no longer loved his wife.

'I want you to stay with me, Belle. Please don't leave me!' Rosamunde's voice had a frantic note of appeal in it, like a frightened child's. 'It's too dangerous for me on my own. I've never been alone in my life, you know that. We can stay here with the children and the servants until Benjamin returns. I know he'll return, Belle, soon. He promised.'

In growing despair, Arabella realized that Rosamunde had convinced herself of this fact; there was no way she could make her change her mind. She stared about the bedroom. Its soft curtains were drawn, and potted plants bloomed in delicate rose, trailing glossy greenness from a shelf below the window. The mirror's curves and her cousin's brushes and stopped bottles gleamed on the dressing table. She thought of the bleak walls and shabby furnishings of her own room back home. This was luxury, and she had learnt to appreciate it again, after so long away from Allenbury Manor.

A knock at the door startled her from her reverie. She answered it, and found Rashida standing in the doorway, smiling apologetically.

'Madam, Mr Squires he want to leave now. He say it very late. He want to catch the train in Pietermaritzburg soon.'

Arabella felt treacherous tears gathering in her eyes. She could walk away from all this, and go with Mr Squires – she could reach Durban, and then leave for England. None of this had anything to do with her. Her heart fought her reason in a silent, intense struggle as she stared at the Indian woman without speaking.

She could hear the chiming of the clock in the hall; and the voices of the servants, all dim and far removed, as if in a dream. She could still leave. She still had time. She had done her best for her cousin, there was no more she could do ... Or was there? Ben had made her promise to see that his wife arrived safely in Durban. But was that really her responsibility? After all, Rosamunde was a grown woman, not a child.

Then a sound rose from behind her – a heartrending series of sobs, punctuated by broken, hysterical words. 'Bella, please! Please don't leave me! I couldn't bear that! Anything, but not that!'

Somehow Arabella found herself beside her cousin, with her arms around her, trying to reassure her. Her hands were trembling when at last she turned away and walked back to the door, where Rashida still waited, her eyes large and frightened. She managed to keep her voice steady and matter-of-fact.

'Thank you, Rashida,' she heard herself say, 'but Lady Stradcombe is not well enough to travel. We will not be going to Pietermaritzburg today. Please inform Mr Squires that we shall not be requiring the wagon.'

Then she walked slowly down the passage, unpinning her toque. Rosamunde's emotional outburst had set her nerves on edge. She must try to relax and prepare herself for the ordeal of staying at the farm indefinitely, until Rosamunde came to her senses.

Mr Squires' wispy brows shot up as his brown eyes fixed her with a questioning stare when he met her in the hallway. 'It be a crazy notion to stay here, Miss – and I am not sure I 'eard Rashida right.'

'It's true, Mr Squires,' Arabella said. 'Lady Stradcombe is in no fit state to travel.'

'Well I'll be darned!' He wiped the back of a shaky hand across his mouth, while his small eyes searched her face, convinced of her insanity. 'If I may say so, Miss, this is the wildest notion I ever 'eard. There'll be fightin' like you never seen and them troops not seein' a woman for weeks! There's no sayin' what'll happen once the guns start boomin' out, and them Boers cross the border.'

He made a cutting sign across his throat. 'Them Boers is not wot you thinks they is, Miss. They is cunning as foxes and resourceful wi' them soft veldschoen shoes. As silent as Red Injuns, they creep up on ye, slow and easy. I know, Miss – I fought 'em in the last war on that bloomin' Majuba Mountain.'

A slow fear began to spread through Arabella as she looked at the old man with the small shrewd eyes, and she knew instinctively that these were no idle words. She summoned up a wan smile. 'We have you to look after us, Mr Squires. I am sure that'll be enough to chase the Boers away without firing a shot.'

But he missed the irony, and shook his head. 'Miss, you don't know what you'll be facin' out 'ere with Her Ladyship in her condition and two small kiddies, and a 'andful of blacks. I'm an old man, Miss – not wot I used to be –'

'That will be all, Mr Squires,' Arabella interrupted firmly. 'I shall ask Rashida to make some tea.'

She turned and walked towards the kitchen at the back of the house, avoiding the old man's bewildered stare.

7

Every day now, small straggling lines of starving Zulu mine-workers from the Witwatersrand gold mines, who had lost their jobs when war broke out, would arrive at Suncrest Farm with their women and children, begging for food and bringing fresh news of the conflict. The first battle, at Dundee, seemed to have proved victorious for the British, who were moving on to a place called Elandslaagte where another big, bloody confrontation was anticipated.

And now the silence which Arabella had once loved, had become menacing and hateful, something to dread.

Eventually, another party brought news of the horrendous rout at Elandslaagte, where the dead and wounded from both sides lay littered on the veld. They thought it was another British victory. Then came news of the death of the British Commander, General Penn Symons, who had been shot at the mountain called Talana Hill.

For the next few days everyone moved about the house like frightened animals, waiting for fresh revelations, starting at every strange sound. Ben and Robbie seemed to have been swallowed up in the conflagration that was taking place miles away. The mail was disrupted, there were no newspapers, and no more information about the fighting.

Arabella sat down at the parlour table where only days before there had been laughter and security, a pot of tea and a plate of thinly cut bread and butter on the tray before her, and except for the slow tick of the squat marble clock on the dresser, the room was strangely quiet. It was then that the beating of hoofs on the gravel driveway outside disturbed her. Swiftly she reached a window, and pulling back the curtains, peered out curiously.

A small body of horsemen was fast approaching the farmhouse, but they were too far away for her to see whether they were allies or enemies, for now that the British troops wore khaki, it was not easy to tell the difference. All the Imperial troops wore regulation khaki, the corps distinguished only by the smallest badges, while the Boers wore no uniforms, except for those in the Police Force and State Artillery.

Arabella wondered if these were Colonial troops, Ben's perhaps ...
For a moment her heart leapt and stopped as they came closer.
Perhaps Ben had found out that they were still here, and had come to
take them away ...

But the first rush of hope died as the men drew nearer, and she saw
the strange beards and ill-assorted clothes. They were the enemy. She
was so surprised that for a moment she could not believe her eyes.
Then, as she watched them dismount their small Boer ponies in front
of the house and stride to the door, Mauser rifles glinting in the
sunlight, a deep chill went through her.

Rosamunde appeared as a loud knock sounded at the front door.
She was about to walk towards it, when Arabella reached out to grab
her wrist.

'No, Rose – don't answer that door. There are Boers out there.'

Rosamunde stopped, her face suddenly white. Then, with her
hands over her mouth, she said in an agitated, trembling voice, 'What
are we going to do? They've come to commandeer the farm, just as
they did to Rietfontein! Bella, they can't take it! Benjamin will be
ever so furious.'

Arabella closed her eyes in an effort to think more clearly as
Rashida entered the room with Zareena and the children, but she
found no answer. There was another loud rap at the door, more
impatient this time, and a harsh voice demanded something in Dutch.

As she stood there, listening to the frightened hum of voices about
her, her mind was busy. Then she opened her eyes with a sudden
glint of green and looked at the little group before her. Suddenly
rallying, she straightened her shoulders, and smoothing the long beige
skirt with shaking hands, she exclaimed, 'Oh, damn these Boers!
They can't just come here as if they own the place! I'm going to the
door, Rose, to tell them to go away and leave us alone.'

Rosamunde's hazel eyes widened in horror. 'They are rough, cruel
monsters, Bella. You must be mad! They'll never listen to you. You
know what we've heard, about small parties of Boers injuring and
insulting British refugees.'

Arabella clasped her hands together, feeling them damp with a cold
sweat, and said with irony, 'We have also been led to believe that
General Joubert has severely scolded them, that he won't allow such
behaviour from his men.' She drew a deep breath as the knocking on
the door became more impatient and the Dutch voice more abrasive.
'We must just trust that they have listened to him.'

At this, she tried to move forward, but the two children clung to
her, hampering her progress. Somehow, thus encumbered, she reached
the door, with the three women cowering behind her. Overcoming a

sudden rush of terror, she flung it open and stood facing the small party of Boers outside.

Most were bearded, except for two younger men, and nearly all were wearing cord riding breeches, broad felt hats with a variety of hatbands, and black or b-own leggings. Their leader was an enormous man, whose black bushy brows rose as he took in her diminutive figure, the children clinging to her skirts.

Doffing his hat, he spoke in a deep gruff voice, using surprisingly good English. 'Good day, madam. I am Commandant Jopie de Beer, now in charge of this area. I must order you to leave this farm.'

Rosamunde gave an involuntary gasp of protest, but it was Arabella who stared up at the big man seemingly unabashed. This arrogant farmer had come to Suncrest, demanding that they leave the land Ben had built up into one of the finest farms in the Colony, as if he had a right to it! She thought of Ben and, in an instant, all fear vanished; a murderous rage rushed through her, so strong that she could barely withstand it.

'This farm belongs to Lord Stradcombe,' she cried, with flashing eyes. 'His wife, Lady Stradcombe, and I refuse to leave until he returns, and there's no way you can force us to go against our will. Now please leave at once!'

Rosamunde's jaw sagged in dismay as a swift glint of something close to annoyance flashed through the dark eyes above her, then it vanished. 'Madam, there is a war going on in this area. This farm is to be commandeered by us for our headquarters, is that clear? That is an order you have to obey. We can force you, but I would rather not have to do so. I give you the chance to go of your own accord.'

'We will not leave here!' Rosamunde burst out, bolstered by Arabella's courage. 'We will *not* leave this farm!' There was a sudden sob in her voice, which she tried to stifle, then the children claimed de Beer's attention. Luke stood beside Arabella, quietly and warily studying this giant of an enemy who had come to his home.

It was a dangerous situation, Arabella thought, noting the frightened reactions around her, looking from the children to the Boer who was regarding her with narrowed eyes, and his men, now standing restlessly behind him. But she did not see why they had to obey a foreigner who had no claim on their land. It was his hateful people who had caused the war, and not only did they think they owned the gold fields, but the whole of this Colony too! When she thought of their arrogance, her heart pounded so hard she could scarcely breathe, but she knew she must not antagonise the big man any further.

She squared her shoulders, and there was a stubborn lift to her chin. 'There are many other farms in this area that you can use to

57

make your headquarters without any trouble. In fact, the next farm belongs to Mr Vermeulen who has gone to fight on your side. Go and make your headquarters there!' Her voice was like a whiplash. 'This is our home and we refuse to leave. Now please leave us alone.'

Jopie de Beer stared down at her from under lowering brows. She felt the other Boers regard her curiously, and for a moment met the gaze of one of the younger, cleanshaven men.

There was something about the way his alert brown eyes were staring at her ... something that seemed to set him apart from the others. He could not have been more than three years older than herself, but held himself with great confidence. Like the others, a bandolier filled with ammunition was slung across his chest and he carried a long-barrelled Mauser carbine with the ease of experience. The men had all doffed their hats when she opened the door, and now his slouch hat, with its brim upswept on one side, was pushed back on his blond head. She saw that he was surprisingly handsome, with a deep cleft in his chin.

She wanted to feel righteous and superior to these men, who had tried to keep the Transvaal and its goldfields all to themselves, but for some reason she could not.

She returned her gaze to Jopie de Beer who stroked his beard, his eyes downcast for a second. Alarm ran through her. He was going to force them out into the veld, to go ... where?

'You make it very difficult for me, madam,' Jopie de Beer said finally, observing her pale, defiant face. 'You may stay here, and we will leave you alone, provided you remain in the boundaries of this farm and do not, at any time, leave it. If you disobey, it is out of my power to give you any protection, you understand? If there is any trouble, you must tell the mischief-makers that General Louis Botha has given you permission to stay, and that you will complain to him if there is any misconduct. Do I make myself clear?'

He paused. 'I have to tell you, madam, that we will be taking your cattle, except for a span of oxen to plough your land, and your horses – this is a stud farm, I understand. We leave you one cow and two horses.'

'The horses are gone.' Arabella held her head high in unconcealed triumph. She could feel the stare of the young Boer as she continued, 'Before the war they were taken away, and so was the cattle, except for two cows.' She remembered the two hacks Ben had left, and the place where she had ordered Pendulu to hide them only the day before.

De Beer nodded. 'Then we will take one cow.' He walked back down the verandah steps, and stood looking at the side of the house, where part of a hillock could be seen, rising behind the land at the back. He pointed in its direction. 'Is that kopje outside your boundary?'

Rosamunde grudgingly said it was, and he nodded, once more smoothing his beard with one massive hand. 'Right, then no one from here goes further than the kopje. It is out of bounds, do you understand?'

With the cold realisation that they were now surrounded by enemy territory, Arabella turned away and closed the door, but not before she had detected a faintly amused smile on the face of the young Boer with the cleft chin. Her nerves vibrated with hatred, and for a moment she wished she had a gun. With suppressed fury, she heard the deep growl of their voices outside as she leant against the door. But even more than the anger and the hatred, she knew she was frightened, more frightened than she could ever remember being. She wondered if it would be only a matter of time before the Boers changed their minds, and turned them out of the house. She could not bear the thought of the dirty, uncouth enemy living in this beautiful home, despoiling the graceful furniture, and laying the gardens and the surrounding lands to waste, then boasting about how they had taken the land of an English lord.

With ominously light footsteps, the Boers moved away and she allowed Rosamunde to hug her in delighted relief.

'You did it, Bella! You made that horrible man back down. I really did not know you had it in you!' She smiled now, and Arabella was reminded of how Rosamunde had been years ago. But the vision lasted only a brief second, as the smile faded from her cousin's face, and faint lines took its place about her mouth.

'We shall have to be very careful, Bella – but how I hate those devils! How dare they come here demanding this land! And how insulting that they leave us with only one cow!' she burst out angrily, two red spots of colour flaming in her cheeks.

'I suppose we should be thankful for small mercies, Rose, After all, there is a war going on.' Arabella felt suddenly weary.

'Where are the horses Ben left?' Rosamunde's eyes suddenly widened. 'You don't think they've stolen them without telling us?'

'No,' Arabella said briskly, pushing back a stray lock from the soft knot of hair on top of her head. 'They are well hidden, safe for when we need them. No filthy Boer hands will ever find them, Pendulu and I saw to that.'

Just then they saw fourteen-year-old Umfaan, the youngest of the Zulu servants, standing in the kitchen doorway with an old rifle over his shoulder. 'I come to say goodbye, missus,' he said. 'I go to find Baas Lord in the war.'

'No, Umfaan. You can't go – you're too young,' Rosamunde protested.

'I go, missus, to help Baas Lord fight the Boers – those that were here, in this place.'

'You don't know where he is, Umfaan!' Rosamunde went forward, almost pleading with him.

But Umfaan only grinned broadly. 'Missus not to worry. Umfaan find him.' He turned away and walked rapidly across the yard, never looking back. Arabella saw that there were tears in Rosamunde's eyes as she watched him disappear.

Another straggling column of frightened Zulus arrived later with the news that thousands of British troops were retiring southwards to Ladysmith. The Boers routed at Elandslaagte had reappeared in great strength, having been reinforced by another commando at a point seven miles nearer Ladysmith. Then they heard the most alarming news of all from Mr Squires.

The Boers were now in command of the road between Ladysmith and Dundee, along which the British column was retreating.

Before the visit from the party of Boers, Arabella's room had become a magnet for Luke and Cynthia. They loved visiting her, unconsciously immersing themselves in the atmosphere she created. The room had been transformed by her paintings, and the whole place was ablaze with colour. It was warm, bright and inviting, as if continual fun and childhood laughter were locked there in her room and in her presence.

But after the Boers had gone, the women and children, black and white, stayed close to each other and did tasks that made no noise, because things were happening that they did not fully understand.

No more Zulu miners came to the house, and there was no news filtering through about the war. Arabella no longer painted much and the rooms, usually fresh with the scent of flowers, were strangely desolate, the vases empty. Rosamunde, usually fastidious and keeping her women busy, now withdrew to her room, and the floors and furniture were dusty. It was almost as if there was a conspiracy of silence. No one talked much at all, and if the children did venture into Arabella's room, she appeared preoccupied, although she always welcomed them.

The world had changed in a few short weeks. Ben and Robbie had gone, the Boers had come, and they themselves were trapped inside the boundaries of Suncrest Farm. These were almost unbelievable happenings, and Rosamunde's mind could not take them in. To her, even Arabella had changed. She had taken charge of everything in a way Rosamunde would never have believed possible. All that had ever been sweet and shy and submissive was gone, and a strange, independent, strong-minded woman stood in her place. And if Rosamunde had only known it, Arabella acted in the way she did because she was too worried and too strained at having the entire responsibility on her shoulders of those who were left, and because it helped to keep her mind off her own frustrations.

She had begun to worry about Luke, who had not seen another child besides his sister for days. He was now six, and becoming restless and naughty. He grew stubborn and aggressive in his mother's increasingly disturbing presence, only wanting Arabella. And Arabella too, had come to dread the uneasy, highly emotional shadow that Rosamunde was casting over the atmosphere. It troubled her to feel that she and her cousin were growing further apart each isolated day. Nothing she talked about interested Rosamunde for long, and her loneliness deepened.

In those long hot days, Luke began to spend hours on a little rocky outcrop on the sloping hillside rising behind the stone-walled cattle enclosure; it lay beyond the outbuildings at the back of the house, but just inside the boundary defined by the hillock rising above it.

One day, soon afterwards, Suncrest suddenly lost its isolation. It was still misty, but patches of sunshine splashed the plain below as Arabella clambered up the rocks in pursuit of her cousin's rebellious little son. She sat down breathlessly on a large smooth rock somewhere near the top. It was a beautiful spot, quiet and unspoilt, and immediately she felt at peace. She watched two old Zulu men far below, under an acacia tree, leisurely smoking dagga with ox-horn pipes and mealie-cob bowls. It was hard to believe there was a war going on over the hills, or that they were within enemy territory.

Suddenly Luke clambered down a rock, and clutched her arm excitedly. 'Look, Cousin Bella – there are men down there. I saw them riding through the trees.'

As she stared in the direction of the small, pointing finger, she saw what looked like a troop of khaki-clad British soldiers moving along the row of trees beside the twisting line of the river.

'Those soldiers have the same clothes as Papa. Papa's come to fetch us, Cousin Bella!' Luke was beside himself with excitement. 'I'm going down to see.'

'Oh no you don't, young man. I don't think it's your Papa. And if it is, it's very dangerous down there. Those men are riding in enemy land.' She gripped his shirt to pull him down beside her. 'Besides, it's so far away, Luke. By the time you get there, they will have gone. And we did promise Commandant de Beer to stay here.'

'I don't like Commandant de Beer!' Luke cried. 'I hate all the Boers! They kill British soldiers!'

'Hush! Quiet, my child, there must be something going on down there.' Arabella pulled him close to her as she watched the soldiers move forward and walk round the knoll on their right, then go out on to the plain in the direction of the surrounding hills.

Something caught her eye to the left, and she was startled to notice the gleam of a heliograph. It was an eerie sight, the intermittent flicker of light reflected on to the pack of dense clouds above. The valley was ominously quiet as the strengthening sun danced along the rows of steel points of the guns high above the horses' heads. But just then, as the fog lifted, a small commando of Boers appeared out of the mist, firing from the saddle as they galloped with alarming ease across the land.

'Look, Cousin Bella! There are the horrid Boers – they're going after the soldiers! We must shout to the soldiers and warn them!' Luke jumped up and down excitedly, nearly knocking Arabella over. Hastily, she pulled him down again.

'Sit down, you naughty little scamp! They won't hear you, and it's too dangerous to let the enemy know we're here. We're already far too close to the boundary as it is.'

They watched the soldiers riding towards the farmhouse, then disappear near the stone cattle kraal at the back. Now, for the first time, they heard the sharp hiss of rifle bullets, and experienced the terror of the reality of war. Arabella could see nothing of the soldiers, except for an occasional helmet and the spurts of dust flicked up around the Boers who were closing in fast, and soon they were firing at the kraal. She heard distant sounds and echoes of the disturbance, and feared instantly for the safety of those inside the house.

'They're at our house – they're at our house!' Luke scrambled up again, but was speedily brought down. Then the world exploded with the noise of guns, with more Boers arriving from every direction, and Arabella knew, with a sinking heart, that it was only a matter of time before the English troops would be overrun.

A large Creusot gun was brought up, and to her rising horror, it was fired. The first shell tore into the British horses, causing the frightened animals to rear and stampede. Luke threw himself into her arms, his small hands tightly covering his eyes. She held the little boy close and comforted him as she watched the horses thunder past below their rocky hiding place.

Her attention was sharply drawn to a raised white flag at the kraal. 'It's all over now, child,' she soothed, stroking the soft, dark hair, so like Ben's. Slowly Luke raised his head, and watched with terrible fascination as the soldiers threw down their arms and fell behind their officers, amidst the ghastly heaps of their dead and wounded comrades strewn on the bloodstained ground.

Just then, Rosamunde burst from the house with one of Ben's hunting rifles. With the servants cowering behind her, an altercation started between her and the Boer Commandant.

'Mama is shouting at the Boers. It serves them right for killing our men!'

Arabella could not hear what went on, but she could make out the gestures, as the British officer in charge stepped forward. After what seemed like some anxious moments of hard talking, the Boers stepped aside, and Rosamunde ran back into the house, with the servants behind her.

A cold little fear was beginning to throb in Arabella's breast, as she watched the British prisoners marching away in fours, between the escort of Boers. She took Luke's hand, and slowly climbed down the hillside. Her hat had been lost; her shawl was untied about her shoulders, and her face was pale and dusty, but all she could think of was how to shield Luke's eyes from the staring, sightless eyes of the dead.

Shatteringly, she now understood that what Mr Squires had said of the Boers was true, and that perhaps this war would not be over in a few weeks or even months. Perhaps it would drag on for years ... they would stay here, isolated from the world for ever, or until they were finally overrun by the enemy.

8

The day was oppressively hot, and flies buzzed through the open windows, as the tide of smells and pain rose about Arabella in her bloodstained apron. She and the two Indian women had groped their way among the dead and wounded outside, where high above hovered giant black and white vultures. Rosamunde, her wild eyes betraying her deep horror, had gone back inside, utterly revolted by the cloying stench of death.

Perspiration soaked through Arabella's dress as she placed a basket of bandages on the floor beside her, then stretched her sore and cramped body after ordering Pendulu and Sijan to bury the dead in the family burial ground beyond the orchard, beside Rosamunde's two stillborn babies. Buckets of well water were brought for the wounded men, who were carried into the drawing room, with its deep rich Axminster carpet, where in that world that had vanished forever, she had played the piano for Rosamunde's guests.

Here each man was covered with a quilt or a blanket. All of them suffered from bullet wounds, which she had never seen before, and she discovered that some of them had been able to apply the sterile field-dressings with which they had been issued, with safety pins; these she removed later to allow the wounds to dry. Others were more badly hit, however, and it was to these she applied herself at once.

Of each man able to talk, she and Rosamunde asked anxiously of Ben, but none of them belonged to the Imperial Light Horse and had not heard of him. Arabella tried to comfort her cousin by telling her that Ben was sure to be all right, that he must still be alive, because somehow they would have heard if he wasn't. She said it was too early to tell exactly where he was, and deadened any private fear that maybe he was no longer alive. One thing they did learn, however, was that martial law had been proclaimed in Durban, also that the authorities had seized the South African Bank and the town was seething with excitement.

Arabella was washing and binding wounds, re-rolling bandages and lint, and trying to deal with the babbling delirium of a soldier lying near the window with a head wound, when Rosamunde appeared in the doorway in great agitation.

'How can you bring these wounded men into our best room, Bella! Look at the carpet – it's ruined for good!' she cried out, staring at the bloodstains and scuff-marks on the deep soft pile. 'I'm going to tell Pendulu and Sijan to take them out.'

'You know it's the largest room in the house, and the most convenient, Rose,' Arabella answered, trying to keep her voice calm. 'We have to let the men lie here – there's no other way. Have we any more laudanum?'

Rosamunde caught the look in Arabella's eyes, and closed her mouth. Then, turning away angrily, she disappeared.

Arabella had a little iodine left in her box of nurse aids, but no morphia or chloroform, and only a small quantity of laudanum, which she had raided from the household medical supplies. This she explained to Zareena, who followed her about the room with frightened eyes, a basin in her hand. The smell of a roast rooster filled the house from the kitchen, where Rashida was cooking a meal that would be shared by those soldiers who were able to eat.

One young white-faced corporal lay on the couch, moaning, and Arabella looked at him with concern. He had been shot through the left arm, and he could hardly speak, owing to the dryness of his mouth. She noticed that his good hand was clamped tightly across the wounded one, where blood had already gushed through the dressing. As she gently pulled it away, fresh, bright blood seeped on to the blanket, and she braced herself so as not to vomit. Never, in all her time at St Albans Hospital, had she ever attended a patient from the battlefield.

Then, as he closed his eyes in stifled agony, she reached out to the small table beside the couch, and lifted one of Ben's finest crystal decanters of brandy. Tugging the top free with her hand, she poured some into a glass and passed it to him. 'Here, drink this brandy – it will help a little. I'm sorry I don't have anything else.'

The soldier turned his head slowly and looked at her. 'Take it first to my pal, ma'am – he's over there, near the door. He's hit worse than me.'

She shook her head. 'Your friend is over the worst. Now please drink this before I apply some garlic to your wound.'

Shakily he took the glass and downed a good swig, then, coughing at the sting of the spirit, he relaxed, his face loosening. 'Garlic, ma'am? I've never heard of that being used for wounds.' He passed the glass across, and fell back on the couch, a violent spasm of pain knifing his face as he moved his wounded arm, but not one word of complaint crossed his lips.

'Louis Pasteur, the French chemist and biologist, observed that garlic could destroy harmful bacteria. I've already used it on some of the others to prevent septic poisoning and gangrene.' Arabella tipped a tiny drop of spirit into the jagged little hole in his arm, wiped away the blood, then carefully applied the garlic.

'Oh, God.' Rosamunde collapsed into a nearby chair, a hand covering her pale face. 'How can you do that, Bella! I think I'm going to be sick.'

Arabella bit her lip with annoyance, but did not answer, although she felt like screaming, 'For heaven's sake, you selfish woman, stop complaining and go away!' She knew she was not treating Rosamunde with enough sympathy, but the weariness and strain had returned, more pressingly than ever, and Rosamunde was no help at all. 'Go and lie down, Rose. I can manage here with Zareena,' she said without lifting her head from her work.

'You don't want me here! You just want to get rid of me, like everyone else!' Rosamunde flared up in an instant.

'You know that's not true. Now don't be so sensitive – we have to help these poor men who are in a far worse plight than any of us.' Arabella raised her head and on her face was the first expression of raw emotion that Rosamunde had ever seen in those calm, determined eyes.

'Don't speak to me like that, Bella. After all, I hate the sight of these poor men as much as you do – and I've never worked with dying and wounded patients as you have.'

Arabella looked away, wordless. But as Rosamunde left the room with unsteady steps, there was a tight feeling of remorse in her heart.

The soldier's mouth twisted up at one corner, as he stared at her. 'Are you a nurse, ma'am?' Arabella nodded, a tired smile flitting across her lips. 'And a bloody marvellous one, too! A doctor couldn't have done much better, ma'am, without the medical supplies, than you've done. We haven't many nurses, y'know – there are some sisters from the Convent at Ladysmith, and the few others are not well trained.'

He bit back a gasp of severe pain as she packed a dressing into the bullet hole. 'And what about the doctors?' she enquired.

'There's a few, ma'am – civilians and army surgeons – for both our boys and the Boers.'

His words came slowly and she was worried that it hurt him too much to talk, so she deliberately abandoned questions she wanted to ask, and said instead: 'It seems strange that we are fighting each other, and yet our doctors attend our enemy wounded.'

The young corporal drew a long, gasping breath and she winced, almost feeling his pain as he spoke. 'The Boers may have contempt for our soldiers, ma'am, but they send their wounded to the Boer hospital that's been set up in Ladysmith.' He lay back, panting, and she pressed a wet cloth to his feverish forehead. 'But then, my pal was tended by a good Boer doctor on Talana Hill.'

'Don't try to speak any more – just lie back and rest. I'm nearly done. I've just got to tie up the new bandage.'

He was exhausted, and Arabella felt a rush of intense feeling for him. He seemed so young, and she forgot that she, too, was young as time seemed simultaneously to telescope and expand, as she left him to work on the others.

She became like a machine. The heat, already intense, seemed to be coming at her in scorching waves, with the insistent buzzing of the flies. The room, though large, was very hot, the atmosphere nauseating, and the soldiers' blue shirts pale blurs. She realised just how very exhausted she was when Sarah, the Zulu maid, came in carrying a cup of tea. She also realised that for the first time in weeks, she had been immersed in her work again; and a bright flame of exhilaration sprang to life within her. It was her vocation to help the sick and the wounded, and it kept her alive. Then her eyes became remote again, and she thought with a sinking heart of the wounded soldiers in Ladysmith where trained nurses were scarce.

By the next day, most of the Zulu servants had run away in panic, and the household at Suncrest Farm had shrunk to a few faithful retainers. Arabella's beige skirt, freshly laundered only the day before, was already streaked with blood and sweat. She stared around at the moaning figures on the drawing-room floor, and the empty place near the window where the delirious soldier had died during the night, and wondered if she was going insane. Men, who had once been whole and healthy, who had laughed and lived fully, were now reduced to the half-living, in this room where Archie Mungo had brought the new of the war. Archie Mungo . . . she wondered where he was now.

At midday, she heard Rosamunde cry out, 'Come quick, Bella. There's a wagon outside with a Red Cross flag!'

Gulping down the sickly-sweet brew that was now a substitute for tea, Arabella picked up her skirts and ran to the front door. Sure enough, a medical wagon drawn by ten mules driven by a black man, swung down the driveway, the Red Cross flag waving in the shimmering heat. From the coolness of the verandah, they could see a field kitchen sending up black smoke signals down near the river.

To their surprise, young Umfaan sat beside the driver, waving frantically as the wagon jolted to a halt. He was wearing a ragged khaki tunic, and a helmet with a bullet hole right through the crown. He jumped to the ground, a newfound dignity fighting with pleasure at seeing his old place and people again, then a grin as wide as a split-open watermelon parted his lips.

'Missus, we come for the wounded soldiers. Yes, missus,' he declared with unconcealed pride, 'we hear of the killings here and we come to take the soldiers back to Ladysmith.'

The driver smiled indulgently and nodded as Rosamunde turned her astonished eyes on him. 'We come with the soldiers, missus,' he said, 'to take away the men that are not dead.'

Rosamunde addressed Umfaan, her mind forgetting everything else but the young boy. 'But Umfaan, fancy you being here with the Red Cross wagon!' She wiped her hands on her soiled apron. 'Did you find the Baas – Lord Stradcombe?' Her voice was intensely anxious, and suddenly Arabella felt her heart in her throat. She almost did not want him to say anything, if the news was bad.

But Umfaan's grin was broader than ever. 'Yes, missus – Baas Lord a major now. Major Saville, yes, missus. The Baas he go all the way up Talana Hill with his men. Baas General he very pleased with Baas Lord. Baas Lord he very fierce fighting man.'

'Where is he now, Umfaan?' cried Rosamunde, passionately eager, as she ran down the verandah steps. 'Tell me, where?'

'Baas Lord – he gone from Ladysmith. He gone with the soldiers.' Umfaan shuffled his feet hesitantly. 'Baas Lord he not let me go – he say too dangerous. I stay in Ladysmith.'

'Did you tell him that we're still here, Umfaan?' There was a frantic note in Rosamunde's voice as she stopped and looked straight into the young black boy's eyes. 'Tell me the truth now, Umfaan. Did you tell him?'

For an awful moment Arabella braced herself for the news.

Umfaan looked suddenly shy and sheepish. 'I tell Baas Lord – he very cross. I never see Baas Lord so cross, missus. He say you go to Durban.'

'So he knows. He knows and he hasn't come back,' Rosamunde answered unhappily. 'He doesn't care what happens to us, surrounded by the hateful enemy!'

'He cannot return, Rose,' Arabella said, coming up beside her. 'He's fighting a war. There's no way he can leave his men, you know that. And we are supposed to be in Durban.'

They all turned just then, as a troop of British horsemen rode up and reined in behind their commanding officer. They were shocked to see that the soldiers were scarcely recognisable as men. All were burnt a reddish-brown by the sun, their faces covered with sweat and dust.

Many were blistered by the scorching heat. Some were without tunics, and the blue army shirts they wore were stiff with blood. Some had helmets while others were bare-headed, and the khaki had changed in colour from a yellowish-brown to dirty-red, blotched with mud. Down near the river, another wagon was crawling along, its Red Cross flag slowly moving in the slight breeze. The officer, a ruddy-faced man with a fair moustache, dismounted and doffed his helmet, announcing that they had come to remove the wounded and bury the dead.

He was amazed to find the women on the farm, surrounded by enemies, and when he heard that Arabella was a nurse, he told them that he and his men would return to escort them through the Boer lines that evening. By that time, Rosamunde was eager to leave, and she agreed – much to Arabella's relief.

How slowly the time passed! The afternoon dragged on, and the house seemed more isolated than ever now that Umfaan and the wounded soldiers had gone with the wagons. At six o'clock, Arabella sat tensely at the table in the sitting room. She could hear the pendulum of the tall grandfather clock in the hall, swinging backwards and forwards. She was still alert as silent-footed servants lighted the lamps. The children were waiting restlessly to see the soldiers and their horses, and the mule wagon stood ready outside the door, the two hacks inspanned, and snorting restlessly as they pawed the gravel.

It was just after eight, when they had eaten a hurried cold meal, that the disturbing news arrived with Sijan that the troop of soldiers accompanying the medical wagons had been ambushed by the Boers and wiped out. In terror, the black drivers had run away, leaving only Umfaan and one of the wounded soldiers to whip up the mules and drive the rest back to Ladysmith.

Rosamunde sank into a deep depression and remained in her bedroom with the curtains drawn, crying in despair. Arabella hid her acute disappointment from the children, but deep inside an anger burned, and a growing hatred towards the foul brutes who had killed the soldiers.

9

A fearful foreboding settled on the farmstead. Night after night, Luke woke from terrifying dreams of screaming horses and dead soldiers, and it was all Arabella could do to calm him down. During the day, she began to grow increasingly worried when he wandered too far from the house. He did not understand the real dangers, apart from what he had seen, and he went further each day.

One particularly oppressive afternoon, she discovered that he was missing. Not wanting to distress Rosamunde, she went out to look for him, heading for his favourite haunt among the rocks. Torn rags of blue had opened between the heavy-bellied clouds, lying ominously low over the curving spine of hills, as she ran quickly towards one of the easier paths leading up to the forbidden kopje. She knew she was approaching enemy territory, but intuitively sensed that Luke had gone that way. The great, heavily-treed plain stretched below, bursting with blue and white lilies, and the small white candles of bushman's pipe glimmered here and there among the flame of aloes, as she pushed her way through the waist-high grass rippling in the eerie light before a storm.

Something drew her attention to a rocky cave further up the trail and she stopped to listen. Nothing seemed to move as she looked back towards the hostile hills stretching away, then her eyes were brought back to the rock faces closer at hand, draped with the dainty orange rosettes of aloes growing on the edges of the sheerest places. She was about to move forward, when something stirred at the edge of the rocks, where the bushes ended.

She stood very still in the terrible quietness of the magnificently wild countryside, where danger lurked behind every boulder. This side of the river, the homestead and its lawns seemed very distant. She hesitated, glancing around. Nothing. Nobody. Just the vast hillsides, the dark heavy clouds and, far away, the muted boom of shellfire. She was alone in enemy territory, with nothing to protect her!

Then she heard sounds of feet scrambling over the rocks, and a bloodcurdling shriek. Her first terrified impulse was to hide in the bushes, or run back along the track. There was a rattle of stones, and stealthy movements in the bush – something else was beyond those rocks ahead. Was it Luke?

Arabella forced herself to call out, knowing that somehow the boy was in danger.

'Luke! *Luke!* Where are you? It's me Bella!'

She heard movements above, and froze in horror. Then she thought of the small boy, shaking with fear, and of the Boers who had shot the soldiers, and rage suddenly leapt up in her breast, so sharply that it jabbed at her heart like a knife-thrust, and fear fell away before her overpowering fury. Let them just touch Luke! Damn them all to hell with their arrogance and contempt of the British!

Quickly and noiselessly, she hurried through the narrow defile above, making her way towards the top. The trail twisted alarmingly, and showed dim through the flowering shrubs, broken by patches of light and shadow where, alarmed by her presence, chattering birds fled. Suddenly she glimpsed a form out of the corner of her eye, and heard a human voice raised in terror.

It was Luke – she was sure it was he! Visions of the rough enemy torturing the child rushed through her fevered brain as she approached the top of the kopje, breathing hard.

'Wie's daar?' shouted a voice in Dutch, and she stopped suddenly, the blood thudding in her ears so loudly she could hardly hear anything else.

Three Boers rose from behind one of the rocks. They were dressed in dark, dusty coats, slouch hats, and had bandoliers slung across their chests. She found herself looking at the cold muzzle of a Mauser pointing straight at her heart.

The leading man came out from behind his cover, sturdy and menacing, and she stood perfectly still, sensing but no longer seeing the gun. He shouted something in Dutch and then he was advancing towards her, his strong muscled legs taking the rough track with ease. He stood before her, and touched the brim of his clipped-up hat politely with his free hand.

'We meet again, mejuffrou from the farm of Lord Stradcombe.'

He spoke excellent English, with the cultured accent of a Free Stater, and the mocking tone made her look at him more closely. His voice was very deep and unexpectedly musical. With a start, she recognised the arrogant young Boer with the cleft chin who had come with Commandant Jopie de Beer to the house. Arabella's legs felt cold to the knees but rage scorched her face. She wanted to scream hateful things at him, but could find no words. She could only watch his face change from hard tension to faint mockery.

'I thought you understood you were not to leave the boundaries of your farm, mejuffrou. You are in our territory."

He loomed over her, now joined by the other two men, bringing the wildness of the veld and the lonely, craggy hills with them. Her heart was beating frantically, but her back was erect and her head was high as she met his stare.

'I came looking for my young relative Luke, who wandered up here as small boys will. I know I heard him scream a few minutes ago. If you have done anything to hurt him, you'll be very sorry!'

The alert brown eyes of the first man watched her sceptically, then he said, 'Now what should we do to a small boy, mejuffrou? Slice him up for biltong? Unfortunately for your British Press, which lampoons us as monsters, we are not savages.'

'I know what you're like – you're all a lot of –' She halted, flustered, suddenly remembering that she was alone against these men.

'Filthy swine?' For an instant a gleam of humour lit his face, then he chuckled suddenly, an infectious, melodious sound, and for a moment she was transfixed by the sheer carefree quality of it. Then it stopped, and he was looking down at her with mock humility.

'Lady, it is a fact that we have been known, on occasion, to bleed. We are, contrary to popular British belief, sometimes as human as you are.'

His words conveyed such cynical contempt that Arabella seethed with suppressed fury, but before she could reply one of the other men had come forward.

'Oh, c'mon du Rand. Let's help the lady find the kid,' he said in English without the slightest trace of an accent. He was slightly younger, and had a broad, attractive face, fierce red eyebrows and a full, uncompromising mouth. He doffed his hat and smiled grudgingly at her. 'Our blood, ma'am, is the same colour as yours, believe it or not.'

A mass of red curls flowed about his head and she wondered, with sudden amazement, why this English-speaking South African should be fighting with the Boers. Both men turned as the third one said something in a harsh, angry voice. He spoke in Dutch, but looking contemptuously at her, he broke into heavily accented English.

'You are mad, Brandauer. This woman is a spy! I don't trust these people. Why did she stay on her farm when everyone else left, I ask you that? I tell you there *is* no missing boy.'

Arabella turned on him like a small fury. 'There *is* a boy! This man has seen him at the house when he came with Commandant de Beer – and it's utter nonsense that I'm a spy. Now I want to find the child before it's too late.'

'She should have left, man – like the rest. I tell you, du Rand, there is something I don't trust about this woman.' The third man came closer and continued talking to the first man in Dutch. He was taller than the other two, and lean, with a dark, sombre face, the light-blue eyes deeply set beneath heavy brows. He levelled his rifle at her, breaking again into English.

'These rooineks are treacherous, my friends. They say one thing and think another – that's how they deceived President Kruger, man, with their doubletalk. This woman's clever, anyone can see it.' His lean, sullen face was hard and suspicious, and a cold little fear began to throb in Arabella's breast.

'She doesn't look like a spy to me.' Brandauer was grinning suddenly – a disarming, enchanting grin like a mischievous schoolboy. 'And she doesn't smell like one, either. Trust me, I have a Jewish nose for these things.'

Arabella forgot her fear for a brief instant, and bit back the sudden amusement. 'That's enough of this nonsense,' she said coldly. 'I have a child to find, so if you'll just let me pass –' She dropped her eyes before the penetrating look du Rand gave her, feeling frightened once more, and increasingly worried about Luke.

'Let's help the lady – what harm can it do?' Du Rand's eyes mocked the fear in her face. 'What's his name, mejuffrou?'

Annoyed that she had shown her trepidation, she cried: 'Let's get on with it, then! His name is Luke.' She turned away. 'Luke! Where are you, darling? I know you're down there somewhere.' The rocks took her voice and threw it back tauntingly at her.

'You're mad to trust this woman,' the lean dark man spat out venomously, still pointing his gun at her.

Arabella was about to call out again when they heard a faint cry from somewhere below them.

'Luke! Luke! He's there ... he's fallen over the rocks!' she cried, running towards the edge of the hillside. In her haste she stumbled against the rock face, nearly plunging over the edge. But du Rand was there before her. He put out a hand to steady her, and without hesitation she caught it; the grip was like an iron band, the muscles of his arm under his coat swelled under her full weight, as he helped her to her feet.

'Keep back,' he said. 'It's a dangerous drop down there. Hey Herman, Isaac – come and help here. We've got to pull the boy up or he'll fall to his death.'

Tucking her muslin blouse into her skirt, Arabella steadied herself and stood back, trembling as she watched du Rand pull off his hat and coat. He now took shape before her with extraordinary vividness, and she saw with a start that he was the most handsome man she had ever encountered, with hair as gold as cornsilk and very thick, with a tendency to curl at his neck. Immediately distancing herself, she drew a deep, shuddering breath, and wondered what he would do.

Stretching himself on his hands and knees, he looked over the steep edge of the cliff where the rocky rampart rose above the valley and in places the granite had worn away and was very smooth. Below was the cluster of farmstead buildings; nearby, only the rustlings of small creatures could be heard while vultures wheeled and dived, already coming in from the east. A small mongoose darted out of the undergrowth, and a colony of greyish-brown dassies stared at them with unblinking eyes, before vanishing.

Du Rand looked up and spoke in Dutch to the other two men, then he turned to Arabella. 'The boy is on a ledge, wedged into a rock.'

'But we can't pull him up, Deneys – there's nothing we can use.' Brandauer looked around with a frown on his face.

The other man sat back on his heels, a sullen expression on his face. Du Rand thought for a moment, then a smile lit his dusty features. 'There is something we can use – but it depends on the mejuffrou here.'

'Why me?' Arabella stiffened. Visions of being lowered down the steep hillside because she was the smallest and lightest swept through her, and a small knot of fear tightened in her stomach. Then it subsided. 'All right, I'll go down and fetch Luke,' she announced.

For an instant, amusement flashed through du Rand's eyes and he grinned. 'You're not dressed for such a hazardous expedition, mejuffrou but if you'll be good enough to give me your petticoats, I can make a strong rope with which to haul the boy up.'

Brandauer burst out laughing, but the dark man scowled. 'Next you'll be having tea, rooinek style, in this woman's kitchen – where she'll have you ambushed.' Arabella knew that he deliberately spoke in English so that she would know of his bitterness towards her people.

'Your honour is safe with us, mejuffrou,' du Rand said, adding insult to injury. 'Good Boers never molest women, even of the enemy.' His voice hardened as he spoke, and his brown eyes cooled. 'I'm not trying to humiliate you, mejuffrou – but if you want us to rescue the boy, your undergarments are the only things we can use.' He rose from his knees. 'The choice is yours.'

Acute anxiety raced through Arabella. Luke had to be saved, and the cost of her petticoats and her embarrassment were insignificant compared with his life. She drew a quivering breath. 'Turn around then, and don't look.'

A surprisingly warm grin flashed out on du Rand's face, and the hardness seemed to disappear. 'On our honour, we will keep our backs turned. Now, c'mon Brandauer, and don't cheat!'

She heard a low chuckle as she turned away and began awkwardly untying ribbons and tapes that no man had ever seen. Then she stepped out of the petticoats, and handed then to du Rand, who passed one on to Brandauer, and proceeded to unceremoniously tear the lace trimmings into long strips. They then tied them into a rope, fastening one end around Brandauer's waist as the third man held him back against the rock face. It was anchored in this way as du Rand made ready to climb down.

'See that it is anchored at all times, you two,' he said, 'and when I shout the word, haul it up.'

Arabella tensed herself as slowly and carefully he lowered himself over the edge. At one point he jerked the rope and it lurched dangerously, but the other two men steadied it, and hung on. Then he disappeared and they could hear him descending as loose stones rolled away, hurtling into space, before hitting some rocks near the bottom with a crash. From then on, there was nothing to do but wait ...

Something touched Arabella's face, and she flailed her arms wildly, biting back a scream.

'It's only a bat,' Brandauer reproved, holding firmly to the rope tied about his waist. 'It won't harm you. It's probably more frightened of you than you are of it.'

'Why are you fighting for the Boers?' Arabella glanced at the other man, who now sat on a nearby rock, his gun at the ready.

Brandauer shrugged. 'I'm fighting for justice – for the land that is by right and conquest, Boer land. As a Jew I understand that – my father was a Russian refugee from the filthy Tsarist pogroms.' His heavy-lidded eyes regarded her curiously. 'It was my deluded father, Jacob Brandauer, who helped set up the regiment Lord Stradcombe fights in.' He smiled mirthlessly. 'He never would understand that he's on the wrong side. The whole world is against this war – and the Boers are going to win.'

Arabella drew a deep breath. 'The world may think that we're wrong, but now it's started, we have to think of our honour. We would be terribly humiliated by defeat.'

'Honour?' Brandauer retorted scornfully. 'Dead and maimed men are no heroes, lady.'

'There is another side to this war that you seem to have conveniently misunderstood, Mr Brandauer, and that is the way the Uitlanders were made to feel alien and inferior and suspect by the ruling Dutch caste of the Transvaal.'

He gave her an aggressive, searching look. In the distance, the muted sound of thunder began to rumble. 'Du Rand's father, the State Secretary of the Transvaal, old Sarel, could give you a number of reasons why they were treated as such which would make all you conniving British shut up once and for all.'

'This man du Rand – he's the son of the State Secretary, the former President of the Orange Free State?' she asked, with ill-concealed scorn. She had heard all about Sarel du Rand from Ben, and had gathered that there was little to like about the man. 'If he's as clever as he's made out to be, he should have been quicker to find a better solution to an explosive situation.'

'I'd like you to know that we're not all a bunch of ham-fisted fools and country bumpkins, as Alfred Milner seems to think. Deneys du Rand for instance, holds a Law Tripos from Cambridge. Only last year he accompanied his father on State visits to France and Belgium. Sarel du Rand has entertained most of the well-known figures in this country, even your infamous Cecil John Rhodes.' Brandauer fixed her with his intense, fiery eyes. 'Deneys du Rand knows you people and the way your minds work – he thinks you are self-righteous bastards.' He looked moodily ahead at the wall of massed clouds. 'Sometimes I think that Herman Muller sitting back there, is right. He doesn't trust you British one scrap. He thinks you're only out for your gain and our gold.'

'And we think you are arrogant and nearsighted,' she began heatedly, but was interrupted by du Rand's voice, coming from below. She could not hear what he said, but Brandauer leaned forward and shouted something in reply.

After what seemed like an eternity, Brandauer pulled at the rope, and motioned Herman Muller to help him. Reluctantly Muller rose, and slowly the rope was pulled up. Soon, Luke lay panting on the edge, alive but obviously in pain. Arabella inched her way towards him and knelt at his side. Moving her experienced fingers over him, she felt dried blood on his right arm, and the sharp edges of broken bone under the bruised skin. As she shifted him gently into a more comfortable position, du Rand hoisted himself over the edge of the cliff. There was the faintest of clicks as Muller put up his rifle, and she saw the gleam of the barrel; she knew, with chilling certainty, that he would fire the weapon if necessary.

Breathing hard, Deneys du Rand knelt down beside her. 'How is the boy?'

'There are no complications, thank goodness. It's a greenstick fracture of the ulna – the inner bone of the forearm. As there's no displacement, he will heal quickly. I need to make a sling, though, before he can be moved again.' Her voice faltered in sudden confusion as she saw in the brown depths of his eyes, a tiny light that flickered for a brief moment, like a small raw flame, before it died. 'I need a large piece of your shirt,' she told him.

'My *what*?' He spoke with pretended amazement. 'Now why would you want that? Not for a souvenir, surely?'

'I need to make a sling, and seeing that I surrendered my petticoats, I think it's a fair exchange,' she said tersely.

'I suppose it would be most ungallant to refuse,' he said lightly, and proceeded to unbutton his shirt. He wore breeches and no braces, and averting her head, Arabella staunched Luke's blood with the hem of her skirt, talking to the small, frightened child all the time.

'Here.' She looked up into two amused brown eyes, and took the crumpled shirt he held out to her. He had replaced his coat, but it gaped open and she was very much aware of the tough, hard chest matted with fair hair that was partially exposed. His body seemed so hard and strong, as did his obviously keen mind, and his easy, confident agility quite disconcerted her. She took the shirt, and was surprised to notice that it was made from the finest linen, then she remembered that this man was the son of a former President of a State, who was helping President Kruger to run the war.

Arabella expertly tore the cloth into a square, then made a rough triangular shape. She tied it firmly around Luke's arm and shoulder, and stood up to let du Rand carry him down the kopje.

'Are you a nursing sister, by any chance, mejuffrou?' Deneys du Rand's manner was mildly teasing but she knew there was a certain seriousness behind the question.

'I am,' she replied, tossing her small, expressive head. 'Now will you please carry the boy carefully.'

She comforted Luke, who cried with tears of pain and fear as Deneys du Rand, followed by Isaac Brandauer, carried him carefully down the trail, Muller keeping a resentful distance behind.

The sky was heavily overcast, with an unearthly stillness. There was a sudden flash of jagged lightning and large drops of rain started to fall. The sky darkened dramatically and a deafening crash of thunder followed, as the men quickened their pace, agile as mountain cats. Then the heavens opened, and the rain came down fast, whipping across the hills and deadening all other sounds. Arabella was already soaked, and her skirt clung in dripping masses to her legs, making her progress halting. There were frequent flashes of lightning now, followed by a savage drum-roll of thunder.

Once down, within sight of Mr Squires' shack, Herman Muller glowered at Deneys du Rand. 'Leave the boy, Deneys. We must get out of here, now we are in their ground. There could be a party of rooineks waiting for us near the house.'

Du Rand turned to her. 'Herman's right – we can't come any closer. Will the boy be all right in that hut?'

Arabella nodded, knowing it would be wise not to bring the enemy any nearer the house. 'Yes, please take him inside. An old man lives there – he won't mind. I'd better go ahead and warn him, though, or he could shoot and ask questions afterwards.'

Water dripping from his slouch hat, the blond man nodded. 'Wait here, Brandauer – and when the mejuffrou gives the signal, we'll carry him in.'

Herman Muller swore furiously in Dutch, then after a vigorous argument, lifted his hand heavenward in disgust and vanished into the driving rain. Then Arabella appeared in the doorway of the shack and beckoned to them. Luke was carefully laid on a makeshift bed of packing cases while Mr Squires peered at the Boers curiously from under his wispy brows.

'I'd offer you some brandy, but there's none left,' he said finally, 'so now you'd best be gettin' back to shellin' our troops – for all the good it'll do you. Give me regards to ol' Joubert – I fought 'im back on bleedin' Majuba Hill.'

'We'll send you a postcard from Maritzburg, Oom,' Deneys du Rand said, as they turned to go. 'When we take the town.'

'And a telegram from Durban,' Brandauer added, grinning suddenly like a far-from-harmless Cheshire cat.

Mr Squires stroked his grizzled beard. 'Oh, go on with ye. We'll be knockin' on doors in Pretoria before Christmas has come and gone,' he replied, whistling through his yellowed teeth.

'Don't bet on it, Oom,' Deneys du Rand advised, a slow smile spreading on his face. 'We're going to chase you back into the sea.'

Arabella stared up at him, and saw that now the dust and grime had been washed from his face, it had a warm, healthy glow. Beneath the well-sculptured cheekbones the flesh was firm over strong muscles. There was something about him that she could not ignore, an almost reckless air and that intangible, arrogant assurance that he knew who he was, and why he was here.

He felt her looking at him, and turned his head, glancing sharply at her pale face with its liberal sprinkling of freckles, and enormous green eyes. Her hair was plastered to her scalp; rivulets of water were shining on her face and trickling down her neck; her clothes were soaked and clinging to her body. Then he looked away as Brandauer darted his head outside.

'We'd better go, du Rand. It won't do to fall into British hands after all this!'

Then he and du Rand tipped their hats, and noiselessly melted through the trees into the curtain of falling rain.

10

Once back in the house, Arabella was able to make a proper splint for Luke, and over the following days, she was able to keep him from becoming too restless, She had asked him to remain silent about the three Boers. She sighed inwardly, knowing that the thought of the Boers had become for Luke the symbol of pain and the signal for tears. She dared not mention them usually, or anything that was happening beyond the house, and Rosamunde, hovering at her son's bedside, wringing her hands and scolding him for his accident, only made it worse. It was at those times that he and she behaved like conspirators, and he constantly looked to her for reassurance when his mother nagged him. He tossed and turned at night and cried, and Arabella had come to dread the occasions when she could not comfort him. He was confused; the Boers were his father's enemies, and his own, and yet they had saved his life. And all the time, while Arabella was busy amusing him, cutting out pictures and telling him and Cynthia stories until her voice grew hoarse, the British and Boers were clashing all the way from Elandslaagte southwards and drawing nearer to Ladysmith with every passing day.

The air on the morning of Rosamunde's twenty-fifth birthday was as oppressive as ever. Everything lay silent outside. No wagon creaked by. No horses raised the dust with their clattering hooves, or whinnied in the pastures. Arabella missed the clink of silver as the table was laid; the clatter of pans in the kitchen where Rashida gave orders, ruling her domain like a queen, and the muted chatter of the houseservants in starched aprons dusting and polishing the furniture or sweeping the floors. For weeks there had been no sounds of the gardeners' voices singing rhythmically as they tended the lawns and watered the plants.

She rose quickly and went outside. Nothing moved; there was an ominous silence. A fairly large hawk-like red-chested cuckoo sat still on a high branch of a tree, watching her, but as she approached it flew away. Somewhere, she thought tensely, and closer than they knew, was an enemy force, numbers unknown, bringing the danger closer at every turn. And they were trapped at Suncrest Farm . . .

Just then, from down near the river, she heard the crack of a rifle, and then it seemed as if the air was full of the echoes of rifle-fire, coming from the ridge above it. For a second, there seemed to be confusion, and Arabella ducked behind the verandah railing, her heart racing with fear. Two men galloped past below. One was rocking in the saddle and she could hear his faint screams of agony. Then more men chased after them, but she could not distinguish between friend or foe.

She lifted her head cautiously above the railing. Now a riderless horse was running loose alongside the river, and two figures lay still in the dust. The other riders had disappeared. Hardly daring to breathe, she crouched down again as she heard more rifle-fire; it seemed like ages that she stayed there, paralysed with terror.

Some time later, she never knew how long, a sound in the bushes aroused her from her numbness. A man crouched there, the muzzle of his rifle glinting every now and then in the light. Her terror returned when he threw a small pebble at her feet to gain her attention.

'Psst! It's me, Isaac Brandauer. I helped to save young Luke,' he hissed, before she could move away. 'Now I need your help.'

Slowly, as if she was sleepwalking, she made her way down the verandah steps to the bushes where the gold magnate's son waited. 'What do you want?' she whispered, crouching down so that she could see his eyes, which were now on her level. 'You must go away from here – your Commandant promised you'd leave us alone.'

'I know, but I need your help urgently.' He looked at her for a moment, the heavy-lidded eyes serious. 'Deneys du Rand had been hit badly by one of your soldiers up on the ridge, and I want you to look at him. I know you're a nurse. Will you come with me?'

Arabella was stunned. 'How can you ask me that? We are enemies – go and fetch your own doctors!'

She was about to move away, when he caught her wrist. 'Please don't go – come and help my friend. We're too far away from our Commando ambulance to call our doctor. If it was peace-time you wouldn't refuse to help a patient, would you?'

'Well, it's not peace-time! Go back to your friend without me.' She stood up, determined to walk away from this detestable man. How dare he come to ask her for aid when he and his comrades were mowing down British soldiers without a scruple!

'Deneys told me you would refuse. He said you were too English for your own good!' Isaac scowled, picking up his gun from the grass beside him.

'He said that, did he?' Her voice was lofty in the extreme. 'If you ask me, Deneys du Rand is far too arrogant – a lesson he will have to learn sooner or later. Did he ask you to fetch me?'

Isaac shook his head. 'No – he asked me *not* to fetch you. It was my stupid idea. I should have known that you are too callous and unfeeling to help another human being in trouble, even when he put himself in danger to save that child's miserable little life for you!'

His words stung. Arabella hesitated, then said, 'Where was he shot?'

There was another second in which she could see him make up his mind. 'In the chest.'

She stood for a moment, ankle-deep in the dew-damp grass, as the sound of more gunfire exploded, but further away this time. 'I'll go with you, but let me fetch my medical bag. Wait here.'

Isaac's scowl turned to open amazement, then to delight, and his eyes twinkled suddenly at her. She retreated into the quiet house, and was soon out again, carrying the small case and a folded-up sheet. She followed him noiselessly down the ridge to the river, and along the bank, keeping under cover all the way.

He took her across to the other side of a narrow cleft where the old massed trees ran along the twisted line of the river, and they walked cautiously along the track, round the knoll on their right and on to land sloping gently towards the hills that cupped it and where, off to one side, they could make out the winking of a heliograph.

They climbed up a gully where Isaac stopped, head cocked, then he turned to Arabella, who was following closely behind, her breathing laboured. An elderly man with a long grey beard, a longer dusty coat, whipcord trousers and a bloodstained shirt sat on a nearby rock, keeping a lookout for British soldiers. He frowned suspiciously at her as she walked past.

Isaac turned to her. 'We dragged Deneys into the shelter of the rocks.'

Arabella looked around. Beyond her there was only the sky over the ridge, which commanded a good view of the surrounding countryside. A quick look over the ledge showed a party of Boers streaming for their horses, and above, on another ledge, was posted a very young man with a rifle.

The heat crept into her cheeks as she saw Deneys lying in an awkward position against the rock face, the sun brightening his bare blond head. The vital spark had gone from his face and he looked drawn and pale. Then she saw that he lay in a pool of his own blood. There was a dark red stain on his shirt, and she wondered, her heart suddenly heavy with dread, if he was still alive.

She placed the medical case on the ground beside her, and then she was bending over him, and trembling as she felt for his pulse. She gently opened his shirt and ran a hand across the wound and around

82

it, feeling the sticky dried blood. Then she loosened his leather belt to enable him to breathe more easily.

He was quite a tall man with broad, powerful shoulders and a lean waist, with an expanse of hard, tapering chest, covered with light golden hair that dwindled into a shadowed line as it trailed down his flat, hard belly. He was neither thin nor massive, but appeared to be in superb physical shape, for which she was grateful, knowing that his good health would help him recover fast. As she examined the small, clean bullet-hole – very much aware as she did so of his all-too-noticeable physical attractiveness – she thought that he had much to be arrogant about.

'Will he be all right, mejuffrou?' Another man, a little younger than Deneys but with the same blond hair, slid alongside them, while others clumped against the rock face. 'I'm Deneys' brother Daniel. Most people call me Danie.' He smiled in an engaging way, and she could see that good looks seemed to run in the family.

'I don't know yet,' she said quietly. 'I'll have to clean the area first. He needs to be X-rayed as soon as possible to locate the position of the bullet. Even though it's a new invention, only four years old, X-rays can be very helpful.'

As she spoke, her mind was busy with the rules she had learnt during her training in London. First, attend to the breathing, then the circulation, and then stop the pain. She looked up, and caught Isaac's eye.

'We must move him into a more comfortable position,' she instructed. 'He seems to be lying on his left arm. I don't want to hurt him, as he's been shot in the chest, but luckily the bullet has missed the bone and lungs.'

Isaac nodded, and together, with the help of Danie, they managed to lift Deneys carefully, so that his arm was freed.

'He fell, mejuffrou – from up there.' Danie pointed to the top of the kopje. 'A sniper got him, but not before he got one of those –' His voice hailed off as his eye caught hers.

Arabella lifted her hand and stared down at the blood covering her palm. Her heart began thudding. It was light red blood, from fresh bleeding, and it came not from the chest wall, but from his arm. Very carefully, she pulled aside the torn shirt-sleeve, to expose the bone at the elbow revealed through the oozing blood; she controlled herself to remain calm. Never had she seen such a jellied mess of blood and tissue. She wondered what she should see to first – the chest or the arm? She decided to attend to the chest as there was less to do there, and then give her full attention to the arm.

Deneys raised his head and looked at her as she tried to gently pull away the torn edges of the shirt at his chest. There was a long, rending tear as the garment split away, and he grimaced in agony. The emerald eyes settled on him with instant concern, and Arabella bit her lips contritely. 'I'm so sorry. I don't mean to hurt you, but the blood has dried on your shirt.'

'Isaac said you would come,' he muttered.

'He did not give me that impression.' She spoke softly as she completed the work on his chest, then quickly she eased away the rest of the cloth around his arm. 'Has anyone got any *more* alcohol? I must clean this wound.'

Isaac nodded. 'We've some French brandy – from our French comrades. I'll fetch it.'

'What a waste of good cognac.' Deneys winced, but held back a groan, as she cleaned away the blood with the spirits and worked out small chips of bone that were sticking through the skin of the arm. Danie sucked in his breath as she proceeded, and started to whistle the *Marseillaise* low between his teeth.

'I'm worried that gas gangrene may infect the dead tissue,' she said, sitting back on her heels and pushing the hair off her forehead. 'If the injured tissues are not removed, infection will probably occur.'

'Can you do something, mejuffrou?' Danie asked, anxiously staring at his brother, who had closed his eyes in silent pain.

The smell of stew wafted back towards them from behind the rock face, mingling with the smell of spent cordite. Arabella became suddenly aware of her empty stomach, but had too much to think about to focus on it. She addressed Danie as he crouched beside his brother. 'It's something no nurse does, and I have only watched doctors perform this operation in the hospital twice. In peace-time, we do not usually tend such wounds.'

'What can you do, then?' Isaac asked, looking down with a frown at Deneys, as he wiped the sweat from his friend's forehead. 'You must do something. Of all the men I've fought with, there has not been a braver fellow than he. Please, ma'am, I beg you to do something.'

At this note of appeal, her heart sank. She knew all too clearly what should be done, but had no experience of doing it. She had read about the time-honoured principle of debridement on flesh wounds many times, imagining what it would be like to operate as a doctor, but it was only theory. Yet she knew if she left it, this man could die . . .

Arabella knew Deneys du Rand was her enemy, but he had saved Luke's life, and he had done it without thinking of the consequences. Could she do the same thing? It was ludicrous, she thought, observing the anxious faces of his brother and friend, that here she was, faced with saving the life of an enemy, who had shot and killed her own people, and who, if he lived, would go out and do the same thing again!

'You're asking a lot from me.' She looked down at the swab in her hands. 'But if Deneys is agreeable, I shall try.'

'Anything, mejuffrou!' Danie broke in hastily. 'You must do it.' He bent down and spoke to Deneys, then Isaac joined them.

Arabella strained to hear what they were saying in their soft, mingled voices but as they spoke in Dutch she could not understand. Would he agree? Time was precious now.

Then Danie looked up and nodded. 'Deneys says try anything – he is too much in pain to care.'

When the discussion was over, the men fitted themselves around the rock as best they could, still keeping a sharp lookout for British soldiers, and the space seemed suddenly too small to hold this collection of bodies. Arabella felt her head begin to swim as she tried to answer the eager, anxious questions from the brother and his friend; to listen to the rare words from Deneys, and to keep her eyes on her work.

'I have no morphia or chloroform, I'm afraid. Give him some of the brandy. You'll have to be very brave,' she told her patient, 'because it's going to hurt a lot.'

She looked at Deneys, who nodded his haggard face. His lips, which had been mocking and teasing the last time they had met, were now grim with pain, but his eyes held a strange expression which made her feel suddenly elated and uncomfortable. For one brief, intense moment there was no war, and they were a man and a woman with sudden, unexpected chemistry forking between them like lightning – something she had never experienced before, not even with Ben.

Feeling her face flush, she lowered her eyes as Isaac fed Deneys the brandy, forcing him to drink as much as he could, then he told Deneys to bite hard on the leather belt held now by a wiry little black man with the unlikely name of Samson, while Isaac and Danie held him down as carefully as they could.

A spasm of pain shook him as Arabella forced the flesh fragments down as evenly as she could, the blood oozing out between them. Deneys held his breath as she took his pocket-knife and started to cut away all the dead tissue that was easy to distinguish from the healthy tissue, trying to remember exactly what she had seen or read about this type of operation.

'How do you feel? Just nod if it's all right,' she kept asking, and he nodded each time, but gave a muffled groan at one point, and she tried not to wince as she cut in and along the tissue, gently wiping the blood away with the torn sheet. She was aware of the long, shuddering sound of distress, and could only admire his enormous courage in not crying out. She strained to raise her eyelids, but the blinding glare and the blur of faces that looked at her, turned her dizzy again. A wave of nausea overcame the momentary blackness, and the stickiness of the warm, wet blood made her conscious once more.

'I have finished the operation itself,' she managed to whispèr to Danie. 'Your brother is very brave.'

She heard Danie's reply through a haze of faintness, and then they were all silent for a time; only the faint explosions of gunfire and men's shouts sounded from the veld far below.

'I will now swab the wound with brandy, then dress it,' she ventured at last. 'Have you anything to give Deneys besides brandy?'

'We have coffee, mejuffrou, but it's cold.' Danie's dark brown eyes blinked fiercely out of his dusty, good-looking face. 'They've made a fire there behind the ridge. I'll heat it – it'll take no time at all.'

His Mauser in his hand, he crept quickly away along the edge of the rock face.

'Coffee laced with brandy will soon restore his usual good spirits.' Isaac wagged his head so vigorously that a lock of red curls fell over one eye.

Arabella soon discovered that there was no more clean sheeting left, and no safety pins. Slowly, she unpinned the brooch that held the fine lace-edged collar around her neck. It had been made for her last birthday by Aunt Matty, but it was the only clean material she had. She weighed her decision as she gazed at the only brooch of real value she owned, a treasured gift from Rosamunde. It was modest but exquisitely designed – a circle of gold filigree enclosing a large round opal. She held it in her fingers for a long moment, watching the prisms of rainbow colours catching the light. She knew she would never see either brooch or collar again, and a spasm of acute distress welled up inside her, but she knew it was a small price to pay for a man's life, even if he was the enemy. Somehow that no longer mattered. She had used her skills, she had expanded herself by attempting something she had never done before, and already new energy and resourcefulness flowed through her at what she had achieved.

She pinned the brooch firmly to the binding around his arm, and saw that he was made as comfortable as possible. A little later, she forced him to drink some warm black coffee from a silver mug, containing a liberal dash of brandy. Then she sat back on her heels limp and exhausted, scarcely aware of those who came and went, though she knew that other Boers had come to sit with him, men who glanced at her curiously.

Then there was a period of quiet when she rested, and looked up at the sky, which was a deep warm blue. Voices started up once more, sounding as if they were a hundred miles away, and she saw Samson dart towards Deneys, and kneel beside him, speaking rapidly in Dutch. He carried an enamel dish of stew, which Deneys wearily pushed away. As he stood up, the sunlight playing on his small, wiry body, she was aware of a deep strength of purpose and devotion to his masters, and an extraordinary dignity in the man's bearing that she could not ignore.

'Who is that little man?' Arabella asked, peering curiously at him, as he vainly urged Deneys to eat.

'Samson has worked for our family for a long time,' Danie said, grinning. 'Since we were little kids in Bloemfontein, all five sons. He followed us to the battlefield, because he said he must look after us, but we will send him back to my Pa in Pretoria when it becomes too dangerous to keep him here.' He paused. 'Would you like something to eat, mejuffrou? You must be very hungry after that operation.'

He spooned thick meat stew into a dish from the pannikin in his hands, as the acrid smell of smoke rose behind them. Smiling wanly, she shook her head, saying that she must be getting back to her family. Suddenly she felt desperate for news. 'What has been happening on the battlefield, Danie? We've had no news for days.'

Danie frowned, and cocked a golden head at her. 'It's bad news for your people, mejuffrou. We hold most of these kopjes, and the road from Elandslaagte to Ladysmith. Your men have been beaten back all the way. They have nearly reached the town, and there is every evidence that we will soon fight a big battle there.'

Arabella felt as if she had been hit in the stomach. Danie eyed her sceptically for a moment, then he said, 'We can defeat your people, mejuffrou, because we have more men on our side, and we have excellent weapons. Our commandoes are mobile, fast, and at home in this countryside.'

She lifted her chin a fraction higher. 'Don't underestimate our soldiers. They are brave and well-trained.'

'But most of them have not been trained *in this country*, mejuffrou.'

The final word had been said, and when Samson left, she went over to check on Deneys, who lay back and greeted her with a faint, apologetic smile. 'Forgive me for putting you to so much trouble, mejuffrou. You have saved my life and I don't even know your name.'

She saw that a mask of exhausted pain had settled over the fine, handsome features. 'Arabella Allen. Now you should rest. Your friends must take you to a doctor as soon as possible. You'll recover, I have no doubt about that.'

She stood up, rubbing her cramped muscles, tears of weariness and relief gathering in her eyes. She found it difficult to speak, as she turned away and followed Isaac down the ridge.

I I

Rosamunde was waiting for her on the steps of the verandah, her hands on her hips: 'Wherever have you been, Bella? We had breakfast ages ago. We had to share the last of the eggs and now there's nothing left.'

'It's all right, Rose, I'm not hungry,' she lied as she walked across the driveway in the shimmering heat, wishing now that she had accepted Danie's offer of meat stew.

'Why are you carrying your case of nurse aids? And there is blood on your skirt and your blouse –'

Rosamunde was suddenly bearing down upon her with hostile eyes and a defiant rush of long skirts. Arabella felt herself go cold inside. The last thing she wanted now was a bitter confrontation.

'I had to help someone who was badly wounded in the veld.'

'It was a Boer – I can see it in your face! You went to help the enemy! Bella, how could you?' Her cousin's voice filled the air with frightened accusations.

'What does it matter who I helped, Rose? I'm a nurse,' Arabella told her. 'And there are British soldiers out there – a small battle was fought near here earlier this morning.'

When she and Rosamunde came together these days, Arabella was conscious of a new confidence in herself. It no longer mattered to her what her cousin thought of her. Rosamunde's outbursts and tantrums now left her unshaken, but outwardly she appeared concerned.

'You're lying, Arabella! You've been with the enemy!'

A tumult of bitterness and fright began to gather and take shape in a storm of protest which Arabella knew she had to stop.

'Rose, please, not now, not here!'

'And why not here and now? I have a right to know what goes on around me. I'm not going to shut up when my cousin consorts with the enemy.'

'But I can explain. Listen, Rose! It may look suspicious to you, but it's not really. I went to help a British soldier who was in great pain. He had been shot by the Boers –'

'I don't believe you, and I won't stand here and be made a fool of!' Rosamunde's voice rose shrilly before it broke into devastated sobs.

Arabella hated lying, and especially to Rosamunde, but she realised that if she told the truth, there was no knowing what Rosamunde would do. And there were the children to consider.

'Rosamunde, you mustn't say these things, it isn't fair. Now trust me. Have I ever lied to you? Well, have I?' Her voice, which had been soothing at first, had grown cool, and she held Rosamunde's eyes without flinching. Now not only am I become indifferent, I am also turned liar, Arabella thought, depressed. Where will it all end?

Then she saw that her cousin's eyes were large and tortured, that the tears pouring down her cheeks were real. This was no pretended anguish. She knew then that she could never tell her the truth, and she saw that it was necessary for her to take the initiative. Summoning all her remaining strength, she went to Rosamunde, arms outstretched.

'I was half-crazy with worry about you, Bella,' Rosamunde sobbed. 'I looked for you everywhere. You never told anyone where you were going. Nothing is normal any more. The whole world has gone mad, and I have come to believe anything, anything at all.'

'Come, Rose, no more of this. You're not well – you must rest. Now come inside out of this heat, and I'll see if there's anything left for Rashida to make a hot toddy for you. I know there was still some honey, though no milk. The cow was stolen only yesterday by some unscrupulous thief.'

With the medical case still clutched in her hand, she gently led Rosamunde inside to her bedroom, praying that she would have the energy to go on calming this unhappy woman.

'What is to become of us, Belle? I grow more frightened each day.' Rosamunde gave a familiar deep sigh, as she lay back on the lace-edged pillows.

Arabella wondered how Rosamunde would react if she knew that the British had retreated nearly all the way to Ladysmith, and were preparing even now for another bloody battle with the Boers.

'We are not defeated yet, Rose. Our troops are fighting for every inch of territory –' She broke off, for it was obvious that Rosamunde was no longer listening. Her attention had turned to a sound outside. The distant scrape of an opening window had distracted her.

'Do you think that could be Benjamin? He said he'd come back, he did!'

Seeing the blonde head tilt almost secretively in the direction of the noise, and the sudden excitement that showed in her face, Arabella knew that even though Rosamunde had locked Ben out of her bedroom, and even though she hated him for his affair with Mrs Prendergast, all reality for her would always be centred in the magic of his physical presence. By now, Rosamunde had forgotten her as she strained to hear further sounds, waiting for Ben's return, and Arabella left the room.

Arabella was quite unprepared for the blow when it fell. Being honest herself, and free from a malicious spirit, she had reckoned without the vicious emotion of jealousy.

A strange, brooding uneasiness had crept over her that night, and she had lain awake a long time, wondering why she was being drawn into a war she had tried to avoid. She did not want to think about Deneys du Rand, nor any of the enemy, but for some reason, she could not stop herself. Something had happened to her that morning; feelings had been awakened she did not want to acknowledge. He was a stranger to her, he fought against her people, so why should she be so affected by him?

Why do I feel like this, she had cried into her pillow. I don't want to feel this way. I don't want to have anything more to do with the enemy! But Arabella knew that for the first time since the war began, the enemy had assumed a human face.

Sleep came at last, and she awoke renewed, the dark mood of the night before having fallen away. Now it was afternoon and the house was very quiet. Rosamunde rested, and so did the children. Arabella found herself lying tensely in her room, starting up when an insect buzzed through the window and stunned itself against the glass shade of the lamp. She was becoming deeply frightened on this farm, now that the Boers and the British soldiers were fighting in the near vicinity. She imagined a thousand things: stealthy soft-leather boots silently surrounding the homestead, the phantom sound of horses' hooves, the snick of cartridges in the long guns she had seen at close range ... then she thought of Deneys and Danie, and Isaac, and the conflict inside her deepened. She knew she had to forget Deneys, for he fought to kill British soldiers, men like Ben ... And then suddenly her door opened, and Rashida stood on the threshold in a state of suppressed agitation. Arabella sat up in bed, her heart beating rapidly.

'What is it, Rashida? You look as if you've seen a ghost.'

Rashida clasped her hands together over the apricot sari, silver bracelets jingling on her arms. 'It's the Master, Missy Allen. He come home up side path, so no Boer soldier see.'

'Are you sure, Rashida?' Arabella could hardly believe her ears. 'It could be some other soldier, or even a Boer – they all look so alike from far.'

Rashida shook her sleek dark hair, which shone like satin, and again there was the tinkling of many thin silver bracelets.

'No, Missy – it *is* the Master, Lord Stradcombe. I know him. I tell you first, because madam not well.'

'You did the right thing, Rashida. Go now and make something that resembles tea. I'll get up and see him.'

Smiling at the dusky-skinned woman, she rose quickly, pulling a thin shawl about the shoulders of her muslin blouse with trembling hands. Ben ... Ben had returned. But what could she tell him? He would want to know why they were not in Durban. She remembered Umfaan telling them how angry Ben had been when he found out they were still at Suncrest.

With her heart thumping loudly in her breast, she hurried downstairs and into the wood-panelled hallway. Then she checked herself, for there he was, in a mud-spattered uniform, standing in the light of the half-open front door.

'Ben! It isn't safe for you to be here. We are surrounded by Boers, and we're only here on sufferance from one of their Commandants.'

'Hullo, Arabella. And why the deuce *are* you all still here when you should be safely in Durban? You have put yourselves in the devil of a stew.'

He stood, conspicuously thinner and worn, and after she had recovered from the initial shock, she was alarmed at the heavy toll the war had already taken of him. Quietly he closed the door and she took a deep breath, clasping her hands before her in an effort to stop them trembling.

'Rosamunde refused to leave. She was in such a state that I had to agree –' She broke off, fearful that she had gone too far. She took another steadying breath. 'So we stayed. We've been given a circumscribed freedom by a Commandant Jopie de Beer. We were going to leave some days ago with a British escort but all the men were ambushed and shot. Now we have to stay, though it gets more dangerous every day. Ben, they could have killed you out there – there was a skirmish only yesterday between our soldiers and the Boers.'

He nodded, looking upstairs towards Rosamunde's room, an expression of instant anger on his face. 'Is she there?'

Arabella nodded blankly and his eyes returned to her. He was watching her with a sudden intent approval, lingering at the lines of her throat and shoulders, so that she wished he would turn his eyes away. She felt her cheeks grow warm, and an unwelcome glow of animation spread over her as it had always done when he appeared unexpectedly. She stared at him fascinated, while the artist in her attempted to fix that image clearly in her mind.

'You've changed,' he said softly. 'I don't know what it is, but it's there, somehow ... I heard how expertly you nursed the wounded men here. They were brought back to the hospital in Ladysmith by that reckless young devil Umfaan and a wounded private, who raced through the Boer lines like bats out of hell. They say you were as good as any doctor, under the circumstances.'

'I wouldn't say that, Ben. I only did what I could, but Umfaan and that private deserve medals for bravery.'

He was so close to her there in the dimness of the hallway that she could hear him breathing. Even without him saying another word, she was acutely conscious of his inner tension and frustration.

'Is Rosamunde resting?' he asked in a low voice.

She wanted so much to take his hand that she had to keep both her own pressed to the small hall table at her back. She nodded. 'Ben, what is going on – outside in the country? We only see what is happening in the immediate surroundings. I do know that our men have been forced back almost to Ladysmith, and that you may have to fight another battle there.'

'How on earth did you know that?' His eyes narrowed suddenly, and she stiffened, realising she had said too much.

'From Mr Squires – he goes out now and then.'

He sighed, shrugging his shoulders. 'We've been pushed right back in great numbers. The victories at Dundee and Elandslaagte were not decisive enough. Both Kimberley and Mafeking have been surrounded by those devils – Cecil Rhodes himself is imprisoned in Kimberley.' There was bitterness in his voice, and his grey eyes were suddenly smoky and hard. 'What we need to do now is to cut them to pieces with one decisive victory, but they're so disorganised, they turn and run away, or hide in the hills.'

Arabella fought against her mounting fears as he drew a letter from the inner pocket of his uniform. It was then that she noticed that his hand was bandaged. A dark stain had oozed through the lint, as he fumbled awkwardly with it, and the gesture went to her heart.

'What happened to your hand?' Her own shook as impulsively she laid it on his. The gesture had been instinctive; only when she felt that live heat under her cool fingers did she realise her rashness. 'Your hand is feverishly hot – let me see to it,' she commented, withdrawing her fingers.

He shook his head. 'It's not serious, dear girl, only a graze. I have a letter for you, by the way, from England.'

She looked up at him, alarmed by his tone and the grave expression on his face. 'What is it, Ben?' Her eyes dropped to the crumpled letter in his hand, the bandage showing white in the dimness of the hallway.

'It was waiting when I returned from Elandslaagte. Then Umfaan found me, with the news that you were still on the farm. I blew my top, and asked for leave on compassionate grounds, which luckily was granted. The letter looked important – it's from your Aunt Matty's lawyer. I hope it's not bad news.'

His dark brows drew close in a frown. 'I believe you did all you could to persuade your cousin to leave. I know how stubborn Rosamunde can be, once she has made up her mind about something. And now she's put you and me in the devil of a mess, not to mention the children, and the remaining servants.' He stopped abruptly and handed her the letter.

She took it from him and read it, hardly seeing the words in black ink from Aunt Matty's lawyer notifying her that the old lady had died of a heart attack. Aunt Matty had left her all her personal belongings, while her small cottage reverted to Mildred Allen, having been bought by Reginald, her late brother – Rosamunde's father – and leased to her during her lifetime.

Arabella walked trancelike into the sitting room, and was vaguely aware of Ben pouring the last of the sherry into a glass and handing it to her. 'Aunt Matty is dead,' she heard her voice saying. 'I must tell Rosamunde.'

It was only after his own glass was drained that he said, 'I'll tell her, Arabella, if it'll make it easier for you. I know how much you thought of the old lady. Didn't she persuade your father to send you to that very proper girls' school?'

'Yes. She never wanted me to have to depend on others the way she had been forced to do. She even lent me the money to pay for my nurse's training. She wanted to give it to me as a gift, but I asked her to let me borrow it, until I could afford to pay her back. It was a sacrifice for her when she was struggling to make ends meet. And now it's too late.'

Arabella's face had fallen into deep lines of sorrow as she thought of her aunt. If only she had known she was ill ... but Aunt Matty had said nothing. She had unselfishly let her come here to South Africa, knowing that her own days were numbered. Arabella envisaged that sweet dear face, framed with white hair, and the faded blue eyes; she heard again the concerned, slow voice which had spoken so many words of wisdom – many not heeded at the time. Oh, how she would miss her!

A movement arrested her attention, and she knew that Ben was there. He reached out and laid his hand on her shoulder. The pressure of his strong fingers came hotly through the thin muslin blouse. 'I'm sorry, Arabella – you should have been with her. We've only brought you trouble, Rosamunde and I.'

'That's not true, Ben. I'm an adult, I can make my own decisions, and I decided to come out here and to stay.'

'Because we both asked you to.'

She moved away from him towards the windows where the warm sunlight poured in. 'I could have refused, but I did not.' She wavered there, then impulsively turned back to him and the room. She felt the warm strength of his tall frame, and for a brief moment, let herself lean against it. The soft chimes of the mantel clock intruded into their mood and reminded her that he was her cousin's husband.

She drew away resolutely. 'How is Robbie?'

It was suddenly deadening, the silence around them, broken only by the sharp sounds of the birds outside and the agitated drumming of her own slender fingers on the rim of her glass.

'He was killed on Talana Hill. He never wanted to fight, God knows –'

'Oh, no – not Robbie! What did he ever do to anyone?' She turned her head away to hide the sudden rush of tears, and stumbled forward, the room swooping in a new, confusing orbit. And then he caught her, and she was in his arms, and she looked up to find him regarding her with an expression so intensely caring that she began to weep unashamedly.

'Benjamin! How could you, and in this house!' Rosamunde's voice suddenly broke over them like a whiplash as she bore down upon them with smouldering hazel eyes and a furious rustle of lavender silk and lace. She was looking at Arabella and completely misunderstood the green eyes, shimmering with tears, in the pale, strained face.

'You've been having an affair with Benjamin!' she cried murderously. 'There's been something between you ever since you arrived. I should have seen it – you, Arabella, of all people!' She stood, rigid with jealousy, and glared at Ben as he faced her with a calm but haggard expression.

Something dark rose inside Arabella, as she stood staring at her cousin. It sat on her chest, almost stopping her breath and wrapped tight tentacles around her heart. For an instant, as her eyes met Rosamunde's, the air between them trembled with the friction of weeks.

'You've misunderstood the whole thing, Rosamunde. I can explain everything, and it's not what you think,' she said at last, in a tight voice Rosamunde had never heard before, but soon afterwards Rosamunde's furious voice filled the room with withering accusations, and there was something in her expression that turned Arabella's face ashen.

'You have nothing to explain! Living as an honoured guest in my house, and turning on me like a snake in the grass! You've taken everything from me – my husband, my children who no longer want to be near me! Oh, how cruel you are!' Her voice rose shrilly before it broke into wild weeping.

'Rosamunde, don't talk such nonsense!' Ben looked full into her demented eyes. 'I was comforting Arabella, that's all. Your Aunt Matty has died, and she received a letter from the lawyer.'

'And you made it an excuse to come and see her behind my back!' Rosamunde's voice vibrated through the whole quiet house.

'That's not true!' A chill spread through Arabella's heart as she watched her cousin's pale, oval face and felt the jealous rage in her. 'Here's the letter – read it for yourself. And Robbie is dead, too, killed on Talana Hill.'

'You get out of this house at once!' Rosamunde shrieked. 'You Boer-lover! She helps Boer wounded, Benjamin!' She turned to him in a fury. 'She's a spy – a dirty, treacherous little spy!'

'It's not the way it appears – ' Arabella tried again, but Ben cut in, his voice harsh and authoritative.

'Enough! I've had as much as I can stand of this petty quarrelling, do you hear? If you want to believe something as monstrous as that, Rosamunde, God help you, but I'll not stand here and listen to it! You'll both be ready to come with me to Maritzburg in the morning. I will see that Commandant – what did you say his name was?' He turned to Arabella, his face stern and fierce.

'De Beer – Commandant Jopie de Beer.' For a painful moment, Arabella thought of Deneys du Rand. 'He's somewhere outside our boundaries.'

'I'll arrange for a Boer escort as far as the railway line and you'll stay with Clare Mortimer, do I make myself quite clear?'

'I will not go anywhere with that husband-stealer and Boer-lover! She's got to go!'

'Rosamunde, please calm down and look at this reasonably. We have to go – it's too dangerous to stay.' Arabella went impulsively towards her cousin, who instantly recoiled.

'I don't want to listen to you! And I never want to see you again, not for the rest of my life!' Rosamunde screamed, putting her hands to her ears to shut out the sound of Arabella's voice.

'Rosamunde, listen to me! There's been a serious misunderstanding. You can't break a friendship like ours, that goes back such a long way, because of a misunderstanding.'

Rosamunde stared at her through narrowed eyes. 'There has been no misunderstanding. You are in love with my husband and you couldn't wait to get your greedy little hands on him. You couldn't get a man of your own with your plain boring face and straight-laced ways, so you stole my husband. Get away from me! I don't want you near me! You've been cruel and unkind. You don't care how I suffer as long as you can do exactly as you please. Benjamin, send this bitch out of the house!' Her voice broke, and there was a horrified silence.

Ben laid a restraining hand on her arm, but his touch only seemed to make her more furious. Arabella stood transfixed, a feeling of guilt and grief so deep coming over her, that she could hardly breathe. She saw that there was nothing she could do to change Rosamunde's mind, for her cousin was right. She did love her husband, if that's what love was ... She had tried to control her feelings for him, but she had failed. And nothing Rosamunde screamed at her could change that.

She had wanted his arms about her, she had wanted his comfort and his strength in her time of weakness, and she was suffering the terrible consequences.

The room and the figures in it turned hazy before her eyes, and she felt a dull pounding in her ears until she could scarcely focus her attention on the flow of angry words that came from her cousin.

Then, with her eyes blinded with tears, she fled the room, away from the tearful children crowding around her, clutching at her skirts. Knowing that she had nothing to give them emotionally for the moment, she asked Zareena to take them away and shook herself free. As she entered her bedroom and threw herself on the bed, her face wet with tears, she had an intensely unreal feeling about what had happened, as if her life had moved forward into another, more terrifying dimension.

Zareena brought her warm water to wash in. The Indian servant was subdued, her dark eyes lowered, and Arabella was far too miserable to speak to her or offer reassurance. Half of her wanted to escape, to get away from the terrible shadow which loomed over her, and grew menacingly nearer with every breath she took, and half of her wanted to face it and put everything right with Rosamunde. But she was suddenly too weak to do anything but lie there, staring at the drawn curtains.

She lay still. Soon night would come, and with it, fear of the danger outside would creep around the house once more. She felt trapped. She was in an invisible net which had been woven around her ever since her arrival – by this house, this family with its insoluble difficulties, and by this land at war.

She could never go to Pietermaritzburg with the others ... it would never work, it would only make things worse. Rosamunde would never forgive her, Arabella knew that, and she and Ben must never see each other again.

She dreaded facing Ben. He had come to her room earlier, but she had pretended to be asleep. She had heard him leave, and her heart had ached with a longing to call him back, and the misery of knowing she could not. She suddenly felt deathly cold. It was all so unbelievable, but the vision of her bitter cousin continued to stalk her mind like a violent spectre, and she feared what Rosamunde would do.

For the first time, she resented her cousin fiercely. This woman had everything she had ever wanted; she had always been forced to take a back seat with Rosamunde, because Mildred Allen had seen to it that she always played second fiddle to her daughter, even making her wear Rosamunde's cast-off clothes. She thought then that Rosamunde had never deserved a husband like Ben.

She remembered her father's austere vicarage long ago, and her Easter holidays spent in that well-ordered but joyless environment, and how she had always yearned to return to Allenbury Manor to be with Rosamunde, always Rosamunde with her gaiety and her careless enjoyment of life, then later Ben, who had stood out in colourful relief.

There was the slightest tap on her door. Before she could answer, it opened and she heard Ben's voice. 'Arabella.' He spoke to her through the darkness. 'What Rosamunde said was unforgivable. I'm so sorry.'

'She's distraught,' she managed to answer, unable to rise and light the lamps. 'I'm just worried that she will really harm herself this time.'

'She's calmer now. Rashida and I found some laudanum hidden away in a closet. I've given it to her, and I don't think she'll try anything. But I want to ask you to stay with her at Maritzburg – see that she doesn't harm herself.'

Arabella sat up slowly. 'You ask too much of me, Ben. She hates me, and I resent her. It won't work. When we arrive there, I'll try to reach Durban and return to England. My place is there, back at the hospital. I should have returned long ago.'

He had come into the room and was pacing the floor, his body charged with a restless, angry energy. 'Confound Rosamunde! She doesn't know when she's fortunate, that's always been her problem. To throw away your friendship after you've supported her for so long ... Anyway,' he whipped round, and she could sense rather than see him. 'Don't go away!' His voice was tense with appeal. 'It's asking a lot of you, I know. But stay in Maritzburg – for my sake.'

'I can no longer make such a promise, Ben.' She hesitated for a moment, then hurried on. 'It wouldn't be fair to any of us, and especially not to the children.'

'Well, promise then that you'll think about it. I found Commandant de Beer this afternoon, and he's agreed to take you all through their lines with an escort to the railway line near Colenso – the next largest town south of Ladysmith – and over the Tugela River to the borders of British-held territory.' He paused, then said dryly, 'Apparently they knew of the assault of my men on Talana Hill and said that in recognition of my outstanding courage, or some such thing, he would do it.'

'I'll think about it, Ben,' she told him at last.

When her strength flowed back some hours later, Arabella turned up the wicks of the lamps and went to the wardrobe, where she began to take down the few garments she would need and could carry in flight to Ladysmith, the nearest town. She had decided not to go with the escort the next day, but to leave secretly that night. She knew it would be too dangerous to try to return to Durban on her own, so she had decided to help nurse the wounded men in the hospital at Ladysmith. At least that way she could make herself useful until the war ended, and it would take her mind off her own personal suffering.

Mechanically she laid out the few clothes and possessions she was able to take, for she planned to ride one of the hacks that had been well-hidden in the bush, and packed her case of nurse aids into a small bundle.

Pendulu had promised to show her the way to the town. They were to leave at midnight so as not to upset the children, whom she knew she was going to miss dreadfully. She bent over the desk, deciding to leave a letter of explanation for Ben. It was going to be a difficult one to compose. She had never written to him before, and suddenly felt inadequate to explain her decision, to describe the complexity of feeling that filled her as she sat in that room which she now had to leave – of the terrible emptiness at the thought of leaving him ... Then her mind cleared, and she knew what she must say.

She began the letter simply and to the point, making it as brief as possible. Before closing, she asked him to see that the rest of her luggage was taken and deposited in Pietermaritzburg for her to collect when the war ended. The darkness outside seemed peculiarly intense, the elusive night noises drifting across to her from far off, blending with those nearer at hand, as she finished the letter. At midnight she crept out of her room for the last time, and placed the letter to Ben on the hall table. For a brief moment, she glanced about the darkened hallway, feeling a sharp, piercing sadness then, bracing herself, she stole outside to meet Pendulu, whose own father had killed five British redcoats in the great Battle of Isandlhwana, and who now waited in the shadows of the bushes. She was carrying two saddlebags holding nightwear, a few dresses, her nursing apron, toiletries, the nurse aids and a brush. She had never owned less, but just then, she could carry no more. It seemed like a hundred years since she had first arrived at Suncrest Farm, not knowing what to expect, but all that was behind her now, like a whole life lived and ended . . .

12

Arabella paused at the top of the main street of Ladysmith in the October morning light, to take in the town, surrounded by its wild amphitheatre of hills hiding thousands of enemy commandoes, through which she and Pendulu had taken two exhausting, nerve-racking days to ride undetected. She knew she would never see a more welcoming sight than the town hall, with its distinctive square clock tower, which was currently being used as the central British field hospital. During the journey, stealthily passing the hundreds of Boer ox-wagons sited beyond the British army camp outside the town, she had imagined arriving – the excitement, the anticipation of nursing, and the doctors delight when they heard she was a trained sister.

Fear fell away as they left behind the screaming horror of what seemed like the whole force of enemy wagons camped on the plain, but as she and Pendulu stopped before entering the main part of the town, all Arabella could feel was relief. They were safe ... they had reached their refuge from the enemy fire in the hills.

Gazing about her, she hardly recognised the place: houses and shops on both sides of the street were almost hidden by carts, limbers and gun-carriages. Four-wheeled traps with hoods went jolting past, while soldiers on horseback clattered ahead, and those on foot stood in groups under the shop awnings, sharing tobacco, chocolate or liquor. There had been a great number of casualties from the recent fierce and bloody battle at Tinta Inyoni, which the British had finally won, and wagonloads of wounded were being brought in to the hospitals in various parts of the town.

Everywhere there was movement and noise, horses neighing and stamping, the jingle of bridle-irons, and people talking, oblivious of the volley of gunfire outside in the thirty-mile ring of hills, its dreadful noise seeming to echo on and on. Multitudes of bullets still whizzed back and forth between the enemies, and off to one side a heliograph winked in the sunlight. A party of red-faced soldiers carried kegs across the street, helped by a crowd of chattering, turbanned Indians, while groups of Zulu men staggered past carrying cases of stores on their heads, and mules with musical-sounding harnesses drew carts of ammunition towards the military camp on the outskirts of the town. But everywhere, beneath all the noise and apparent chaos, Arabella could sense a feeling of waiting ... of some sort of crisis building up.

As Arabella and Pendulu came abreast of the red-brick town hall, with its Red Cross flag floating high above it, a young civilian trotted past. He was some way in front, when suddenly there was an almighty crash, sending waves of noise echoing through the town. A shell from Bulwana kopje had flown down and burst right under his horse. The sound was deafening, even with all the other noises going on, and before Arabella knew what was happening, her own mount went down on its knees as a heavy piece of flying shrapnel plunged into its flank. Then, with a loud snort of fear, it scrambled up again, with Arabella still clinging desperately to its neck.

Once on its feet, it charged down the street in a panic swerving to avoid a bullock cart carrying a gun limber. Soldiers, shopkeepers and townsfolk rushed forward to see what was happening, and a young soldier leapt nimbly to one side and loaded his rifle as the horse, with its frightened rider, came stamping towards him. While he was ramming the bullet home, the animal suddenly swept round in his direction, knocking into a four-wheeled trap, and throwing Arabella with a heavy crash into the dust.

Before the soldier could fire, the horse was upon him, the rushing hooves catching the rifle and sending it flying into space, and the young man on to his knees. Then another soldier, coming up behind, aimed and fired, the bark of his rifle awakening the echoes in the sudden deadening silence as he yelled for everyone to keep well out of range. The shot rang out as the animal stampeded past.

Arabella was conscious of herself as one slowly stirring to life from a total void, and for a few moments everything floated in a timeless vacuum. Then she woke to the grim reality all around her. She heard a bellow of pain, and saw the hack lying on the ground, dark red blood from a wound in its neck staining the macadamised surface of the street. She looked with pity at the dying horse, and heard with physical loathing the hideous end of a once warm and living animal.

There was a rapid clatter of heels and confused chatter of many voices, then someone close by asked, 'Are you all right, young lady?'

Her distress mounted as she was drawn against her will into her present surroundings. She blinked her eyes and the indistinct shadow beside her helped her up, resolving itself into a man with a neat beard and side-whiskers, his face wrinkled with advancing age, his eyes peering at her alertly through wire-rimmed spectacles.

'I'm Dr Savage, my dear. I'm relieved that you're uninjured. I'm afraid your horse had to be shot.'

Arabella opened her mouth to speak, but a hoarse croak was all that issued from her. Shards of painful brightness hurt her eyes as she looked up at him.

'How do you feel, my dear?'

'I'm just a bit bruised, Doctor. How is Pendulu, the Zulu – and the young man on the other horse?'

Dr Savage slipped an arm beneath her shoulders, as a male orderly in a heavy khaki serge uniform hurried up.

'That fancy German prince wot's in the Boer 'ospital – 'e's gone, sir, not more'n five minutes ago,' the orderly said, as they helped Arabella to the pavement.

'Ah, Count von Zollern. Poor fellow!' Dr Savage replied. 'Not that he could have lived much longer with that bullet exposing his brain. He was a real gentleman, and his father distinguished himself so gallantly during the Franco-Prussian War. Find young Dr Stevens, will you? I'll be along shortly.' He turned to Arabella. 'You look shaken, young lady – suffering from slight shock, no doubt. Your manservant is somewhat bruised, but otherwise unhurt. He was very worried about you, but I packed him off to help the other stretcher-bearers. He's an uncommonly big and strong young man – very good for dhoolie-bearing, y'know. As for the young rider, he's seriously wounded, I'm sorry to say.' He shook his head as he led her towards the town hall. 'Come into the hospital and we'll give you some sal volatile.'

As Arabella turned to look further down the street she could see that the smoke had begun to clear away, and with growing horror she noted that the young rider who had been flung on to a footpath, had a long piece of shell embedded in his side. He was being attended by another doctor, and two orderlies, and his horse was lying in the roadway, completely disembowelled. Already a busy stream of flies was buzzing over the carcase.

A flame of intense rage licked through Arabella's blood. Shrugging off the physician's arm, she ran towards the rider.

After a moment's astonishment, Dr Savage hurried after her. 'Come back, young lady – you're in shock!'

He drew up, panting, beside her. The rider stared up through the knot of people around him, looking very pale and obviously in great pain.

'This means two more Dutchmen killed, Dr Savage,' he whispered.

'Just lie still, young fellow,' replied the doctor, bending over him, as he suddenly smiled and died.

Arabella blinked back the tears that blurred her vision, and in that moment she had never hated the Boers more.

'Come, my dear. There's nothing more to be done here, and you really must rest,' the elderly doctor said, firmly taking her arm and leading her away, while somewhere a woman screamed and gave way to deep, heartrending sobs.

'That young man was innocently riding his horse down the street when he was deliberately shot at!' Arabella cried. 'And now his mother has lost a son. It was totally unnecessary – what had *he* done to the Boers? What kind of monsters are they, who fire into a town and kill civilians?'

'Innocent people have a habit of getting in the way during a war, my dear, and now that the British force has accomplished its object – to facilitate the junction of their two retreating columns – and have retired to this town, the Boers are determined to get Ladysmith one way or the other, because it's the gateway to Natal and the port of Durban.' He shook his head, and escorted her up the steps of the imposing red-brick building. 'One sees dreadful injuries in the field. Ever since I left my Harley Street practice to take up an appointment here as consultant physician when the war broke out, there have been appalling casualties – but it's essential not to let it get you down.'

Arabella stopped and looked at him. 'I'm a qualified nursing sister, Dr Savage, and I've come to help the wounded. I was trained at St Albans Hospital in London.'

Surprise filled the doctor's face, then a deep scowl drew his eyebrows down sharply, and the muscles in his cheeks twitched. 'Soldiers, my dear, prefer to be nursed by male orderlies. They do not like women about them when they are sick and wounded, and an army field hospital is no fit place for ladies such as yourself. The convalescent patients sit about and chat, and women interfere with their freedom, and become flirtatious. We have no need of your services.'

'But how can you have no need ...?' Her voice trailed off and she frowned in amazement. 'I can't believe you really mean that, Doctor. That cannot be the reason for withholding competent nursing service from the sick.'

Dr Savage's answer was cold and deliberate. 'That is my considered opinion, madam, – backed by the Army Medical Department. *Men prefer to be nursed by men.* And I have it on good authority that many young women from the best families in England have recently landed in Cape Town, under the pretences of volunteering as nurses, and are merrymaking behind their parents' backs, with such to-do's it would make you cringe. We most certainly don't want that here.'

Arabella stood very still as the shock of his words sunk into her brain and settled as a cold lump in the pit of her stomach. It was unbelievable! Where were the welcoming arms for a trained nursing sister? She could not credit the man's reason for rejecting her services.

She felt a desperate need to try again. 'But Florence Nightingale's nurses achieved great success in the Crimean War, Dr Savage, bringing comfort and care to the wounded and sick soldiers at Scutari Hospital, and reducing the death-rate from forty percent to two per cent.'

She waited breathlessly for his reply. Pursing his lips, he said, 'Since the Crimean War, very few nurses have been used in the British Army, despite Miss Nightingale's efforts. You know yourself that female nurses are employed only in general hospitals. Stationary army and field hospitals are staffed solely by male orderlies.'

Much to her consternation, he turned as wounded men were being brought in on dhoolies – stretchers hooded over with green canvas to keep off the sun and rain, and suspended from bamboo poles carried on the shoulders of black and Indian bearers. He lifted the hood of one as it stopped beside him.

'Well, my lad, and what's the matter with you?'

The soldier feebly pointed to the card attached to the dhoolie. Dr Savage read it carefully, then nodded. 'You have a bullet through the chest – we'll do you first.' Then he noticed Arabella still standing beside him.

'Please give me a chance, Doctor. I'm a trained ward sister, and belong to the Royal British Nurses' Association. I've tended wounded soldiers before – on the farm belonging to Lord Stradcombe. It holds very little horror for me.'

He stroked his neat grey beard thoughtfully. 'We are short-staffed at the moment, but that is only temporary. Report to the Matron and the Medical Superintendent – but it's only temporary, mind.'

'Oh, thank you!' she breathed in relief. She stared at him more closely, and felt a pang of pity for the elderly man; his shirt was soiled with sweat and bloodstains, and rumpled, as if he had slept in his clothes.

He responded with a stiff smile. 'Your duties will be purely supervisory – the dressing of wounds, preparation and serving of meals and such, do you understand? Tell the Matron that I suggest you help out for a while in the Boer hospital. They are very short-staffed.'

'The *Boer* hospital?' Arabella's voice was defiant. 'I'd rather start with our soldiers, sir.'

'You'll do as you're told if you want to work here, Sister! In war, we tend both the enemy and our own soldiers, showing no bias whatsoever.' The man's eyes were frosty behind his spectacles. 'You can't pick and choose. If you want to work here, you will go where you are needed. The Boer hospital is at the back of the building. Once there, you'll please tell Dr Stevens I am in the midst of emergency surgery.' He turned to the orderlies. 'Take this young man to the operating theatre at once.'

As he motioned the dhoolie away, Arabella knew with a sinking heart that she would have to do as he said, or not be allowed to work there at all. The Boer hospital was the very last place she wanted to be. The thought of tending the enemy who had coldbloodedly killed a civilian, totally repulsed her. Then she froze as she thought of Deneys du Rand. Perhaps he was there ... She tried to marshall her thoughts, and bring her rising emotions under control. What would she say to him? How would she react if she saw him again, in this British camp?

Her bruises were by now quite forgotten as these questions rose to haunt her, but she knew she had better get used to the idea, and once the other medical staff noticed how good she was, she would arrange for a change.

Arabella forced her mind to take control as she went in search of her saddlebags. She had a strong will, and she would not let herself be governed by chaotic feelings, no matter how powerful. After discovering that Pendulu was enthusiastically helping the stretcher-bearers, she snatched a quick meal at the patients' cookhouse before tying on her crumpled, starched apron and making her way to the Boer hospital.

A series of large, high-ceilinged rooms opened out from the impressive entrance hall and along the passages, now converted into wards crowded with cumbersome, old-fashioned iron bedsteads, cots and stretchers. All around, the pungent smell of iodoform mingled with the stench of sweaty unwashed bodies and the sweetness of gangrened limbs; flies buzzed incessantly. Through the door to the operating theatre, she could see a soldier having bullets removed from his thigh. Several nursing sisters moved along the rows of beds with dippers of water from buckets just inside the doors, and white-aproned dressers hurried to assist the surgeons, as more dhoolies arrived. Convalescents sat and chatted in the passages, dressed in the regulation flannel trousers and ill-fitting jackets of vivid blue with red neckties and yellow slippers.

Stepping carefully over the reclining figures of wounded men, covered with grey Army blankets, who slept fitfully on stretchers in the passageways, waiting for beds in the wards, Arabella made her way down a flight of stairs to the Boer hospital, too preoccupied with her first impressions to be aware of the booming gunfire from the hills outside.

The Boer hospital contained about eighty wounded, mostly young men. Here they lay, sat or sprawled on cots and stretchers. Many of them were wounded in the left arm, shot as they had taken aim. Some moaned, one or two muttered in delirium, but most endured their suffering in silence. A few doctors, orderlies, and one or two nurses moved among them. Many spoke perfect English, and to judge from the freedom with which those who were convalescing chatted with the visiting British officers, few of the latter needed to speak Dutch to make themselves understood.

Even though they obviously expected to be treated fairly, many still seemed to be surprised by the care of their captors. But there was a look about them which was still proud and self-contained, even a sullenness in the expressions of some.

She found Dr Stevens – a man of great height, in his forties with an enormous brown handlebar moustache – working in one of the wards. He was attending a man with a smashed leg who was lying on a bloodstained blanket. He nodded absently as she reported to him, and once more, she was disillusioned that no welcoming arms awaited her. The staff were all so busy that she was waved to one side, and dismissed.

Chagrined, Arabella watched him as his fingers, bloody and expert, explored the leg, while the man bit his lip in agony.

'I'm sure you can manage to clean it up, Sister,' he said finally, noting her presence. 'The orderlies will bring splints to set the bone. He should be up and about in a few weeks.' He wiped his fingers on his khaki serge breeches, and spurs clinking at his heels, walked away.

With quiet determination, Arabella took up the scissors from her apron pocket and began, with utmost care, to cut away any remaining clothing, and then to swab the wound, before bandaging it with dressings, the quality of which, she observed with mounting alarm, was antiquated.

As she finished, a Boer nearby spoke with great agitation. 'My brother – he's gone, Sister. He just sat up and went!'

She went over to the cot beside him, as an orderly appeared.

'That one was shot near his heart, Sister. Sitting up like that was too much for him,' he announced, opening up the dead man's shirt, where the bandage across his chest was soaked with blood.

'But he was so young,' she exclaimed, looking down at the Boer's pale, unlined face. 'He couldn't have been more than sixteen!'

'When your numbers up, Sister, it's up, and there's no arguing about it,' the orderly replied matter-of-factly, when there was a call from outside. He looked up with annoyance, then nodded to her. 'See to him, will you, Sister. I have to go and help Dr Stevens with an emergency op. They're still comin' in like flies from Tinta Inyoni. We'll be up all night at this rate.'

Then he was gone, leaving her in the gloom of the stinking room with its clouds of flies. The heat outside had been bad enough, but inside it was like an oven.

'He would have been sixteen next month,' the Boer explained brokenly. 'He's the youngest of the whole family, and with Pa gone to fight in the Siege of Kimberley, I had to look after him. Now he's gone, and there's no one to tell Ma.'

'I'm so sorry,' Arabella said, as she bent to her grisly work. 'Is Kimberley still in a state of siege?'

'Oh, ja.' The young Boer nodded his head vigorously. 'We've got them well and truly surrounded. It's only a matter of time before we starve them out.'

A trickle of sweat traced a cool path down her temple as she fought the revulsion against unnecessary death that was beginning to tear at her, leaving her trembling and tense. This boy had not even seen his proper manhood, and now he was gone ... too young to really understand the full implications of the war.

After a short eternity, she managed to claim a small measure of victory as she washed the body, and crossed the still-warm hands over the exposed breast, then pulled down the eyelids.

'I'm Christiaan du Rand, Sister,' a pleasant voice said beside her in perfect English, with the rounded inflection of the cultured Boer. 'My brother, Deneys, was tended by an English nurse in the veld. She saved his life.'

As her fingers closed over the dirty bandages that had bound the dead young Boer, the image of a handsome golden-haired man flashed through her mind. The vision was brief, but vivid.

A Boer shell crashed somewhere in the distance. Trembling, she gazed into two striking hazel eyes, appearing in that moment more green than brown. The man wore a neat sun-streaked beard, and his left arm was in a sling, but even in shirt-sleeves, she could see the flawless tailoring of the shirt, and the superbly fitting cord trousers. He appeared both smaller in build and older than Deneys.

She cleared her throat. 'And why are you telling me this?'

He shrugged. 'You're new, Sister, and you're small with green eyes. I've been watching you working on this young fellow, and I can see you know what you're doing – just as you did when you operated on my brother.'

'And what if you're wrong?' She cast a worried glance about the room, but no one seemed to be taking any notice of them. It would not be a good idea if any rumour spread that she had been fraternising with the enemy, nor did she want to be drawn into the world of the du Rands – it was alien to her, foreign and repulsively cruel, but she knew that it was no use trying to deceive this man.

Curious, she lifted her eyes to search his face and he raised a quizzical brow. 'I know you are that nurse.'

She answered with a slow and hesitant nod. 'Has your brother recovered? Is he here?'

'No, he's not here. As far as I know he was taken to a doctor. His commando is somewhere outside Ladysmith waiting for the big battle that will soon take place.' He paused as his eyes appraised her, then a small reluctant smile curved his lips. 'It seems as if Deneys and I owe a certain debt to you English. Not that it should be so strange, considering we had English neighbours in Bloemfontein when Pa was President, and we got on very well with them. We've all been to England – Deneys was educated there – and now I am your captive.'

Arabella could find no adequate response, and she straightened, steeling herself against the disturbing knowledge that this man and his family were the hateful enemy, that Deneys' commando was one of those battering this town ...

She was sure that Christiaan du Rand and his brothers, and Isaac Brandauer, were sincere about their cause, and more than anything else, in that tortured moment, she wanted to keep some concept of their humanity clear. After all, Deneys had saved Luke's life, and risked his own. But there was too much against it, too many irreconcilables, and the killing of innocent townsfolk ...

'I have to go,' she said crisply. 'There's so much to do, now that your commandoes insist on firing shells into this town.'

His brow slanted up. 'Your gallant troops are not slow to answer back, Sister.'

Her eyes briefly marked his words, then she turned away as two orderlies hurried up to remove the body of the young boy.

'Well, well, I do believe it to be that hoity-toity miss from the port of Durban, no less.'

She was brought up short by that sneering Irish brogue she would never forget, marvelling in spite of herself, that it was an accent and a delivery which, even used in contempt, had an underlying soft velvet lilt to it. Turning around slowly she faced Sean O'Shea, who was lounging against the door jamb, his left arm in a sling. He was looking evenly at her, and she could hear a giggle somewhere behind him.

She remained as coldly aloof as she could manage. 'I have nothing to say to you.' Her voice was low and firm, but the intonations carried and it stopped the mutter of talk in the near vicinity, as curious eyes swivelled in her direction.

'You're an uppity dame, to be sure – and who do you think you are, anyway? A common little nursing maid – a butcher's assistant, that's what you are, darlin', nothing more or less.' The others round about laughed and there was another giggle. O'Shea fingered the green cap in his hand, watching her as she strove to remain calm.

'And where's that fancy pants captain you were nobbin' with in Durban? Learnin' his lesson, is he, now that the bloody lot o' Saxons have retreated all the way into the town like toothless dogs, with their tails between their legs.' His dark eyes shone with malice as he looked her up and down. 'You look as though you're used to dirty work, darlin', and you'll have to get used to a whole lot more when we win this war.' There was more sporadic laughter, and one voice, jeering.

Arabella lifted her head proudly, her face flushing. Then her emerald eyes settled on him with cool disdain, while her well-shaped mouth managed a mirthless smile. 'And *you*, I take it, are part of the dirty work?'

A snap of silence fell as the salvo found its mark, and renewed laughter broke out, more robust this time. O'Shea's face darkened, and he scowled. As Arabella turned and walked away with her head held high, and her back as straight as a poker, she was acutely aware that he was a dangerous enemy.

At noon, a large cauldron of hot soup was brought in from the cookhouse and the orderlies served it out. A certain anger tore at Arabella's spirit as she went to help. It was not a pleasant thought to know that she would have to endure nursing the enemy – however cultured and intelligent and pleasant some of them happened to be – when their shells continued to rip through the town ... and especially when there were those amongst them like Sean O'Shea. She knew she would have to deal with him relentlessly as time passed. Control would have to be her ally. Or at least as much of it as she could muster.

13

It was 30 October, and in the streets, on the station platform, and all through the British lines in Ladysmith, were the visible signs of a large conflict with the Boers, who had mustered in great numbers around the town, in a far stronger position than before. Army mules clogged the streets, as more and more soldiers were evident, and the excited shouts of Zulus and Indians filled the air. Guns still boomed at intervals and the atmosphere simmered with suppressed tensions.

Arabella had left her food untouched the night before and gone to bed in anguish as she recalled the memories of that day. The next morning, she had woken with her mind grown coldly calm as she dressed and made ready to resume her duties. If she was to survive intact, Arabella knew that she must learn to minimise the fatigue, the heat and noise, the vile smells, and the fact that the orderlies knew very little about disinfectants and there was no time to teach them; some even failed to wash out slop-pails, or their hands after dealing with the patients, if she forgot to tell them.

She had taken bed and board with Mrs Saunderson, a middle-aged widow who had refused to leave town, and a nurse's uniform had been found for her and sent to an Indian tailor for alterations.

The golden radiance of the day seemed to dim as she heard the news that the Boers had surrounded the town. Guns boomed as tall pillars of red dust rose in all the streets except the main thoroughfare. Columns of Transvaalers and Free Staters continued to close in on the surrounding forces, while British infantry moved forward outside the town in successive waves, and there was all the bustle and activity of a battle forming.

At noon, there was a tremendous crash of shells and the loud reverberating din of thousands of rifles echoing across the hills for great distances. Arabella was frightened. It had never occurred to her that the town would be unsafe, possibly more so than the open veld, and she wondered what new agonies lay in store when the wounded were brought back to the central hospital and the various pavilion hospitals around the town. She had learned only too quickly that the most depressing part of it all was when the dead and dying were brought back and buried under cover of darkness.

Suncrest Farm was so far away, and as she thought of its silent lawns, deep cool verandahs and luxurious rooms, it seemed now like a safe haven, yet when she had been there, she had felt so afraid ... but it was nothing like this fear that held her in its grip, day and night. There, she had cared for the soldiers unencumbered by the orders of any doctor, free to nurse as she thought right under the circumstances, to practise what she had learned, read or heard in lectures. Now, not only was she right in the middle of the conflagration, but she had to submit herself to dubious orders from doctors working in an outdated, ironbound system, clogged with petty trivialities.

As this dreadful day passed, she hugged the hope to herself that the British, with their years of training and knowledge of fighting around the world, would be sure to win this battle, and push the Boers back for ever. But in the evening the news came that mostly British dead and wounded men lay littered outside the town, and the summit of Pepworth Hill, in the outer ring of hills guarded by the Boers, was covered in smoke and flames, as the roar of bursting shells shook the ground. The town was now completely surrounded by the enemy.

Arabella wondered how she could ever have dared to speak of the British Empire as glorious, of the Boer farmers as backward, of the rights of the Uitlanders, like a presumptuous child prattling of the unknown. As a cloud of snow-white smoke belched out from the big guns on the hills, and hung like a huge woolsack in the sky for a few seconds, all her romantic notions of the British Empire at war, with its stirring bands and heroic cavalry charges against the enemy, vanished for ever.

The following day, at noon, the sound of a bugle rose in the still, hot air. The observation balloons went up to chart the Boer positions, and the British troops under Sir George White withdrew into the town. The Siege of Ladysmith had begun.

The wounded and dead came thick and fast in the ambulances, and there was even more of a crush of cots and stretchers in all the rooms, which were now crammed to capacity. The air was rank with rotting flesh and medicines, and there was an endless succession of young faces and broken bodies, which all had a terrible sameness. As nurses and orderlies moved from bed to bed from cot to cot, a few subdued moans escaped, and now and then an involuntary shriek of agony. Everything, except abdominal wounds, was operated on, with chloroform as the only practical form of anaesthetic in this dry climate. The nurses were set to washing and rolling bandages, preparing appropriate meals, administering medicines and dressing wounds

– a restricted routine which continued to frustrate Arabella, who longed to get back to her own British soldiers and to be able to do more actual nursing at the bedside.

At daybreak the following day, she hurriedly dressed and rushed out on to the verandah of Mrs Saunderson's house, amidst the reverberating thunder of the guns in the hills. She was just in time to see a mass of splintered shell come hurtling over the British camp and smash in the street, catching an unfortunate black man standing only yards away from her.

She rushed over to him, calling for a doctor, as a crowd of people gathered. Desperately trying to staunch the appalling flow of blood from his leg, she quickly applied a temporary tourniquet. A woman screamed, and others stood at their doors, waiting anxiously for another shell.

'Here, Sister, let me help you,' an Australian voice suddenly drawled, and a khaki-clad man pushed his way through the onlookers and knelt beside her.

Arabella looked up in surprise, and great relief. 'Archie Mungo! How glad I am to see you! Please help me with this man. If we don't get him into hospital for an emergency operation at once, he'll die.'

Archie looked at her thoughtfully, noting the bloodstained pinafore. 'Let's get him in, then – we've no time to waste.' A slow grin began to crawl over his lean, deeply-tanned face under the flap-brimmed hat. 'Fancy you being here, Arabella. I thought you would've turned tail and gone back to good old England when war finally broke out.'

'I had to come and do my duty –' She lowered her eyes quickly with embarrassment under his close scrutiny.

'Here – let us pass. This is an emergency. Move back, please,' Archie's voice announced as he and a bystander carefully carried the wounded man, now screaming in agony, up the street towards the hospital.

Once inside the imposing entrance hall, Arabella hurried off to find a spare bed and a doctor.

'There are no available beds, and there's no time to take him to the section for black people,' she said breathlessly, arriving back a few minutes later. 'We'll have to put him in this space here. I did manage to filch an Army bedroll. All the doctors are busy with emergency ops – apparently there was a rush of dhoolies in the night bringing in the rest of the wounded from the battlefield. Some had lain there in the hot sun for hours, and the surgeons are way behind in their routine.'

Archie straightened his long, lanky form after carefully placing the man on the bedroll. 'He'll die if he's not seen to, Arabella – there's no doubt about that.' His forehead twisted in a heavy frown, as he stared into her troubled green eyes.

'I know.' Arabella shivered as a sudden chill went down her spine. She glanced around in growing dismay. 'If the injured tissues are not removed, gangrene will affect the dead muscle.'

She stared down at the man, whose face was shining with sweat. 'Please, missy, take away the pain,' he gasped in agony, trying to hold his leg.

A nervous fluttering attack her stomach as an idea began to take form in her mind. She heaved a sigh of frustration, then her anxieties disappeared and she knew what she had to do.

'I must do it myself. I've done it before, and as none of the orderlies will help me – not that most of them know anything about nursing – I need your help, Archie. Are you up to it?'

Archie's sandy brows shot up. 'But you're not a doctor, Arabella!'

'There's no one else, and if I don't do something, this man will die,' she chided crisply, her small hands placed determinedly on her hips. 'I'm going to scrounge a surgical knife, scissors, sterile solution and dressings from the dispensary. I know I'm taking a chance, but I'll cross that bridge when I come to it. Are you going to help me?'

'You bet. I'm willing if it will help this poor bastard. Now hurry – there's not a moment to lose.'

Arabella returned with a basket filled with medical aids. She quickly administered a heavy dose of morphia to the patient, and he relaxed as the pain started to subside. Then she picked up the scissors, with Archie kneeling beside her.

'Well, here goes, Archie. Last time I had to use a pocketknife, believe it or not.'

'Well I'll be blowed!' Archie muttered, shaking his head in open admiration as she carefully peeled away the torn trouser leg, soaked in blood. For an instant she gazed at the bright blood on the dark skin, and took a deep breath, as Archie handed her the surgical knife.

'And by God, what do you think you're doing, Sister Allen?'

There was a sudden commotion as Dr Savage burst through one of the doors leading into the entrance hall, followed by two orderlies. 'Thank God I got here in time. If it hadn't been for these orderlies, anything could have happened.'

Arabella looked up, startled. 'There was no one else to tend him, Doctor, so rather than wait and let him die, I did the next best thing.'

'The next best thing for you is to leave, Sister. This man needs an anaesthetic, which you are not qualified to give him, nor to operate – for that was a debridement you intended to do, was it not? Only a Matron is allowed to assist in an operation, and then only in emergencies.' The doctor's eyes were cold as they met hers.

Arabella was astonished. 'But I've done one debridement already, Dr Savage – and it saved a man's life.' Her head swam with angry, confused feelings. She knew she could do it, and every minute was vital.

'She was only trying to help the poor chap, Doctor,' Archie interrupted.

The physician responded with a derisive snort. 'You will leave at once, young man,' he barked. 'You have no right to be here. And as for you, miss, you are suspended from nursing in this hospital. I shall inform the Medical Superintendent and the Matron immediately. I do not like your attitude towards the patients in the Boer hospital, and now this gross abuse of the rules! We do not want troublemakers, nor do we want interfering nurses here. Now go – and don't come back! Do I make myself clear?'

Arabella's amazement was complete. She saw no reason for him to fly into such a rage when she had only been helping at an extremely busy time. 'I had a responsibility to save this man's life, Dr Savage,' she said steadily, 'when there was no one else available.'

'Go! I have no time to argue with you!'

A line of dhoolies rushed in, as Archie and Arabella exchanged a meaningful look.

'I'm afraid you'll have to do as this chap says, old girl, otherwise you'll be in for the chop,' Archie said quietly. 'Take my advice – don't make it worse by arguing. That can come later.'

Arabella looked up at him for an instant, then she hurried briskly away, her white headdress bobbing up and down on her angry little head.

Like a woman in a nightmare, she wandered where her limbs took her about Mrs Saunderson's cool, high-ceilinged sitting-room, drained of all emotion but an overriding desire to nurse again. Mosquitoes whined in the room, but she hardly noticed them. She was unable to read or to concentrate on anything for more than a few seconds, her mind too full of the confrontation with Dr Savage.

Intermittent explosions of cannon-fire could be heard outside on the hills, where temporary fortifications were being hastily erected by the Boers. Shells now regularly arched above them, plunging down the veld and into the town. Only the night before, there had been chaos at the railway station when three trains, their carriages filled with women and children, and open trucks packed thickly with Zulus and Indians, had moved out on their uncertain journey across the veld, hoping to reach Maritzburg safely. Arabella could have gone with them, but her proud spirit would not give Dr Savage or any of the other doctors that satisfaction. She was determined to stay and nurse again.

The wounded black man had been attended by Dr Savage, but had died soon afterwards. The physician blamed his death on Arabella's reckless behaviour, while she maintained that the man had been left too long. It grieved her to think that he could have been saved . . .

Now that she had time to brood, her thoughts returned more frequently to the quarrel with Rosamunde. She tried to remember her cousin as she had once been, but all Arabella could recall now was the last furious rage distorting that beautiful face. She had been close to Rosamunde once, had known and admired her deeply, but none of that had substance any more. Only the pain was real. She missed Ben and the children, and wished that somehow the situation could be changed. After a long, dreadful moment, she walked out on to the cool verandah, shaded by its vine creeper, blinded by sudden tears.

The tree-lined street stretched away on both sides; horses cantered past, and one or two four-wheeled traps drove by. There was the squeaking of the axles of a bullock-cart, and in the distance, the Red Cross flag above the town hall drooped forlornly in the heat. All morning rumours had run riot, claiming that the Boers were mounting guns on many commanding points on the outer rim of hills, and that Ladysmith would soon be at their mercy.

There was mounting suspicion that the town was filled with Boer spies, for the commandoes seemed to be familiar with every move made by the British forces. A message had been sent by the enemy, declaring that if the newly-invented explosive lyddite shells were used, there would be reprisals, and the town would be shelled. The British had replied that if the enemy stopped pitching shells into the town, the lyddite would not be fired. But as neither side would give way, there was a stalemate.

Arabella shielded her eyes from the glare of the sun, and looked up towards one of the enormous observation balloons hovering way above the town. Behind lay the rugged folds of hills reaching up to touch the sky, where the herds of Angora goats that had whitened the hillsides before the Boers came, had disappeared. She watched the flash of guns over the inner ring of British-held hills producing a booming sound like the beat of far-off drums, and further back where the Boers were steadily bracing their dreaded Long Tom gun with further earthworks on Pepworth Hill to the north-west.

Her gaze dropped, falling on the tall, lean figure of a priest in a black cassock who was walking swiftly towards her. It took a few seconds for her to recognise Father Sebastian, whom she had last seen at the fateful dinner party at Suncrest Farm.

'The last time we met, you were expounding on the virtues of Mr Oscar Wilde, I believe,' he said, smiling widely as he stepped in through the small gate and strode up the path to greet her at the verandah steps.

'I had forgotten you were posted here, Father,' Arabella said slowly. 'It's the most terrible place to be in at the moment, with all the dreadful suffering and grief.' She was looking into a face that was more gaunt and drawn than she remembered, but it was still commanding and she felt strangely comforted by its familiarity.

He took the glasses off his nose. 'Suffering and grief are part of the experiences of the heart, my child – but they give birth to that which produces compassion, healing and justice for society and for our lives. It helps us to grow in grace.'

She drew a small breath. 'No, Father, I cannot agree! All I have seen is needless destruction and pain caused by men such as the Boers who shell innocent people to get their own way. I see no compassion or justice in it.'

He turned his light-blue eyes on her, and for a moment regarded her in silence. Her face was devoid of expression, yet now and then the sunlight caught the hard, almost brittle gleam in the depths of the green eyes. No one looking at her diminutive form in the white muslin blouse with its high neckline and demure sleeves, and knowing her innate gentleness and caring about her patients, could believe that there was not a trace of that warmth to be found in the small, determined face under the tumble of soft brown hair.

The priest shook his head slightly. 'Human beings are deeply carved over thousands of years by the flowing tides of pain,' he said gently. 'When we have suffered deep pain, my child, and worked through it we learn to rise above it. We learn not only in our joy and ecstasy but also in our pain and sorrow that this is the birth of something better.'

'I would like to believe that, Father,' she said with unexpected harshness, 'but there is too much against it.'

Father Sebastian replaced his glasses and watched a· gun being hauled down the street. They could hear the strain of the bullocks against the yoke and the crack of a whip. Further away lay a mound of rubble where a building was holed with shot and scarred with shrapnel. Strong Zulu men were carting away the debris, and somewhere near the observation balloon a dense pall of smoke writhed upwards, where it had been targeted by the enemy. A couple of soldiers limped up the street towards the hospital, one supporting the other. There was another open-throated roar from the guns in the distance as they belched once more into action, and a party of soldiers and civilians dragged sandbags up the street. They were making for the protective barriers set up at high points in the town, with a shelter trench, where soldiers and civilians stood and aimed their guns at the enemy, and where the women of the town, dressed in their finery, regularly went to stand beside their men.

'Once your mind is dominated by anger, my child, as it is now, it becomes almost mad, to be sure,' Father Sebastian said, after a while. 'You cannot take the right decisions, and you are blinded to reality. But if you calm your mind, and let it become stable and more free of emotions, you will see everything as it is.' He shrugged his shoulders. 'The ideal way in life is the middle way – neither hostile to the world, nor hostage to it.'

Arabella had been avoiding his eyes, but now she turned and looked into his firm, compassionate face. 'My father was a clergyman, Father, and though he preached tolerance and love, he never practised it. I think he turned me against the middle way forever.'

The priest folded his arms and stared at her. 'You were born, like the rest of us, into the eternal cycle of living, with its struggle for perfection through redemption, and you must work through it.'

They were silent for a time. Heat haze shimmered over the street, and only the large syringa beside the gate seemed to have any real substance.

'But how can I work through anything if I am barred from it because I am a woman, Father? One cannot work in a vacuum!' Arabella burst out, at last.

'Your nursing, you mean? Well, it just so happens that I have come straight from the central field hospital,' Father Sebastian said, leaning his long frame against the verandah railing. 'And I have very good news for you. Some of the doctors want you to return immediately. Dr Stevens has spoken on your behalf to the Medical Superintendent and the Matron.'

'But why? Did *you* speak to them?' Arabella's eyes widened in surprise, her heart suddenly racing with suppressed hope.

'That I did. I was administering the Last Rites to a soldier in the hospital when I heard about that poor soul who died after you tried to help him. There and then I decided to see the medical staff. Dr Savage was against it so I put my case to Dr Stevens and the others, and told them how you had nursed those wounded soldiers at Suncrest Farm. They cannot afford to throw out good nurses such as yourself, as they are battling to keep up with the ever-growing numbers of wounded.' He looked down at her. 'The Medical Superintendent has agreed to take you back, provided you behave yourself and abide by the rules set by the doctors.'

'But what about Dr Savage?'

'Keep out of his way as much as possible.' Father Sebastian peered at her with a slow spreading grin. 'That shouldn't be too difficult in all that dreadful overcrowding.'

'I can't thank you enough, Father,' she whispered, clasping her hands together to stop the trembling.

'Before you do that, my child, promise me you'll stick to the rules. They're willing to take you back on a trial basis.'

'I promise.' Arabella nodded vigorously, the sternness of her small face broken completely by her mounting enthusiasm. 'I won't let you down.'

Father Sebastian unfolded his long, gaunt body and stood up. 'Well now, you'd best be changing into your uniform and go on over there without delay. And perhaps, in time, I shall also have the chance of saving your doubting soul.' Then he was striding down the steps, his cassock brushing the ground. At the gate he turned and waved, then lengthening his stride, he was gone.

14

Arabella's discomfort was obvious as she left Dr Stevens and made her way down the corridor to Ward One, after a severe lecture in which he told her that she was never to attempt to debride a wound again; she was only to dress wounds and attend the seriously ill, as her duties and those of the other sisters were merely supervisory. The good part of it was that she was out of the Boer hospital, never to see Christiaan du Rand or that dreadful Sean O'Shea again, and she was nursing once more – but she would have to be extra careful as Arabella knew she would be watched like a hawk.

She was so busy from then on, that she had very little time to think about anything else. The day passed supervising the nurses on Ward One, as the roar of cannon continued, the cannonade southward becoming so heavy that it sounded as though a serious attack was being mounted from that direction.

A small party of infantry was brought in on dhoolies just after noon, wrapped in the British ensign. Two of them were shot through the lungs, but they were tended immediately, and after very little haemorrhaging, soon began to recover. Typhoid (enteric) fever and cases of dysentery had broken out, to the horror of the medical staff, as more wounded soldiers were brought in from the recently built sangars and several deaths had already been caused, not by the high body temperature, but mostly as a result of complications. Only Phenacetin, the new wonder drug, seemed to stop the temperature in its upward course.

Now as Arabella wrestled with the lighting and putting a pot of water on to boil in the cookhouse, she cursed the chronic shortage of bedpans and commodes, hospital clothing and general nursing utensils. While she waited for the water to boil, she gazed out of the window at the gathering dusk, wondering where Ben was ... In that moment she longed to see him again, but with those thoughts came the remembered pain, and quickly, she shut the longing out of her mind.

As she supervised the preparation of the strong broths, puréed vegetables, port-wine jellies and milk puddings, she wondered when this war would end. It seemed to her that it had been going on for years, and whatever had happened before it was another life, indistinct and shadowy, one in which she had been another person. She knew she would never be the same again: so much had happened to change her.

The next day, the isolation of the town was complete. The wires were cut in the morning, and as no train arrived from Pietermaritzburg the day after, it was presumed with mounting dismay that the rail southward was in enemy hands.

Boer guns were now trained on them from three sides of the town. Shells rained down into the streets, and the big gun, a six-feet Krupp, looked straight down the main street. The second gun was so perfectly hidden that no one knew its exact location, though they came to know its sound, and the third was to the north-east at Surprise Hill.

There was growing nervous tension among those still in the town; most people could not believe that the Boers were actually shelling a place filled with women, children and wounded soldiers, but the following afternoon there could no longer be any doubt about it. From midday to sundown, shelling continued at irregular intervals. Waiting for the next Krupp shell became the depressing order of the day.

And even worse news was on its way. Fighting now covered a circle of twenty-five miles, and the British were threatened from all directions. So far, however, the Boers had not come on in force. Inside the town, no one made any more facetious remarks about backward farmers. The British troops would drive the Boers back at every point, but as soon as they retired to camp, the enemy re-occupied their ground.

Outside the hospital, the noise of the guns increased, and became deafening as explosions shook the plaster from the ceiling of Ward One. Arabella was in the process of trying to help two patients with bedsores, when a shell dropped through the roof further along, and exploded with a mighty crash in the passage outside, showering the door with shrapnel.

'The Boers are going to kill every one of us,' one of the nurses said tearfully, as she groped her way towards Arabella. 'It isn't fair, Sister. What have we ever done to the likes of them? Why, we're even nursing their wounded! If they come down those hills, they'll take this town, that's what everyone is saying ... and then there's no way our poor patients and doctors can fight them off. Oh, Sister, I don't want to be – you know ... !'

'Raped, you mean, Nurse Miller? A lot can happen before then. Now pull yourself together and come with me to see how best we can help these poor men.' And Arabella led the way, seething at the bombing of helpless patients, her rage increased by the knowledge that she could do nothing about it.

Some hours later, all the patients, nurses and doctors had been evacuated and re-housed in rows of tents behind the town hall.

The Boer guns now had total mastery over the town. This gloomy fact was proved when there was a sudden hurried movement of British cavalry, mounted infantry and artillery southward to meet a threatened attack by Free State Boers. As the British troops hastened out, the three Boer guns shelled them at long range, right over their own camp and the town. There were about seven thousand civilians left in the town, and southward of it, where the Klip River ran close under the hills, hundreds of residents now dug out caves in the soft banks near the milk-bloomed syringas, as protection from shrapnel. Here they either stayed or returned to their homes for the night.

There was now every possibility that the Boers would take Ladysmith, or so batter it to pieces that the ruins would be scarcely worth claiming. A meeting of the local council was hastily called, in which Sir George White was urged to communicate with General Joubert, to request that the wounded in the hospitals, the women and children, and the civilians, be allowed to leave the town.

The crimson globe of the sun just edged the masses of the hills to the west, and small puffs of clouds dissolved, disappeared and re-formed in the last shafts of light gilding the roofs of ruined buildings and rutted pathways gouged by flying shrapnel as Arabella dressed a wound on Archie Mungo's shoulder, where a bullet had grazed the skin.

'General White's reluctant message from the townsfolk found old Joubert seated in the shade of an ox-wagon, smoking away,' Archie said, sitting heavily on a trestle table in the dispensary tent.

Arabella frowned as she tied off the bandage around his shoulder. 'What was the old brute's reply? I doubt there's an ounce of humanity in his bones,' she responded with asperity.

'He's only allowing those who have not taken up arms against the South African Republic to go southward by train.'

'The old devil!' Arabella breathed. 'First he orders his men to shell us day and night, partly destroy the hospital and send us to cower in tents, and now this!'

Archie's lips twitched, but his eyes looked at her with serious attention. 'Cowering – you? Not on your sweet life, Arabella.'

For a moment his eyes held hers. So she broke the atmosphere by saying, 'The Boers use smokeless Mausers, I believe.'

'That's so. Hour after hour I've heard the faint call of wounded men amongst the rocks, but not a sign of gunsmoke. Arabella,' he said, his face becoming very still. 'There's something I'd like to ask you, and there may not be another chance for a while.' Arabella knew he was looking at her averted face, then she heard him continue, softly, so that only she could hear. 'When we get out of this mess, I'd like you to think about a life for us, together. We have a lot in common, and I know you'd get on with my family back home.'

A strained silence ensued, in which neither of them moved.

'You're overlooking one very important thing, Archie,' she said slowly, trying not to think about Ben. 'I don't love you. I like you very much – but that's not enough. It's not enough to marry, for that's what you're asking of me.'

'But love can come, Arabella – it often does, given the chance. We can make it, I know we can.'

Tears came to her eyes at the unfamiliar pleading in his tone. She looked up for an instant at his face, now so thin and strained, with shadows of fatigue and pain under the sunken eyes.

'No, Archie. There's much more to it – there has to be.'

'But isn't there enough already for you to try?'

She shook her head. 'No, not for me.'

'Is there someone else then, is that it?'

She began to speak coldly, and in a precise and distant fashion to cover her own embarrassment. 'No! There's no one. Now let's forget this matter, and never speak of it again.'

'I don't get it.' For a moment he was puzzled. 'You just don't want to try ... are you sure there's no one else?'

She nodded, drained and miserable. His eyes travelled over her drawn face, her enormous green eyes encircled with weariness. In the silence that separated them from the noise and bustle around them, she gazed at his face and saw the quiet determination there, and suddenly she was filled with a deep affection for him.

If only I did love this uncomplicated man, she thought, how much simpler my life would be. But she knew that there was so much he could never share with her ... too much.

'I'm sorry, Archie, I just can't explain my feelings,' she said wearily, at last. 'I'm truly sorry.'

Then without another glance, she picked up a spare gauze pad stitched to a bandage in preparation for the next patient.

The townsfolk of Ladysmith were subjected to another heavy bombardment for several hours the next afternoon. To their great relief, the British guns were soon thundering back, but not before it was discovered that the drinking water was filled with mud and filth and more cases of dysentery broke out. The typhoid fever cases rose alarmingly and the price of coffins shot up.

In the midst of all this, Arabella had two other concerns – one for Pendulu and Umfaan, who were now taking mail out of the camp. They had joined a regular string of black runners who carried messages once a week through the Boer lines, running the gauntlet of their guns, to villages called kraals out of town where the mail was collected and taken from kraal to kraal across enemy territory until it reached the coast. A pigeon-post to Durban was sometimes used by Archie and the other war correspondents who wanted to get messages to England and other countries, but more often they risked using the black runners, taking uncoded messages and letters for family and colleagues overseas.

Her other concern was for Ben. She was in an agony of ignorance as to his whereabouts, and the strain of not knowing if he had been killed or wounded was becoming more unbearable to her as the hours passed.

Then, at last, a message was received by heliograph, stating that General Redvers Buller had arrived in Cape Town to lead the army in the field and was departing immediately to relieve Ladysmith. At once the atmosphere was elevated; smiles reappeared on downcast faces, and there was a lift to the steps that had begun to drag heavily, as each day had interminably followed the next without any sign of respite. All hopes were now pinned on Buller.

However, the peace of the town was once more shattered a week later when the enemy opened fire, their shells hitting the streets with terrific impact. One went through the roof of the Church of England, blowing the porch out and disembowelling one of the Natal policemen.

The King's Royals could be heard sniping on the western ridges of the hills, and later that day, one of the war balloons was completely destroyed. In return, a shell from one of the British naval guns fell right on the Boer Krupp gun, killing or wounding nearly every man working it. The nursing staff were kept very busy as the dhoolies of wounded were brought in, victims of the rattling Mausers, which mowed then down like a grass-cutter in summer hayfields.

The night was split open with an almighty thunderstorm which had threatened for days, so that the bombardment from the Boer guns and the clash of the natural elements together made a catastrophic noise. And later, when the thunder had died down, the tum-tum of a banjo and the drone of an accordian were heard on all sides, except on the ridges where motionless, great-coated figures, rigid with cold and drenched with rain, stared out through the darkness, listening for the quiet tread of the Boer veldschoen, and hearing from their own camp below, the strains of 'The Old Folks At Home.'

'They said you were here, dear girl. I must say, it's appalling to find you working such abominably long hours.'

Arabella started in sudden panic at the familiar sound of Ben's voice as he entered the overcrowded tent, where patients were hidden in shadow, the fever-ridden men pressed together with the wounded in a festering pool of stench and cross-infection.

'There's an acute shortage of nursing staff,' she said, peering at him in the light of a paraffin lamp. 'We lost two nurses today from dysentery, and we're now using untrained convalescents from the ranks as orderlies, even though they're not fit enough nor knowledgeable in this type of work.'

'Haven't you complained about it?' The brightness of Ben's eyes was reflected in the low, pulsating light from the paraffin oil lamp, and he appeared much taller and darker than he really was. Her chin lifted suddenly and she had time to notice that the khaki greatcoat emphasised the bronze of his skin and the piercing grey of his deep-set eyes.

'I've complained until I'm blue in the face, but no one wants to listen.'

He stared down at her for a long moment, then he said softly, 'May I speak to you for a moment – outside?'

Signalling to one of the overworked orderlies, she followed him, her face set in a frozen mask of turmoil. The change in her was not only in the fact that Rosamunde had shattered their long friendship; it went deeper than that, into her very soul – a wound that would never completely heal. Even though she had longed again for his presence, and had worried about him desperately, Ben's unexpected appearance had brought her inner conflict painfully to the surface.

Outside the tent, he turned to her. 'I'm sorry to call you away from your duties, Arabella,' he apologised, 'but I had to see you. I was confoundedly worried after I read your letter. Then to run off into the night like that ... You really are the most reckless creature.'

'Did Rosamunde and the children get away safely?' she asked quietly.

'Yes. They're in Maritzburg with Clare Mortimer, as arranged.' He spoke guardedly. 'Rosamunde has settled as well as can be expected. There have been no more – surprises.'

'Ben,' she said, 'if anything I said or did before Aunt Matty's letter came – if in any way I was the cause of Rosamunde's distress, you mustn't spare my feelings.'

There was an electrifying silence before he answered. The expression on his face, full of remembered pain and disgust, wrung her heart, and she would have given much to see it replaced by his usual confidence.

'The cause, as I once tried to tell you, goes deeper than anything you could have done or said.' He sighed, and brushed a moist lock of hair from his forehead. 'It always comes back to me.'

She looked at him closely for a moment, trying to see into his mind, and was shocked at how thin he had become, and how the well-formed mouth bore the unmistakable imprint of bitterness. She said no more. She felt he had no wish to continue the subject, nor had she. He suddenly looked away and broke the silence.

'You had a damn lot of pluck to come here with Pendulu – I've just been to see him with his company of runners. Umfaan is off tomorrow – what on earth would we do without those ragged young urchins? I returned here in time for the Battle of Ladysmith, if that's what one can call it.' He cursed softly, then went on: 'Those confounded Boer idiots made a serious mistake by letting us retreat into the town and not following up their victory. Because Joubert was not strong enough to deliver the coup de grâce, he's pinned down thousands of his men for weeks, and in doing that, he's successfully pinned us down too.'

'How long do you think it will last, Ben?'

He shrugged wearily. 'God knows, Arabella. I only hope to heaven Buller gets here soon while there's still a town to relieve. Randolph Churchill's son Winston was captured at Chieveley recently, on an armoured train while reporting for the *Morning Post* – and there have been Boer advances in the eastern Cape. But on the more optimistic side, Lord Methuen has taken over command of the Orange River, thank God, and started his advance into the Free State, and reinforcements have arrived, including Canadian and Australian contingents.'

'I hope it won't go on too long, Ben. The sick and wounded can't take much more, and the overcrowding gets worse every day. We're at our wits' end to know how to deal with it all.'

'It may last longer than we anticipate, my dear,' Ben said soberly. 'The Boers have completely surrounded and cut off three important towns – and their ability to pick off British officers has led to a general order that we dress as private soldiers. All medal ribbons are to be taken off, buttons dulled and Infantry officers are to carry carbines in place of swords. All haversacks are being stained with Condy's fluid.' He paused, the lines deepening on either side of his mouth. 'Of course the devils are triumphant that the "khakis" are retreating everywhere towards the sea, having lost nearly seven hundred dead and left thousands of prisoners in Boer hands.'

The expression on his face was suddenly fierce. 'Photographs of columns of captured men have been flashed around the world, and their publication has caused an outcry in Britain, where the public are not used to the idea of our troops surrendering. In all African and Indian campaigns up until now, capture usually meant immediate execution.'

He paused, his eyes suddenly far away. 'Isn't it ironical that you ran away from Rosamunde, and no doubt myself as well, only to be thrown back with me again,' he said, almost thoughtfully.

'I'd better get back to my patients,' Arabella said hurriedly trying to maintain her calm under his watchful gaze. 'I've been out here too long.'

He nodded reluctantly. 'I've just come from the officers' hospital – not a pretty sight. We've lost so many already. I really admire the way you can face all the stench and horror of it so calmly.'

He turned away, and watched the flash of gunfire over the hills as it rose, then flickered and fell with a sudden flare. The hospital camp lay in almost total darkness as there was no electricity. Here and there a glimmer of a paraffin oil lamp brightened the gloom, where an emergency operation was being carried out in the theatre tent, or a patient was undergoing a crisis.

Standing beside him, Arabella felt a deadening return of the old fear, anxiety and longing, which she had suppressed during the busy, back-breaking hours tending the patients. She would have to get used to being in the same town as Ben ... she would have to become detached and sensible. Then there was the war itself, where every day they were being pounded to ruins, and elsewhere in the country, the Boers were excitedly anticipating victory!

The Boer guns were never silent for the next few days, and most of the damage done was to the houses on the ridges to the west, which became the playground for shrapnel and plugged shell. The Boers began with one gun, and then went on, gun by gun, until they gradually completed their firing to the south and west, leaving fewer ridges behind which British troops could shelter.

Hunger and thirst had, by this time, reared their hideous heads, as every shop was closed, every hotel kitchen demoralised and most of the provisions commandeered by the Army. The military authorities put black people on a diet of mealie meal, and commandeered all the liquor in the hotels – a most unwelcome move to the hard-drinking, hard-swearing Tommies.

Towards the end of November, some particularly nerve-shattering days occurred, ending with another terrible storm and Boer bombardment producing a paralysing din. Almost every night the enemy forced everyone out of bed. Men in pyjamas and women, half-clad, thronged the streets, fleeing to the shelter of the sand-bagged cellars and barricades. Some hurried away to the tunnels in the river bank, without wraps, and remained there, shivering, until morning.

During the day the town hall was struck more than once and Sir George White wrote to General Schalk Burger, who was in charge of all the commandoes in the area, pointing out this flagrant violation of the rules of civilised war. For a short while this protest was respected, but at the end of the month, shots began to drop all around the hospital again as the enemy gunners were clearly experimenting for the range.

In the hospital camp, Arabella could hear the muted cheers drifting across from the Army camp, where a cricket match was in progress between the Natal Carbineers and the Imperial Light Horse. She marvelled at the men's undaunted attitude in the midst of the ever-increasing hostilities, and the slow starvation spreading throughout the entire community.

It was hot, and the sun beat down on the tents, which retained the fierce heat. Her uniform stuck to her body, the folds of the bloodstained grey skirt dragging on the dusty ground as she cleaned a wound and re-dressed it, surrounded as usual by buzzing flies and the high whine of mosquitoes. Then she crossed over to another cot and was reassuring her patient – a young man from Manchester – when there was a blinding flash of light followed by a tremendous noise. She looked up to see a wall of fire come towards her. The whole tent was filled with a mushroom cloud of evil-smelling smoke, but before she could react, she was knocked violently sideways, and everything spiralled into blackness.

She came around within seconds, and frantically struggled to free herself from the wreckage of the cot and the tent-pole which had been mangled and thrown upon her. The whole place had been transformed in a second. She could hear the sound of screaming and people outside running in all directions. Putting a hand to her forehead, she felt the sticky dampness of blood from a gash. The young man whose wound she had re-dressed was lying on his stomach under some wreckage further away with half his face blown off. She realised with a blinding revelation that she had been standing beside him only thirty seconds before the explosion occurred.

The soldier from Manchester's leg was a mass of blood. There was no skin left and it looked as if it had been scorched off. He was alive, but in a great deal of pain; she tried to move him away but he was too heavy. She had to get help immediately.

With an ashen face, and lungs bursting from the smoke-filled atmosphere, she crawled over the mangled mess in search of a doctor or an orderly, but could find no one. Young Nurse Miller, who had been in the tent seconds before it had exploded, was lying sprawled near the entrance with blood running from her head, only just conscious.

Total pandemonium and confusion had broken out outside, as Arabella staggered into the open air. A mass of people had gathered – soldiers, patients with bloodied faces, orderlies in the tattered remnants of uniforms, excited and frightened Zulus and Indians. The town hall nearby was holed again; a wall had collapsed, and the roof partly fallen in. She saw the plumes of greenish-black smoke rise in and around the hills, where explosive lyddite shells were pitched towards the enemy positions.

She shut her eyes and for a moment was overwhelmed. Nothing in the war up until then, however horrific it had appeared at the time, had affected her so deeply as the sight of patients killed in their cots. Running footsteps approached, and voices. She screamed for help.

'Arabella! God damn it, are you all right?'

It was Ben.

'Patients – there are patients in the tent – killed – wounded terribly – mangled! Help me! They need help urgently,' was all she could sob.

'Yes, yes, there's a doctor on his way right now – but thank God you're all right!' He firmly put his arms around her and led her away.

Some time later, he appeared in the officers hospital tent with a bottle of brandy and two tumblers hidden under his khaki jacket, and went over to Arabella, who was sitting with her aching, bandaged forehead resting on her arm at a trestle table.

'This'll do the trick. I managed to get it from Army rations, commandeered no doubt from the Royal Hotel, for it's a very fine brand.' He smiled as he set the bottle and tumblers on the table. 'I'm relieved the doctor has patched up your forehead. It looked really nasty.'

'I must go back to the patients, Ben. They need me.' Arabella tried to smile as she accepted a tumbler of the topaz-coloured liquid. All she could think of, all she could picture were the dead and the wounded from the shell that had exploded before reaching the ground.

'You're in no condition to go back there now – you're still faint. Drink up, you'll feel better afterwards,' Ben said, his voice very low and reassuring.

'But I must see them. They're terribly helpless and in such pain,' she mumbled, her shaking fingers tightening around the tumbler for comfort, as her teeth chattered violently for a moment.

'Arabella, look at yourself! You're as pale as a ghost, and shaking as if you've got the ague. Now do be sensible. You'll see them soon enough, dear girl – when you can walk steadily again.'

'How I hate those Boers!' she whispered fiercely. 'They have no right at all to shell wounded men!'

'We'll get them, Arabella, once we're out of this stinking town. Buller will be here any-time now – he's well on his way.' Ben finished his tumbler of brandy in a gulp, and wiped his moustache with the back of his sleeve.

Arabella, with a hint of colour in her cheeks, looked across at him. 'Thank you, Ben, for coming to my rescue once again.'

'I somehow slip into the role quite effortlessly.' He rubbed a hand over his brow. 'It was just too painful to think anything had happened to you.'

He cleared his throat and sighed, and bent his dark head to look at the tumbler before him. The tent was suddenly hushed, as only the mosquitoes whined and the flies buzzed around the empty tumblers. Arabella's hands became white-knuckled fists as she clenched them in her lap. The horror of that day had taken its toll, but this latest admission on his part, nearly rent her soul. If only Ben was free, if only . . .

She stared at him while she fought the urge to cry out. 'Yes . . . I am glad you care about me! I want you to care, as much as I care about you!' She wanted to scream the words to everyone within hearing. Then her eyes filled with despondent tears. Ben would never be free. He belonged to Rosamunde.

Rising unsteadily, she forced herself to meet his gaze. 'I really must go to the patients now, Ben. Thanks again.' And then she was gone, almost running from the tent.

The shelling of the hospital tents excited such anger and indignation that it was decided to move the field hospitals. The wounded and those civilian men, women and children who chose to accompany them were to be taken, in agreement with the Boers, to a spot on the railway line selected as neutral ground, and called Intombi Camp. It was fairly close to the Boer stronghold at Umbulwana Hill, but it was safe from attack. Supplies were to come from Ladysmith, and one railway train, under the flag of truce, was allowed to travel between the camp and the town each day.

The first trainload was ready to move out at noon. It was very hot, and the noise soon had Arabella longing for the cool tranquillity of Mrs Saunderson's back room. She stood inside the train, supervising the stretchers being loaded into the carriages, while the jostling crowds pushed and heaved around them. They were now extremely short-staffed. There were only two nurses on the train, three medical officers and sixteen orderlies newly pressed into service. So many patients were loaded into each of the four carriages that the passageway was soon blocked with stretcher cases, or with men sitting or lying on all the available floor space. Women and children were crowded into the back.

A hard lump formed in Arabella's throat as the couplings hissed, and the train lurched forward, almost causing her to lose her balance. Children cried, and some of the husbands and soldiers ran alongside the tracks, with messages and last-minute instructions. She thought of the agony of the wounded with their broken bodies, and the sick, wracked with fever and pain, being jolted on the rails during the short but nightmarish journey.

And as the flag of truce fluttered with the motion of the engine, and they steamed out of the crowded station, her last sight was of Ben's tall, khaki-clad figure standing on the platform in the crush, his hand lifted in a farewell wave.

Then, turning her head away, Arabella consciously shut all thoughts of him from her mind.

15

In Intombi Camp, now called 'Camp Funk', Arabella stared at the train making its way back to Ladysmith for another load of human cargo, and then at the straggle of stretchers and orderlies, making their way towards the tents under the shadow of Umbulwana Hill. She wondered just how safe they would be here in this isolated home of flies, mosquitoes, gnats, heat and dust.

There was no water, no rations, and the whole place was in total disorganisation. If she had been disillusioned with the fact that the doctors, even the consulting surgeons, in Ladysmith had had no training in the duties of ward-masters and stewards, such as the disinfection of clothes and utensils and the inspection of food, and the possible range of responsibilities expected of hospital orderlies – she was now even more dismayed to discover that they had no idea about camp sanitation or the pitching of tents.

There was only one operating tent and one dressing room; they were to be kept open day and night until all the wounded had been tended. One paraffin lamp was available for the whole camp. There were five nursing sisters and twenty-seven nurses for nearly two thousand patients, and only twenty-two medical officers. Due to the lack of space, the enteric cases lay so closely packed together, the dying against the convalescents, that there was no room to step between them. Many of the patients complained of bedsores and boils, but there was nothing with which to relieve their discomfort. To make matters worse, Dr Hickory – an Australian civilian who agreed with Arabella's suggestions that the nurses be given all the actual nursing, whilst the untrained orderlies act as porters, bathmen, scrubbers, messengers and stretcher-bearers – had sent despatches to the Army Medical Department, only to be told not to criticise the medical organisation of the army, since the only important aspect of the war was the fighting!

Now, holding the hem of her pinafore to her nose as she hurried past the open latrines, Arabella thought longingly of Suncrest Farm before the war – a paradise of peace and comfort, with the quiet efficiency of Rashida and Zareena, the delightful tinkle of teacups, and plates piled with home-made delicacies, the rhythmic voices of the Zulu men in the yard, and the excited, happy laughter of the dear children ... she wondered if she would ever see Luke and Cynthia again.

She thought critically of the self-righteous, all-knowing person she had been then, despising Rosamunde's friends, intolerant and judgemental of Rosamunde herself ... then of the satisfaction she had felt in managing Suncrest when war broke out, and in tending the wounded soldiers there. All of that seemed so straightforward, so simple in comparison to what she now faced.

Only weeks ago, she had undergone experiences beyond her wildest imagination – but in that time, a void had opened up between the sensitive young girl she had been, and the woman she now was.

The creaking of military carts carrying in water dragged from the river, the scurrying footsteps of dhoolie-bearers and the snorting of mules drifted towards the dispensary tent where Arabella was sorting out medicines, surrounded by trestle tables crowded with jars, bottles, wooden boxes for instruments, lotions, medicines and ointments. Outside, in the mercilessly bright sunshine, two nurses were cooking mealie-meal porridge over an open fire.

Just then, an orderly stepped to the entrance of the tent, and peered in. 'There's an officer to see you, Sister – says he knows you,' he announced, glancing over his shoulder at someone behind him. 'Sister's in here sir. She won't be a tick.'

Arabella glanced up, wondering wildly if her visitor was Ben. The sturdy figure of a British officer in khaki jacket, puttees and boots strode through the flap with confident ease.

'I heard you were here, Sister Allen, and as I was passing I dropped in to thank you for saving my life.'

'*Deneys du Rand!*' Arabella whispered in amazement, recognising the deep, musical voice instantly, but baffled by the uniform. Her colour heightened as he doffed his helmet, and she wondered if it was a trick of her mind that he seemed even more handsome and dashing than when she had first met him on the hillside at Suncrest Farm.

'I never expected to see you again – and recovered so quickly!' As her astonishment dissolved, she appraised him with a reserved air.

His blond hair was brushed into a typical English style, and he sauntered forward, with the careless swagger of a British officer.

'My arm has recently come out of plaster, Sister. The bullet, however, will live with me for life, but as you see, I am in the peak of health – much of it thanks to you.'

She remembered him lying against the rock face above Suncrest Farm, his face drawn, his body bloodstained – then, without warning, her heart began to beat with overwhelming intensity ... Disconcerted, she asked: 'How did you know I was here?' A blush warmed her cheeks as his gaze wandered over the scarlet 'Netley Cape' she wore on top of her long grey gown with its sweeping skirts and long tight sleeves, the stained pinafore, and the white muslin headdress.

He smiled easily. 'I keep my ear to the ground.'

'I met your brother Christiaan in the Boer hospital in Ladysmith.'

'I know. He escaped with one of those renegade chaps from the Irish Brigade, a fellow by the name of O'Shea.'

At the sound of O'Shea's name, Arabella braced an arm against the table, struggling to subdue a feeling of dread. After a long moment she could breathe evenly again. 'Why the British uniform?' she said, in an effort to change the subject. 'You know you could be shot for wearing enemy clothes.'

A strange smile played upon his lips. 'It was the necessary accompaniment in the line of duty, as was the gelding outside. Not as fast as a Boer pony, but one must use what one can find.'

Her cheeks grew even warmer as their eyes met and held, and she felt again the unwelcome surge of blood pounding in her temples. She could hate his people, she could hate what they did, but seeing him again broke through all those angry, bitter feelings.

Then her eyes widened in alarm. 'You're a spy! And you're here under false pretences!' she managed to gasp, backing up against the table. 'You could be caught and shot – right here.'

He shrugged broad shoulders and casually sauntered about the tent, halting beside one of the tables. 'You have chlorodyne, I see. Our commandoes are in urgent need of it as cases of dysentery have broken out.' He looked up, his brown gaze cool and unswerving.

He was thinner, and there were lines about his mouth, but in comparison with the patients and the others in the camp, he looked remarkably fit and well-fed. Remaining aloof, she returned his gaze without giving him the benefit of a reply, as she thought about the many officers who had been killed by his people, and especially the dead officer whose uniform he now wore.

'You intrigue me,' he murmured, searching for the appropriate words that would draw her from her shell. 'You think nothing of coming to save my life, like an angel of mercy, and yet now you act the self-righteous, cold-hearted enemy.'

Arabella lifted a bottle from the table, averting her gaze from his curious regard. 'How can I be anything else when I know you've been spying on my people?'

'It's no different from those British nationals of yours who've been using the Red Cross as a cover for espionage in the Transvaal, and who were conveying British soldiers to the lines in Red Cross ambulances. They are so-called spies, surely?'

She raised her head at this and retorted. 'Your own people have flagrantly escaped by sheltering behind the Red Cross flag on several occasions!'

'Only because the burghers were ignorant of what the Red Cross symbolised and what the Geneva Convention prescribes in regard to its use,' he replied easily, 'but come, this is a pointless argument. It's a necessary part of warfare.' He gave her a slow grin. 'This camp is a meeting place for both Boer and Briton, Sister. We have never been sent away empty-handed by your people – can we not call a truce?'

Swiftly she shook her head from side to side. 'There will be no truce until this war has ended, and men have stopped being unnecessarily killed and maimed.' A trace of bitter anger crept into her voice. 'This camp is a meeting place only for men on the legitimate business of fetching medicines for their sick – *not* for those who come in the pretence of peace with information in their minds that will cause more suffering to my people.'

It unnerved her to find him watching her with unswerving attention. It was deathly still in the tent as a soft wind blew through the open flap, bringing the fetid smell of disease. Arabella opened a box of medicines and studied the row of bottles filled with precious chlorodyne. She knew she should call for the soldiers to hold Deneys – she could do that right now ... but it did not ease her dilemma to remember that he had saved Luke's life once. The appearance of this handsome and audacious man had thrown her completely offguard. She felt vulnerable in his presence, knowing that he was extremely clever, that he was so familiar with the British way of thinking and acting that he had totally deceived the soldiers and the orderly. For some reason this made her feel as if she was transparent to him.

She knew that she could never turn him over to the soldiers ... but he was a spy, and for that reason she could never accept him, never be anything else but withdrawn and distant. And he was surely insane to come here under the very noses of his enemies! Fear assailed her then – he had to leave immediately. She stood small and straight, and when she looked up at him again, his brown eyes had hardened perceptively.

'If that's the way you see it, Sister, then I had better go, before you betray me to your people. I wouldn't like to have my head served up to your Lord Stradcombe on a plate.' His words fell with a thud against her heart.

'Leave at once – I won't turn you in. You saved a child's life once, and because of that, as far as I'm concerned, you were never here.'

There was a tight, dangerous little smile on his face, as from the nearest kopje came the sound of guns booming out across the countryside. 'Without the chlorodyne?'

'I'm afraid so,' Arabella said in intense frustration. She turned away quickly as he strode out, before he could see the utter hell in her eyes.

Quite suddenly one morning, the camp was awakened with the news that a band of Imperial Light Horse, led by Lord Stradcombe, a hundred Carbineers and a small party of guides and Engineers had crept up Lombard's Kop during the night and destroyed Long Tom. The excitement in the camp was tangible. From now on, there would be no more fear of that large monster of a weapon.

By now, too, news was circulating that a spy had stolen a British uniform and a horse from the Army camp in Ladysmith. This evoked different reactions – anger in some at his audacity, disgust in others for the incompetence of the sentries, and open admiration in some people, who maintained that had the roles been reversed, and the spy a Briton in a Boer camp, he would never have got past the first line of defence.

The matter soon died down, but it lived in Arabella's memory. Ever since she had seen Deneys again she had been disturbed and angry. Only she had known his identity, and she had let him walk away. Resentment at his utter impudence, visiting her in stolen clothes as casually as if he were stopping by to see a friend – and the weeks of outrage against his people were locked deep inside her.

She had been on duty for several hours when she learned that Archie Mungo, by now the most well-known and popular of all the war correspondents, had gone out with the assault party and been hit twice. One shot had almost torn away his thumb, while the other shattered his leg below the knee; he had died while one of the doctors had been trying to arrest the bleeding.

Arabella thought about the lanky, friendly Australian who had asked her to marry him. Later she went to the tent she shared with the nurses, and sat down on her cot, amidst the buzzing flies and the stink and the noise, and tried to make sense of it all. At first she could only stare at nothing like a shocked statue, and then, shaking all over, she wept and wept . . .

Soon, to make up for the loss of Long Tom, the Boers opened up on the town and its inner ring of hills with every available gun. The British guns were prompt to answer back, and the din reached an almighty crescendo. Not long afterwards, the gun on Surprise Hill was taken, but hope had faded concerning the relieving forces under General Buller. The distant rumble of their cannon had been heard, but it never came any nearer and there was news of heavy fighting southwards on the Tugela River.

Then the dispiriting information arrived that Buller had suffered a reverse. The Boer position on the river was almost unassailable; beyond it, for miles, lay an open valley across which the British must come without a scrap of cover.

Christmas Day dawned hot and cloudless. A cease-fire had been called and the streets of Ladysmith were surprisingly gay, with men in straw boaters and women wearing their prettiest white dresses and carrying parasols. The children's party drew to a close, and Arabella, who had travelled in from Intombi Camp to help organise it, walked back to the station, the air almost eerily quiet without the gunfire. In its place, the music of the banjo and the accordian, and the singing of Christmas carols brought back poignant memories of past Christmases at Allenbury Manor ... the house full of the excited chatter of guests, a great tree in the hall, silver charms in the pudding, and Rosamunde, beautiful, vivacious, golden Rosamunde, with her tinkling laugh and shining hazel eyes ... and dear Aunt Matty, smiling as she was hugged and kissed for her thoughtful and appropriate homemade gifts.

Aching loneliness gripped Arabella then, and she closed her eyes against the jostling mass of humanity in the station. She felt that there was no past or future, only an endless, present which was the only reality, and always would be ...

A voice startled her from her reverie, and she was surprised, and not a little disconcerted, to see Ben standing there.

'What a sad face on a day of long-overdue festivity!' His face was serious despite the forced smile. 'I've been looking for you everywhere, Arabella. You seem to have dodged me the entire day.'

'You'll think I'm ridiculous,' she said impulsively, 'but I was thinking of past Christmases at home –'

'I know!' His deeply tanned face broke into a pleased smile which caused the lines to disappear and made him look suddenly boyish. 'I remember, too. The warmth and cosiness behind closed curtains and carol singers outside the window – the steaming-hot plum pudding straight from the kitchens – the holly and mistletoe ...'

'Yes,' she agreed, with a soft laugh, 'that's exactly what I meant! Somehow it doesn't seem like Christmas here, in the heat with the flies and the dust, the wounded and the sick.'

'It certainly is hard to believe.' He looked down at her, his grey eyes searching her thin, freckled little face. Then he took her arm and led her to a small oasis of peace near the ticket office.

'The Boers are very quiet today.' Her green eyes flickered up towards the hills. 'I thought we'd be hearing cheers by now, what with their commandoes holding down the relieving force and the surrounding countryside for miles southwards.'

Ben's brow puckered into deeper furrows. 'The Boers, my dear, regard Christmas Day as a religious holy day. They've most likely spent it praying and reading their Bibles and looking down on the Sodom and Gomorrah of their degenerate foes.' He paused, then smiled sardonically. 'But there is some good news, thank God. A truce has been called and there've been some major Boer defeats near Colenso to the south.'

'But there's also been news of appalling British casualties, and the need for relief of this town is urgent, Ben. I hear that there are only five days' supply of fresh beef left. Butchers are no longer allowed to sell meat to their customers. Everyone is on rations – which is still better than in the camp.'

'Buller will get here eventually, Arabella. He has enormous obstacles to surmount, but come he will. Lord Roberts of Kandahar has been appointed Commander-in-Chief and an Army reserve has been called out. He has left England with Kitchener. When they arrive on this soil, we shall see a turn of events, I guarantee.' Ben stressed his words as he stared into her anxious green eyes. 'But let's talk of more pleasant matters. I have a gift for you.'

'A gift? But Ben you shouldn't,' she burst out, as he handed her a small box tied with string.

He flicked an experienced eye over her scarlet cape, the white head-dress bringing out the soft brown of her hair as she looked down at the gift in her small, capable hands.

There was no card or mark on the wrappings, and wonderingly, she searched the grey eyes for some clue to its contents, but they gleamed back at her above mute, smiling lips. Carefully, as if she had a great treasure in her hands, she explored the cotton inside the box, feeling an object light and smooth. She had it in her hands at last – an exquisite pendant wrought in the finest gold filigree set with pale peridot stones and seed pearls on a slender chain. She stared, fascinated. She had no jewels since she had pinned Rosamunde's brooch to her collar on Deneys du Rand's arm, and this was the most beautiful piece of jewelry she had seen in a very long time.

'Oh, Ben ...' Tears gathered to blur her vision as she looked at it. 'It's so very lovely.' She held it for a long moment, turning it this way and that between her fingers. She could see it was in the finest taste, and the sort of gift a cousin may give another, but somehow, she knew it had been chosen with particular significance.

'I bid for it at an auction held last week,' he told her, a note of pride creeping into his voice. 'I was damned fortunate to get it, I can tell you – and it's genuine, not the usual paste.' He stood close to her, a light kindling in the smoky grey of his eyes. 'I also came by a coveted bottle of St. Julien claret which I want you to share with me – and a box of apples, for seven pounds ten shillings, if you can believe that! The apples are for you and the nurses at the camp.'

For a moment, her eyes left the strong lines of his face, the assertive set of his jaw. She hesitated briefly, bewildered by his generosity. She could not utter the words she wanted to say, the pleas that would caution him to be careful of her feelings. She wanted love, but not like this, when she could no longer clearly discern right from wrong, when she had no more sure knowledge of herself. She thought of Deneys du Rand, and wondered what Ben would say if he knew she had let a spy walk away, and her guilt deepened.

'Ben, I really can't accept this gift. I have nothing for you,' she said finally, shaking her head as she caught his quizzically lifted eyebrows.

'That's no reason for not accepting a gift, dear girl.' His lips curved in that disarming slow smile she knew only too well, and he looked at her steadily until she dropped her eyes once more.

His words came to her as from a long way off because she could hardly keep her mind on what he said. She could only be acutely aware that he stood so much thinner, but seeming so tall in comparison to her lack of inches, above her, faintly fragrant of brandy and a recently smoked cigar. Somehow it was always like this; she could never be completely logical about him, even though she knew his weaknesses, even though she knew he was a married man, because she was always aware of that subtle scent of masculinity that aroused the romantic notions in her again and again, notions she would much rather forget . . .

He was still looking at her with an amused expression, and she said with an over-elaborate casualness, 'Ben – this gift should be for Rosamunde, not me.'

She started on seeing that his that his mouth had taken on a bitter curve, and his dark brows were drawn close in a frown. 'Rosamunde, is the mother of my children, that's all. It seems strange for you to be thinking of her after the way she drove you from our house.' The sharpness had suddenly left his tone, leaving a trace of thoughtfulness, as though he was trying to discover another meaning behind her statement.

'I know you compliment me, Ben, by giving me this gift,' she said, trying desperately to explain herself adequately. 'But I'm no longer the girl I was back at the farm. Too much has happened to change all that, and I hardly know what to think any longer – not about Rosamunde and me, or anything.'

'When this war ends, we shall all be able to untangle ourselves, Arabella ... There's a dance this evening, and the young people not on duty will celebrate until midnight, before the fighting resumes tomorrow. I would like you to attend with me.'

She shook her head, feeling drained and miserable, conscious of her thin cheeks, and sunken eyes and the appalling state of her clothes. She was aware, too, that he did not understand her scruples.

'Thank you for the invitation, Ben, but I must return to Intombi Camp as soon as possible. The number of typhoid fever cases has reached dangerously high levels, and the medical staff is in a critical state, having lost two more nurses and four orderlies.'

'Can you not forget your duty just for a few hours?' he pleaded wearily. 'Who knows if some of us shall see another Christmas, and those who are going tonight, are going anyway. There's frustration and boredom enough waiting for Buller's troops ...' His lips closed tightly on those last words, and glancing up at the profile of his face, she was struck by the grim set of his jaw and the way his eyes took on a sudden blankness as if to hide something intensely painful.

She did not answer. The crowds, jammed with more dhoolie-loads of sick, were now milling around so intensely that it was impossible to speak.

The train hooted and steamed up. She said goodbye, and he sighed, and moved back as she climbed aboard. As she settled against the hard seat in the carriage crammed to overflowing with groaning sick men, she felt tears gathering in her eyes. Clutching Ben's gift tightly in her hands, she was suddenly afraid of her own heart, as she had been afraid of it before, but now with more intensity.

It had been a dubious reward in the midst of all the weary waiting and dreadful suffering, to see Ben again, to see his face light up in pleasure when she opened the gift. More and more she realised that if he were free, she would have no hesitation in accepting his love. One of her sharpest sorrows was knowing that it could never be. And the gift would remind her of that, every waking moment of her days.

She could force herself to face not ever having him, but what she could not endure was grim prospect of a life of duty without the chance to give or receive real, deep and enduring love. The last thing she wanted to do was to live a loveless life. She, who had always been so proud and happy in her independence was now helpless in the face of this new demand.

Chilled at the thought of the future and what awaited her, she shivered a little and closed her eyes as the train steamed out of the station.

16

That night, a soldier who had been brought into Intombi Camp the previous day became very excited and slightly delirious. Dr Hickory, who was short-staffed, called Arabella in to assist him in the bell-shaped operating tent. He held up the paraffin lamp to reveal a young figure stinking of gas gangrene lying on a stretcher, and obviously in great pain. The face had a ghastly yellow tinge; the man's eyes were closed and his lips were drawn back over his teeth. The soiled dressings on his left leg had been removed, exposing the stump where it had been amputated up to the thigh, and the ominously dark discolouration from there to the abdomen.

Dr Hickory wiped his blood stained hands down the side of his khaki serge breeches. He stood for a moment facing Arabella, his sweat-stained shirtsleeves rolled up to the elbow, then he placed the lamp nearby to examine the infected parts with minute care as the soldier moaned in agony.

A grave expression appeared on his usually cheerful, ruddy face, and he flicked the ends of his ginger moustache in a frustrated gesture. 'Do you want to know the truth, Corporal?' he asked, in his slow Australian drawl.

'Yes sir, please, sir,' was the muffled reply from the stretcher. ''Tis better that way.'

The doctor pursed his lips. 'The same sort of gangrene which affected your leg has spread to your abdomen, my lad. I'm sorry.' There was the slightest pause, then he went on, 'You have only a few more hours to live, old son – there's nothing more we can do to save you.'

The young man gave a small, painful sigh that went to Arabella's heart, then he said in a quiet, steady voice that shook ever so slightly, 'Thanks for telling me, Doctor. At least now I'll not live on false hopes any longer. Up until this evening I really thought I was going to make it. But, if you can choose, I suppose Christmas night is the best time to go, when all's said and done.' He lay back, wincing with pain. 'Could you get one of my pals to send a message to my ma back home?'

'Of, course we will, lad. Now don't you worry – we'll make you as comfortable as we can.' Dr Hickory caught Arabella's eye and she realised that he was no more immune than she to this blow dealt to a young man, who had arrived in the country fit and healthy and ready to fight the Boers . . .

He called her to one side. 'Redress him, Sister, and give him as much morphia as it takes to put him out of his misery.'

He walked away wearily as she set to work, and dosed the Corporal heavily with the drug before attending to the stump, which was stinking from the putrid discharge. She spoke gently to him as he was carried back to his cot, where he half slept, weary but resigned, dimly aware of the comings and goings of the doctors and orderlies, of the muted voices and the giving of orders that would continue the whole night.

Another young soldier, lying on a mattress on the ground, lay exhausted after a dreadful choking fit. He looked as white and pinched as if he were dead when Arabella bent down to help him. The tent was only half-lighted by a candle on the ground, in a corner, while through the open flap the moonlight streamed in on to his bandaged hands and white face. She stiffened as she heard yet another patient's last long-drawn struggles for breath as if he was drowning, and then it stopped with that rattle she had come to dread, and all was still, except for his friend's sobs and the singing of *'God Bless Ye Merry Gentlemen'* in the distant Army camp.

She was suddenly overwhelmed with the terrible sadness of it all, and felt like running away to weep, but all she could do was to assist the young soldier into a more comfortable position, and help one of the exhausted nurses to lay out the body of the dead patient. They tidied up his cot, and she walked outside, to find Dr Hickory smoking a hurried pipe in the darkness.

As she stood beside him, she could see nothing but the densely-packed stars, and to the right, vast shadows against the sky, where the rugged black humps of the Boer-controlled hills rose sinister and lonely, the flicker of enemy fires kindling the ridges, as they waited for the dawn and the end of the Christmas celebrations.

In the darkness, the pipe bowl glowed like a firefly, waned and grew, as the moon rose above the eastern shadows, now almost full.

Dr Hickory stared out into the darkness for a long moment before saying, 'I wonder how many times I've had to tell a man his life is at an end, a young man, with a future and the whole world ahead of him. There's always that moment when you wonder – should I tell him, or not? But what's the use of hiding it! It's just so damned difficult, breaking up a man's life with a few stark words.'

'The Corporal's very brave. Let's hope he goes peacefully at the last,' Arabella said quietly, her eyes looking unseeing at the humps of hills, knowing that out there somewhere, a golden-haired Boer and his brothers and their Jewish friend were waiting it out until the morning, to kill again with deadly accuracy, more young British soldiers ...

The Australian doctor was silent, preoccupied with his own thoughts. Then suddenly he said with soft viciousness, 'I don't know what's worse, Sister – telling them they're going to die, or making the decision that they cannot be treated and *leaving* them to die! Way back in Adelaide, it would never have entered my head that I would be called upon to make such grotesque decisions so often.'

Arabella turned around, her back to the menacing hills, and folding her arms, she stared at the entrance to the operating tent, at the bright pinpoint of golden light from the oil lamp shining through the open flap, where another operation was in progress.

She knew he was referring to the standard procedure for sorting out the patients into three categories when they arrived: the lightly wounded, who needed no immediate attention and who were simply given pain relief, the severely wounded whose survival was impossible, and those on whom the most effort was made – men with injuries which, although life-threatening, were curable.

Shivering imperceptibly, she said, 'I suppose it must be the same as when women die giving life to children they will never see grow into adulthood ... like a flower withering before its fullest blooming. She has to make that choice when she loves her husband, the choice that she might die giving birth to his child.'

She thought suddenly of her own young mother, who had died giving birth to her stillborn brother. She had only been nineteen and she had loved her husband so much that she had given her life having the son he wanted ... and after that, her husband had grown into a bitter, angry man who had died with ice in his heart.

'Do you know, that the patients call you the Angel of Intombi, Sister Allen?' Dr Hickory said gruffly, breaking into her thoughts. 'It doesn't seem fair that a talented young gentlewoman such as yourself should be here, in this muck and suffering, seeing to the needs of dying men when you should be home, tending a devoted husband and children of your own.'

Arabella stiffened, thinking of Ben. Loving him, she would never be able to marry and have her own children ... She forced a laugh. 'Perhaps, when this war is over and forgotten.'

'This war will never be forgotten.' Her colleague's voice was uncharacteristically harsh. 'It will only cause more problems, more complications, more bitterness, before it ends. Wars never solve anything, Sister, and no war is forgotten, not by those without limbs, without sight ... They are our eternal monument to man's inhumanity to man. Those maimed by war will live with the memories forever in their hearts, and we doctors will never forget the terrible decisions we've been forced to make on the battlefields ... we will always be haunted by the dreadful spectres of those we allowed to die!'

The days passed, bright and merciless. Conditions were chronic in the town and the camp, as fever spread and depression mounted. Food supplies were low, and the nurses were back to serving the patients bread alternating with Army biscuit soaked in water first and then slightly toasted; they had to increase the coffee in bulk by mixing it with burned maized meal. Seventy horses and mules were now killed daily, their flesh boiled to make beef tea for the sick. The heartbreaking thing for all the nursing staff was that, though they might pull a man safely through the crisis of his illness, they had no chance of building up his strength again with a decent diet and no opportunity for the careful nursing which to the fever patients was so important.

In order to make room for extra patients, the dispensary was moved into the operating tent. One of the doctors had fallen ill with the dreaded typhoid, and two more patients were on the danger list with it. As there was an acute shortage of coffins, the dead were now rolled up in blankets before they were buried at nightfall.

General Buller's relieving force was still unable to reach the beleaguered town, and hope was fading fast that the reinforcements would get through at all. Ladysmith itself now stood in an even more dubious and vulnerable position. Even though it was held by a British garrison, there were several hours during the day of 6 January 1900 when the question of ownership hung in the balance. A major attack was expected – very soon.

A force of picked men were massed to the south-east of the town in preparation for the anticipated Boer offensive. The point chosen for the assault was called Caesar's Hill, the south-eastern end of the horseshoe forming the outline of the British defences and the highest of all the hills surrounding the town. The range there was irregular, in the form of a rough triangle, and the position of it would give the enemy absolute command of the town and cramp every operation of the British troops, bringing under fire every ridge still left to them.

Everyone knew it would be a life and death struggle, that having determined a course of action, the Boers would carry it out with the daring and disregard for the consequences worthy of the boldest trained troops in the world. A new dread enveloped all those in the town and in the camp, for they had learned only too well of the strength of the enemy, his bush-craft, and his quickness of resource in emergencies. They feared it was a matter of days before Ladysmith was overrun.

It was just daybreak on that fateful day, in the faint blush of dawn, that the blaze of gunfire across the hills intruded into Arabella's uneasy sleep. After measuring out doses of sleeping draughts the night before for patients in extreme pain, she had desperately wanted to sleep herself, and refresh her aching limbs. But it was not to be.

As the dawning rays spread slowly across the hills, the sound of gunfire increased in volume. Coming fully awake, she flung herself from her cot, and pulling on a muslin veil and scarlet cape over the crumpled, slept-in dress, she flew out of the tent. Casting her gaze around the camp, where the ambulances were ready to start, she saw Dr Hickory hurrying out of the operating tent, carrying his small black surgeon's bag. Her knees began to shake as invading impressions of a bloody battle sought to push their horror upon her. A cold sweat made her skin clammy as the image faded, but it was a full moment before she could clear her mind. She stopped the doctor, touching his sleeve.

'Dr Hickory, whatever is going on? Why are you going off with the ambulances?'

'Last night our troops strengthened all the defences on the hills, particularly on Caesar's Hill, in preparation for the rumored Boer attack which came in the night.' He paused to adjust his unbuttoned khaki jacket. 'The fighting was the heaviest on Wagon's Hill, held by the Imperial Light Horse. As some of the doctors in the field hospitals are down with fever, as are many of the orderlies, I've been called out to help the wounded on the battlefield. You'll have to manage, Sister, as best you can with the remaining doctors until I return.'

'The Imperial Light Horse?' A chill coursed through her veins, as she realised that in all probability, Ben had been in the thick of the fighting on Wagon's Hill. 'I'm coming with you, Dr Hickory – you'll need someone to assist you,' she gasped as he turned to hurry away.

His eyebrows came up in astonishment as he whipped around. 'You'll do no such thing, Sister. The battlefield is no place for a woman! You'll stay here and see to the camp patients and the wounded when they are brought in from the field hospitals.'

She gazed up at his tired ruddy face as footsteps came towards them. His chin was unshaven, and beneath the jacket his shirt was crumpled and bloodstained and she knew he had been up most of the night. He looked around to see the ambulance driver and the dhoolie-bearers approaching with long, hurried strides. She stood for a second in indecision, as he stalked away and climbed into the nearest ambulance drawn by six mules, then, without another thought, she picked up her dusty skirts and ran to the back of the ambulance where the black stretcher-bearers were sitting.

Calling for a hand up, she was hoisted with much surprise into the ambulance as it jolted to a start, and rumbled away across the veld in a cloud of dust. Her heart was thumping violently as she sat on the crowded hard seat running along one side of the uncomfortable vehicle, bracing herself against the jolts, as it swerved to miss some obstruction in its way, and bumped over the ruts in its path.

She knew that Wagon's Hill was so-called because of the curious shape of a tree growing on its crest, and she was now told by one of the bearers, with graphic hand gestures, that the face of the hill was as steep as a wall, and covered with enormous boulders. She winced when a battery of artillery was heard on the outskirts of Ladysmith, as all calibre of guns and rifles seemed to rake the area into which they were heading.

Her mind was working swiftly as they neared the heat of the fighting, where the noise rose to a deafening pitch. Though one part of her was afraid of the next few dreadful hours, and knew that she should not be there, that she could easily be killed or maimed, the other part had sprung to life. Dr Hickory needed her assistance – and against all reason, she had to find Ben. She had to know where he was, and if he was still alive ...

The ambulance drew up sharply, pitching her forward. Putting out an arm to save herself from getting hurt, Arabella shakily allowed herself to be lifted down by two bearers. The surrounding hillsides were a terrifying sight – a moving tide and counter-tide of British troops and the enemy. As she wiped the dust from her forehead, she saw a hail of shell splinters burst downward over the largest rocks, searching every corner of Wagon's Hill, where the boulders were piled in such confusion that amongst them the men were safe except from shrapnel directly overhead. Beyond that and stretching right across the valley to the Boer ridge, the country was covered with thorn trees, and now she could see that the enemy attack, which covered a front of over two miles, had been very well timed.

It was all far worse than she had ever imagined. Near at hand was the horrible aspect of a bloody battlefield where men lay with seemingly not a single whole bone in their bodies. Arabella saw that the bodies were totally torn to shreds, and her growing nausea rolled up like an ugly serpent.

She climbed over a mound of Boers who had died trying to chase the British from the hill. Scattered everywhere were the pathetic reminders of human existence – rifles fallen from lifeless hands, water bottles and hats in the stinking corruption of dead and rotting flesh, mingled with dust, smoke and the ear-splitting barrage of gunfire.

A sudden slight noise alerted her. A man was coughing painfully as he lay outlined against the rocks a little further up the hillside. She made her way towards him, and as she bent down he opened glazed eyes for a second, a twisted smile crossing his haggard face.

'You've come again, mejuffrou – but this time, it's too late,' he gasped, then lay back, exhausted from the effort of speech.

Her eyes widened in disbelief when she recognised Danie, Deneys du Rand's younger brother. She felt a shooting pain near her heart, and then it was gone. For a second, all the terror of the war seemed to stretch between them: Deneys shot on the hillside, the siege, the shelling of the hospitals. She looked at him again, as he moaned in agony.

Here was a man in grave need of her skill. Gently she pulled away the blood-soaked shirt, until she could see new blood welling from a bayonet wound in his lower lung. She knew he was dying. His lungs had collapsed, he had already lost a lot of blood, and he was in shock. She gazed down at his filmy eyes, hopeless in the knowledge that there was nothing she could do to save him. She remembered Danie as he had been when they first met – young, robust and eager, blessed with shining blond good looks, and full of concern for his brother Deneys who even at this moment might be here, on this hill.

Before she could call to Dr Hickory, Danie's dark brown eyes flickered, and a few matted and bloody strands of golden hair fell over his forehead. He clenched his left fist in pain. 'We Boers – hold – all nurses – in – very – high – esteem,' he gasped, every word painfully wrung from his lips.

'Don't talk,' she said gently, folding her scarlet cape into a pillow for him. 'I'll try to make you as comfortable as I can, then I'll call our doctor.'

'I don't – want – to die, mejuffrou,' he said with agonising gasps of breath, 'but – there – is nothing – you or I can do. We cannot choose – the day to go. It just comes –'

'It's all right, Danie,' Arabella whispered thickly as she tried to stem the blood pouring from his chest. He coughed and a trickle of blood ran from his mouth.

Almost in tears, and on the verge of fainting, she shrieked: 'Dr Hickory, please help me! There's a man here who desperately needs you!'

She heard a brusque male voice bark suddenly, 'Bloody hell! I thought I told you to stay at camp, Sister Allen!'

Arabella looked down at Danie. He was dying, and she did not want him to. She wanted to pull him back into life . . .

Then she came to her senses to hear Dr Hickory say, 'He's gone, Sister. There's nothing more I can do.' There was a small silence, then the doctor rose to his feet, his mouth stern but his eyes contemplative. 'Did you know this man, Sister?' he asked curiously.

She shook her head, unable to speak. When she could her eyes were expressionless. 'He was just another Boer, Doctor.' It was said so quickly, and yet she knew at the moment of utterance, the horrible lie for what it was.

'Even among enemies, there is a certain compassion,' the Australian said gravely, as he stumped off over the hillside. 'But all the same, I told you not to come here.'

Arabella bent down and gently reclaimed her crumpled cape. She placed Danie's mudstained hat over his face and crossed his arms over his bloody chest, then she crawled away with an ashen face, afraid to break down completely. How she wished she had not come.

Over the hill on the enemy's side of the slope, more Boer dead were lying, their Red Cross men dotted among the thorn trees in the valley, and a queer Boer ambulance with little glass windows rattling along under an enormous white flag, bringing British wounded in exchange for wounded Boers. Not far away, a British ambulance van stood with several of its mule team dead, the black driver hiding at the rear in panic. Another wagon stood further away, dead bodies clumsily piled on it one upon the other.

Arabella wondered if Deneys and Isaac and Christian were among the dead . . . then she thought of Ben, somewhere on this terrible mountain. Stumbling over the bodies in her path, she hurried towards Dr Hickory, who was kneeling beside a wounded Gordon Highlander. As he bent over slightly, carrying out his examination, a stray bullet cut through his side, just above the hip. It made a nasty wound, but fortunately missed the vital parts. Though his clothing was fast staining with blood, he stayed there continuing with his work.

Arabella, keeping her head well down, approached him cautiously. 'Let me help you, Doctor. You're lucky to be alive!' she gasped.

'You should not be here, Sister,' he reiterated doggedly as another fusillade of bullets flew past them. They both ducked, but Dr Hickory did not falter in his task of dressing the soldier's wound. 'If the authorities hear about this, you'll never be able to nurse again, and I, for allowing you to help me here, will be hauled before the Army Medical Headquarters in Cape Town. We're both in enough trouble as it is, with our constant complaining against the authorities.'

'I had to come,' she persisted. 'I know it was against orders, but these are exceptional circumstances. And now that I'm here, I can be of great help, even if I am a mere woman.'

He looked up briefly. 'You insist on sticking your neck out, don't you, Miss?'

Arabella lifted her head and spoke hoarsely. 'Yes, Doctor, I suppose I do.'

He looked at her, seeing the determination in her small, freckled face, and the strength of purpose. Then he stared down at his patient thoughtfully. At last he sighed, 'Oh, very well. If you want to help, then keep well down. The last thing I want to have to do is to operate on you, too.'

His eyes flickered towards her briefly, and received a strong smile of courage. After he had allowed her to staunch his own wound, they went to work further up the hillside, where the casualties were heaviest. And all the time there was an ache in Arabella's heart for Ben, intensified by the knowledge that this time, he might not have survived ...

All over the hill, clips of Mauser bullets could be found behind rocks, where the owners had left them when they retired in a hurry. And far below, they saw the incongruous sight of a small red mongrel dog threading its way through the welter of mule wagons and water-carts. The fire was so heavy that the pair were forced to move snake-like along the hillsides as they went from one casualty to another. Rumours flew about that the Imperial Light Horse had lost thirty men, fourteen officers being killed instantly. Arabella found it a dreadful experience to move amongst the slain, not knowing if the next dead soldier would be Ben.

Clouds had been gathering all morning, and in the early afternoon, the distinct roll of thunder electrified the air. Then the heavens opened, and the mightiest thunderstorm Arabella had ever witnessed burst over Ladysmith.

As hailstones the size of small pebbles, fell in blinding torrents, she ran with Dr Hickory for the cover of the rocks, being forced to leave the wounded lying out in the open, many too badly injured to shield their faces from the lashing hail. Everything was blotted out, and the sixty guns were temporarily silenced. Then, at the height of the deluge, the Boers, who had the storm at their backs, came on again to the hill with a burst of firing.

As the storm subsided, Dr Hickory decided to return with the next ambulance; he ordered Arabella to go with him. Drenched to the skin and shivering convulsively, she agreed. She was hurrying down the slope when a stretcher carried by four turbanned Indian bearers passed them.

'Put me down beside the ambulance, chaps, then get on with your work with the other poor bastards.' She stopped, transfixed. She knew that voice – it was one she would never forget.

'*Ben!*' she cried, and leapt forward to the stretcher. She looked down, hardly daring to breathe. Ben lay there, wincing, a large bloodstained bandage tied around his left leg.

'Arabella – what on earth? You do crop up in the most God-damned places, dear girl,' he grunted painfully, seeing her anxious face bent over him.

'Don't worry, Ben. We'll get you off this terrible hill as soon as we can. I'm going with this patient,' she announced as he was carefully placed in the ambulance van.

There was no sign of her colleague, and she knew she would have to see that Ben survived the journey. She saw with deep dismay the deathly pallor of his skin, against which his black moustache stood out in striking and dreadful contrast.

'I'll live, old girl, you can count on it,' were the last words he said as she climbed up beside him. With relief she saw the lean figure of Father Sebastian mount up after her and seat himself on the other side of the stretcher, among the others that were crowded together in the stinking space.

He produced some brandy which Ben gulped down with the greatest relief, and said, 'God really does work in mysterious ways, to be sure, Sister Allen – sending us an angel of mercy in Major Saville's great distress.'

'Father.' She looked anxiously at the priest through the shifting dimness from under the roof of the ambulance as it jolted away from the mayhem of the battlefield. 'Will he live?'

The priest's slender, well-cut features were grave. He sat upright like a soldier, his shoulders back. 'That, my child, is in the hands of God.' His light-blue eyes behind the spectacles were gentle. 'Our friend has been shot in the thigh, and the main artery is severed. Some would say he is fortunate to have survived this long, but then,' he gestured with his lean, scholar's hands, 'miracles are performed every day. We must have faith – it is essential.'

Suddenly the bandages tore apart, and fresh blood gushed from the gaping wound in Ben's thigh; Arabella feared the great loss of blood. As he lay there in silent agony, she quickly called for a bandage from the medical box, and applied it as a temporary tourniquet. Never had she felt so desperate as she sat looking out at the passing scene between the bars of the van. She could not bear the thought of him dying . . .

There was a sudden jolt as the van halted, and Father Sebastian peered out. 'We've stopped at a dressing station, Arabella. We'd better get the Major out as quickly as we can. It's too far to take him all the way back to the camp.'

Arabella shook her head. 'No, Father. Major Saville needs a more complex operation than that performed at a dressing station – a mobile field ambulance is more suitable. Are we anywhere near one?'

She glanced imploringly at the priest, who immediately rose and climbed out of the van. Looking down at Ben, whose breath was now ragged and loud, she felt a trickle of blood running down her hands. Blood was clotted on his cheeks and forehead, and she wished she could clean it away. There was great activity as the more lightly wounded men were carried out to the dressing station, but Arabella felt strangely remote from it – her only concern now was the saving of Ben's life. Never had a few minutes seemed so long ... then the priests was back.

'There's a field hospital some way ahead. It should take us another ten minutes to get there,' he said in his soft-spoken way.

'Oh, God,' she complained without thinking. 'Ten minutes is too long when a man's life is in danger.'

Father Sebastian shook his head, noticing the sudden glint of tears in her eyes. 'We must never give up, Arabella – it will not help the Major. This is not the time to panic. We must use all the spiritual resources God has given us to rise to the challenge.'

Eventually, they arrived at the field hospital, and Father Sebastian climbed out and helped the stretcher-bearers carry Ben to the nearest doctor. Arabella hurried alongside, still holding a compress in place.

The hospital consisted of an operating marquee, and a few wagons and bell-tents. It was to the marquee that the bearers carried Ben's stretcher. Outside a large number of wounded men lay waiting for attention and a place in the overcrowded tents. Two surgeons stood at the entrance, checking over the new load of patients arriving. When they saw Ben, they shook their heads.

'It's too late – there's nothing we can do. There are others with more chance of living,' one of them said, waving the stretcher away.

'No!' Arabella cried hoarsely. 'You'll not send this man away. He has a good chance of surviving if he is attended to right away. I demand that you give him that chance!'

The surgeon who had spoken frowned heavily at her. 'We make the decisions here, Sister, and we do not think he can be saved. Now take him away!'

Arabella's eyes flashed green fire, as defiance and anger whipped through her, lashing her emotions into a great fury. 'This man is Major Lord Stradcombe of the Imperial Light House. He deserves to live as much as any of the others. We will not move from this spot until you examine him properly.'

The other surgeon, who had remained silent, came forward and looked at the wound, then he nodded. 'I'll see what I can do. Get him up on the table at once.'

He led the way, with the clink of spurs at his heels, into the tent where half the wall had been turned back to give the surgeons room to move, so that it was practically in the open air. The grass around about was trodden and heavily stained with blood and other body fluids. Ben was lifted on to the operating table, while the surgeon in his shirt-sleeves and riding breeches bent over him, assisted by a dresser, the anaesthetist who placed a cloth over Ben's face and slowly dripped chloroform on to it, and a couple of orderlies with burnt-sienna complexions, unshaven chins, and dressed in Army shirts, breeches, and helmets. Of nurses there was no sign.

Arabella was forced to release Ben into their hands and to stand at a distance, trying to control her fear while the surgeon began the operation.

'The femur has been smashed, Sister,' he announced a few seconds later. 'I shall have to amputate just above the knee. There's no other way to save him.'

The blood drained from Arabella's cheeks. Ben would never be the same man again: could he accept such a condition? But it was a desperate remedy, she knew, and in order to save his life, there was nothing else to be done.

Just then, Ben's heart began to fail. There was a sudden flurry inside the tent, which by now was baking hot.

'Strychnine! Give me strychnine, dammit,' the surgeon snapped. 'We have no time to waste, or we'll lose him.'

Arabella turned away and stared outside as Ben was injected with large doses of the drug. With conscious thought, she began to pray for the life of this one man.

'He's not going to make it. I'm sorry,' she heard the surgeon say, and she turned back to see Father Sebastian standing beside the operating table, reverently crossing himself.

She walked outside, where the sun struck her like a hot blade. Everything glared whitely and the air was suddenly so still she seemed to stand in timelessness, placelessness. For a moment she seemed very near to Ben – although she could not see him.

The field hospital with its tents, and the hills beyond danced before her eyes and turned blood-red – the whole world turned violent red as she heard voices around her, and the tramping of feet. '*Please God, don't let him die,*' she heard herself pray, as she fell through the redness to blackness to nothingness ...

17

She had no memory of being taken back to the camp. When she awoke on her cot, faint and gasping, she found Dr Hickory bending over her.

'Try to keep calm, Sister Allen. You're in a grave state of shock,' he urged. 'Major Saville will live. He was given enough strychnine to kill a normal person, but he rallied, and is here in the camp.'

Gasping air into her lungs, she struggled up on an elbow and rubbed her bruised face. She was given a battered tin mug of amber liquid and drank it, numbly. It was brandy, prickling her parched tongue, and almost immediately she felt a strong warmth spreading to every nerve in her body.

'Are you ready to have some food, now? There isn't much, but at least it's something,' the doctor asked, his eyes narrowed with concern. 'We can't have our best nurse wasting away. Your patients have been asking for you – they say it isn't the same without you.' A slow encouraging smile spread across his wide lips under the ginger handlebar moustache.

Their eyes met briefly, and in hers he read the gratitude she mutely conveyed before she rose unsteadily, brushing down her skirts. 'How is your wound, Doctor? Are you sure you're all right now?'

'I was patched up well enough and am mending fast. Now we've got to get you right. Rest is the main thing. Only come back to your duties when you're completely well again, understand?'

Arabella opened her mouth to object, but slowly closed it, unable to put forward an adequate argument. He strode away and gestured for the nurses hovering at the open flap to return to their duties.

Arabella stared after him, then the full memory of Ben's operation leapt at her. She pulled on her apron and veil and ran from the tent in search of him. Ben was in a tent in the outer row. Her feet carried her towards him, and a great fear possessed her as she stopped and looked down at his pale, drawn face on the bloodied blankets.

And so began the days and nights of tireless care at the bedside of a man unaware of his own grave plight. As her body strengthened, her brain and hands had never been so active; preparing special dishes for him, cleaning his wound and applying garlic as often as she could, administering his medicines and talking to him between her other duties until her head ached and her voice grew hoarse.

Later, she learned that only three officers of the Imperial Light Horse had survived, even though the British had been victorious on both Wagon's Hill and Caesar's Hill. Ben, who was slowly recovering, was promoted to the rank of Major-General.

On hearing this news, Arabella walked outside, renewing herself in the sunshine, her eyes falling on the tents filled with unwashed, hungry, suffering patients, and the rows of men on stretchers lying with their helmets over their faces against the glare of the sun, awaiting treatment from those overworked doctors who had not succumbed to fever.

She was aware of a gnawing feeling of persistent hunger, and it was now painful to think of the delicious meals of the past. The mere memory of a hearty English breakfast brought such pangs of untold misery that she snuffed them before they could take hold. Never, she thought, would she ever take food for granted again, and she immediately forbade her nurses to talk of it.

Hearing the rusty-sounding call of fork-tailed drongos overhead and seeing the wheeling of vultures far above the two lines of attacking and defending ridges, her eyes turned to the silhouettes of Boers on the outer ridges, moving about like small dots. She wondered if there was something fatally wrong at the very core of the human soul, that it should forever court war and destruction. For a fortnight or more, they had known of the alarming British defeat at the battle of Spionkop, to the south-west of the Tugela River. Spionkop, the key of the Boer position, was a high, double-pronged mountain known to the Zulu people as *N'taba N'Yama* – the black mountain – and to the Boers as Spionkop.

The most frustrating aspect of the current situation was that relief for the suffering inhabitants of Ladysmith was only beyond the next town, but between the relief and the town lay a country infested with enemy commandoes ...

As Ben recovered, he seemed to swing between moods of biting cynicism and a kind of moroseness. Arabella tried to be tolerant, knowing his impatience with any kind of disability. He was forced to walk with crutches, and her heart turned over with anguish, to see how grey and breathless he became after even the smallest effort at walking. She admired the courage with which he forced himself to practise, hour after hour, refusing to rest in his cot.

Towards the middle of February, news of British successes reached them, but at this stage, wild optimism was as dangerous as deep pessimism. General French had swept aside the last Boer commando blocking his entrance to Kimberley and relieved the town with a classical charge, and the victorious battle of Paardeberg had forced General Cronje to surrender with four thousand Boers. These feats brought a few ragged cheers from the small groups of pale, emaciated patients, shrunk in their shabby, dirty clothing.

The cannons to the south had been silent for some time, and there was hope building up that Buller was getting through ... Then came the amazing news that the enemy were in full retreat! For five miles, a long, dense train of wagons stretched across the country beyond the hills. Galloping black-coated horsemen were moving forward in groups of varying numbers, like a continuous living stream around the corner of End Hill, before disappearing northward behind Telegraph Hill, where the British heliograph was stationed, in the direction of their railway base.

A great hole had apparently been torn across General Louis Botha's line, and now it seemed that only the northern kopje on a mountain called Pieter's Hill, stood between the entire Natal Field Force and Ladysmith. At last, the town was on the verge of rescue. The final battle of the great Tugela Heights had lasted six hours, and in Ladysmith, the townsfolk and the Army sensed that their problems would shortly be resolved.

At the end of that terrible month, Arabella became aware of an unusual stir towards the outer row of tents in the camp. Hurrying footsteps sounded, and a hoarse male voice suddenly cried out, 'British horse – riding for the town!'

Those who could walk poured outside, and the convalescents sitting in small groups in the shade staggered to their feet and made their way to the outer edges of the camp. Ragged children ran after them, their mothers following behind with haunted, disbelieving eyes. Arabella picked up her skirts, and joined the dingy, emaciated throng. No one needed to tell her that she looked the same – a small, gaunt figure, wearing clothes that were much too large for her.

They stood and watched as three squadrons of British soldiers came down the nearest hill to Intombi Camp. Arabella caught the gleam of steel when horsemen from the town raced out to meet the column, howling like wild dogs, and churning up the road into clouds of dust.

'We're saved! Our soldiers have come to save us at last!' a woman cried beside her, embracing the little girl in her arms.

There were hoarse cheers from those clustering around as the two columns met, gripping each other as they flourished their guns and waved caps and helmets. Tears of relief began to course down Arabella's cheeks while the cheering grew in volume, echoing around the silent hills.

As the horsemen galloped, whooping, towards the town, she turned and ran back to the camp to find Ben, who was limping painfully on his crutches towards her. She flung her arms about his neck.

'Ben! They've really come – Buller's troops are here!'

A warm glow came into the smoky depths of his eyes as he stared down into her tear-streaked, excited face, then he reached out a hand and gently smoothed an errant strand of hair from her cheek.

'Arabella, I can hardly believe it.' He grimaced, but quickly masked the pain.

She gazed up at him and smiled, admiring the still-fine figure he presented. His khaki shirt, though crumpled and stained, was tucked into the long narrow breeches, and his dark hair was ruffled, but on closer inspection, the deep lines of fatigue and pain around his mouth and down the prominent cheekbones where the flesh had fallen away, showed the strain and tension of the past weeks.

Then he lowered his head, and she lifted her face to meet the full force of his hunger. The green eyes flickered uncertainly, then she yielded, her lips meeting his, the bristles of his moustache, rough against her skin. The kiss began as a gentle questing, with his mouth slowly moving upon hers, but the fire ignited like dry kindling into a roaring blaze.

A shout from someone nearby jolted them back into reality. Ben let his breath out in a long sigh, and moved a little away from her, clenching his teeth, and she knew that his stump had become one long anguish of pain.

'I've wanted to do that, ever since I first saw you on the quayside in Durban,' he said. 'You are rooted in the very core of my life. I want you, Arabella – as I've never wanted any other woman ...' he went on hesitantly, 'but I have no right any more to the feelings of a full man. I have nothing to offer you ... except my love, for what it is. Do you understand that?'

'Yes.' She did not dare to meet his gaze. They stood close together, seemingly united in some strange, intangible way. Her heart cried out to him, and yet it had to remain silent.

'I'm leaving this place, my dear. I'm going to find Kitchener and join his staff, for my fighting days in the field are over.' She heard the trace of bitterness in his voice, then he added, 'but I'm not finished with the Boers yet and I want you to come with me.'

'I can't, Ben.' Her voice was tiny. 'I must help our troops wherever I am needed.'

'*I* need you, Arabella – don't you understand that? You saved my life,' he pressed. 'I want you with me. For years I was a man, accepting the standards of my kind. I had this burning hunger in me which my wife forbade me, so I went with other women. But I could find no real satisfaction. Call me a stubborn idiot, but I am totally and hopelessly in love with a dream that only you can fulfil. I know what life is like without you, and I want no more of it.'

She said slowly, 'We make a pair, you and I, wanting what we may not have. You ask me to become your mistress, Ben, but I cannot accept. I want to be a wife, and that you cannot give me. I must go on and help the men, and you have your own path to follow –' She stopped suddenly, not wanting to think of Rosamunde, and her cousin's claim to him.

He slowly shook his head. 'I cannot make such an offer, even though it would serve to ease my present desire, but, perhaps in the future . . .'

She heaved a weary sigh. 'A divorce? No, that cannot be – the children don't deserve that. I must go.'

A deep scowl drew his brows down sharply, and he glanced away, tormented with jealousy. 'I don't like the thought of you leaving me.' He reached for her hand, and the gentle pressure made her tremble with longing. She wanted him to take her in his arms again but knew there would be no turning back if she yielded to her desire.

'I must,' she whispered. Giving him a last light brush of her lips against his, she slipped away from him.

Arabella stood once more in the main street of Ladysmith, having said a tearful goodbye to Ben, who had repeatedly tried to persuade her to stay with him. It was an impossible situation; her love for him had grown stronger with every passing day . . . but she could never stand at his side as his wife, the mother of his children. Now she felt she had to get away from this town with all its associations. It was a heartbreaking decision, but one she felt compelled to make.

The atmosphere around her was euphoric; flags of victory fluttered up and down the streets, and bright bunting waved from the latticed balconies of shell-scarred buildings. Strangers of all races clasped each other and embraced, and Arabella felt terribly lonely in the midst of these celebrations – an outsider who was forced once again to face the future alone, in a strange country without much money and no long-lasting friends. She had been asked to help the wounded soldiers to the north as the British Army under Lord Roberts made its way to take Bloemfontein, the capital of the Boer Free State, then on to Pretoria, the Transvaal capital.

She was still undecided when Fate intervened in the portly, well-corseted form of Mrs Pickering, a colonel's wife who had accompanied her husband from Durban. The couple had stopped off in Ladysmith for a brief stay after its release before proceeding with the British forces under General Buller. Mrs Pickering had suggested taking Arabella with them, as a nurse and her companion.

It was an overcast day in the autumn of 1900 when Arabella finally left Ladysmith with the Pickerings in their mule wagon, and it took her all her time to keep back the tears. The hardest part of leaving was saying goodbye – to the doctors, especially Dr Hickory, to those survivors she had nursed for so long ... and also to Father Sebastian, with his slow, charming smile.

The journey north was a revelation to Arabella. Where there had once been fertile and smiling acres of land, were now only tumbled masses of blackened earth. Here and there, ruined Boer farmhouses dotted the desolate veld, reduced to rubble by the British forces under the authorisation of Lord Roberts. The Boers now lived off their burning land and the British retaliated with long lines of barbed wire and blockhouses stretching across the countryside, with massive sweeps of mounted soldiers.

At one evening stop, Arabella and Colonel Pickering climbed a steep stretch of hill on foot. Arabella halted some way from the top and regarded the countryside spread out below them, looped and laced by the pale threads of wagon-wheels and mule carts, and the impress of thousands of dusty Army boots.

She stared out across the great plain, her eyes following the slow wheeling arc of a large, dark bird in the vast sky overhead, then moving closer to a pathetic herd of cattle travelling with the wagons below, their ribs visible as they hungrily trekked on in search of grass in a land parched and brown and quivering with heat. There was only four days' food left for the animals. Then she proceeded up to the top, where she stood beside the Colonel, gazing out at the enormous views to the horizon, across the plain to where green hills broke the far distance. She had turned around to look in the opposite direction when she noticed fire pouring out of the windows and doors of a farmhouse far below. Black volumes of smoke rolled up.

'Look!' she cried, pointing towards it with an agitated hand. The Colonel whirled around, and then they stood, transfixed, unable to believe their eyes.

Clustered around the house were at least two dozen British soldiers, holding horses, while a small group of women clung together, some with their faces in each other's laps. In the background, more soldiers were chasing poultry, flinging stones, and throwing themselves on maimed chickens and ducks, whose dying squawks could be faintly heard. Even further away, herds and flocks and horses were being rounded up and driven off, while on top of a nearby hill, a party of soldiers, rifles in hand, stood guard against a surprise attack from the enemy. The figures of several Boers were silhouetted against the skyline as they watched the destruction of their home.

After her first exclamation, Arabella stood petrified, and when the agonised crying from the women echoed across the still, hot air, her heart began to burn with a sense of outrage.

'I really cannot think that punishment needs to take this wild form, Colonel!' she cried impetuously, unable to restrain her outrage. 'This is going too far!'

Colonel Pickering's face had darkened, the twisted scar along one cheek, which pulled his mouth aside, standing out in deep contrast. 'The troops are often upset by what they are told to do, m'dear, but it's not for them to question an order,' he said grimly. 'However, I cannot for the life of me see why Kitchener cannot make a real attempt at conciliation. He seems to see this as the best way to deal with the commandoes, without pausing to imagine its effect on the people who are thrown out of their homes.' His large blue eyes, were full of quiet intensity.

Arabella had found the Colonel to be a perceptive man, giving shrewd and lucid comments on the situation in the country, and the Army Medical Department in particular. Once more she fixed her eyes on the burning farmhouse, and something broke in her with unbearable pain. The whole centre of that family's life had been destroyed. She lowered her head, her eyes blinded with tears.

Colonel Pickering stood beside her, watching the scene. 'There have been some instances, it is true, of colonial troops gratifying their feelings of hatred and revenge, but on the whole, that's not the case. If these farms are to be confiscated – as the most vindictive loyalists desire, and then given over to settlers – why burn the houses? The new occupant will only have to build another homestead, and building is a serious matter here where wood and the means for dressing stone are so very scarce.'

'Yes.' Arabella nodded emphatically. 'The ends achieved seem so very small when punishment, if it be really necessary, could otherwise be inflicted, and the evils as one sees them on the spot, are so many.'

'Kitchener is a desperate man in a desperate cause, m'dear.' The Colonel stared down at her, and saw a tired, but intelligent young face. 'By the way, Sister Allen, I am writing to the Royal Commission on Hospitals in South Africa, roundly condemning the unhygienic services everywhere, especially the open latrines, which are nothing less than disgraceful, and I would like you to add your comments.'

Arabella's eyes clouded as they met his. 'I'd gladly do that, Colonel, but I'm sure the authorities will take very little notice of a nurse's opinion. They're still so wretchedly antagonistic towards female medical staff in the military hospitals.'

'I want you to do it, Arabella. I shall see to it that they sit up and take notice, and I'm not the only one who is appalled by the conditions of the sick at the war front – the breakdown in medical arrangements and the miserably insufficient equipment, medical staff and nursing which completely falsifies the statements sent back to England. I want you to back me up on this, for you are one of the finest nurses I have ever seen, and deserve to get the credit for what you've done.'

She felt herself answering his quiet command. 'Very well, Colonel Pickering. I shall set about writing a report for you without delay.'

They turned away from the sight of the women and children from the looted Boer farm being loaded on to wagons to be taken to one of the points of 'concentration,' where special camps had been built, protected and supplied by rail. They hardly felt the ruts under their feet as they descended the hill, a brilliant orange sunset flaring before them, and they did not speak even when they came in sight of the wagons and tents.

Arabella drew a deep breath and steadied herself to enter the first camp inhabited by the Boer women, children and ailing elderly men, which the Pickerings were visiting after crossing the Transvaal border on their way to Johannesburg. No one in the convoy had needed to go too far out of the way to hear some report of the miseries of such places.

As they neared the camp, and were able to distinguish the rows upon rows of tents, an open horse-drawn wagon passed them, containing two large coffins and four small ones. Behind the Pickerings' party was a column of mule carts and cattle trucks, driven by soldiers bringing more people into the camp. Hundreds of cattle had been driven before them, and were now gathered outside the camp, bellowing agonisingly from lack of food and water.

As they approached the gate, Arabella felt more and more dismayed. They were conducted to the Commandant's office – a prefabricated wooden hut towards the centre. She followed the Pickerings as they were led past the rows of inadequate bell tents and several wooden huts behind a barbed-wire fence where guards were on duty at intervals. There was a strange mixture of humanity collected in suspicious and sullen groups, as they moved from one tent to another.

Shocked and sickened, Arabella looked at the howling, hungry infants in the arms of their older sisters or mothers, wearing elaborately frilled white bonnets and surrounded by grubby children with gaunt, frightened faces.

Over and over, she told herself: 'I must control myself,' as the intense realisation hit her, that these people were the ruthless harvest of the war. For them, one war was over and another more merciless one was beginning – against disease, overcrowding, death and bitterness. She looked at a small boy with dark tousled hair, and thought of Luke. She could not bear the idea of him and Cynthia and Rosamunde being herded into such a place.

Each tiny tent space had to serve as a sitting room, kitchen and bedroom for one family – most consisting of numerous children. It was obvious that many of the women who had been forced to flee their farms had not even brought a bedstead. The whole place was an ugly concentration of tents, some distance from the nearest water supply, with tanks of boiled water set up on one side, and a maternity ward in a square marquee at the other, beside the marquee for infectious diseases. Rows of washing were strung out beside the river and an inadequate number of foul-stenching latrines had been dug far too near the drinking supply, in a hollow near the railway line.

Some of the women were already making small fires in front of the tents, to be shared by up to thirty families, to cook the one hot meal of the day, while others were laboriously carting water from several miles away. Arabella thought of the horrors of the Siege of Ladysmith and those dreadful months of deprivation and despair. But here, conditions were far, far worse. The camps were meant to house the refugees in comfort and safety after the confiscation of their farms ... but it was all too clear that the administration, unprepared for the vast numbers of people arriving each day, had already run into insuperable difficulties.

As they left, passing open cattle trucks ferrying more women and children to the camp, Arabella wondered why she had allowed herself to come here. Had the death of Danie du Rand, and the meeting with his brother, changed her more than she was willing to admit? Did these people affect her in a way she hardly understood?

By the time she had visited more camps, she was beginning to condition herself, and it was on a visit to a camp further on, where there was no medical officer or trained nurse, that she decided she must stay and help. Neither the Colonel nor Mrs Pickering were happy about leaving her there, but they respected her decision and, armed with two letters she had written – one to the Royal Commission of Hospitals and one to Ben – they reluctantly waved goodbye and departed. For a moment Arabella stopped and watched their wagons disappear, feeling a strange loss, then, crying silently for everything she had left behind, she turned and walked back into the chaos and disorganisation of the camp – and another terrifying future.

The morning light filtered through the open flap of the smelly hospital tent on to the pale face of a small girl in one of the cots. Arabella stood looking down at her for a long moment, pitying the poor little mite who was dying alone. Her mother had died the week before, and only that morning, her sister had gone. A terrible, overwhelming grief filled her as the child drew her last small breath. Then she combed the blonde hair as best she could, plaited it, and crossed the frail little arms over the chest, covering the body with a threadbare blanket. How easily these people were dying, especially the old and the very young, and still the authorities had done nothing to improve the situation.

She turned slowly, like an old woman, the white veil around her head emphasising the pallor of her skin and the almost fevered brightness of her eyes. Outside, the full December glare hit her, and she was conscious of a group of ragged children watching her with furtive curiosity. She met no one else as she walked slowly past another row of large and small coffins lined up ready for burial, but knew instinctively that almost every tent had its watchers, that she was being scrutinised by unseen and bitter eyes. She could feel the camp simmering with hostility all around her. It was a unique sensation, for even in the Boer hospital in Ladysmith, she had been finally accepted.

This elemental atmosphere had a depth of gall and suspicion that frightened her. Every day, as the situation worsened and the people's misery intensified, she was regarded with more and more contempt. She had one nurse aid, a young farmgirl from the district, who was not accepted by the majority of others because her family had surrendered to the British and recently taken the oath of allegiance to the Crown. She was called a 'hands-upper', and was despised by most of the women, who refused to cooperate with her in her duties.

Arabella walked past a few of the starving, pallid figures busying themselves with their daily tasks, and though they ignored her, she sensed the hatred and silent rage in the stiffening of their bodies.

These people hated her because she was English; her people had burnt their farms and brought them to this detestable place. She could not speak their language, and they were deeply suspicious of the British medicines and nursing methods. They preferred their own home remedies, and were determined to keep their children with them – not place them in the hospital in the care of detested strangers. The youngsters themselves screamed at this prospect, if it seemed likely. And there was another reason, as potent and more sinister, for their attitude – they knew of her relationship to Ben, one of the hated Kitchener's closest aides. If she was ever to have any success in her dealings with them, Arabella knew she would have to win their confidence ... and the only way to do that was through empathy with their problems, and an understanding of their backgrounds.

She stood for a moment, bleakly looking out at the low kopje not far away, and at the miles of burnt grass outside the camp. Every day, puffing red clouds of dust along the deeply-rutted track announced the approach of regular convoys bringing in more people, and with them the only news of the outside world. Every afternoon enormous clouds gathered, with the hope of rain. But even that was denied them, as the vast sky darkened into indigo shot with jagged spears of lightning, and thunder was tossed about the immense lonely space. Far off, the clouds would split open and rain peal down, but never on them.

The camp was near the railway line, and sympathetic stokers threw down large lumps of coal as the trains passed; the inmates rushed to retrieve them as fuel was extremely scarce. Food rations were received only three times a week, hence both the inmates and patients suffered great privation. The Camp Commandant, Mr Andrew Jervis, an unsympathetic man with prematurely wizened eyes and a pinched nose with a sharp and quivering point, maintained that there was sufficient to eat. He blamed the Boer commandoes for constantly blowing up the railway line, saying that this was the cause of any difficulty in obtaining food supplies. Arabella had taken an instant dislike to him, and even though she refused to be intimidated by his manner, she knew it was useless to argue with him.

She felt so powerless, and then angry at her impotence. Why was she here? Had she given up everything only to bury hundreds of children who were dying like flies, every hour of every day – so many that they were already falling short of coffins? Why had she come to live and work in the midst of women who hated her very presence, who resented everything she tried to do to help them?

As she walked on, the stale dank air hit her in the face at every turn. A small cluster of women and an old man watched her silently as she entered the small tent which she shared with the nurse aid, and she stood for a moment at the entrance, stiff and unmoving, knowing that she was alone in a sea of hostility. She let her hand tighten on the skirt of her apron, and now her heart quickened. Then she let out her tense breath slowly, and unclenched her hand. She would have to find a way to get through to these people, somehow. She had to, if she was going to help them.

The opportunity arose in a most unexpected way. Scarlatina had spread through the camp, adding to the rising death rate. One night, Arabella entered her tent, threw off her cape and veil and sat down on the single, hard chair, her head aching and her weariness like a tremendous pain all over her body. The suffering in this detestable place of the starving refugees, many of whom did not possess bedding of any kind, and the non-cooperation from Mr Jervis were too much for her soul. Nothing could assuage her desperate exhaustion, both mental and physical.

Outside, she could hear the continual cry for the chaplain: 'Mijnheer, kom tog heer.' (Sir, please come here.) The weary man trudged from tent to tent, to one more dead or dying victim. He had already taken short services at several gravesides that day, and prayed beside the dying. A shrill whistle called for another corpse to be taken to the mortuary tent, and then Arabella heard the clatter of a train passing nearby, and the hissing of its steam, and something began to stir in her mind. The only solution was to get on the train and go to Pretoria herself, see Ben and tell him all about the maladministration of the camp and the sufferings of the refugees.

She returned from Pretoria two days later, to the intense displeasure of Mr Jervis. The Commandant only held back his anger because he knew of her relationship with Ben, and of Ben's connection with Kitchener. Unfortunately, Arabella had been unable to see Ben as he was out of town after escaping unharmed in a train with Kitchener that had been blown up by a party of Boers led by Deneys du Rand. After overcoming her intense disappointment, she had demanded to see the Military Governor, General Neville who, after listening to her complaints with amazement, promised to visit the camp himself.

She was able to ignore Mr Jervis' open resentment when, true to his word, General Neville inspected the camp a week later, and was so shocked by what he found that he immediately commanded that supplies of bedding and food be forthwith released from the stores for the use of the inmates. He demanded that more slop-pails and buckets be issued, and more latrines built. Another medical officer and two locally trained nurses were despatched to the camp from Pretoria.

After this episode, a cold hostility settled between Mr Jervis and herself, but there was a subtle change in the attitude of some of the refugees. There were always those who would never change their attitude towards her – and she wondered if anything *could* ever eliminate this horror from the spirits and memory of these people, for there were very few places now in the former republics which had not been ravished, very few smiling acres of free land for the future of those who were now forced into this condition of chaos, and reduced to panic and fear for the survival of themselves and their children.

But there were those inmates who now turned to Arabella for advice, and who regarded her with more acceptance.

Sir Alfred Milner sailed to England to arrange the details of the new Crown Colony rule which was to follow the conclusion of peace, and peace seemed to be near, at last.

But the Boers fought on, while Kitchener slowly enmeshed them in his barbed wire, sent scores of them, including the two du Rand brothers, Michiel and Christiaan, to prison camps in the Cape Peninsula, St Helena, the Bermudas and Ceylon. He gathered more men, women and children by the day into the concentration camps, setting up separate ones for black women and children whose kraals had been burnt in an attempt to stop the Boers hiding there.

Then the weather turned, bringing the worst winter for a hundred years.

Arabella pulled her shabby blue coat about her shoulders as she left the little tent where yet another child had died, the hacking coughs of the young and the elderly, and the crying of children in pain ringing in her ears. It was sundown, and the bitter wind hit her with an icy blast as she trudged away past the neat row of small coffins, half-shrouded by snow, waiting for burial the following day. Only the old and the ill were dying of the cold, but sickness was spreading like a dark stain among the children, and was already reaching the adults with unbelievable rapidity.

With the distant sound of a train whistle and the crunching of snow under her feet, she made her way to the tent she now shared with two local nurses, from whom she was learning a simple form of Dutch. She had been amazed to discover that the Transvaal nurses had been registered by the State for nine years – an enviable status not enjoyed by British nurses or others elsewhere. Shivering uncontrollably she went inside and sat down at the small trestle table beside her hard, uncomfortable cot where one candle flickered. The rest of the tent was already in darkness, and she knew that the two nurses were away, still attending patients.

She was suffering from a particularly severe depression, and her frustration had never seemed more terrible. Only the day before, the camp medical officer had died of typhoid and, fearing a renewed epidemic, the medical authorities had given strict orders not to allow in food or water which might be contaminated. Fresh vegetables were forbidden, water was boiled and kept in large sealed tanks, and fresh meat from outside had been stopped. Tinned beef from America had been issued instead, and a careful watch was kept on the tins of meat, which were constantly tested for infection. But in spite of all these precautions, the death toll continued to rise, and rumours were circulating in the commandoes that Boer women and children were being systematically poisoned with infected meat.

Various reasons were put forward for the cause of the deaths, but Arabella, and many of the Boer mothers, believed that the suffering was caused largely by malnutrition – by the poor quality and monotony of the ration and by the lack of essential nutrients to the diet, like fresh vegetables and milk. Dr Harvard, an overworked and ill man, had maintained that everyone was given enough to eat, and due to the typhoid scare there was nothing else he could do. There seemed to be a kind of scurvy running right through the camp. Many children had sore and dreadfully smelly mouths; in some cases their teeth fell out, and in most, death soon followed.

Arabella was in a dilemma. She could no longer approach Mr Jervis; there was no doctor in whom she could confide and her last letters to General Neville remained unanswered; she wondered if somehow Mr Jervis had intercepted her correspondence. Another journey to Pretoria was out of the question because of the constant derailing and blowing up of trains by the Boers.

She felt helpless against the mighty avalanche of disaster in the camp. By this time it seemed to her that the filth was everywhere, on the faces of the people, under her own fingernails, in her hair, on her clothing, in her food. And worst of all, in her very soul.

Then Marie Roussouw, one of the refugees who could speak passable English, came to her rescue. Marie was part of the secret communication service of Boer women who sent uncensored messages out of the country. She suggested that Arabella use this service to send letters to England describing the conditions.

Now, drugged from lack of sleep, she picked up her pen and filled the coarse sheets of paper which Marie had found for her with one more in a series of detailed reports she had sent to various members of the Liberal Opposition in the House of Commons, and to certain prominent Liberal newspapers. She had started a personal crusade, and had to keep going until it was completed.

Suddenly the tent flap was pulled aside, and a tall young woman in a thin black dress under a patched coat hurried inside, looking nervously around. It was Marie, a woman of generous proportions who had become emaciated through the long months spent in the camp. During this time she had lost three children and her mother. Her dark hair was already flecked with silver, her face carved by sorrow and suffering, even though she was only twenty-six years old.

'You writing another letter, Sister? That is good – good for our cause,' she said, shuddering for a moment in the chill of the tent.

Arabella looked up in surprise, then smiled. 'I only hope someone out there is reading them, Marie. Sometimes it feels as if they're falling into a void.'

Marie smiled back with suppressed excitement. 'Someone *is* reading them, Sister. I have a letter here for you, brought by one of our Boer scouts from Bloemfontein.' Her eyes darted here and there for fear of being overheard.

Arabella raised an astonished eyebrow. 'But I don't know anyone in Bloemfontein!'

Marie vigorously nodded her head. 'But there is a woman who knows about you, Sister – an Englishwoman like yourself called Emily Hobhouse. She came out to this country to see for herself the camps. She has read all your letters.'

Arabella immediately forgot her own wretchedness. She rose and stood behind the table, holding the much-handled, dirty envelope in her shaking fingers. 'It can't be possible! Who is this Miss Hobhouse? I've never heard of her.'

Marie smiled. 'But she knows you, Sister. Many of the commandoes now know you are trying to help us – your letters have crossed the sea to your own people. That monster Kitchener hates Mejuffrou Hobhouse because she was looking into the conditions in the Free State camps.'

Arabella opened the letter and started reading as Marie waited expectantly. Emily explained how, after hearing various reports, including those from Colonel Pickering and his wife, and reading Arabella's letters of the appalling conditions in the camps, she had come out to South Africa as the Secretary of the Women's Branch of the recently formed South African Conciliation Committee in London, to find that everything she had heard and read was true. She had tried to reach Arabella, but Lord Alfred Milner had forbidden her to visit any camps further north than Bloemfontein. She had returned to England but asked for more information. The previous letters had been widely debated in Opposition British journals, causing a wave of consternation throughout the country.

When Arabella had finished reading, tears began to run from her eyes and over her cheeks. 'Oh, Marie – at last someone out there is going to do something to help us!'

'Are you going to write to her then, Sister?' Marie was watching Arabella intently.

She smiled shakily. 'She has given me an address in London. Yes, I shall write straight away.' She hesitated. 'What is the news of the war, Marie?'

'Good and bad, Sister.' Marie's voice was deliberately impersonal. 'General Botha has raided Natal, and General de la Rey's new commandoes are fighting fiercely here in the Transvaal with the men specially chosen and trained by Sarel du Rand's son, Deneys. They say that Deneys was attacked while trying to cut off the main water supply to Johannesburg. He was driven to the nearby kopjes and held off the British troops for a long time. When the firing stopped, the British were surprised to find out it had been only one man – and he escaped.' She gave Arabella a slight, almost apologetic smile, then her eyes sharpened at the quick intake of the Englishwoman's breath. 'But they say that Lieutenant-Colonel Saville is in charge of catching him.'

Arabella had listened with dread in her heart, realising that Deneys du Rand had fast become a Boer hero, and that even though she and Marie worked together to help the women and children in the camp, as far as the war itself was concerned, they were still enemies.

Marie continued, more bitterly: 'General Smuts marched secretly through the Transvaal not long ago to get the Cape Boers to rise up against the British, and they were nearly caught by Kitchener's soldiers – how you say? – sweeping in the area.' Before Arabella could respond, she went on, 'It is believed that after his escape, Deneys du Rand joined General Smuts in his raids into the Cape Colony.'

When Marie had left, Arabella suddenly thought of Rosamunde and the children, and was overwhelmed by memories of Suncrest Farm before the war – memories the more bitter because they had once been so sweet. Everywhere in the camp, these memories loomed without warning – recalled by the sight of an old man singing a tune, or a child's eyes shining up at precious chocolate offered by a British soldier. A chance remark could make her eyes fill, or her throat constrict as the screws of memory tightened her heart. A man's tall figure dressed in a khaki uniform, swinging towards her past the interminable rows of tents, a woman with blonde hair, hugging a child ... she was at the mercy of them all.

19

Winter gave way at last to spring, and beyond the barbed-wire fences of the camp, the veld sprang to life with carpets of delicate pink, white and purple cosmos, from the seeds that had arrived from South America in the fodder for the British horses. Arabella had never been so aware of a season before; so awakened by unseen natural forces. It seemed to her that a different quality crept into the voices of the refugees, along with a feeling of hope that now the deaths must surely end.

Milner had returned from England to Johannesburg, bringing with him a large loan for relief at the end of the war. To hasten that end, Kitchener's headquarters had become the centre of an enormous war machine, driving through the northern Free State, and the Transvaal, giving notice that all who did not surrender before 15 September would be permanently banished, and the cost of maintaining their families charged against their property. His tightening grip on the country was having an effect! He made endless attempts, in his obsessional thoroughness, to catch the remaining Boer commandoes in the annexed territories, but this threat was followed, if anything, by increased enemy activity.

Cattle trucks and open carts still brought fresh refugees every day to the camp, but instead of lessening, the death-rate continued to rise. Tuberculosis was now spreading, as was whooping cough, and still the inmates were being systematically starved of vital vitamins, in the Army's desperate effort to keep everyone isolated so that these diseases would not spread to the towns.

As the warmer weather advanced, Arabella learned that she had helped to stir up a hornet's nest of dramatic proportions in Britain. Emily Hobhouse published her findings and an uproar followed which successfully polarised British opinion. Women's organisations were now in the forefront of the campaign that raged to help the Boer women and children, and for the first time in British history, a broad spectrum of women became politically active.

It was with incredulity that Arabella learned that Emily had returned recently to the country, but as the Cape Colony was under martial law, she had immediately been arrested and deported on Kitchener's personal order.

One day, Arabella was attending a desperately sick woman, when the tent flap was suddenly thrown back, sending in a burst of light and air where the stench of sweat and sickness was almost unbearable.

One of the orderlies stood in the entrance, a pipe hanging out of the pocket of his khaki serge breeches. 'Lieutenant-Colonel, Lord Stradcombe from Pretoria to see you, Sister. He's waiting in the Camp Commandant's office.'

There was a smothered cursing from the sick woman's two daughters as Arabella looked up, amazed. Ben, here? It could not be possible! 'Are you sure?'

'As sure as me ruddy life is worth, Sister. He's there, I tell you, large as bloody life with his wooden leg and all.'

Arabella left the tent, her knees shaking ever so slightly as certain thoughts buzzed through her head: Ben was working closely with Kitchener, and Kitchener had deported Emily . . . *and she was working with Emily* . . .

A group of women caught her eye as she walked towards the wooden hut of the Commandant, and when she was only about ten paces from them, she suddenly glanced up. There was murder in their eyes. She knew it was because of Ben's presence in the camp. Her mind became clouded with doubts; she did not know how she felt at seeing Ben again after almost eighteen months, and she was concerned about the reason for his sudden visit at this time. What would have excited her before, have held a special meaning for her, had become something ominous, with sinister overtones.

She entered the severe hut. Mercifully, Mr Jervis was not there. With rising apprehension, she glanced around the room. In one of the corners sat the figure of a khaki-clad man, silently smoking a pipe. It was hard to see him in the shadows, but she caught the impression that he was tall and lean, with one leg projecting awkwardly before him. He puffed at his pipe, the bowl of which he kept in his hand, and in spite of the dimness, she felt that familiar strength in him, that strong intelligence, that smell of Macassar oil and highly polished leather, and she knew it was Ben. She tried to see his face more distinctly, but the hand holding the pipe partially concealed it. However, her face was illumined by the sunlight pouring through the open doorway, and it was evident that he was studying her.

'Excuse me for not standing up, Arabella,' he said, his eyes measuring her slowly as she drew nearer, but there was no welcoming smile on his face. 'It's so confoundedly awkward getting up and down.'

There was an enigmatic expression in his grey eyes. His face was a little more weary, and strangely keyed-up.

'Why are you here, Ben?' she said, before she could stop herself. 'It's dangerous for you to travel about like this, especially after –'

'After your Boer friends nearly blew me up?' His voice was crisp, and she knew with terrible clarity that he was not here as her friend, not as the man who had once professed to love her.

'That's not true, Ben, and it's very cruel of you to say such a thing,' she whispered. 'You speak to me as if I am a traitor.'

'And so you are!' he said fiercely, leaning forward. 'You have been sending hostile accusing letters to the Liberal Opposition in England, denouncing the camps. The Opposition press has been having a field day because of you and that bloody Hobhouse woman. There have been outcries of the most slanderous kind. Questions are being asked and suspicions raised by downright lies. You have discredited the Tory Government and endangered the management of all British affairs in this country.'

Arabella started up in amazement. 'My honesty and that of Miss Hobhouse have endangered nothing. It's time that the British Government were informed of what is happening under their authority here! It is their full responsibility to put matters right for the women and children in the camps, and I'm not ashamed of exposing it all.'

A curious flicker, like the flash of a bared knife, passed over Ben's face. 'Kitchener wants to deport you, Arabella, but I prevailed upon him to give you a chance.' His face darkened. 'I managed to persuade him that you did not fully understand what you had done. He's giving you that chance, on condition that you retract everything you have written, in a public statement, and stop all criticisms as of now.'

Arabella was both frightened and enraged. She began to tremble and her face and hands were ice-cold. But when she cleared her throat and spoke, her voice was quiet and strong. 'If my concern for the treatment of the women and children has caused embarrassment to the Government, then they must put it right by improving conditions. I stand by what I have said, every word.'

Again that knife-like flash passed swiftly over his face. He leaned forward on one of his crutches. 'You must promise to discontinue this madness, Arabella, for once and all. Otherwise there is no other course but to believe that you are a traitor to your own country.'

There was deep consternation in her green eyes. 'How can you, of all people, believe that of me, Ben? You know I could never betray my country! But I do believe in justice. Problems cannot be swept under the carpet, with hopes that they will remain there, quietly.'

Ben stroked his dark moustache deliberately, and she noticed the tensing of his features, which hinted at a tumult of restrained emotions.

'I see. You are determined to cause as much trouble and embarrassment to the Tory Government and the British Army here as you can – you and that Hobhouse bitch.'

'No, you don't see,' Arabella said passionately, 'and you won't see, because to see clearly what I am doing and why, is to see the truth and all its implications. Look for yourself at the emaciated children outside, little living skeletons, dying by the thousands. Go and see for yourself the foul stinking latrines which one can hardly approach because the buckets from the previous day and night are not emptied and remain outside in the sun. Just as the lack of adequate sanitary arrangements in the British Military hospitals has contributed to the loss of thousands of British lives, so it is affecting mortality among the refugees. Go and look at the overcrowded conditions, which increase by the day –'

'Bloody rot, Arabella!' Ben leaned more heavily on his crutch, a sudden glitter firing his eyes. 'The camps have increased in size because Kitchener has failed to persuade that idiot Botha to leave surrendered burghers on their farms – and the refugees have joined the families from the destroyed farms. Many of these people, as you very well know, were already in poor physical condition when they arrived here, and in some cases they are unsuited by their primitive ideas of hygiene and suspicion of officials to adapt themselves to life in crowded camps.'

He sat staring fiercely at her, and she flinched at the harsh, stabbing words. 'I don't care any more why it happened, Ben, or what was before. I'm only interested in the supervision of our administration *now*. I want the conditions improved,' she shouted, 'and I won't stop until it is done!'

Ben continued to look at her coldly, but she was determined to convince him. '*We* set up the camps, and *we* must organise them in a decent manner, do you not understand that? We need more medical staff with a high standard of technical skills who are sympathetic towards these refugees, and can understand what they are going through, even though they *are* Boers. We have only one hospital here, containing a mere forty beds. There is no doctor, only myself, with two trained nurses and four Boer women assistants from among the refugees themselves, for the entire camp.'

'What do you need more staff for,' he demanded, 'when these women refuse to cooperate with the doctors and nurses who are sent? Most of the deaths could be prevented if this was not the case.'

Arabella's mouth worked, but she managed to remain calm. 'Too much has been made of this, Ben. I am using this very misunderstood devotion of the mothers to their children, and their fear of our methods which they do not understand, by leaving the children in the care of their mothers who are trying to carry out their responsibilities as parents. But they struggle with alarming obstacles and wear themselves out caring for their sick, only to succumb themselves in the end.'

Ben suddenly rose, a bit unsteadily at first, but once he was on his feet, with the aid of both his crutches, which he managed with surprising dexterity, he hopped forward agilely, his eyes glittering like some dangerous animal.

'This seeming inadequacy of the medical staff quite contradicts the many reports received from Camp Commandants in both former republics, that the nursing staff is sufficient for the workload. I think you have made an issue of it, as with everything else, because you are determined to bring down the Tory Government. But from now on, you will do as you are told, Arabella.' He took a deep, rasping breath. 'Dammit, the entire medical organisation has broken down. We desperately need nurses with your skills and experience on our side.'

Completely distraught, Arabella cried: 'It has broken down no more so than in these camps!'

'These people have brought their own suffering upon themselves, can't you see that? If they had all surrendered when they were ordered to do so, this would never have happened. They are prolonging their own agony. You belong on your own side. Now pack your things and be ready to leave with me in one hour.'

A chill went through her. He had become another person before her eyes: his expression was cold, his jaw rigid, his mouth set in a tight thin line. I have failed, she thought, as they stared at each other for a long, agonising moment. I cannot get through to him. He just won't understand.

'You will not be writing any more letters to England, Arabella – I shall see to that. Nor will you evade the censorship of mail again.' Never had she seen such inflexibility and such hardness in him. He had changed so much she could hardly believe it.

'No one, Ben, not even you, is going to stop me!' Something strange rose in her mind as she stared up at him – a new emotion, startling in its intensity. She was no longer afraid of him, of what he would do. She no longer felt helpless, or oppressed.

As she turned away, he caught her wrist in a vice of steel, and swung her around to face him. 'Listen to me, you little fool! You're playing a dangerous game that you'll live to regret, against powerful people.' He was breathing hard. 'You are bringing the greatest shame on your family – on your cousin –'

'Since when have you ever considered Rosamunde's feelings Ben? I bring no shame on anyone except what they bring on themselves!' She saw the unspoken contempt in his eyes, and something more, much more.

'I could almost believe you have been stupid enough to fall in love with some Boer rebel!' he suddenly broke out, the jealous hatred hardly concealed in his face. 'You have betrayed my trust and my love, Arabella. And all because I am no longer a complete man!' His fingers dug viciously into her wrist.

Shaken to the core, she fiercely pulled her arm away, and stood back, her face on fire. 'Even you would not stoop so low as to accuse me of that! Your condition has nothing to do with it, and well you know it.'

The sudden silence in the hut had the weight of iron, and prolonged itself to an unbearable point. Ben had paled, and she could only stand and stare at him, sickened and shocked by what she saw. Suddenly they were released from their terrible spell, and half-stumbling, she ran from the hut.

'You'll be sorry, Arabella,' she heard him mutter with awful bitterness. 'You'll be sorry you turned against me!'

As she reached the door, she glanced back over her shoulder. The sunlight struck full on Ben's face, and it was the face of an enemy.

Several weeks later, two young British officers entered the hospital marquee where Arabella was working. They ordered her to pack her things and leave with them at once for Pretoria Gaol, pending a hearing before the High Treason Commission, a recent body created to investigate cases of persons charged with high treason who were not tried by the Special High Treason Court.

Mechanically, she dressed, brushed and combed her hair, felt for buttons, lacings and ties. But once outside, her mouth fell open in astonishment. Neither of the two soldiers who had come to fetch her noticed her; they were staring at the flood of humanity facing them, sending out disorderly waves into the rows and rows of tents. The howling that issued from it was the anger, frustration and hatred of the women of the camp. Hundreds of shabby women closed in around her, shouting and waving their fists at the soldiers who had hurried up to control them. And in the forefront stood Marie Roussouw, shaking her head violently as the tears poured down her cheeks.

The river of human beings divided to allow Arabella to pass, after several of the women had tried to snatch her from the soldiers, but they were held back. And as she walked forward between her two tense escorts, her eyes circled with black rings in a pale face, the women ran behind them, cursing and screaming and gesticulating in protest.

Suddenly Marie threw herself in Arabella's path. The soldiers stopped abruptly, pulling their prisoner roughly out of the way.

'You can't take this woman – you must leave her here. We need her ... she is the only one who cares about us,' she pleaded in English.

Arabella sorrowfully looked into Marie's tear-streaked face, as the young Boer woman clutched the jacket of one of the soldiers to hold him back.

'Get out of the way, woman!' he ordered sharply, jerking himself free from her anguished grasp and raising his rifle instinctively. There was a gasp from the crowd, which now fell back, silent.

He was about to lead Arabella away when she twisted herself free, and threw her arms about Marie.

'Listen to me, Marie. I have to go with these men, but I will speak to somebody about you, about this camp – all the camps. I will never remain silent while there is still life in my body. Please believe me. My work is not over yet.'

Marie clung to Arabella's hand. 'But why are they doing this to you, Sister? You helped us, even though we were your enemy. No one would have known about us if it wasn't for you and Mejuffrou Hobhouse –'

'I will speak up for all of you,' Arabella promised again, speaking in simple Dutch to the crowd clustered about her. 'Everyone will know what has happened here, I –'

Before she could say another word, the soldiers pushed her to the waiting wagon, past the triumphant face of Mr Jervis, and the crowd was lost to her.

20

As drought continued to ravage the parched land and dry up the rivers, Arabella was placed in the cheerless gaol which had once held the Jameson Raid conspirators. All the way down the long, gloomy corridor she could sense faces here and there swiftly appearing at the grilles of the cells in the women's section. Her escorts halted at a door at the far end, and produced a long steel key, which unlocked it, grating on her ears.

Not guessing the full meaning of her predicament, she entered the small, barren cell in a state of numbed calmness. Once inside, the door slammed behind her with a hollow knell of finality, and as soon as she heard the sound of the key turning in the lock and closing her in, she was jolted into a wretched sense of panic, and beat her fists against the door in terror. When only the overwhelming silence answered her, she pressed her face to the chill bars and let the tears course down her cheeks. It was all Ben's fault – he had done this to her. Not for the first time, she felt the terrible weight of female powerlessness in a world that was controlled and operated by men.

She looked at the dreadful place she was locked into – at the icy cold stone slab floor, the stone-blocked walls, and the cell door of strapped wood and metal bars that shut out her world. She glanced up at the one narrow and close-barred window that was too high for her to glimpse even a bird or a flower or a tree, even if she stood on the hard, unyielding bed. It was all so grey, even the wooden ceiling, and all in an instant it seemed to her to be an affront to her dignity, her whole self.

Food was brought twice during the day, and she was allowed the two books she had packed in her luggage at the last minute when she had fled from Suncrest Farm. There was an oil lamp on a hook by the door, the eerie yellow of its light falling at a sharp angle through the bars across her favourite Jane Austen, smelling faintly of the roses from the gardens at the farm. She opened it in the middle. A dried rose petal little Cynthia had given her lay between the pages, and a lock of Luke's hair. Cynthia, Luke ... she could not bear to think of them now.

Swift dusk settled down over the brooding building, deepening in all the narrow, dreary cells. She heard the guard's heavy boots tramp down the corridor, and all the lamps were turned off, except the ones at the end. Then she rose and lay fully dressed on the bed, staring into the blackness and trying to stifle her fears. All that night, she tossed about restlessly, torn by conscience and betrayal, rent on the rack of her love-hate feelings for Ben.

The food in Pretoria Goal was good solid fare, and one of the more sympathetic guards was able to supplement it for Arabella now and then, even though she had no extra money. Though she found it difficult to swallow, Arabella forced herself to eat, knowing that she had to keep up her stamina and put on a little weight in order to survive the coming ordeal. She must not succumb to illness, which had been her greatest dread in the camp. Much later, she was to discover that, throughout her period of incarceration, even the most conservative papers read like lurid gossip sheets, with descriptions of Ben's courage and daring against the Boers, the tragic loss of his leg, the blowing up of the train and his miraculous escape. Rosamunde was the beautiful, devoted wife, while Arabella was branded as the worst of all creatures – a dangerous feminist and a traitor to her family and her own people.

On the morning following her imprisonment, she was taken to a room in the building beside the prison, which appeared to be a meeting hall of some sort. It was furnished with a few hard chairs set around a long trestle table covered with green baize, on which lay several heavy books, piles of printed sheets, pads of paper and pencils. Then the door closed, and a guard stood to attention beside it.

Facing her at the table was a British officer of senior rank, and two other officers who looked up alertly as she halted before them. The senior officer, a man with a heavy bristling fair moustache and red veins on his nose, gestured her to sit and the questioning began.

Arabella had a feeling of unreality about the whole procedure as she mouthed words and watched the man before her making gestures, his voice brisk and clear as he asked her question upon question about her work and her criticisms of the concentration camps. The room grew imperceptibly warmer but she met the questions with the same unflinching directness she had shown since her arrest. All her answers were recorded meticulously by one of the other men. At one point the officer in charge of the proceedings stared at her in absolute silence, his mouth grim under the fair moustache, as he listened to her descriptions of the running of the camps.

He interrupted her as she paused for a sip of water. 'Sister Allen, did you, or did you not, make use of the Boer women's secret communication system in the camp, to send uncensored letters to the Liberal Opposition in England?'

Arabella hesitated, turning her head to glance at the other two men, who were leaning forward, with sudden interest.

'There was no other way,' she began. 'I'd tried –'

'Just a brief yes or no, Sister Allen. Did you, or did you not, use the system?'

She paled, looking at his fair, aristocratic face, at his probing, detached eyes, and felt small and powerless. Then she squared her shoulders, her voice firm and decisive. 'Yes.'

'Did you work with Miss Emily Hobhouse in your criticisms against the concentration camp system?' He sat there and slowly and deliberately waited for her reply, every flick of his eyes condemning her.

She nodded. 'I did, after some months – after she left this country to return to England.'

One of the other men stopped writing, and once more leaned forward. He was short and portly, with bristling grey hair and restless brown eyes.

'Is it not true to say that you were used by Emily Hobhouse and the Liberal Opposition, to bring about the downfall of the Tory Government to end the war which you despised?'

'No, sir. At no time had I any plan to discredit the Tory Government. I have never been used, as you call it, by anyone. I started my – campaign alone, only hearing about Miss Hobhouse later, when I discovered that our views were similar regarding the camps.'

The portly officer steepled his fingers, thoughtfully. 'But you are against the war, are you not, Sister Allen?'

She answered carefully, knowing that anything she might say would be twisted against her. 'At first I thought the war was a just one, that the Uitlanders had a just cause. However, as I nursed first our men and then the Boer women and children in the camps, I found it abhorrent, yes.'

The senior officer smiled unpleasantly. 'Is it not true, Sister, that the terrible suffering among the British soldiers whom you nursed, and then your disenchantment with the disease among the Boer women and children, caused you to want in some way to change this state of affairs – in fact *to join* the Boer women in attempting to bring about the downfall of the Government?' There was a small eloquent pause, before he continued, watching her keenly, 'I put it to you, that you not only sent condemning letters to Opposition newspapers and Parliamentarians, but that you also passed valuable information to other countries – countries unsympathetic towards Great Britain – in an effort to undermine the British Army, and through it, the Tory Government.'

His tone was dry and Arabella caught the quick glance between the other two men.

'That is not true!' Her voice was defiant. 'I had no need to discredit the Government of my own country. They have done a good enough job of it themselves!'

There was a sudden silence, and Arabella realised her mistake.

'So! You admit that you are against the Government. Are you an admirer of the Liberal Party, Sister? A brief yes or no will suffice.'

Arabella knew they were waiting for her to fall into the trap they had set. 'I have no interest in politics. I am only interested in justice.'

'Justice, Sister? For whom – the enemy of Great Britain, the country you profess to love?' he asked, with interest.

She hesitated, but stood her ground. 'For the innocent women and children,' she answered, with calm simplicity.

The second officer held out his hand and the third man passed him a paper. 'Innocent, Sister? By whose assumption – yours? The Boer women cannot be regarded as innocent when they actively help their men by acting as spies in the field, and set up the secret system already mentioned, which you yourself used until your arrest.'

Arabella was silent, but she was not cowed. She just sat and calmly looked at the officer, who narrowed his eyes and put a monocle to his eye.

'I have copies of the letters you sent to members of the Opposition in the House of Commons.' His voice was suddenly curt as he lowered the monocle. 'You are an articulate and highly intelligent young women, Sister Allen. These letters are not those of a woman suffering for concern of those under her care. They constitute flagrantly defiant anti-Tory propaganda against the work of the British Army in erecting the camps for the safety of women and children who, if left out on their isolated farms, would perish, in far more terrible ways than any you have described.'

Arabella, her face now bright with anger, made her point. 'Those letters were letters of despair and anger at an inefficient system which was doing nothing to improve their lot.'

He stared at her and let a silence build before making his next statement. His face was grim as he asked, 'If you were so dissatisfied about the conditions, why did you not approach the doctor in charge, or the Commandant before you sent these inflammatory letters?'

'We only had one doctor, for a very short time before he died of typhoid. I did approach him, but he was too ill to do anything about it. When I broached the matter with the Camp Commandant, he refused to listen to me. I did visit General Neville, the Military Governor, to complain about the shortage of stores and bedding, and he visited the camp soon afterwards and was shocked by what he saw.'

There was another silence, as the officer frowned, then turned to the others in muted discussion.

'Why were we not told of this visit of General Neville, Sister?' the portly officer said, after a long contemplation of her.

'I do not know.' Arabella shook her head, relieved at the new evidence. 'All I know is that the letters I wrote to him subsequently can never have reached him, since they were not answered.'

'You wrote to General Neville?' The first officer queried. 'We have no record of it here.' He shuffled among some of the papers before him. 'The Camp Commandant, Mr Jervis, is of the firm belief that you were working with the Boer women – one woman in particular, a Mrs Marie Roussouw, a suspected collaborator with the Boer commandoes. He states that you never cooperated with him in his difficult task in the camp, and did everything in your power to undermine his authority over the refugees.'

Arabella's face was now deathly pale. 'Marie Roussouw and I were only concerned about the health of the women and children. Mr Jervis was most unsympathetic towards those under his charge.'

'He is not the only one who gives evidence against you, Sister. We have here a report by Lieutenant-Colonel Lord Stradcombe himself, stating that when he arrived to ask you to refrain from your malicious undermining of the British Army, you refused.' He indicated the report in front of him with a long forefinger.

Arabella swallowed. 'I never tried to undermine the British Army – I believe Lieutenant-Colonel Saville knew that.'

'Then why should the Lieutenant-Colonel, who has fought most bravely for his country, have cause to believe you did, Sister, and an overworked Camp Commandant such as Mr Jervis? They are both loyal subjects of the Crown, doing their best in a situation plagued by violence and hostility. I put it to you that these letters are not the only ones you wrote as an agent of the Liberal Opposition bent on the destruction of the present Government and the war effort.'

The implication was clear and Arabella felt a wave of desolation as she answered, 'That is not true. I wrote no other letters than those to England.'

'It would appear that you are a danger to your country in a time of war – a danger to the law and order of this country, now under British rule.'

Arabella stared at him, unable to respond, as he declined to question her further that day. After she returned to her cell, she panicked again. Rivers of sweat ran down her back, and she wept tears of anger and horror for what the man she had once loved had done.

How she missed the sun, its light and warmth! And so it went on, every day – the endless questions in an attempt to make her confess to being an anti-Government agitator, and through it all, she felt Ben's subtle, restricting hand, keeping her virtually in chains. But she met her interrogators' questions day after day with the same unflinching directness she had shown from the start. Only back in her cell, did she allow the despair to come when the spirit that had carried her through the ordeal left her, and she felt limp and exhausted and could not swallow the food that was brought her.

She tried to pray, for she knew that without prayer she was finished. After a while, the old words returned: '*Our Father, Who art in Heaven, hallowed be Thy name . . .*'

In the war that was still being fought outside the prison walls, it became increasingly clear that even in strategic terms the camps were a failure, for although conditions in the veld made life hard for the fighting Boer men, in an ironical way, instead of ending the war as Kitchener had intended, the camps, and now their great losses, became the very reason for the 'bitter-enders' to continue fighting.

After the severe winter of late 1901 and into 1902, Arabella little realised that this whole experience, beginning with that last meeting with Ben, marked a distinct transition in her life.

One afternoon, she received a surprise visitor. She was standing at the grille of her cell door having heard footsteps approaching with the guard, and wondering who they belonged to. It was with incredible amazement that she saw the tall, black-cassocked figure of Father Sebastian stop before her.

'Father, whatever brings you to this terrible place?' Her voice was breathless as she pulled herself as close to the barred grille as she could get, using her books and everything else she could find, to stand on.

'My dear child,' he said, his voice grave. 'When I read the newspapers with the dreadful news of your imprisonment, I hurried up to the Transvaal without delay. I tried, without success, to see Lieutenant-Colonel Saville. It was through the Military Governor, General Neville, that I'm here at all.' A slow smile lit the pale eyes behind the spectacles.

She gripped the bars fiercely and he noticed the pallor and extreme thinness of her face. The impression was one of fragility, reminding him of a delicate piece of fine porcelain.

'I hope I haven't endangered your reputation, Father – your

coming to see a dangerous feminist.' For a brief moment, the familiar humour spilled out, only to be stemmed immediately.

'A priest should be above concerns for his reputation,' he said gently. 'I have come to be of support and assistance to you, and to tell you that your courage has not been in vain. Your deeds in the dark hours of despair have been an inspirational light of hope for so many women. Your vision and strength in attempting to bring about change and understanding in a violent conflagration, is the hope we should all cherish.'

Father Sebastian looked at her with quiet intensity, and continued: 'A commission of women was sent out from England to visit the camps, Arabella, and their findings have corroborated everything you and Miss Emily Hobhouse said. The breaking point seems to have come at last.' He gazed at her with deep admiration. 'Something positive has indeed come out of this tragedy.'

Arabella leaned slightly back from the bars, and the light caught her pale face. 'If only they had listened sooner,' she lamented, 'so many deaths could have been prevented!'

'But now Sir Kitchener is setting about remedying the situation.'

'Sir Kitchener!' she gasped, letting out her breath painfully. 'That devil!'

'He's doing his best, my child. Accommodation and food are now carefully supervised, and better medical assistance is being provided. None of this will make the Tory Government any more popular, I fear, since it will cost the British taxpayer a considerable amount of money.'

Arabella smiled faintly. 'Do you know if they will let me out, soon Father? After all, there's no proof that I wrote anything to unsympathetic countries, no matter what they say.'

Father Sebastian's brow creased in a pained frown. 'To be sure, it would seem as if you're being used as a kind of scapegoat, my child. You're an embarrassment to the authorities, and they're afraid the Tories will fall down on the war issue. It seems that they have to keep you shut up and out of the way until the war ends. To release you now would only damage Kitchener's cause, and Milner's.'

He peered at her anxiously. 'I urge you to write to Ben Saville, Arabella and prevail upon his generosity. After all, he is your only kinsman in this country, and he has great influence with the powers that be.'

She stood deathly still. Then she said, 'He'll never help me, Father, for it was he who had me imprisoned here.'

'Arabella,' he spoke quickly, and glanced around to make sure they were not heard, 'I'm sorry to hear that, and I'm greatly worried about your health which has obviously suffered – I can see that.' He looked at her intently. 'You *must* see a doctor! He will be able to get you out of here with a good reason.'

'Oh, Father,' she sighed, and made a small futile gesture with her hands. 'No doctor is going to do that for me – a pariah to the British Army and all who work in it. Besides, I wouldn't trust anyone I don't know.'

'If you want me to send or bring anything for you, anything at all – letters to England, extra comforts . . .'

'Are you conspiring with me against the authorities, Father?' A faint ghost of a smile lit up her features for a brief moment. 'No, but I thank you for your generous offer.'

'A world of women and their children has depended on you, a whole world of fear and despair and suffering. The Cross has been yours, my child, and you have carried it with courage and dignity. What you do tomorrow, and every tomorrow from now on, will be God's work, and may He go with you.'

A deathlike stillness followed Father Sebastian's departure. Arabella willed herself to sleep that night, for sleep had become her most valuable possession. Sleep was freedom . . . Days had passed – several months on her calendar – and she had not gone mad. *Not yet.*

Some weeks later, Father Sebastian was able to visit her again, with news of the continuing uproar following her revelations. Arabella garnered all the information she could, like a squirrel hoarding nuts for the winter, as a lifeline in a lonely, frightening present. But even this could not dull the longing for other people's company, the chance to walk outside the prison walls free and feel the sunshine on her face, the wind in her hair, and the rain beating down on her body. Freedom had never been so inaccessible, and it had never seemed so precious. Never again, she vowed, would she allow anyone to take it away. She would fight until she had no breath left in her body to attain it once more, and when won, she would do all in her power to keep it. No one, and especially no man, was ever again going to be her gaoler, either in body or in mind – she would see to it.

At the end of May 1902, acceptance terms were finally agreed to among the Boer leaders. Gradually the commandoes rode in to surrender at the nearest military posts and to hand over their weapons. Most of them signed the Oath of Allegiance to the British Crown, but among those few who refused were Sarel du Rand and his four surviving sons – Michiel and Christiaan recently returned from the prison camp at St Helena, Deneys, who still had a price on his head, and young Johan. The old man chose exile in America and took Johan with him, while Michiel went to Holland, and Deneys and Christiaan disappeared into the wilds of French-ruled Madagascar.

Reparations began immediately the fighting stopped, and soon afterwards, Arabella was released. At the same time, the Army Medical Department finally agreed that trained-female nurses were essential in the military hospitals, and an Imperial Military Nursing Service, with a permanent Army Nursing Service, was established.

As she gathered up her few belongings, prior to departure from Pretoria Gaol, Arabella pushed a hat pin through her grey toque, and felt a strange emotion take possession of her. She examined it and, with surprise, recognised it for what it was – pure hatred and revulsion directed against Ben Saville *and against herself.* She had betrayed Rosamunde as surely as any traitor, and yet she had not known it. She realised then the depths of unkindness and greed to which every one is prey, and she was shocked at it in herself. Arabella remembered that when her feelings for Ben had been strongest, there had been no virtue in her at all, nothing but selfish egotism. There had been no compassion for Rosamunde, no real guilt. All she knew in those moments, was that she was free – and yet she was guilty.

Arabella was led by two guards towards the entrance of the gaol, and then she was outside in the clear winter light. Suddenly the deep heaviness left her. She was alive and she was free! She cried silently and tried to make sense of her emotions, feeling as if she had walked into some kind of heaven. She made her way towards the silver-haired priest, waiting silently on the pavement, and as she stood before him, she was rendered speechless. But Father Sebastian, gazing down at the tears of relief and gratitude in her eyes, understood.

PART TWO

1905–1915

I

All the old pain and revulsion came back to Arabella undiminished, that hot night in late January, as she stood in the marble-floored hallway of a retired gold magnate's Johannesburg mansion, staring up into the face of her former enemy, Sean O'Shea. The Irishman had undergone a transformation since she had last seen him during the Siege of Ladysmith. He was wearing an immaculately pressed dark evening suit, his collar standing stiff in white splendour almost to his ears, his black tie neatly folded and held by a pearl pin. He was clean-shaven, except for a black moustache, and there was a smug look about him as Maria, Siegfried Heinz's youngest daughter, introduced him as her latest beau.

'It's been a long time, Miss Allen,' he drawled, weighing Arabella up maliciously. 'And here you are, living in the home of one of the richest pro-Boer German industrialists – and the governess of my dear little Maria. How very, very interesting.' He looked down at seventeen-year-old Maria, who was possessively hanging on his arm, and a curious expression passed over his sneering features.

'There's talk that you had a lot of trouble getting work at the end of Milner's reconstruction programme – that no hospitals nor any of your worthy English wanted anything to do with you after the Hobhouse connection. From what I heard, you walked the streets of this Uitlander stronghold in desperation until Herr Heinz came to your rescue.'

Arabella felt furious, and a familiar knot tightened in her stomach. This man knew too much about her. 'I'm very grateful to Herr Heinz', she said guardedly, 'especially as work is so hard to find during the post-war depression.'

The large hallway, with its omnipresent mahogany – banisters, wall panels and heavy furniture all made from the same wood was warm, yet to Arabella it suddenly felt chilly. She looked at the pastel velvet draperies drawn over the long windows, the tapestries and animal trophies of every kind which adorned the walls. A long flight of steep stairs rose upwards from where they were standing, its balustrade covered with dimmed blue velvet. From a distance she heard the laughter of men and women in the drawing room.

'Especially for an outcast from all Uitlander society,' O'Shea said smoothly.

'Only until they understood fully what I was doing,' she said, immediately on the defensive. 'But I'm quite happy here, I assure you, teaching Maria painting and English.' Arabella's hands were clenched stiffly at the sides of her plain white blouse buttoned high on her throat, and the full long skirt of blue cotton. The lines of her chin and the faint lines of her cheeks had sharpened. This made her green eyes very large. The big gas chandelier flared down on her hair, coiled about her face, and its brightness lit up the dark, precisely-placed furniture and expensive rugs, making her own lack of colour more evident.

Before responding to this O'Shea lit a cigarette. The flare of the match revealed his swarthy face and hard, squinting eyes. He shook the match, waving it back and forth in the air.

'It must have been quite something, visiting those farms after the war, that were ruined by your English soldiers, and offering the defeated wretches clothes and comforts with that Hobhouse woman – all on the funds from that self-righteous English newspaper. Oh yes, I know all about that! Did you enjoy seeing the humiliating desperation of the Boer women and children and the ruin of the little war-orphans, knowing that they are now well and truly under the heel of Milner and his swinish administrators? Meaning, of course, your bloody cousin and his friends?' O'Shea guffawed crudely, enjoying himself at her expense. Never had she detested him more, Arabella decided.

Maria suddenly tapped him on the arm, giving him a wide, beaming smile, gaily unconscious of the atmosphere between them. 'Sean,' she cried, in her heavily accented English. 'I did not know you knew my dear, clever Fräulein Allen!'

Arabella let her face clear. 'Only as a nursing sister, Maria – and that, for a very short time.' But Maria was not really listening. She was smiling dreamily up at Sean, in a cloud of sweet perfume and red curls, in her expensive lemon silk gown, all angles and thin limbs, gold bracelets and dangling turquoise earrings.

O'Shea took his cigarette from his mouth. He held it in his short, ruthless fingers and regarded it pensively. His forehead wrinkled. 'It seems very strange to me, that an English nurse with a cousin who is bosom buddies with Kitchener and Milner, should become a traitor to the cause and then live with pro-Boer Germans after some desperate years of struggle existing below the breadline, abandoned by all her fancy friends.'

190

He stuck the cigarette back in his mouth, and stared at her, his expression cold and full of enmity. A feeling of suffocation overcame Arabella. Then her anger vanished, and all at once, terror struck her – a quite unreasoning terror, like a blow. She did not know why she should feel so afraid, but sensed that somehow, this man was a threat to her and to her position in the Heinz household.

'Oh yes,' he went on now, slowly, his smile malicious. 'I know a lot about you, Miss Allen. How you worked your skin to the bone in Mrs Smythe's infamous boarding house in the poorest part of town, mending socks for her single male boarders, and washing dishes for your keep. Oh, how the mighty have fallen!'

There it was. He enjoyed her discomfort, the fact that she had been made to suffer. It was as though he had some secret knowledge about her, his black eyes were suddenly so sly. Apparently he was pleased with his life these days, especially with Maria, an heiress to the Heinz millions. He ground out his cigarette on a silver ashtray set beside two Dresden figurines on a mahogany table, Maria watching him as if he was doing something very important and interesting. Not for the first time Arabella became aware that, in some strange, indefinable way, Sean O'Shea was an evil force to contend with – to destroy, if possible, or let herself be destroyed ... The tension in the hallway was very strong, as she studied his thin, cruel mouth. He had pushed his hands into his trouser pockets, and was the picture of the bitter rebel, out of place in his dinner jacket.

The sound of a gramophone crackled from the drawing-room, playing Wagner, and a servant came down the passageway with glasses and liqueurs on a silver tray, and disappeared into the room. They heard the doorbell ringing, and the steps of a maid in starched black and muslin going to answer it. By now, the smile had left Maria's young face.

'Ah, our guests are here for the theatre,' she announced: 'Come, Sean – we go to drink liqueurs and coffee with Mama and Papa before we drive in your very wonderful car to the Standard Theatre to see – what is it? – *The French Maid*, yes? I am glad you and my very best teacher now meet again. Goodnight, Fräulein Allen.'

The guests came in, in a body of five couples. Arabella knew them only slightly. They were, like Siegfried Heinz, wealthy retired gold barons. The hallway was instantly a-flutter with rose, white and yellow evening gowns, rustling like a soft wind among the solid black of the men. Maria tugged Sean along with her in the direction of the drawing room, from where the voices of her father and eldest brother, Werner, could be heard, amidst the more subdued strains of her mother, Magda, and now and then, the voices of her sisters and their husbands.

Before they disappeared into the room, Sean turned his head and looked at Arabella. He touched his forehead lightly with his hand in a mocking salute, and the grinning enmity was there for her to see.

Her mouth went dry with hostility and fear. She would have to be careful if she wanted to keep her job, the only worthwhile one she had managed to obtain in months. The war had been followed by the enormous and painful task of reconstruction, and while Milner and his young administrators had worked diligently with the assistance of Boer Commando leaders to overcome the post-war problems, she had assisted Emily Hobhouse to supervise the care of war orphans and the relief of the poverty and famine among Boer families. She remembered them, starving on their isolated, ruined farms, trying to eke out some kind of existence in the bare veld, and how, day after day, her spirit had reached out to these people, touched by their pride and courage, wishing that there was more she could bring them.

All her sorrow came back to her, and with it, deep loneliness. The pleasure of the evening was gone. She feared the humiliation of having to walk the Johannesburg streets again, as she had been forced to do at the end of the reconstruction programme in 1903. She feared having every Uitlander door slammed in her face because of what she had done during the war, just as her feet were touching ground again, and she was fast reaching the stage where she could save for her fare to England and a new post in nursing, perhaps that of Matron in one of the county hospitals. But she would have to remain calm.

She walked slowly up the stairs to her room on the second floor, her head pounding with a single thought – the sickening realisation that Sean O'Shea would stop at nothing to marry Maria Heinz. Ambitious and ruthless, she strongly suspected that he would plot to remove her from the Heinz household, so that she would not be able to turn Maria against him and that, in his new position of power, he would humiliate her at every opportunity ...

A nearby clock was striking midnight. Unable to sleep, Arabella crouched by her bedroom window, peering into the garden below, with its tidy lawns, excessively neat shrubbery and pruned hedges, like green walls, surrounding exotic, imported plants and potted trees clipped into the shape of birds. A lone lamp glimmered feebly near one of the few swimming pools in Johannesburg.

Every sight and every sound stabbed her now with the sharpness of personal futility. She leaned her arms on the polished wooden window ledge, and buried her face upon them to shut out the vision of interminably stretching, disillusioned years. She was twenty-seven years old, alone and frustrated as she had been for as long as she could remember. Sweat broke out on her brow and under the folds of her nightgown. Father Sebastian had said she had courage. Perhaps she had, but did she have enough to face the new threat of Sean O'Shea?

She thought of the Irish priest with deep affection. After her release from gaol, she had refused to accompany him back to Natal, knowing that she could never let herself accept charity, especially from someone who had done so much for her already. He had seen that all her belongings were returned to her. Her thoughts went back to the hated menial jobs she had been forced to do to earn a living, based in the south of the town where the ugly mine dumps thrust their dirty yellow backs to the sky, enveloped in its perpetual pall of red dust.

She leaned out on the windowsill, breathing in the heavy air, suddenly back again in those dead, pre-war days on board the *Sandringham Castle*, when she had felt so brave, so sure, before she had become ensnared by Ben's magnetic charm, and ruined by his jealousy.

Her life seemed to have changed for the better in the boisterous Heinz household as she accompanied Maria, who had a temper to match her fiery red hair and absolutely no talent for painting, on shopping expeditions in Herr Heinz' landau, to the centre of town. Maria had an extraordinary ability for spending fortunes in the small expensive shops, or in the fashionable upstairs tearooms where in the new Edwardian society of Johannesburg, money was the passport to everything, and especially into upper-class society.

Johannesburg never ceased to surprise Arabella, with its townhouses and large palatial homes, racing stables, blocks of elaborate ironwork-façaded offices belonging to the gold magnates, and the slender-pillared shops, arched with fussy Victorian cast-iron decorations. The small blocks and narrow streets had been laid out as a grid in the 1880s in order to maximise the number of gold-bearing lots of the sprawling town, which had originated on five farms, and been constructed out of a desert in an amazingly short time. For about thirty miles on either side of the town ran a reef of gold-bearing quartz, which seemed consistent and inexhaustible, promising the Witwatersrand – 'the ridge of white waters' – a long life and an ever-growing population. For this reason, even though it was the place where the rebellious, disenfranchised Uitlanders had helped to spark off the war, and although it still needed a great deal of reconstruction, it had ironically been untouched by the conflict.

Johannesburg was a place of excitement and opportunity and Arabella continually marvelled at the sense of sturdy independence and activity which seemed to charge its very air. Here, everyone appeared bent on some definite purpose as they moved at a brisk pace about their business.

Siegfried Heinz, like so many others, had come out as a penniless young man to South Africa years ago during the unprecedented gold rush on the Reef. He had made his fortune, built his fine house and educated his son at the best boarding schools. His five daughters had been educated at home to become perfect German wives and mothers, and now all were married, except Maria. Werner, who had been studying medicine in Scotland, had recently returned home, prior to setting up his own practice, and whenever his father was away, the house was filled with his friends gathered around the swimming pool drinking and laughing, which his mother, a woman much younger than her husband, indulgently tolerated. But as soon as Herr Heinz arrived back, the house immediately returned to the strict rules and etiquette he demanded.

Although Arabella deplored Werner's irresponsibility and lavish extravagances, she envied him the freedom to pursue his medical studies in preparation for his chosen profession, while she was forced to shift from pillar to post ...

She rose and lay down on her bed, relaxing in the darkness. The air outside had freshened slightly; the room was less oppressive. Perhaps Maria would tire of O'Shea, and there would be nothing to fear ... But Arabella knew it would be foolish to cling to that hope. She had never seen Maria so flushed and excited as she had been that evening, hanging on to the Irishman's arm with such possessiveness ...

There had to be some way out. Later in the day she would face it with new eyes. She would speak with Herr Heinz – he had always liked her and valued her opinion – and she would explain everything to him. Perhaps he could prevent O'Shea from jeopardising her job.

She fell into a dreamless sleep. Dawn slowly slipped into the spacious gardens of the Heinz mansion, as the milk-cart laden with churns and drawn by a sleepy horse rattled up the driveway, and a dog barked.

A scraping sound somewhere in the room awakened her with an instant feeling of deep unease. She heard the sound again and still only half-awake, stumbled out of bed, blinking in the dim light. Wide-eyed, she stood in her white nightgown, staring at the man who grinned back at her, in the middle of the room. She stifled a scream as she recognised Sean O'Shea, still in full evening attire.

'Oh come now, Miss Allen – I couldn't have frightened you that much!' he said with a contemptuous snort.

Wondering what mischief he was up to, and very aware of her nakedness beneath the nightgown, she stepped back, the antennae of her mind beginning to quiver. Instinctively, she folded her arms across her breasts, and glared at him. 'Will you please leave this room at once!'

O'Shea ignored the demand, and looked swiftly around the room, throwing his shiny black top hat on to the chair.

'You hate being a governess with all your bleeding little guts, now don't you? How it must infuriate you to see the Heinzes having everything you enjoyed with your filthy cousin, eating off the fat o' the land! Perhaps your calculating little eyes are set on Werner – now that wouldn't surprise me at all. But Werner Heinz is too clever for you, English bitch!'

Arabella's eyes narrowed with hatred. 'Get out of here at once, or I shall call for help.'

He shrugged leisurely. 'I don't think you have the guts, governess, nurse, maid, or whatever you call yourself – because you value your hoity-toity little reputation above everything. But if you are so stupid, no one will ever take your word above mine.'

Arabella was thinking rapidly. O'Shea had been drinking, possibly with Maria's brother Werner, after he had accompanied the family home, and left the house. Then he had secretly returned. How did he know her room? Maria, no doubt, with her usual chatter, had innocently told him. Outwardly, Arabella's expression was one of calm disdain at his behaviour, but her mind was a red cloud of hatred. 'It will look very bad for you if you are found in my room, Mr O'Shea, so will you please leave!'

'If they ever found out, Miss Governess, I should make it quite clear that you invited me here, and not wanting to cause a scene, I agreed – to keep your stinking little mouth shut!'

Quickly, she darted to the door, hoping to escape, but it was locked, and she knew that he had pocketed the key. Turning, she faced him like a hunted animal as he advanced towards her.

'Now that was a stupid thing to do, you silly bitch.'

'Don't come any closer, or I'll scream!' She held her breath and tried to flatten herself against the door as he stood before her, reeking of whisky fumes.

'No, you won't – you'll do just as I say.' He grabbed hold of her two arms with the steel pressure of his fingers. His face darkened, in contrast to the false softness of his voice with its deceiving Irish lilt. 'You don't approve of Sean O'Shea, now do you, English bitch, you and that mean bastard Lieutenant-Colonel Saville and his wooden leg. God, do I wish I had roasted his liver good and solid when we had the chance! He with his fancy-pants Military Intelligence gents, living it up while we starved, fighting for a lost cause!'

Picking her words carefully, as his dark eyes watched her with the intensity of a stalking animal, Arabella said quietly, 'I think you must unlock the door and just leave. The servants will be up soon with early morning coffee and Mr Heinz likes to stroll around the garden very early –'

'To hell with Mr Heinz and the servants! If you ever tell little Miss Maria or anyone else about this, you'll live to regret it, I promise you. I'll see to it that you never work in this town again!' His voice was low and deadly, and Arabella saw the naked spite on his face. The last shreds of her assurance fled.

She cleared her dry throat. 'You are very unfair to Maria, Mr O'Shea, by coming to my room like this. Whether you tell her or not, she'll know something is wrong – that I cannot hide. Now will you please unlock the door, and go, and nothing more shall be said.'

'Nothing will be said anyhow,' he snarled, and pulling her over to the tumbled bed, he forced her down and bent over her, his face chalky and twitching. 'Maria Heinz will do anything I say, and through her, that dolt of a father who grovels at the feet of his spoilt baby daughter.'

Arabella almost lost her head. 'You must go! Go before it's too late!' she pleaded wildly, in a frantic whisper.

'Too late for what, you stupid bitch? Losing your ridiculous virtue?' He seemed to tower above her, as she shrank back in her nightgown. 'I'll be glad to ruin you forever, so that you'll never be able to look at another man for the rest of your worthless, miserable life. I want you to burn in shame for what you and your kind did to us.'

'Let me go!' At last she spoke loudly, for panic threatened to overwhelm her. He saw the fear glimmer in her eyes, and in triumphant savagery, he closed in.

'They'll find out – they always do,' she said fiercely, as she felt his body press against hers, his lips on her neck. As he yanked her head up by the hair, she placed a hand on his chest and desperately turned her head aside. 'Stop it!' she cried. 'Stop it!'

'Just shut up, you understand? This is for that Stradcombe bastard! I'll ruin his woman as we've been ruined by his filthy English swine!'

He pushed her head cruelly into the pillow until she could hardly breathe. As he began ripping her nightgown, she kicked out with her legs as furiously as she was able, and with all her strength, threw out an arm and grabbed the heavy pottery ewer from the side table and brought it down on his head with the force borne of utter desperation ...

Instantly, his arms slackened and loosed their hold, and he fell back on to the floor. Bright red blood oozed from his forehead on to the carpet.

Stupefied with terror, tears of shock pouring down her face, Arabella forced herself to bend down and feel his pulse. With sickening relief, she discovered that she had not killed him, but only stunned him. She searched frantically for her bedroom key in the pocket of his dinner jacket. Dragging on a dressing gown, and shaking all over, she unlocked the door at the third attempt, and raced down the passage to the opposite wing where the family slept.

Opening Werner's door, she cried, 'Mr Heinz – Mr Heinz, do wake up! Something terrible has happened. I've knocked Mr O'Shea unconscious. He – he came to my room to – I hit him with the water jug in self-defence! Please come quickly! I can't tell Maria yet. She'll be far too upset!'

Werner was up in no time, running towards the other wing and shouting for his father. Soon the whole passage was buzzing with people rushing along its length, and into Arabella's room.

2

It was after breakfast that Arabella was called into Siegfried Heinz's wood-panelled study. Despite her protestations that O'Shea had come into her room and forced himself upon her, her employer, a big, white-haired, white-bearded man, stated with rigid inflexibility that she must pack her bags and leave by the end of the week, when his landau would take her to the station. He told her that finding the Irishman unconscious on her floor, with blood all over the wildly disordered bedclothes was too much for the fine reputation of the Heinz family. To shelter her would give substance to the lie that the family, and especially Siegfried himself, supported her part in the shocking affair.

His usual dignity absent, his deeply lined face appalled and flushed, he told her that O'Shea, having regained consciousness, had been forbidden to see Maria or any other member of the household again.

Returning to her room, Arabella prepared to leave the comfortable shelter which had closed around her in her most destitute days, and to go out once more into a hostile town. She asked herself if there was any true justice left in the world. For all she had suffered in the past, this latest experience was a shattering awakening leaving her feeling degraded and unclean.

Maria refused to see her, imprisoning herself in her room in weeping hysteria – a state which Frau Heinz blamed entirely on the Englishwoman. And as Arabella struggled to keep quietly to her room before she left, the buzz of morbid interest in her rose to a dull roar; once more, she was the most notorious woman in the vicinity.

It was late in the afternoon. After she had washed her hands for the tenth time in an effort to erase the filth of the experience from her, and finished listlessly checking the remaining possessions on her bed, she stood, holding a sheet from the evening newspaper, *The Star*. Her shaking fingers moved in the direction of an item someone had circled with red pencil and pushed under her door. Nothing had prepared her for the shock of the words that declared that she, the well-known concentration camp feminist, now working as a teacher of painting to the daughter of the mining magnate, Siegfried Heinz, had tried to seduce Maria Heinz's fiancé, Mr Sean O'Shea from Dublin, in her bedroom and, having failed, had attempted to murder him. He had suffered a serious blow to the head, but was recovering after defending himself while trying to protect Miss Maria Heinz's position, of which it was alleged, Arabella was insanely jealous.

The words swam before her eyes, bringing back the horror and humiliation of the experience. She let the paper fall from her fingers, the words sinking like lead weights into her mind. So, O'Shea had already talked to the press, and now everyone was against her! Who could she turn to this time? She realised to the full her intense loneliness and saw the future stretching ahead of her, insecure, bleak and tragically joyless. The time had come for her to move away – but where to? This time lodgings would be almost impossible to find.

She moved to the window and opened it. The garden, lying bright and warm with summer fragrance, had looked secure and prosperous only days before. But now, as the carriages and one or two smart cars of consoling Heinz friends, rolled up the neatly swept gravel drive, the house and its surroundings took on a furtive, secretive aura. Shame and scandal had come to it, and she had been part of the cause. She caught a glimpse of the pool, as a flock of sparrows landed on the lawn around a Japanese evergreen privet. It was beautiful and peaceful, but the house itself stood there, seeming to have shrunk and drawn in upon itself, simmering with deep tensions.

She drew a deep, unsteady breath in the room that suddenly seemed stifling, with its heavy, ebonised furniture faintly shadowed with the heavy drapes.

Even though she could not bear returning to Mrs Smythe's boarding house, perhaps it would not be so bad for a few months, just until she had enough money for her fare to England. Then she would rid herself of the soil of this country and its memories forever. Called by the fresh air outside, she turned impulsively and made for the door. She was supposed to stay secluded in her room until she left, but all at once it became intolerable to her. She had to get out of its suffocating atmosphere, and for one last time, go and sit in the quietest part of the luxurious garden, and forget for a while everything connected with Sean O'Shea.

She stepped into the long dark corridor and crept down the stairway, holding on to the velvet-draped banister where a gargoyle held a lamp aloft at the foot. As she reached the floor below, she passed two maids, who looked at her and then at each other. When on impulse she glanced over her shoulder, she found they had stopped to watch her instead of continuing on their way, making her painfully aware that the entire staff knew about the ugly incident; once again, she felt as unclean and despised as a leper.

She opened the massive hall door, breaking the reflections thrown on the highly polished floor from its stained-glass panels, and walked out into the garden. Aimlessly, but breathing more easily, she moved away from the house toward the conservatory. It was basic instinct which drew her; in that glass-domed building there was peace and solitude, an escape from fear and loneliness. The coolness in the conservatory, with its pleasant splash of fountains, the waxy greenness of the many exotic ferns, soothed her overburdened mind. Sitting on a small ornamental bench, hidden by the fronds of brilliant foliage, she could try to plan her future.

It was then that a movement near the doorway made her stiffen. She sat very still in real fear, praying that whoever it was would not see her and go away. Holding her breath, she shrank into the heavy greenery surrounding her, as a figure pulled back a long fern frond – and she found herself staring into a pair of familiar, heavy-lidded hazel eyes.

It was the Jewish Boer, Isaac Brandauer, whom she had last seen before the Ladysmith Siege! But it could not be ... this man's round face was framed by a neat red beard and a handsome moustache, elegantly twirled at the ends. His mass of red hair, however, instantly brought back memories of Deneys du Rand and his brother Danie ...

But why was he here, in this house?

With silent swiftness, surprising for such a thickset hulk of a man, he stood before her, raising his fiery eyebrows. 'Miss Allen – at last! I've been turning the entire household upside down in an effort to find you – and here you are, in the last place I would have thought of.' He pursed his lips, appraising her astutely. 'You do recognise me, don't you? Brandauer – Isaac Brandauer, who helped save young Luke during the war.'

'Yes.' She swallowed hard and looked at him with growing interest. His jacket and trousers, red bow tie and checked waistcoat with the gold watch-chain were expensively flamboyant, so different from the dusty cord breeches and coat he had worn when they last met, and he looked older, but the ebullient, energetic manner of speaking had not changed.

A generous smile broke out on his face. 'Good, because from the sound of things, you are going to need my help.'

'I am?' Arabella's eyes brightened with suspicion for a moment, but there was nothing in his manner to suggest a threat.

He sat down beside her and she shrank from him, her face suddenly ashen. 'I read the account in the evening paper about you and O'Shea

– we all knew him, back in Ladysmith, when he belonged to the Irish Brigade led by that Yankee Colonel Blake. A mean bag of tricks if ever there was one. None of us trusted him. He damn well signed the Oath of Allegiance to the Crown, but he's obviously using that as a cover for his own far-from-legal activities, because he still hates you English like poison.' He gave her a keen, searching look. 'And now he's been up to his nasty tricks again. Knowing a little about the nurse we met during the war, and your experience in the camps and Pretoria Gaol, I knew you would never have encouraged that Irishman, and God forbid, try to seduce him!'

Arabella frowned, then lowered her eyes, but not before he had seen the expression in her pale face with its large, appealing eyes, of one who has suffered a great deal. For all this, he was instantly aware, too, of her extraordinary personal magnetism, which had attracted many who had come into contact with her.

'How did you find me?' she asked, almost shyly. 'Do you know Mr Heinz, perhaps?'

He was smiling. 'I met Werner during the war, and our paths crossed again when he returned to this country from Scotland. His father and mine never agreed about the war – although Mr Heinz was a good friend of my wife's late father, Theodore Bernstein, who helped Paul Kruger to build his railway from Pretoria to Delagoa Bay before the war.'

'You're married?' she ventured, nervously clasping her hands together.

Isaac cocked his head to one side, considering. 'I married Rachel after the war, a few months before her father died. She and her mother had been sent to Cape Town during the fighting, and most of her brothers, except Benjamin, the youngest, fought against their father's wishes, for the British, to their eternal shame. Rachel and I – we have known each other since we were children – had an understanding that when the war ended, we would marry. And thanks be to God, that's how it turned out. Her formidable mother is the well-known soprano, Bertha Singer. Needless to say, her mother and my parents have had nothing to do with each other since the war.'

There was a silence as they faced each other, then it was again broken by Isaac's enthusiastic voice: 'I have a proposition to put to you, Miss Allen. I have recently bought a small newspaper, *The Southern Herald*, with money inherited from Rachel's father, and I would like to run your story on the front page – the *true* story, the way it really happened. I have a first-class reporter in my youngest brother, Reuben, and he will write a story that will make the public sit up with indignation and disgust. It's not fair that you have to hide away whilst that scurrilous Irishman has it all his own way. I want to expose Mr Sean O'Shea for what he really is.'

Arabella knew a moment of deep consternation. Part of her wanted to believe him, to agree to the vindication of her reputation, but after the hideously sordid episode, she now wanted to cringe away and hide like a wounded animal from the glaring interest of strangers.

'No, Mr Brandauer – you'll never know what it was like, and I don't want to talk about it. All I want to do now is to disappear quickly from the whole thing. No one will believe your story, sincere though your motives may be, for I have already been damned for my part in the concentration camps saga. Your readers will already be biased before they read one word your brother writes.'

For a while Isaac was quiet, restlessly tapping the ivory-topped cane across his knees. 'My motto is *carpe diem*, Miss Allen – seize the day, especially in the newspaper game.'

'Please! Let's leave it!' she cried suddenly, upset beyond endurance. 'I want to forget the whole thing, and writing another account will only drag it out again, with strangers debating for one side or the other, though they've never met either O'Shea or myself. I couldn't bear that!' Her voice broke and she blinked rapidly, wanting to run away, back to the gloomy security of her room. 'Besides, there is Mr Heinz and his family to consider. He gave me shelter when no one else would, and he does not need any more publicity.'

Isaac rose and there was another silence. 'Mr Heinz, I assure you, my dear Miss Allen, can well take care of himself and his family. He hasn't risen to such great heights unscathed, I can tell you.'

'I'm sorry – it's just that my whole world has collapsed and I have to find employment and a place to stay as soon as possible.'

Isaac shut his eyes, as if her words had somehow hurt him, then he said gently, 'I understand. You are right to say that. Will you forgive me?'

'For what?' she asked simply. 'For trying to get a story to fight your competition in the other papers? It's your business – stories of people and their follies.'

He gave a groan which turned into a chuckle. 'You really are astonishingly frank, Miss Allen. But don't get me wrong, dear lady, it wasn't just the competition that urged me on. There really is a sincere desire deep in my black mercenary heart to help you and to put the record straight as regards O'Shea, believe me. I fought in the war for justice, and I fight for it again through the voice of my newspaper.'

He sat down beside her once more, slapping his well-covered thighs. 'You do believe that, don't you? After all, you did save the life of one of my dearest friends during the war, and I have never forgotten it.' He looked searchingly at her and then, putting down his cane, he took her hand and pressed it warmly. 'One day you will tell me your story. One day, when the experience is not so raw.'

I'm not alone after all, thought Arabella. It was a liberating idea, and she smiled weakly. 'Yes, one day, when the time is ripe and all the bitterness of the war is forgotten – when people will understand that what Emily Hobhouse and I did, and the other women involved, was for justice.'

He studied her soberly for a moment, then his face changed. 'Now on to my second proposition,' he said, releasing her hand. 'I have a home for you – if you want it.'

Her eyes flew to his face. 'A home? I don't understand.'

He coughed, his eyes sparkling with sudden enthusiasm. 'I can offer you shelter in the home of a dear friend of my wife – an Englishwoman like yourself, a widow and a friend of Miss Emily Hobhouse – Mrs Althea Rigby.'

Arabella uttered an exclamation of astonishment. 'The writer? The friend of Olive Schreiner? But she has never met me. And with what the newspapers are printing about me, how can she –' she continued with rising agitation, until Isaac raised a forestalling hand.

'Mrs Rigby knows all about you. She has spoken at great length with Emily Hobhouse in England, from where she has just returned after a visit to Mrs Emily Pankhurst, among others. She's very impressed and wants to meet you.'

Arabella's depression and sadness were considerably lightened by this news, but then her enthusiasm died. It all seemed too good to be true. She rose and walked slowly about, her charcoal-grey skirt dipping and sweeping as she moved. Althea Rigby was one of the most talented writers of her day, and she outspokenly deplored the servile position of women in society.

She swung around to face him, one hand nervously tugging at her high lace-banded collar. 'I haven't any money to pay Mrs Rigby for her generosity.'

'You'll work with her, dear lady. She wants to start a movement for women's suffrage here in Johannesburg, and she is keen for you to help her. She thinks it would interest you.'

I have a friend, thought Arabella. Suddenly, from facing a terrible abyss, this man had come back into her life. She wondered wryly if there were any red-haired angels in heaven. Blushing slightly, she became conscious that Isaac was looking at her, his round face serious and thoughtful.

'How can I ever thank you enough, Mr Brandauer? I cannot believe it,' she said, smiling with genuine sincerity.

'I want you to meet Rachel, my wife. I think you'll like her.' He sat back, his arms folded on top of his cane, an enigmatic expression in his eyes. 'There's also someone else you should meet again – Deneys du Rand.'

Arabella stopped beside a cluster of wild exotic orchids, the flowers like bright birds arrested in flight. She hesitated, then murmured, 'I thought he was in Madagascar with his brother Christiaan.'

Isaac looked at his cane thoughtfully. 'Christiaan died of malaria while they were pushing wagons through the island jungles to the coast and back again as transport-dealers. Deneys continued on his own, until I persuaded General Smut's wife, Isie, who has always had a particularly soft spot for Deneys, to write and ask him to rethink his position and return to help Louis Botha in the making of a new country – with Boer and English working together. He was very bitter, you know, at the outcome of the war. He and his family lost everything. He felt there was nothing left for him after the Peace of Vereeniging.'

He glanced at her, but she was gazing at a delicate lilac orchid, her face full of conflicting and puzzling emotions. She seemed totally unaware that he was studying her, when she said suddenly, 'But I thought that Kitchener had put a price on his head.'

Isaac shot her another swift glance, then he said in a low voice, 'Louis Botha got permission for Deneys to be pardoned and have it lifted – on the condition that he came back to work with us.'

Toying with the creamy brown and white cameo brooch pinned at the neck of her blouse, Arabella said, carefully, 'Why did he agree, if he felt there was nothing left for him here?'

Isaac stared at her, his heavy-lidded eyes narrowed. 'It took some persuading, I can tell you, but we need people like Deneys – clever, resourceful, strong. He didn't like the idea of working with his former enemies, but finally he agreed. I know he missed this country more than he would admit. He's set up a law practice in a small Transvaal dorp called Heideville, where he's the lawyer. He could have gone to the Bar, but prefers to build up some capital first. His father, old Sarel, is still in America, and is totally against his working for unity with the English. So, I might add, is Michiel, his eldest brother – he is even more bitter than Deneys, if that is possible.'

Isaac leaned forward earnestly and fixed her with deeply serious eyes. 'During the war, Miss Allen, most of us were high-spirited, youthful and heedless – Deneys more than most – but we've all changed. We've grown a bit older and, I like to think, a little wiser. Deneys has the ability to become one of the greatest legal men in this country.' His eyes followed the movements of a bee that buzzed above some plants, as a hand plucked at his rich moustache. 'In my view, the British papers did him a serious injustice, giving their public a totally wrong picture of him. They saw him only as a saboteur and a spy, which has made them greatly underestimate him.'

Arabella was touched by his words, yet embarrassed at the implication behind them. She hesitated a moment, then asked carefully, 'And you – why have you changed your mind about working with the English?'

Isaac rose, flourishing his hat and cane. 'We fought and lost, Miss Allen. The war is over, and we have to live in the present and plan for the future so that it won't happen again. Everything has changed and we must change with it. I think Louis Botha and Jannie Smuts are realistic in their belief that the answer is in one nation, and that can only happen if Briton and Boer forget their differences. As you know all too well, the war broke up families, with brothers against brothers, fathers against sons.' He took a deep, savage breath, his face drawing itself in lines of formidable tightness. 'The wounds in my family, and in Rachel's, will take years to heal, and in yours too, but God willing it can be done – for the sake of our unborn children. It's the only workable solution.'

He suddenly shot her a sharp glance from under his thick red eyebrows. 'What about your cousin, Lord Stradcombe? I'm told he has no time for either Botha or Smuts.'

A cold shiver ran down her spine at the mention of Ben's name. Immediately she flinched as if he had struck her. 'I don't know. I've not heard from him since my arrest,' she said.

Noticing her subtle withdrawal, he said quickly, 'If you're ready, I'll drive you to Mrs Rigby in my Cousin Aaron's four-cylinder Gladiator – the very first motor car to drive just over four hundred miles to Durban in five days.'

Her eyes widened. 'Right now? I've never ridden in a motor car before and –'

'There's always a first time! Now go and get ready, but do wear a headscarf. The wind plays havoc with hair, which is the one thing Rachel detests above all else when driving in Aaron's car.'

Arabella's face suddenly sparkled a little. 'I'll be ready in no time – everything's packed.'

Then abruptly she turned, and with a rapid swish of her skirts, she was gone.

3

Arabella was aroused by someone knocking on her bedroom door. Memory, blanked out by sleep, now presented total recall of the events leading up to her presence in the large green and gold bedroom in the Villa Valencia, the home of Althea Rigby. The door opened and a large, dark-skinned woman in a spotless pinafore and bright headscarf woven around her head like a turban, entered, balancing a commodious tray.

'Good morning, Missus. The Madam want you to enjoy the breakfast,' she said in the soft clicking speech of the Transvaal Tswana, a wide beaming smile on her face.

'Yes. Thank you.' Arabella quickly sat upright and watched her place the tray on the bedside table, then leave, closing the door behind her.

Arabella's heart warmed as the scent of good cooking rose from the breakfast tray with its lace clothe. It was so long since she had eaten anything that resembled English food that she could hardly wait to start on the boiled eggs, crispy rashers of bacon and grilled kidneys keeping warm under a silver cover, the muffins, crumpets and crisp buttered toast in a silver rack, accompanied by a dish of black cherry jam and a steaming silver pot of the very best tea.

As she ate, she recalled her first meeting with Althea Rigby in the tasteful drawing room filled with Galle vases, Gustav Klimt paintings and Lalique bowls the previous afternoon, after Isaac, with a cheery wave, had driven away in clouds of dust. She had taken an immediate liking to the writer – a tiny, elegant woman in late middle age with silver hair parted in the middle and looped across her forehead in the style much favoured by the late Queen Victoria. She was impressed by the quiet authority in her voice and the direct glance of her bright blue eyes that were somehow youthful in spite of the soft wrinkles about them.

Arabella finished her breakfast, and proceeded with her toilette in the green and gold bedroom where all the furniture was of mahogany, walnut and rosewood. She fastened a tea rose on the high lace-banded collar of her pale green and white muslin blouse before joining Althea in the morning room for further discussion on the establishment of an enfranchisement league for women in Johannesburg. To her, the older woman's recognition of her intelligence made her equal in status to women who had husbands and lovers. She did not need to beg for the attention of any man, in the old and fixed belief that a woman's only hope of self-expression was through marriage, if she could use her brain to its fullest potential. She had to admit that suddenly there was a new and exciting incentive for her to go on, and the lonely and intellectually thirsty woman was more than delighted by the change in her fortunes.

Arabella was revived by the preparations for the new women's suffrage movement, instantly fascinated with Olive Schreiner's *Story of an African Farm*, criticising the conventional role played by women in society, which convinced her that no evils could be redressed until women became a part of the electoral process. She was further stimulated by the remarkable personalities who gathered in Althea's house. There were those who had not been enthusiastic over her entrance into the league, but once Althea had convinced them of her determination to have Arabella as her protégée, they had accepted the inevitable. Althea's hospitable door was regularly thrown open, and many of the wealthy, well-educated mostly English families, some whom had closed their doors to Arabella on her arrival in the town, now accepted her, firstly because she was Althea's friend, and later because a bond of mind and interest in the suffrage movement sprang up between them.

The new Arabella who emerged from the crucible of her past suffering was a woman determined to put the past behind her, and to throw herself into the ripening of her new life. She found Althea stimulating company, with her shrewd and witty comments on matters foreign and domestic, and listened intently when the older woman discussed the political situation in the country at the frequent dinner parties she threw.

These parties always broke up late, the guests still arguing, discussing and comparing views. Arabella felt though, that some of the women still regarded her with suspicion, that they disapproved of the active part she took in the conversations. She showed too much spirit in speech and far too much independence in her own life, past and present, to be altogether trusted. And yet, her enthusiasm was contagious, and even those, including Isaac's brilliant, dark-haired young wife Rachel, who were prejudiced and sceptical of her, slowly found themselves charmed by her intelligent comments, her quick wit and the first paper she wrote on why women should be enfranchised.

Forty members joined the new Johannesburg Enfranchisement League, electing Althea as the president and Arabella and Rachel as office-bearers. It was decided to hold meetings in the various drawing rooms and gardens of different members.

The early afternoon was beginning to stretch itself into a long, mellow goldenness, as Arabella dressed for the first large meeting in which she was to speak on the paper she had written. It had been published in the *African Monthly*, causing a stir of great interest. Her toilette complete, she stood in front of the mirror in her bedroom, studying the gown Althea had lent her, with growing nervousness. It was the first time she had ever spoken in public, and among the audience would be visiting Australasian delegates.

The gown was the most beautiful one she had ever worn; of silk chiffon in subtle tints of lilac and green, edged with heavy flounces of rich Brussels lace, the softly-gathered lilac belt emphasising her handspan waist. In a cloud of Crab Apple Blossom perfume, she stood for a moment, anxiously appraising the corsage of lilac roses on the triple tier of lace setting off the fitted bodice of the blouse, the floral toque decorated with pink and lilac roses on top of the fashionable bouffant hairstyle.

Suddenly she thought of England. She could now afford to return there, but as she became aware of the twittering of a lively pair of black-eyed bulbuls outside, and the distant tinkle of glasses from the sweeping lawns downstairs, she realised that she still knew too little of South Africa to leave it, and what she had learned, she was coming to love.

The buzz of talk died across the lawn, where long tables and chairs were set out under the spreading trees, as Althea rose from the centre table, elegant in a tea coat of écru lace and chiffon, and welcomed the visiting delegates, the women and the sprinkling of men present.

'Before we listen with great enthusiasm to the success and pitfalls experienced by our Australasian guests in women's suffrage, we welcome one of our own young members who has suffered much under the heels of society's injustice. I have only, my friends, to say the name of Miss Arabella Allen, to capture your deepest attention.'

There was a burst of applause in the fresh, sunny air, and Arabella rose, taking a deep, steadying breath as every eye turned in her direction. She began to speak, hesitantly at first, then more confidently as she warmed to her subject. Her voice was not brittle and strident as some evidently expected, nor was it sharp and forceful. It was clear and sweet, though it carried her words to the farthest seats.

'The price of a good wife and devoted daughters is higher than the most precious jewel. If this is true, then it means that that wife and those daughters deserve to be free and independent and able to contribute to our world fully and joyously as every man does.' She took a deep breath in the silence that had fallen across the lawn, conscious of the sea of eyes staring at her, whether in approval or disapproval she could not say, for it was not the speech they had expected.

Without warning or conscious effort, her mind and her voice fused as one, and suddenly transcended all fear of the reaction of the audience. She broke away from her own prepared speech, and spoke spontaneously of her war-time experiences, the heartache of the nurses and their hardships, of the men who had relied on them in a limited system, of the helpless women and children in the camps. Fearlessly and without bitterness, she reviewed the cause of the injustices of that outmoded, inflexible system that had brought about such misery, like a ruthless surgeon laying his hand at the root of a dread disease, pointing out that if the nursing staff had had more power, it would only have benefited their patients. And so it was with everything else one cared to mention. If women were given the power, they would only bring great improvements and benefits to every aspect of life.

Everyone listened to her, fascinated, absorbed, as all the heated arguments for and against the enfranchisement of women that had raged for months, all the controversy surrounding her own part in the concentration camps, the inconsistencies that had frustrated her suddenly crystallised in the sure simplicity of her words, in the clear conviction that suddenly made them all the more significant. Horror leaped across some of the women's faces; reservation marked others. The men were disgusted, sympathetic, or embarrassed. One or two flushed, but they could not turn away from her face, and her glowing eyes, however much they tried.

Then quite simply, she finished what she wanted to say: 'Let us then go forward in our dedication, fearlessly and constructively.'

She sat down very quickly and closed her eyes for a brief second. There was a clap of hands from somewhere on the lawn, and another followed, and another, until the air resounded with applause. Arabella looked up with relief, her eyes meeting the liquid dark ones of Rachel Brandauer. For a moment both women gazed intently at one another, and then Rachel smiled, the warmth reaching her eyes.

Arabella had planned to melt into the crowd after the lecture given by the Australasian delegates, when tea was served, but many of the guests stood about her, trying to talk to her. Then Isaac and Rachel were at her side, congratulating her.

'So – you finally decided to come out and talk about your dubious past, Arabella. It would make excellent copy on my front page. Have I your permission to publish it as part of the women's movement coverage? It will give your work wonderful publicity.'

Arabella caught the note of wistfulness in Isaac's voice, and looked up at him, surprised. It was as near as he would ever come to pleading.

'Please agree, Arabella. After all, it will be such good exposure for what we are doing.' Rachel stood beside Isaac, the glimmer of jet beads and white chiffon frills at her throat, her dark head moving in a cloud of green and black ostrich feathers. 'I liked the lecture given by our Australasian guests,' she told her, 'but most of all I liked your talk.'

Arabella flushed under her praise. 'I'm glad,' she said. 'But to go really public is such a big step.'

'Just another step in an already adventurous undertaking, it would seem,' a deep, musical voice said behind her, in perfect, softly accented English.

'There's someone I want you to meet, Arabella,' Isaac said as she swung round, his deep-set eyes sparkling with suppressed mischief. 'Someone you should remember.'

'It's been a long time, Miss Allen.'

As the soft clink of fine china rose about them, and the servants moved among the guests with trays full of dainty cucumber sandwiches and small iced cakes, against the backdrop of rose masonry, Italian-style arches and red roof tiles, she stared up at Deneys du Rand in his smart dark clothes with unconcealed amazement, and forgot everything she had ever intended to say.

He was, as she remembered, quite tall, muscular and broad, with an air of powerful vitality and magnetism she could hardly ignore. But she had forgotten how handsome he was. He was older, and his brow showed traces of the furrows of experience, far beyond his thirty years, but genial humour lurked in the strong, forceful patterns of his face, about the expressive and smiling mouth.

'It has been a long time.' Arabella controlled an impulse of responsive warmth to this man who had been her enemy in more ways than one.

'Your speech was very good, Miss Allen – almost as good as your nursing,' he said without preliminaries, as Rachel and Isaac melted away into the crowd. 'I do believe that you are advocating a kind of holy war against the oppression of us males.'

He was looking down at her, faint lines crinkling at the corners of his eyes, and in spite of everything that had happened before, she felt drawn to him as he stood out among the sophisticated crowd like some sturdy shrub transplanted into an exotic flowerbed.

Recovering her composure, she said, 'We have to fight against oppression of any kind, Mr du Rand – in whatever form it takes.'

He considered her for a moment. 'But fighting for freedom is an illusion, if you would only realise it. Once you're free of us, we'll be fighting to get free of you. I shudder to think of a tyranny of women.' She was disarmed suddenly by the charming smile that transformed his features.

For a moment they looked at each other without speaking. She could see that he was surprised by what he saw.

Arabella could at times, as now, convey the impression of enormous personal fascination, especially when she was flowing with enthusiasm for something, for then the radiant quality about her was most apparent. Her face was tremendously alive and she was obviously quite the reverse from what he had almost been determined to dislike, especially after their last meeting in Intombi Camp. There was nothing to suggest the rapacious 'femme fatale', the arch enemy of all decent women, or the militant feminist that her detractors had described.

Then, in spite of herself, she smiled, and her small face looked unexpectedly provocative. 'Well spoken, as only an unemancipated man would speak, Mr du Rand. It's against those like you we have to awaken the majority of women in their chains.'

There was an ironic edge to her words, but her coolness made no impression on him. 'But what will you do once all poor deluded women are awakened?' His voice was low. 'Not all women will have the talent to handle that pot of gold at the end of the glorious rainbow of women's emancipation.'

Her shoulders lifted in a slight shrug as she tried to sort her thoughts. 'We are not poor or deluded. We are intelligent, capable people, quite able to hold our own in every sphere of society, and more than capable of getting the vote.'

His eyebrows came together, but a glint of humour touched his eyes. 'I think you speak for a very small minority, Miss Allen. From my experience, most women are not politically minded, and never will be. They are too emotional, and to make important decisions concerning the governing of a country, there has to be logical balance and objectivity, which is why we men are in Parliament. Besides, they will only duplicate their husband's vote, because they have not the interest to think for themselves ...'

'Please!' She cut him short, stubbornly standing her ground, as he was. She had only just met this man again, and already they were sparring. 'I do not think we have anything more to discuss, Mr du Rand. You are obviously against any kind of equality for women because it threatens your age-old, antiquated position as a man. And now, if you will excuse me, I must find Mrs Rigby.' She had managed to keep her voice chill as an icicle, but she felt her cheeks flush in angry betrayal. Damn this man. He had got right under her skin in a few seconds!

But Deneys did not stand aside politely. He actually came a step nearer to block her path of escape. 'Oh, but you can't leave just when our discussion is becoming interesting!' he went on, ignoring her coldness. 'You do realise of course, that there will be a lot of opposition to your cause. This is a country very much dominated by men and always will be. I think we have much to discuss.'

'You may have, but I don't –'

His jaw tightened ever so slightly, then he looked down at her, smiling steadily. 'Have it your own way, Miss Allen, but don't make the mistake of thinking you'll get the vote that easily. There'll be an ugly struggle before you get even halfway, and I hate to think of you in the thick of it.'

Other people jostled at their elbows, or brushed them with flowing skirts and bustles, but they stood quietly facing each other, as if they made an island for themselves in the moving human stream. Then it caught them up and whirled them apart. She saw him for a brief moment as he spoke on the fringes of an animated group of guests. He seemed to stand out in that gathering, and she could not understand the reason. He was certainly handsome, but it was more than his looks. Then she understood, in spite of her antagonism against him. She saw that there seemed to be some inner sureness of purpose which possessed him completely, and which had angered the woman in her.

Then he was gone, and Althea and several of the other women mentioned him to her. He was a most extraordinary man, they said, even for a former Boer spy. They knew he was a brilliant student of law, and that his family was of the best Boer stock, although he seemed to have nothing of the bitterness and hostility of his father and eldest brother, Michiel.

As Arabella listened, she felt a touch of remorse, remembering how he had saved Luke's life, of how his brother, Danie had died ... Deneys had lost everything for which he had fought, and still he had returned to live under the rule of his enemies in the face of family opposition, to help unite this troubled country. It took courage to return and reconcile himself to the English who had taken everything away from him. She need not have behaved so rudely, trying to snap off his head, simply because he had dared to speak his mind.

The company was thinning out rapidly as she slipped upstairs unseen. She opened the bedroom door and went in, closing it behind her, trying to hide from the fact that Deneys du Rand strongly attracted her. He always had, ever since their first meeting, and she had fought against this knowledge for so long.

She had tried to hide behind a wall of her own making, to shut herself away emotionally where nothing could ever hurt her again. Others had respected her wall – others, like Althea and dear Father Sebastian – but Deneys du Rand had, in one swift blow, penetrated her defences.

4

The Johannesburg roofs were sleek with late summer rains, and the gardens of the Villa Valencia dripped in greens and yellows as the town rocked with controversy over the article covering the suffrage meeting in Isaac's newspaper *The Southern Herald*. The newspaper offices were broken into and the press smashed by a small crowd calling Isaac 'the Boers' Jew' and shouting against, 'that concentration camp woman!' Isaac and his brother Reuben managed to enter the premises, fix the press and clean up the mess.

Arabella felt numbed. She had known the old bitterness would inevitably resurface, and had been prepared for it, but not at the expense of her friends' business. It was evident that some people still considered her part in the war as an irreversible evil. Once again, she was in the midst of heated controversy.

She felt dismayed by this public antagonism, but Althea would not give up the fight, no matter what it cost. With her strong support, Arabella rallied. She was under an obligation to help her friend, who had been goodness itself, and to Rachel and Isaac. All she could do was to give her loyal and unstinting support to the cause, knowing that public opinion could not be changed overnight. That would take months, even years, to alter.

Autumn came and went. Johannesburg was in the grip of its dry, cold winter. Chimneys smoked and people hugged grate fires and stoves as they discussed the undercurrent of discord building up beneath the apparent harmony of the Boer population, some feeling that many Boers were disappointed that Louis Botha and Jan Smuts had not held out against the British for better terms. But Althea, Arabella and Rachel were too busy struggling over pamphlets, letters, and meetings on women's suffrage, to take much notice of these rumblings. There was by now a growing number of labour organisations, particularly the newly formed Transvaal Political Labour League which, for the first time, included women's suffrage in its manifesto. It was the Women's League's intention that somehow, through this type of alliance with labour, the women's movement could be carried into the national political arena. Leagues were set up in all the larger towns and by the close of the year, Johannesburg boasted two. As the suffragists were still very much a minority in the mainstream of politics, they were still regarded with a mixture of amusement, indifference and hostility. The first motion calling for the vote for women was severely defeated in the Cape House of Assembly, and the speech accompanying the motion was received with loud cheers, ribald laughter and applause. In various petitions presented before the Assemblies of the four new provinces, more signatories were against women's suffrage than in favour.

It was a full summer night. There was the hum of conversation and the throb of music in the palatial home of Jacob Brandauer, who was celebrating his thirtieth wedding anniversary with his wife Ruth. Laughter rose from the ground-floor reception rooms in the brilliance of light and colour, as a small group of musicians played soft background music, and waiters glided between the guests, to the cheerful sound of popping champagne corks.

'Welcome to my parents' home, Arabella,' said Reuben, a slender, red-haired young man, in a dark evening-coat and trousers. 'I'm so glad Isaac and Rachel pressured you into coming. Isaac said he would not attend if you were not invited.' He glanced down at Arabella, his blue eyes penetrating but kind in his lean, volatile face. 'Mama gave in, under the deluge. Isaac can be so terribly persuasive.'

In a cloud of Crab Apple Blossom perfume, Arabella stood uncertainly beside Reuben and his wife Bernice in the hall, still buzzing with guests bearing gifts, the heads of the women gleaming with jewelled combs and aigrettes of diamonds, against the black and white of the men.

'I thought that your father wasn't inviting Isaac because of their antagonism over the war,' Arabella said in a carefully controlled voice.

'He wasn't!' Bernice interrupted, in a cold, angry voice. She was a small, brown-haired woman, resembling a shining white butterfly in her fine silk gown and pearls. 'But Miriam and Selwyn had to force their father to agree for the sake of saving face in front of their family and friends, I ask you! It would've been better if they had left it. Isaac is nothing but an embarrassment and so is his feminist wife!'

Amidst the rising chatter of voices all about them, Reuben turned to his wife. 'Apologise to Arabella, Bernice. You know Rachel is her friend.' There was a deep flush on his cheeks, as Bernice's mouth curled in an unattractive way.

She regarded Arabella with distaste. 'I don't like feminists – they're crude and masculine. I'm sorry Arabella – that's your choice,' she said with acid sweetness, 'and you wouldn't have been invited if Lord Stradcombe and his wife were not friends of Reuben's parents. They dote on your cousin's husband, even though they are not exactly ecstatic about you and your association with that Hobhouse woman.'

'Stop that at once, Bernice!' Reuben demanded, his narrow face tightening. 'I really cannot understand you sometimes.'

Bernice fixed the largest aquamarine eyes Arabella had ever seen on her husband, and they hardened. 'I don't like your brother or his wife, Reuben, or anyone who fought for the Boers!' There was cold repudiation in her voice, and catching Arabella's eye, she looked away from her with haughty disdain. 'I'm going to find Miriam and Selwyn.' She took a step forward suddenly, whisking out the back of her bustled skirt, and threaded her way between the guests without a backward glance.

'I'm sorry about that,' Reuben said stiffly, his face changed to a heavy anger. 'Bernice seems to enjoy embarrassing me.'

Arabella looked up into his eyes, and smiled. Reuben was no dissembler. He was genuinely honest. He wrote significant and brilliant articles for Isaac's newspaper, and his taste in art was nothing less than exquisite.

He stared back into the extraordinary green eyes. His voice was gentle when he spoke. 'This is not going to be easy for you, or for Isaac and Rachel, but for my Papa's sake, we must see it through – especially in front of all his family and friends.' Then his blue eyes warmed, and he took her arm. 'Come, let's go and find my rebel brother and his feminist wife.'

Dressed in a creation of Althea's dressmaker, Arabella looked elegant in a gently bustled gown of pale-lime foulard, embroidered with matching beads and trimmed with flounces of black lace, as she walked forward on Reuben's arm into the buffet room, a small aigrette of diamanté sparkling in her hair, upswept in the fashionable Pompadour style. Earlier that evening, she had taken out the peridot pendant Ben had given her and turned it over, staring at it. It matched her gown, but it brought back such painful memories, mocking her as it lay twinkling in the palm of her hand, that she had hidden it away again, out of sight, preferring to wear no jewelry.

An enormous Waterford chandelier was suspended above the large centre table, divided down the middle with every kind of kosher delicacy on one side, and choice offerings for the Gentile guests on the other. Surrounding a large shining silver épergne, the table groaned with claret cup in enormous glass punchbowls with fluted edges, delicious platters of quail, chicken, thin slices of venison, huge game pies, cold salads of all descriptions, fish and vegetable, fancy pastries, open tarts, rich puddings made with thick cream, and butter exquisitely shaped in the form of swans. There were huge bowls of summer flowers on the heavy, highly polished sideboard, with its giant seven-branched silver candelabra.

Arabella, who had dreaded the occasion, found herself moved by the sight of the family and friends filling the rooms with a great press of life, as there was a sudden silence and speeches were made, and letters from absent family and friends read with moist eyes, with rows of faces on either side turned towards the couple who had married three decades ago.

Dinner was announced, and Reuben escorted Arabella to the buffet table, placing a gold-rimmed china plate in her hands.

'The jellied consommé is excellent, Miss Allen, and so is the chicken, and afterwards I recommend the wine mousse. I've not tasted anything quite like it for a long time.'

Arabella turned swiftly at the sound of the familiar voice. Something was trembling in her face, like reflected light, as she confronted Deneys du Rand, who was looking dashingly handsome in a dark broadcloth suit, the narrow black tie setting off the flawless white shirt and golden hair to perfection.

Trying to suppress the immediate rush of blood through her veins, she looked around for Reuben, but he had tactfully disappeared into the throng of guests. She said carefully, 'But you were not invited –'

'I'm a gatecrasher, to put it bluntly.' He raised a glass of champagne, with a most charming and heart-stopping smile. Against all reason, she was suddenly absurdly pleased to see him in these alien surroundings.

'Does Isaac know?' She asked mischievously. 'If he doesn't, you could land him in a terrific mess with his father.'

A sardonic gleam lurked somewhere behind his lively brown eyes and even in repose, a faint smile played around the corners of his mouth. 'Isaac dared me. He said I didn't have the courage to face his father and friends – all my former enemies. He said it was all very well in time of war, but what about peace-time? He thinks his father is callous and insensitive to the new situation in this country. So, to prove a point, I'm here for the hell of it.' He cocked his head to one side. 'Besides, he told me that after much persuasion, you had agreed to come.' His tone was easy, but his face had a strange hard set to it. 'I didn't think I would enjoy it, but I am – every minute of it.'

Arabella was shocked; it showed in her voice and in the tremulous flutter of her small pale hands holding the half-filled plate of food. 'But how did you get in? You couldn't possibly have walked through the front door undetected.'

The lines on either side of his mouth deepened quizzically. 'You seem to forget, Miss Allen, that I've had plenty of practice entering enemy camps.'

Suddenly he was watching her, and her mind filled with remembered visions. Her cheeks grew warm, and though she knew she should hold him at arm's length for her own good, she was increasingly aware of him as a man, acutely feeling his nearness, as she struggled to avoid his waiting, watching regard.

'But if you're caught among all these guests of the Brandauers, I mean – many of them are still very anti-Boer.' Lamely she waved a hand about the crowded room.

A slow smile curved the corners of his mouth upward. 'This is the best place to get lost – in a crowd of people. If I do get caught –' he paused and stared reflectively into space '– I shall just have to cross that bridge when it comes.'

She noticed again that his warm, clever eyes were watching her speculatively, without appearing to do so, and again she was aware of her thumping heart.

'When you have finished eating,' he said casually, strolling beside her as she filled her plate with delicacies she knew she would never eat, 'I think we should go the whole hog, as you English say, and enjoy a few dances. Now what do you think of that idea?'

She blushed with embarrassment. 'Dance? Oh no, I couldn't! I haven't ever danced much, and when I did it was so long ago I wouldn't remember any of the steps.'

'It's like riding a bicycle – once learned, never forgotten.' Deneys considered her closely, as if she had captured his total interest. 'I, too, am rusty, but that can easily be remedied by putting the forgotten skills to the test, wouldn't you say?'

'I don't think it a wise idea in the situation,' she managed to choke out, as she tried to eat a small piece of delicious spiced chicken.

'But an interesting one, and one you really want to accept. You resemble me, Miss Allen, in that you like to take risks – especially when there's a strong element of danger. I enjoy the danger, while you – if you feel strongly about something – will ignore it. Am I right?'

Arabella was suddenly frightened by the violence of her feelings. During their few, brief encounters, Deneys had always troubled her, awakening her to something she did not want to understand. In the past, he had been her enemy, in a bitter and fiercely fought war; in the present it was peace-time, and theoretically, she was the victor, he the defeated – though he hardly looked the part with his strong, proud bearing. And now, standing there, with the light of sheer devilment in his eyes, he looked a hundred times more attractive than she ever remembered.

Suddenly, she wanted with all her heart to dance with him, and she found her initial reluctance dissolving into a strange kind of courage. 'Thank you, Mr du Rand. I am deeply honoured by your invitation.'

'Good girl! For one moment there I thought you would deny me the pleasure.' His grin grew slightly roguish above the deep cleft chin. 'If you're finished with this wonderful spread, let's go.'

He led her purposefully through the guests crowding into the buffet room, buzzing with conversation and merry laughter, and into the elegant drawing room. Arabella faltered for a second as the musicians struck up *The Blue Danube* and Deneys escorted her into the foaming sea of bustled gowns and long black tails. Her heart thumped as she felt his arm about her, and she cautiously placed a hand upon his shoulder, instantly conscious of its hardness.

'Now enjoy yourself, Miss Allen. It can't be often you have the chance to dance with an outcast Boer!'

His eyes sparkled down into hers and she gave him a wan smile in return, realising that they were the most notorious couple on the floor. She was nervous in case she made a false move, and drew attention to them both, but she need not have worried, for as soon as they began to dance, she sensed his strength. It was there in the way he guided her, easily and yet with comforting firmness. With such support she could never slip or make a silly mistake, as chandeliers, shimmering gowns, dark dress-coats revolved around them, while at the centre of it all, only they seemed to exist. Everything else spun away and she was totally absorbed in the magic of his warm, responsive presence.

Then it was over, and Isaac and Rachel, who wore an off-the-shoulder, lemon and black barred-satin gown, stood beside them, in the crush of dancers.

'Deneys, how could you have agreed to Isaac's madness? It's the first time he has stepped into his father's house since before the war, and I was hoping – the whole family was hoping – for a reconciliation tonight.' Rachel was frowning as she nervously patted her shining dark hair swept bouffantly high and wide, and caught up by a jewelled comb.

Deneys was unperturbed. He smiled at her in a disarming manner. 'But Rachel, the war is over. I cannot see what harm I'm doing here. It had to happen some time, so why not now?'

She looked uncertainly at him and then at Arabella. 'It goes far deeper than that, Deneys, and you know it. Hatred still burns in many people. Your father is the same – he refuses to return here under British rule ...'

, 'Rachel, Rachel,' Isaac interrupted, standing steadfast and immovable as a boulder. He surveyed the crowd of dancers with a wry smile. 'Somebody has to do something to change it, to bring people together in a real reconciliation – and who better than their former arch enemy, Deneys du Rand? What real harm is he doing, I ask you?' He smiled mischievously. 'I'm glad you're here, Deneys, and Arabella too –'

Before Deneys could reply, the music stopped and all the guests were staring in their direction as Ruth Brandauer, a tall, regally erect, grey-haired woman in severe black satin and a dazzle of diamonds, bore down on them.

'Deneys du Rand! How dare you show your face in this house!'

Isaac started forward, but Deneys seized his arm. He was no longer smiling. He stood very still, as the lights glimmered on the incredulous faces of the guests, standing in motionless and ominous ranks.

Mrs Brandauer drew herself up to her full height, falling just below Deneys' shoulder. 'You came here to embarrass my husband and now you will leave instantly and never cross this threshold again!'

Isaac threw off Deneys' grip angrily, saying loudly, 'That is no way to talk to my friend, Mama. Deneys has as much right as any one of your guests to be here.'

'It's all right, Isaac – I can speak for myself.' Deneys stood there and did not move, but his eyes flashed about the room like brown lightning. 'The war is over, Mrs Brandauer. You robber barons and we Boers have to shake hands if we are to prevent another one.'

Mrs Brandauer was all acid hostility. 'Robber barons indeed! We will never shake hands with those who deprived us of our rights – rights for which we so courageously fought and won!'

Arabella's heart swelled with revulsion as a ripple of applause ran through the mass of restless, hating faces. She saw Reuben's wife, Bernice, toss her shapely brown head, and eye Isaac with cold triumph. Arabella wanted to shake her, and her face must have betrayed her desire, for Bernice, catching her caustic expression, perceptibly shrank back. Arabella stood amidst that vast sea of faces, not knowing that she had a youthful majesty, that her face glowed and that her eyes were an incandescent green.

But Mrs Brandauer's disapproval made no impression on Deneys. 'I'm not leaving because you order me from this house, Mrs Brandauer. Nothing and nobody is going to drive me away from any place where I belong in this country, ever again.'

'That's the biggest lie yet! You left of your own free will!' a shout challenged him. Then there was silence again, and a shuffling of feet.

Deneys ignored the interruption. 'I shall leave,' he went on with suppressed anger, 'because I do not feel comfortable in a house where there is no spirit of reconciliation.'

'I'm ashamed of the lot of you!' Isaac raised his voice commandingly. 'Deneys and his family have suffered just as much as any of you here. He lost everything –'

'We've lost sons and husbands and brothers. But their deaths will not be in vain – we will never give up what they died for!' a man bellowed, and faces swung angrily towards Isaac and Deneys, as Arabella clenched her hands together in rising fear and apprehension.

Rachel clutched Deneys' arm. 'Go! Go, Deneys,' she urged frantically, 'so that Isaac will shut up! For God's sake!'

Deneys nodded, sensing the ugly mood that now pervaded the room, as other guests began to crowd in from the buffet room. He looked at Arabella. 'I think it would be the better part of valour to leave, though I'd rather fight it out to the bitter end,' he told her, then shouldered his way past Isaac, and was gone.

A thunder-faced Jacob Brandauer entered, followed by his third son Selwyn – a robust, chestnut-haired man of medium height with very pale grey eyes. Jacob himself was a small man with a meticulously neat white moustache and beard, and straight white hair. He wore thin gold-rimmed glasses and had an aura of authority which was evident as soon as he stopped and faced Isaac in the pool of complete silence that had formed around them.

He raised his formidable eyebrows, focusing for a hard moment on his angry, burly son. 'Isaac,' he said sternly, in the modulated accent of Eastern Europe, 'I will see you in the library at once. And your mother will see Miss Allen in the morning room.'

Without another word, he turned on his well-polished heels and walked back through the crowd, which parted before him like the waters of the Red Sea before the Israelites.

5

The ornately decorated door of the morning room swung closed and Arabella found herself in a lavishly furnished room containing ebony furniture, cabinets of buhl and ormulu, heavy gilt mirrors, small tables displaying elegant glass shaped candles, and bronze statues set beside elaborate Art Nouveau ornaments.

Reluctantly her eyes were drawn to the figure of Isaac's mother. Mrs Brandauer was sitting in a high-backed armchair beside the splendid fireplace, her features set in a cold, forbidding look. There was no warmth in her voice as she lifted a gold lorgnette to her eyes, and acknowledged Arabella's presence across the thick, heavy carpet. Arabella's own fingers shook as she clutched her small silver mesh purse and watched the blue-veined hand holding the lorgnette trembling with suppressed rage as it glittered with the fire of diamond rings.

'Why did you choose to disgrace me, Miss Allen, before all my guests, by dancing with an uninvited and hated Boer?'

Arabella looked at her with unswerving directness. 'Because he invited me to do so, Mrs Brandauer.'

Ruth shot her a glance of purest malevolence. 'So! You haven't changed your colours, Miss Allen! I'm not in the least bit surprised that your family disowned you after your disgraceful collaboration with that Hobhouse woman!'

Arabella lifted her chin a fraction higher, refusing to appear at all upset. 'I am not here for a re-trial, Mrs Brandauer. I went through all that during the war.'

'I have no patience to argue the finer points with you, Miss, but as I have said before, the war is *not* over yet, and won't be for years to come – if ever. Deneys du Rand is an unprincipled opportunist. He only returned when he thought he could gain entrance into the doors of power and take back what he asserts he has lost. He is clever and unscrupulous – but a leopard never changes its spots, mark my words. Once he has what he wants, he and his kind will attempt to close us out again. Make no mistake about it, there is no reconciliation in him.'

She paused for breath, one hand fluttering to her breast in great agitation. Then she continued, talking faster, 'I saw right through him, and that's why he tries to humiliate me and my dear Jacob.' Her brows contracted fiercely. 'He is laughing at us, Miss Allen – he's using you and that detestable feminist widow of Judge Rigby, who has many friends in high places and useful contacts everywhere, just as he's using our Isaac. He's not a clever lawyer for nothing. He will always be a most relentless and ruthless enemy.'

Arabella pulled fiercely at the fingers of her white gloves. 'I cannot believe that Deneys – Mr du Rand – would do such a thing! He is sincere about the new cause – as are Generals Botha and Smuts.'

Ruth stared at her. 'You poor misguided fool, Miss Allen!' she snapped, lifting her pale grey eyes so that the glaring white below them shone. 'I do not trust either Botha or Smuts – especially Smuts. They play at being friendly with us because they need our wealth. De Wet at least speaks out honestly for another republic.'

Arabella took a deep breath, sensing that whatever Ruth Brandauer was, and she appeared to be many things, she was not a fool. 'But Deneys du Rand is your son Isaac's best friend!'

Ruth's immaculately coiffeured grey hair became slightly tousled and she was trembling again. 'Isaac will suffer yet through this dangerous friendship.' She looked Arabella over, to see if she understood. 'The way things are, there will be trouble yet between the Boers, which will involve us all, but Isaac cannot see it. My son is a clever man, Miss Allen – but he is harmfully idealistic. The day will come when his so-called friends will turn on him, once they have used him well to their purpose, and that is the day I do not want to see.'

Those cold, dark words, that terrible look in Isaac's mother's face, made Arabella wilt inside for a moment, for she could see that for all Ruth's bitterness towards her son's actions, she still loved him deeply.

Ruth's eyes gleamed suddenly in the lamplight. 'That's why I ask you, Miss Allen, to make my son see sense. He has a great admiration for you. He will listen to you, and so will Rachel. Get him to give up this iniquitous relationship with du Rand – and I will see to it that all the influential doors still closed to you in this town are opened at once.'

Arabella kept her voice even as she said: 'I cannot do that, Mrs Brandauer. During the war, Deneys du Rand saved the life of my cousin's little son – with total disregard for his own safety. I cannot help you. If Isaac wants the friendship, that's his choice and I would be the last one to interfere.'

'Then you will never set foot in this house again, Miss Allen!' Ruth exclaimed, outraged. 'Do I make myself quite clear?' Her face was dark with loathing.

'You will go on fighting the war till you die, Mrs Brandauer,' Arabella said in a low voice. She was suddenly overwhelmed with the horror of it all, the nightmare of suspicion, hatred and bitterness which she hoped she had left behind. The past war flowed like an impassable river, treacherous and deep between them. She took a deep breath. 'I'll leave now, Mrs Brandauer, after I have said goodnight to Isaac and Rachel.'

Ruth Brandauer's face was flushed, her eyes full of loathing. 'You're an evil and dangerous woman! I'll do everything in my power to crush your friendship with my son and his wife!'

Arabella supported herself against a walnut table near the door, then stiffly walked out of the room, a lump of despair in her throat.

The débâcle at the Brandauers' party was raked over thoroughly for days. Arabella could scarcely pick up a newspaper without finding some reference to it, containing exaggerations and falsehoods; soon the whole affair took on an ominous significance, linking it to the underlying Boer-British rivalry. Isaac and his father were still not on speaking terms, and the rest of the family, except Miriam and Reuben, blamed Isaac.

But all this was swallowed up in the preparations for the next large meeting of the Women's League, to be held in a church hall near the centre of Johannesburg. Notices appeared in Isaac's paper, with a prominent write-up, and it was advertised on placards all over the town.

As the women arrived with Rachel and Isaac on the evening of the event, they were told that there had been rumours that it was going to be noisy; there might even be an attempt to smash it altogether by rough elements. Arabella was incredibly nervous. This was the largest meeting they had ever convened, and the most widely publicised.

The church hall was not very large, but it was already crammed to overflowing. People stood in the aisles, along the walls, sat on the floor, or on the deep windowsills. Arabella and Althea, as the main speakers, took their places on the platform before that formidable sea of faces, and never had Arabella felt her lack of height so much as in those first tense moments.

Patting her dark emerald toque, she eased herself into the seat beside Althea behind the central table with its large bowl of bronze and yellow chrysanthemums, shining like ragged golden balls under the few, dim gas-lights. The table, with its largest light, was the focus of shifting brilliance in the darkened hall, casting bright shadows on the walls and stretching up long fingers of light into the hidden rafters of the wooden ceiling.

Straightening the short matching green mantle about her shoulders with trembling fingers, she took a deep breath, let it out – and waited. She looked at Rachel and Isaac, and the other members of the League Committee, sitting in the front row, and smiled as Rachel nodded encouragingly. After Althea's speech, during which the audience became restless and impatient, she rose to address them. 'Ladies and gentlemen –'

Her next words were drowned in a deafening roar of, 'Go home, feminist – dirty Boer-lover!'

'Speak louder,' Althea hissed above the racket. 'You have to gain control of the meeting before they take it from you.'

Without another thought, Arabella suddenly shouted as loudly as she could manage: 'I *am* going to speak! This is *our* meeting!'

There was a burst of applause from her committee, and she outstared the audience for a moment, before putting her fingers to her mouth and letting out a piercingly shrill, discordant whistle.

There was a sudden silence, and Arabella proceeded, her voice steady and defiant.

'Women have traditionally played a major role in the family and the community. Besides their function of childbearing and rearing, women are largely responsible for educating the children and passing on their values.'

'That's their place – at home with the kids!' someone shouted from the body of the hall.

'Ignore those rude boors,' Althea urged, leaning towards her so that her hat tilted dangerously over one eye, threatening to lose its moorings.

Arabella continued, raising her voice with dogged determination. 'Women have not been encouraged to show signs of independence. They have not been given the opportunity to acquire job skills or received an education equal to their menfolk –'

'Women are not equal – and they never will be!' a strident voice informed the hall, and others answered it. Then there was silence again, and a shuffling of feet as she went on.

'Girls need to be trained more like men, which would give them businesslike habits and self-reliance. They should be taught –'

'Girls should be taught to run a decent home, like their mothers! They do not need the likes of you to tell them what to do!' Suddenly a man rose and shook his fist at her. 'I didn't even get a decent meal tonight when I got home from a hard day's work because my little woman was out, gossiping with her friends about all this equal women's rubbish! Neglect of the home and the kids and their husbands, that's what you're preaching!'

There was an instant clamour of dismay and derision from the audience. Isaac rose and faced the body of the hall. 'Let Miss Allen speak! That's what you're here for – to let her speak!'

Faces turned angrily to him, as another man bellowed, 'She's preaching destruction of the home, the downfall of civilisation! If a woman's not in her home seeing to her kids and husband, society will fall into chaos!'

'Who's to pay for all this female education, I ask you?' another male voice demanded. 'Are you going to throw away your hard-earned pay on an education for your daughter that she'll never use when she marries?'

Arabella had prepared her speech, and was determined that it would be heard, so when a lull fell, she took advantage of it and shouted: 'Girls should be taught to think that work is as necessary for a woman as for a man. Their education should teach them that they have work to do outside as well as inside their homes, and neither must be neglected.'

'How can they do both? It's a full-time job trying to do one well enough,' a female voice demanded, and the audience's voices rose again in jubilant response.

Althea leaned quickly across, her hat a flash of silver in the light. 'Don't answer any questions at this stage, my dear,' she murmured. 'Don't get sidetracked, just keep on with your speech.'

Nodding, Arabella began again, 'I say to you –'

'Equality of women is rubbish!'

'– that once women are given their true recognition –'

A crescendo of voices grew like a wind blowing through the hall. 'You don't know what you are talking about! You're going against the order of God and the laws of the Bible! Down with all hateful feminists!'

At this point, many in the crowd stood up, some making threatening gestures. Arabella's voice was drowned in the volume of sound, and Althea quickly rose, trying to quieten them, as Isaac and the committee were attempting to do on the floor, but to no avail. Pandemonium broke out, and there was scuffling in the body of the hall. Isaac drew back his massive right arm like a flash of a piston, his fist crashing on to the jaw of a man who had grabbed his arm, about to smash a bottle over his head. Suddenly there was the sound of whistles, and uniformed policemen rushed into the hall.

The crowd started to scatter in all directions, threatening to rush the platform and overturn the table. Arabella and Althea jumped back in alarm, grabbing their papers as the stampeding grew thunderous. Arabella caught Althea's arm, as a man rushed up, cursing and shaking his fist. Then he was down as someone hit him with an upswept fist, and the hall seemed to swoop into orbit around Arabella.

'Are you all right, Arabella, Mrs Rigby?' a deep male voice was saying at her elbow and there, beside a tousled Althea, crumpled and golden, was Deneys du Rand, who had fought his way through the crowd to reach the platform, and knocked down the attacker.

Arabella nearly fainted with relief. At least, she thought wildly, there is one point of normality in this madhouse – and that is Deneys! She gazed around, very conscious of his hand on her arm. Most of the frenzied mob were dispersing as the police drove them from the hall, and Isaac, his coat torn and upper lip bruised, escorted the ashen-faced committee members towards the platform.

'You can't say you didn't get enough exposure this time, ladies,' he joked painfully. 'We'll have to get you a bodyguard for the next one.'

'Isn't it too dangerous for women to expose themselves to this kind of rough-house, Isaac?' Deneys asked, frowning as he helped Arabella and Althea down the steps to the body of the floor. 'It doesn't seem worth the risks.'

'We are going to get the vote, Mr du Rand,' Althea said with grim determination, 'one way or another – and no one, not even this ignorant mob, is going to stop us!'

'But you're arousing great fears, Mrs Rigby, and in doing so, you're in danger of bringing down the whole order of society by its ears.' Deneys spoke evenly, but his lips were pursed in faint derision.

Arabella's face was pale. Moistening her lips, she answered him steadily. 'It only seems that way, because certain outdated habits of thought must necessarily be eradicated before women can move into their rightful place in our society. Change is always painful.'

Deneys turned to look down at her. 'And what will happen once you have your so-called rights and can tyrannically run society as you please? What will our role be then? You won't need us any more. You'll be able to do it all on your own.'

Arabella was breathing agitatedly. 'We'll always need both sexes, Deneys. That is the balance of society, which will never change.'

A strange smile played about his lips. 'That is very kind of you, Arabella, but it doesn't appear that way to me or to many other men.'

Disconcerted by this rebuke, Arabella eyed him warily as he bent down and collected the rest of her papers, scattered about the floor. Then Isaac and Rachel, and the other women and their husbands were joining them amidst the shambles of overturned chairs. Before she could collect herself properly, Deneys was escorting her out into the darkness of the Johannesburg evening.

Arabella was very aware of his body's vigorous, athletic strength, emphasised in the smart business suit; she noticed how the lamplight in the street outside turned his tousled blond hair into burnished gold. Suddenly something prophetic stirred in her, and she knew that this moment would haunt her always. Then she was saying, 'I know you don't care for the idea of women's suffrage, Deneys – that you fear a female tyranny as you call it, so why did you attend this meeting?'

A mischievous smile played about his mouth. 'Isaac said you people needed support, and I admit I was curious to see how it would go. I left my practice for a short while to observe how the public would react to your outlandish proposals.' He gave her a penetrating look, then a grin. 'I arrived late so stood at the back. I didn't know you had such a good pair of lungs! You had me fooled, behind that gentle feminine exterior.'

Arabella drew herself up, bridling a little. 'It's not a ladylike undertaking, I'm afraid, as you have been so quick to point out.'

His eyes narrowed against the brightness of the small aureole of lamplight, where moths hovered in their self-destructive dance of death. 'That's the whole problem. It turned out to be an ugly rout with nothing achieved. Is that what you really want? Is this what you are selling your soul for – to throw away everything that a women traditionally represents?'

'There's another side to women that no one wants to see, Deneys. Everyone wants to believe we are gentle and submissive with no identity of our own, but we are tough underneath, and it's just as well for the world to know it. In my view, it does not detract one jot from what a woman traditionally represents – it only *adds* to her stature,' she said decisively. 'This is no time for meek acceptance, for acceptance has become a betrayal.'

His brow slanted up. 'Then your troubles, not only as a suffragist, but also as a woman, have only just begun.'

The heat of his gaze set a forbidden flame burning within her. Silence fell between them, as Isaac and the other men shepherded the women towards the waiting vehicles. Though Arabella could hear their voices, and the noise of the far-off traffic, it seemed to her that she and Deneys were set apart in some peculiar intimacy, as if a circle had been drawn about them and they were the only two people in the world. He was like a strong magnet that drew her progressively nearer, despite their differences, and despite her attempts at logic and restraint.

But he was undeniably and forcefully against her cause. A cold little fear was beginning to throb in her breast. It would do no good to get too close to this man; it would only bring pain and disillusionment in the end. She had to forget him – Deneys du Rand had no place in her life.

6

It was early spring, and even though the post-war slump had hit the entire country, Nature did not alter her course. Buds swelled on the trees at the Villa Valencia; delicate tassels and soft dottings that would soon be leaves lay like mist on brown branches. Everywhere the gardens bloomed with pansies, hyacinths and geraniums around the croquet lawns, tennis court, pergolas and summerhouses.

Arabella stood on the freshly swept gravel driveway near the front door as Isaac jumped down from the driver's seat of his new Silver Rolls Royce with its wide running-boards and huge mudguards, and Rachel sat beaming in the front seat, a silk headscarf fastened over her bonnet.

'Come on, stop staring at it like a startled rabbit, Arabella, and get in!' Isaac ordered as he placed her one modest valise in the back with the rest of the luggage, and made a place for her beside it. 'You'd think we were going away forever, with all Rachel's luggage, instead of just a weekend on Johan Struik's farm, only fifteen miles away!'

'Oh, do be quiet, Isaac,' Rachel said, laughing. 'I'm glad you decided to come, Arabella. Deneys will be there too, and he's very good company, when all's said and done.'

The world stilled for Arabella as she stood there in the clear sunshine; she had both dreaded and longed to see him again. However, knowing his attitude towards her work, it would be difficult enough, but to see him again as a man would be very disconcerting, especially as she knew he could have no place in her life.

Rachel handed her a headscarf. 'You'd better tie this on or else you'll lose your gay bonnet.' She smiled affectionately at Isaac as he cranked the engine. 'This car is my husband's new baby – he couldn't wait to show it to you.' She relaxed her slim body against the seat. 'No more begging his cousin for the use of his car on special occasions. My, but we have come up in the world!'

'Well, that's a good way for a suffragette to talk. Soon we'll be driving our own cars!' Arabella chuckled as she settled on to the hard back seat, almost enveloped by hunting rifles and valises.

The car would not start and Isaac, forgetting the ladies present, swore loudly and gustily.

'I would never have guessed that Isaac knew such language,' Rachel whispered, giggling into her handkerchief, in an effort to hide her amusement.

'Why on earth must she do this to me now?' he demanded, quite red in the face.

Trying to stifle her mirth, Rachel said innocently, 'But you said it was as easy as playing a mashie shot, Isaac.' At that, he gave her a black look and with a heavy grunt, opened the side of the bonnet and looked in. She trilled: 'Are you sure you turned on the petrol, darling?'

There was a deep silence as Isaac's head re-emerged. Slowly, as if he was performing a ceremony of great importance, he closed the bonnet and climbed back in the car.

'It must have slipped my mind with all your irritating chatter,' he growled.

'Never mind, Isaac,' Arabella said impishly, as she tied the headscarf over her bonnet, 'Nobody's perfect.'

Pretending not to hear, Isaac fiddled with the button arrangement on the dashboard. He then went around to the front of the car again and seized the starting-handle. There was a short chug, then another and another ... and the car began vibrating loudly.

Then they were on their way, roaring past pedestrians who robustly shouted after them. Isaac hooted loudly and waved expansively as hysterically barking dogs raced madly in the clouds of their dusty wake. Leaning back in an easy position, he called out above the commotion: 'She has a beautiful body, Arabella. Listen to her humming now like a little bee.'

'Spoken like a true man!' Rachel tittered, and Arabella giggled in agreement behind her shawl as, screened by clouds of dust, they left all habitation and mad, howling dogs behind.

The first night in the rambling and unpretentious farmhouse near Pretoria, nestling in a screen of trees, was long and restless for Arabella, who tossed and turned. The afternoon had been relaxed enough with Johan Struik, a large, genial Afrikaner, his lively wife Annie – an English-speaking woman of Irish descent – their five excited young children, and six other house-guests, until Deneys had arrived just before dinner on his fast Boer pony. The company had gone out to meet him, and she had felt the reflected glow of the enthusiasm of their greetings as she stood in their midst. Everyone had milled about him, chatting eagerly, and she was again reminded of his magnetic personality.

During dinner, she studied the manner in which Deneys fitted into this kind of informal social occasion. He talked with ease and authority on the widest range of subjects, always pitting himself subtly against Isaac's original and brilliant mind, and the wit and general bantering of the other guests.

Watching him across the table, she had guessed his power, and she knew he guessed hers. She felt it in him, and flushed, embarrassed at her own thoughts.

After dinner, with the children in bed, she was asked to play the pianoforte in the sitting room. Everyone gathered around as she played Liszt's *Campanello* without leaving out a single note. She then struck up a song, and the company joined in, but it was Deneys' deeply resonant voice and Sarie Struik's pure soprano that soared above the rest. Then Deneys fetched a chair, and placing it beside the piano stool, he sat down and joined in her rendering of Schubert's *Marche Militaire*, which had the whole company beating the accompaniment. She was very aware of him beside her, as her fingers flew over the keys with his, and common sense once again warned her to be careful, to distance herself from him.

Now, unable to sleep, she rose and dressed, lingering for a while at the half-shuttered window overlooking the wild beauty of the veld beyond the narrow border of the garden. Then, suddenly throwing away her caution, she crept out to the stables.

There, in the darkness, Lalique, the snow-white mare she had been given to ride that afternoon, lifted her head as Arabella whistled softly to her. Her ears pricked forward and her lip lifted in a quiet answering whicker. Then, head a little lower, she walked with great delicacy towards the half-opened hand with the little heap of brown sugar in it. She edged her flanks against the stable-post, rubbing it gently, and her muzzle went down to the sugar, silk lips against Arabella's palm.

Later, as they rode down the bridle-path in the very early morning mist towards the river, Arabella lifted her head, smelling the sweet fragrance of wild jasmine clinging to the branches of ancient, tangled trees, their humped roots writhing like dry snakes over the surface of the red soil. Her eyes seemed absorbed in the crystalline substance of the slowly lightening sky where brightly plumed small sunbirds swerved and swooped over the silent jungle of acacia trees. Everything was golden, from the irregular carpet of deep golden botterblom and orange daisies to the delicate, budding yellow stamens of the tall twinkle grass.

Further away, behind the trees, lay the river and the old moss-covered masonry of a long-forgotten broken wall, which seemed to merge into the surrounding bushes. The air was filled with the cries of African birds flitting among the branches of the shrubs and the buffalo thorn trees, and she felt some of the restlessness leave her.

She slowed to a trot, then to a walk, and as she turned the corner of the uneven, rugged path on to the winding river trail, she saw a man riding towards her on a small, dark brown pony, through the long grasses between the trees and the path. She knew at once that it was Deneys from the set of his strong, compact shoulders. He waved as he rode up, and they reined in.

'Good morning, Arabella,' he said, breaking easily into English. 'I see that you too couldn't sleep.'

She wished she did not feel so shy. 'It's so beautiful here,' she said. 'It seems a pity to waste even a minute asleep.'

A smile played about his lips. 'Africa is beginning to seep into your blood, and once that happens, you are doomed to stay forever, did you know that?'

Disconcerted, she looked away, feeling her heart race at the way he was looking at her. Then she turned back and met his eyes, challenge for challenge. 'Only time will tell, won't it?'

He laughed, that same bubbling, infectious sound she had first heard so long ago on the hillside at Suncrest Farm, then he asked, 'Do you mind if I join you?'

'I'll try not to.'

For a moment she could not stop an answering smile from lighting up her face. His strong, handsome features stirred exciting and confusing feelings she found extremely difficult to control. Today, Deneys was casually dressed; she was acutely aware of the powerful shoulders and muscular throat where the white shirt gaped, exposing blond curls that shadowed the bronze expanse of chest. His light-coloured trousers and dark boots displayed the strong length of his thighs. Deneys carried himself with the proud, erect bearing of a man born in the saddle, and well in control of his animal. Everything about him was sturdy, solid, as the early sunlight flooded down between the branches, lighting his face. A golden knight in a golden world ... the sudden thought flitted through her mind, and she chided herself for being so ridiculous.

His pony flicked its head to one side, the mane sliding like dark silk across the brown arch of its neck, and he murmured, 'I cannot fathom you at all, Arabella Allen. You are, without a doubt, the most unusual woman I have ever met.'

They rode along in silence for a while, then stopped at the river and looked across it towards the spreading veld and the clusters of trees rising in the distance, as the sound of a red-chested cuckoo stole clearly through the air.

'The old Transvaal at its best,' Deneys said suddenly, with the boyish enthusiasm that was such a part of his charm.

'You must have missed it,' she said quietly, 'when you lived in Madagascar.'

His brown eyes hooded briefly, and he toyed with the riding whip and reins before answering. 'There were times, I admit, when I sat on a wild hillside on that island and looked out across the lakes and the forest and the swamps teeming with crocodiles, and further, at the vast open plains grazed by herds of wild cattle, when I longed for this country.' He paused, then went on: 'My brother died out there, buried in a lonely grave. And all he talked about before he died, was coming home – ' He stopped abruptly, as if suddenly recalling her presence. Then, 'I am a white African,' he continued, 'for want of a better term. My homeland's history has been short and very bloody – its very soil is dark with blood. The strength of my people has been in the land, and the land in my people, but it has been ravished, annexed and stolen. Everything has changed, but it has not affected that strength, whatever way one looks at it. And it is a strength to be respected, a force that will never die, believe me.'

Then he grinned, exposing strong white teeth, and pointed his whip at a tree. 'Do you know why we call the buffalo thorn the *wag 'n bietjie*?' She shook her head, still shaken by what he had said. 'Well, once entangled in its thorns, it is difficult to get loose and so you have to wait a minute – wag 'n bietjie.'

The tension was broken, and they both laughed as they started to walk on again.

'Is it used for anything?' Arabella asked, intrigued.

'It has its uses,' Deneys said conversationally. 'Our Boer commandoes roasted its dried red berries when we ran out of coffee during the war – which was often, towards the end. You know what we are like for our coffee.'

A hoarse, loudly whispered *waa-waa-dedaa* of the shy Cape robin interrupted him, and his eyes searched under the bushes for the little bird with its distinctive orange breast and prominent white eyebrow.

'We call him *Jan-fred-erik* from the sound he makes.'

'And what is that one?' Arabella pointed to a bird in a hanging cup-shaped basket of lichens and cobwebs, slung between the forked ends of a high branch under which they were passing.

He followed her gaze. 'That is the black-headed oriole. If you listen carefully, you can hear its call – there it goes!' A pleasant liquid *pheeeo* filled the air.

'Where did you learn so much about the birds and animals of the bush?' Arabella ducked her head under an overhanging branch.

233

Deneys was silent for a while and she thought he had not heard her, then, as she was about to repeat the question he said, 'As boys, my brothers and I would take our horses from my father's stables in Bloemfontein, and go out for days in the veld hunting, fishing, and sleeping under the stars. Even though I was a townsboy, I had plenty of outdoor life. I was fortunate to have both, and that, I suppose, was where I learnt most of what I know.'

Arabella took a deep breath, broaching a subject she had wanted to ask him about for a long time. 'But why, Deneys, if you exiled yourself after the war and refused to take the Oath of Allegiance to the British Crown, if as you believe, the British plundered your country ... why then did you return to the very situation you hate most – your country under British rule?'

He looked at her in genuine surprise. 'Times change, and we must change with them, or else we perish. There is only one sensible path for this country now, if we want to avoid another disastrous war, and that is the middle way – a joining of both sides. I cannot see an alternative. We are not strong enough without you British, and Madagascar was not the place to spend the rest of one's life.' He paused reflectively, then added, 'I admit it isn't easy to live under the rule of those who have no time for our language and culture, who try to force us to behave like Englishmen in our own land.'

He smiled at her; he was honest, but not hostile. Then his voice deepened. 'And why did *you* work in the concentration camps during the war, among the very people you hated most – your enemies?'

Seeing that he was genuinely interested, she answered simply and truthfully. 'Because I was there and I was a nursing sister, and they were suffering, in many cases unnecessarily. I no longer regarded them as enemies, but helpless, vulnerable people caught between two fires.' She sighed, trying not to think back to the pain of the past, to Marie Roussouw and the others. 'I saw great suffering on both sides of that war, Deneys, and it was a war caused solely by you men. There's no need for conflict, if only we can understand one another's needs and learn to compromise.'

He measured her with his eyes. 'And now you fight for women.'

They rode on, the clink of spurs and the creak of saddlery pleasant in the warming air. 'It's all part of evolution,' she said crisply. For a moment, a mischievous spark lit up her eyes. 'Perhaps when we tyrannical women hold important positions in the State, and have a say in the governing of it, there will be no more wars, because most women will never easily agree to it, knowing they must send the sons they bore.'

There was a snap of silence, then he commented mockingly, 'I don't know about that. There seems to be a war mentality among British women – flinging themselves into the path of oncoming traffic, tying themselves to railings, and going to gaol to bring attention to their cause. Given power, I don't think those women would shy away from war, if it was in their interest.'

She considered. 'You won't find those goings on in this country, for here it is a purely constitutional movement. I confess to a certain feeling of repulsion at the militant actions of the British suffragettes who, I think, only bring great harm to their cause.'

'But you admitted once that what you are doing is not ladylike, that you are prepared to shout out and fight for what you want. If that is not a kind of warfare, what is it?'

The mocking quality in his eyes had gone. It was as if some vibrant flame had sprung up between them, as if they had touched, body to body, and her heart beat suffocatingly fast. This was the kind of moment she had never dared to think about, which she had forced from her mind for so long. And yet, the longing was still there, still living deep inside her.

She sat there, unable to control the fierce emotions that poured through her entire mind and body, unable to reason herself through it, even though she disagreed with everything he had said about women. Quite illogically, she wanted this man. Deep down, she must always have wanted him, and now that desire was undeniable ... but unattainable.

The moment was broken by Deneys' voice saying cheerfully, 'I'll race you to the edge of the river!'

A nervous fluttering attacked Arabella's stomach as she caught his eyes, which were dancing with a bold challenge. She hated racing, she had always hated it, from the days at Allenbury Manor with Rosamunde and her friends. The speed frightened her, the sense that she was not in control, the awesome power of the animal beneath her.

'There's a hedge in the middle –' she started hesitantly, then stopped as he peered at her sceptically.

'Ride straight then, if you prefer it,' he called. 'Hey, Kitchener, go get it!'

Arabella smiled at the dry humour of the horse's name, but then her eyes flared in open admiration at the sight of the horse and its rider. The horse, feeling the firm lilt of Deneys' voice, checked on the turn and paused, his hooves close, his body perfectly balanced. For a moment, the dark brown horse pranced in high-stepping rhythm while he arched his neck and flagged his tail. The rider was in total control of the animal's movements, and he did it with such ease that the pair flowed together as one.

She watched as Deneys backed him, and then, putting his spurs to his side, galloped towards the high hedge near the river. Flexing his thighs and with a touch of his whip, he set the horse at the jump. Kitchener reached the hedge, gathered himself and soared easily over it into the high yellow grass beyond.

Deneys was, without a doubt, a superb horsemen. Arabella was not a little envious of the trust between the animal and rider that inspired such grace and disciplined power. Her own horse followed, and she clung to the reins, urging Lalique along the straighter path. Breathless from terror and exhilaration, she galloped across the veld as Deneys reined in, and turned his steed to meet her at the far side, mane and tail glittering black in the sunlight. Overhead, birds in flight cast fragile shadows over the thick grass, and the strengthening sun above threw a cataract of light.

'You're too tense,' he called, as she drew up to him. 'Too afraid of your animal. She needs and wants to be driven harder.'

'But I'm afraid to overstrain her,' Arabella objected breathlessly.

'She can take it, believe me.' The flat of his hand gently stroked Kitchener's neck muscles. 'I can see that you do have concern for that mare – and that you're not easy in the saddle, but with practise you can get to know her so well that you will be able to sense her every mood.'

Taking a deep breath, and shielding her eyes from the sun, she said suddenly before she could stop herself, 'However did you get back here from Madagascar? Isaac said you had nothing left except the clothes on your back.'

He regarded her for a brief second with a raised eyebrow. 'You really ask the darnedest questions, Miss Allen – constantly taking me off my guard, which I'm beginning to believe is deliberate. If you must know, I had to sell my last span of oxen and my wagons.' His eyes suddenly crinkled with brilliant humour. 'You won't believe this, but I had no clothes at all. I even had to borrow a smart suit from Aaron Brandauer for the suffrage meeting at Mrs Rigby's.'

Arabella threw back her head and laughed, the peals of mirth filling the air. Deneys frowned, looking at her with mock astonishment. 'And I thought I had earned your sympathy at last!'

She managed to stop and said hoarsely, 'That makes two of us! My gown at the meeting belonged to Mrs Rigby's daughter, and I felt so self-conscious of the fact – the borrowed plumes, I mean.'

Then he was laughing with her. 'Well, I never would have guessed your devious little secret.' As the sky turned to bright azure, he held his whip high in his hand. 'I think that a good hearty breakfast beckons – I'll race you back to the bridle path.'

236

She was sad to think that their ride together was ending, as they trotted towards the bridle path, then stopped to walk at a more sedate pace. She sensed rather than heard him riding alongside her, vibrantly alive to his presence. She knew that she was perilously close to falling into a subtle but insidious trap with this man. If this feeling had anything to do with love, she must dismiss it. Love was an emotion she had come to mistrust, for to her, it represented all the cruelty and betrayal between men and women.

He must never know, she thought desperately, just how much she had come to desire and admire him, no matter what it cost her. Then, facing the broad sweep of path leading to the stables, she urged Lalique on into a short step, then a long stride as she and Deneys cantered towards it.

7

The rest of the spring and the summer stretched before Arabella at the Villa Valencia ... with long uninterrupted days to work for the suffrage movement. She had looked forward to this time, hoping it would give her a chance to find some answers to the many problems and obstacles facing the suffragettes. Yet the days were slipping by, and much of the work remained undone, for Deneys had started to be a constant visitor during the weekends.

He had been working hard at building up a legal practice in Heideville while he made up his mind whether to remain at the Side-Bar, or go on to the Bar. As his number of clients increased, he had time on his hands during the weekends, and began to appear at the Villa each Saturday afternoon. At first, Althea pressed him to stay for supper and the evening, and a new vitality crept into the meals as the guests gathered about the table. However, after a few weeks, something in the way Althea looked at Arabella began to disturb her. She made excuses for the growing disapproval in her friend's eyes. She told herself there was nothing to be concerned about. She had resolutely turned her back upon love, but wanted to keep this new friendship that had blossomed so amazingly; she did not want to lose it just when it was becoming excitingly satisfying and necessary to her, so she tried to overlook what she had no wish to see and hear.

One warm afternoon, as the sun filtered softly through the delicate webs of fine Venetian lace which covered the long arched windows of the sitting room in the Villa Valencia, Arabella and Althea sat on either side of the coffee-table, the silver tea tray between them, in a silence that became harder to break. Arabella tried to put aside all her uneasy feelings, as she allowed herself to study Althea, in her long pale-green tea gown. She was stroking a fluffy smoky-grey cat on her lap, and on one wrist the dainty blue and red stones seemed to leap out of the twisted gold bracelet she wore. As usual, there were flowers everywhere – white narcissi and pale-yellow primroses, jonquils and brightly coloured ranunculus in gleaming silver bowls, the sun striking golden sparks off the massive firedogs, clustered tongs and brass shovels on either side of the fireplace, which supported a large cloisonné vase of the utmost beauty.

'Althea,' Arabella said at last, 'I believe you disapprove of my friendship with Deneys du Rand. I know he is an Afrikaner, and that he fought against us. I know all that . . .'

'Arabella, you may think I'm interfering, but since you have raised the subject, I feel I should have my say in a matter that not only concerns you, but the whole suffrage movement.'

Arabella swallowed hard, a pool of sunlight softly outlining her high-necked white blouse with its two rows of wide lace frills and matching wide lace cuffs. She tried to suppress a growing resentment. 'The whole suffrage movement? Isn't that rather an exaggeration?'

Althea permitted herself an ironical smile. 'No, on the contrary. Every moment that takes your attention away from it, endangers the cause of women everywhere.'

Arabella's voice sounded exasperated, but she was determined to keep calm. 'My friendship with Deneys doesn't make any difference to my wholehearted commitment to female suffrage. I still feel as strongly about it as I ever did.'

Althea was sipping her tea, and looking at her sceptically. 'Arabella, you may not be aware of the change in yourself since this man has come into your life. You no longer spend the same amount of time on your work, nor do you demonstrate the same intensity of purpose. He's very clever, Deneys du Rand, and very charming. You know that I have never held a person's convictions or background against them, not even the opposing side, but this man has no time for the women's movement – he has made no secret of that! He sees no place for it in his life, nor in yours, and I'm very afraid that he will influence you to give it up.'

Arabella rose, her long beige skirt swishing softly as she walked to the window and, drew back the lace curtains. She could see the espaliered pear trees drawing patterns on the walls, and birds fluttering and preening on the sun-silvered roof. She knew that what Althea said was partly true – she *had* neglected her work of late – but she had enjoyed, for the moment, the wild clamour of ecstasy in Deneys' company, the delicious pain of his absence.

'What about Rachel and Isaac? They are married, yet she still does her suffrage work –' she suddenly burst out, turning to face Althea.

Althea's eyes narrowed, and she said, in an angry low voice, 'Isaac is behind Rachel in all she does – *that's* the difference! This man will stand in your way, Arabella – I know he will!'

Arabella paled, then she surprised a sudden wistful expression on the older woman's face. As their eyes met, she saw an unexpected, deep sadness in her friend's face, and she was suddenly reminded of all the stimulating, inspiring times they had spent together.

Full of remorse, she said gently, 'Althea – no one will ever influence me against my own wishes, you know that. – I've come through great opposition in my life, but always on my own terms.'

Althea frowned, then, pulling herself together, she said quietly, stroking the cat, 'Come and sit down, my dear. It's time you should know a little of my life so that you will understand my concern for you.' She sighed, then went on, 'I married my dream husband. Bedford was everything I ever desired – intelligent, witty, handsome, athletic – not unlike Deneys du Rand. We married when I was very young – seventeen. He was ten years older, a newly qualified barrister from Edinburgh. We were very happy during those first years with our four children, or so I thought. Then Bedford went up to East Africa, somewhere near Nairobi, and he fell in love with the place. By that time he was the leading judge of Johannesburg, a man much respected by his colleagues and friends. He gave up everything here, saying he wanted to go and work up there in the wilds. He knew I couldn't join him – not with four young children to raise and not a school anywhere. There was also the terrible danger of malaria and other diseases. I begged him to stay, but to no avail.'

Her lips tightened for a second into a grim line. 'He left me and the children for years. He wrote occasionally, saying he was the only lawyer in the area, living with an English parson and his daughter.' She paused, considering her next words carefully. 'Then, just before the war broke out, he died of malaria and I had to go up to fetch his things. There was no explanation from the parson or his daughter.' A current of anger passed through her eyes. 'He left me and his children, my dear, because he was selfish, as most men are – they put their own desires above all else. I know, I have learned in the hard way, and I gave everything I had to my husband.'

She stared at Arabella, her eyes wide with an emotion the younger woman did not understand. 'I fear the same thing happening to you, my dear,' she concluded, with a sudden great weariness. 'That is why the cause of women is so deep inside me – a cause I will never give up, and neither must you, whatever happens. You are a vital part of it – one of our most outstanding workers. Don't let us down now, I beg of you. You have too much to lose, and so have the women for whom we are fighting.'

Arabella tried to suppress the shock and sadness she felt for her friend. Her face had grown even paler, and when she spoke, her voice was choked. 'I'm so sorry Althea. I didn't know – how dreadful for you, and your children.'

Then the storm within her slowly abated. She turned away, seeing herself as a burned-out shell of a house: the outside walls remained, but the house would always be empty. That was the penalty of her life, the cross she had been forced to bear.

If only she could keep Deneys' friendship as it was, but she knew that the time would come when it would not be enough. She would want more, as she had with Ben.

Yes, she thought as she faced Althea again, the house must stay empty. I owe it to myself and to the women who suffer out there, and to Althea herself who has given me a home and security, who has been almost a mother to me . . .

A strange expression, almost a wince of intense pain flickered over her face, but it was so fleeting that Althea thought she had imagined it.

'Then we can count on you to give up this man, my dear?' Her eyes searched the younger woman's face. 'We're doing such marvellous work together, you and I and the others. We have to sacrifice everything that is detrimental to it.'

Then she rose, and placing the cat on the carpet, she brushed down her skirt and walked out of the room, while unshed tears sprang to Arabella's eyes. As they dried, sadness and bewilderment warred within her for mastery. She thought of Deneys and their times together. She tried to banish the wonderful experience, for Althea's words had torn her away from all the beauty and warm delight. The exhilarating euphoria had burst, vanishing into a dark forest of guilt and frustration.

The afternoon was warm, but a breeze stirred from the hills as Arabella and Deneys sat in the back of Isaac's car on their way to a picnic spot out of town. Arabella leaned back on the upholstered seat and stole a glance at Deneys' strong profile as he chatted pleasantly with Rachel over the chugging sound of the engine. She thought of the bitterly disappointed expression on Althea's face when she had announced that she was going to spend the whole of Saturday with Deneys and the Brandauers. Althea had tried to dissuade her, but Arabella had refused, reasoning that one last day with Deneys could do no harm.

Rachel had packed an enormous picnic lunch, and near the river, where the sun's brightness reflected from the deep blue skies only slightly tufted with white cloud, they sat and ate the large selection of cold meats, pickled herrings, fresh crusty rolls with parsley, hard-boiled eggs, apples, hot-house grapes, and drank a select bottle of vintage Cape wine. On the other side of the river, the veld and the row upon row of grassy koppies began – long stretches of wild green grass dotted by dark glistening evergreen bushes, acacia trees and buffalo thorn. A breeze stirred the long grasses on their side, which were busy with birdlife. There were the snuffling sounds of a pair of large brown francolins as they ran speedily through the grasses nearby, and further away, a large covey of greyish helmeted guineafowl chased one another across a patch of veld.

The place was almost deserted by the time they walked steadily along the sandy river-path, where wild flowers competed with moss-bearded trees. Arabella, picking up her cinnamon-coloured skirts, followed Deneys as his strong muscled legs took the downward path with ease. She pulled the small straw boater from her head and out of the way of an overhanging branch as he turned, holding out his hand at a particularly slippery spot where moss hung like grey lace from the gnarled tree-trunks, and at their feet, little lizards craned their wrinkled necks to watch them pass. Bright flashes of white and pink arum lilies peered from the undergrowth where small sunbirds hovered and darted into the bright cones in their quest for nectar, and beyond the water gleamed through a gap in the foliage.

There was the clear, fresh scent of leaves and wild flowers, as she felt his hand, warm and urgent, on her own. 'Look at me, Arabella.'

Her heart leapt. She ought to draw away, but had no power to do so. In that moment, in that lovely place that was like a wild and ancient garden, shrill with the whinnying trill of the dabchicks in the reed beds and on the river, and the rasping cicadas, she felt the awareness of a piercing sweetness shooting through her entire being. And not even Rachel and Isaac bumping them as they passed could break the isolation of this mysterious world in which they stood alone. As the others' voices drifted away and a kite screamed high above the trees, Deneys gently pulled her to him through the long streamers of moss. Dropping her boater, she felt the touch of his arms like fire, as something inside her struggled to break free, something wild and untouched. It had come, then, all in a moment. Now there was nothing she could do to put it off.

'I've been wanting to kiss you for a very long time, Arabella Allen.' He studied the frilled high-necked blouse under the short, cinnamon-brown bolero, and her hair breaking free of its pins and falling in wisps around her face.

'I think you're taking advantage of me,' she joked shyly, aware of his searching glance.

'If I had wanted to do that, I could have done it long ago,' he considered, a sudden gleam in his brown eyes. 'But I wanted you to be willing, to want it as much as I.'

He had said the words, and she knew that more would come – the words of love she had waited so long to hear. Too late, she told herself; they had come too late. After this one kiss, there would be no more. Yet, his words fell upon her like rain on parched earth, and the deep roots of her loneliness and her need for him responded, in spite of all the doubts her reason could muster.

He touched her as though he held something of infinite value, and almost feared to damage it, and she clung to him as a guide, taking her into an unknown land, knowing that she would be safe as long as he held her, as he lit a fire in her blood, sending all the cold chills of guilt and fear fleeing from her body and her mind. As the firmness of his mouth found hers, she was barely conscious of the surroundings and responded with an all-consuming passion. There was no room for anything beyond this new awareness of her body, of this wonderful man, of being alive to sudden insatiable demands . . .

He kissed her again, before steadying her on her feet, and held her against him, solid and comforting and strong. There was a beautiful, senseless happiness in being in his company and she knew that she was in love with him. Tears filled her eyes as his strong fingers cupped her chin towards him. They came between her and his face, but she still felt his hand under her chin. She could no longer see his high-collared white shirt under the light-coloured jacket, or the golden hair gleaming in the filtered sunlight. Love, she thought desperately, was all the more miraculous, all the more precious because she had never expected to find it again, with this man.

'And now I have seen you cry,' he whispered. 'I have seen you in many moods, but never this one, and I love you in every one.'

Beyond the trees, the hills, valley and river bank were drenched with a clear golden light. Everything shone and glittered, sending sunrays exploding in tiny flashes of gold on the surface of the water. She was aware of every inch of him, of the vitality that surrounded him like an aura, knowing that his sure attempt to reach out to her had penetrated her deepest feelings and her defences.

'I have something for you.' He reached into his jacket pocket and pulled out a small white bundle.

'What on earth is it?' she queried, wondering at the slow smile which curved the corners of his mouth upward.

'It is something you gave me eight long years ago – during the war, when you saved my life. I've kept it all this time. Here – see for yourself.' He handed her the little package.

She unwrapped the lace-edged fichu, brown from old bloodstains, and found inside it her precious opal brooch, which caught the iridescent rays of light dappling the trees. Looking down at it silently,

Arabella saw again that hillside near Suncrest during the war, where Deneys had lain with a smashed arm and a bullet in his chest, and where his young brother Danie had offered her meat stew, his golden head bright with hot sunshine.

'Are you glad to have it back?' he enquired, and at her bewildered nod, captured the wide emerald eyes by the intensity of his stare. 'I carried it right through the war, everywhere I went. There were times when I knew I should get rid of it, because the memory it carried was too painful, but I never did. Somehow, through all the bitterness that followed in the last years of the war, it was a symbol of the good that was in the enemy – a small flicker of hope that some compassion still existed there.'

Her eyes misted momentarily. Then she looked up at him and searched his face. 'But why did you not sell the brooch when you were in dire straits – especially as it belonged to your enemy? It's worth a great deal of money.'

He reached out and closed her fingers over the brooch. 'I always hoped that deep down, you were not my enemy, but my friend.' He gently smoothed an errant strand of hair from her cheek. 'My wicked little feminist, I want to marry you and I cannot think of a better way of uniting Briton and Boer than that, and of proving that we are, from now on, on the same side.'

Suddenly she could find no anchor for her thoughts, seeing and sensing only the bleak, disappointed look on Althea Rigby's face, of her promise to her, and her own precious freedom being snatched away ... of her betrayal of all those miserable, oppressed women in the world.

'Deneys.' Clenching the fichu and the brooch in her hand, she backed herself against a tree, speaking with all the ruthlessness she could summon. 'You must listen to me. I cannot marry you because I am committed to my work, and always will be – that is what I am destined to do.'

His head snapped up in surprise, and she saw the first wave of bewilderment register in his eyes. 'But why not? Why are you saying this, Arabella? We can work that out. When you marry me, your life will be very different. You won't even miss it.'

'I'm a very practical person, Deneys,' she insisted as she remembered the anger and defeat in Ben's eyes when she had refused him. She could still hear the tone of her voice answering him all those years ago – and now, at another similar crisis in her life, she was forced to use that tone again. 'It will not work. I will never be able to be just a wife – I have another mission. It wouldn't be fair, either to you or to me. What you wish is not possible – not after all I have been through.'

He spread his hands in a gesture of impatience. 'If I could only make you feel what I feel, Arabella, you would not think it impossible. We need each other, you and I.'

She heard those words from a long way off, those same words said by another man, in another place.

'It's impossible, I'm sorry. You have offered me the highest prize a man can offer a woman, but I cannot accept.' She tried to smile, but failed miserably. 'I cannot circumscribe my life by purely domestic concerns, Deneys. I have always wanted much more than that, and I know that in this world, I cannot have both until women are fully emancipated. It is for me and others to go on fighting for that day.'

He stared at her in disbelief. 'I can't believe this! What you are proposing is madness – to cut yourself off from a happy married life and live like a nun, fighting for a cause most women wouldn't give you thanks for,' he said with a trace of sarcasm. He considered her for a long moment in deepening suspicion, then setting his jaw, he said with sharp savagery, 'It isn't only the women's rights nonsense that's making you do this, Arabella. It's that Rigby woman and her fanaticism, isn't it? She's made you indebted to her. She's made you promise her something, hasn't she?'

Arabella stared at him, nettled by his tone and aware of the trap that was closing around her. When she spoke, her voice was low and husky. 'Althea has nothing to do with my decision. It goes much further and much deeper than that. Now go away – there's nothing for us.'

'You can't fob me off just like that!' His voice had hardened as he came a step closer. 'All this time you have led me on, encouraging me, and now you tell me the door is closed. I don't for one minute believe it!'

She threw out an arm to him. 'Don't come any closer. I mean what I say – it will never work, and it's better to find that out now before it's too late.'

'You have one damned good way of making a fool of a fellow,' he responded caustically bunching his hands into two strong fists at his sides. The lips which had been warmly expressive only moments before were now angry and forbidding. 'You set a trap, you deceiving little Englishwoman. You caught the fox in your snare, played with it, then kicked it out. Well, that's the last time this fox gets his tail singed!'

She raised a shaking hand to cover her face, and accepted the darkness behind her lowered lashes as he stormed away, his long angry strides taking him to the river where Rachel was watching Isaac skim pebbles across the smooth surface of the water. Through a long, dark tunnel, she heard him ask Isaac to take them home.

That night she lay awake long after she had finished writing letters to various members of the Transvaal House of Assembly and the Labour Party. It was intensely quiet except for the wind that tugged against the shutters, and in spite of all the pillows and comforts around her, she stayed stiff and depressed as she mulled over the happenings of the day. She felt lonely and old, just as a spinster of twenty-eight should feel.

I've hurt Deneys, she thought wretchedly. I've wounded him deeply and he may never forgive me. She vividly remembered the uncomfortable journey back. All the way, his laconic replies to the Brandauers had prevented any further glimpse of his inner emotions, and they had made no further attempt to draw him out.

She turned restlessly on to her back and stared into the darkness, where slivers of moonlight shivered and shifted through the half-open curtains. It had to be done. After all, she owed so much to Althea and the movement. She had to choose and she had chosen her work. He would get over it, she reasoned agonisingly. He could have any woman he wanted ... *but he had chosen her*. She knew that many women would give up everything to be his wife. A pang of anguish stabbed her at this thought, and she tried to forget his warm, smiling brown eyes, lusty baritone voice and his intelligent, quicksilver mind.

A trickle of sweat traced a cool path down her temple as she fought the frustrated emotions that suddenly tore at her, leaving her trembling and tense. She knew she loved him: there was no denying it. But too much stood in the way of a successful marriage. Once she had been almost eager for an experience such as this, but now she was older and wiser, and her wisdom had been painfully acquired.

Kneading her sweating palms together, she turned over to face the window, as horror congealed within her that she had sacrificed something infinitely special, that she had destroyed forever the friendship she had craved. A long sigh slipped from her, and she found herself staring at the opal brooch lying on the fichu on the dressing-table in a pool of reflected moonlight. She felt like smashing the jewelry and ripping the fichu to shreds.

Gradually, a calm deliberation overtook her. She had a strong will, and she would not let herself be influenced by her emotions, no matter how much they tormented her, and as a certain sadness tore at her spirit, she turned her head to the wall.

8

In the depth of the country's Depression, as Arabella continued to throw herself almost desperately into her suffrage work in that crowded year of 1907, deliberately putting Deneys' proposal behind her, a new development in South African politics – one to which she attached little significance at the time – was to mark a distinct transition in her life.

Some members of the many white trade unions that had sprung up along the Rand during the past few years suddenly followed the lead of the Transvaal Miners' Association and prepared to strike against low wages, for which Chinese labourers had been imported for several years.

On one particular bright, clear morning, Arabella prepared to travel across Johannesburg to visit the starving women in Maraisdorp, a poor part of town where she had worked before joining the Heinz household. She and a small group of the suffrage committee had set up soup kitchens there. Althea and the other committee members had declined to go there in the rising atmosphere of unrest, and had pleaded with Arabella to postpone her visit.

She knew of the bitter reactions among white miners to the low wages and the presence of large numbers of Chinese labourers in the mines, but this knowledge could not touch her. She felt equal to anything that morning as, dressed in her favourite blue and white striped coat and gown, she went out to Althea's neat carriage, with its middle-aged horse, and Oubaas, the tall, aging Tswana driver.

She smiled as she sat down on the crimson leather seat, glad it was not Isaac's car – bright and utterly dear to his heart it might be, but so noisy and causing dust clouds that enveloped everything in sight. And she could definitely do without the accompanying wake of barking dogs! The horse trotted sedately out of the driveway and down the dusty road, and she leaned back and enjoyed the sight of the large mansions lying among their gardens far back from the roads.

It was already twelve o'clock as they made their way up Rissik Street alongside the tramcars clanging their bells, their wheels rumbling noisily down the centre of the street, when suddenly, the echo of shots being fired some way to the east hit the air. A carriage passed them, then an open cart and a man on a bicycle, as some kind of commotion could be heard in the distance, but it was soon drowned out by noises closer at hand.

A group of men suddenly overtook them, all moving in one direction. Shortly afterwards, they found their path blocked by a struggling mass of men and uniformed and helmeted British soldiers on horseback. Their own horse shied, whinnying fearfully in sudden panic. Oubaas, perspiration pouring down his wrinkled face, tried to turn the carriage around, only to be met by another large wave of bodies pressing in behind them. Too late he realised they were caught fast between two groups merging from opposite directions, and it took him all his strength to keep the carriage from being overturned in the rush of trampling feet, and to control the panic-stricken horse.

Then, without warning, the animal reared violently and broke loose. Maddened with fear, it galloped into the crowd. Oubaas was pulled from the carriage and dashed to the ground. Arabella tried desperately to reach him, but she was borne helplessly along by the great throng of angry men.

'Down with lower wages! Down with scabs! Down with yellow-skinned coolies!' furious male voices shouted all about her. There was the dull thud of distant gunfire and the drumming of plunging hooves as the soldiers bore down, trying to clear the street.

Arabella caught hold of someone's arm to keep from falling as the soldiers pounded by. The coarse cloth of the jacket belonged to an Australian miner, who was loudly cursing and shaking his fist at the soldiers. Up the street they surged and she was swept along with them, her feet scarcely touching the ground. Never in all her life could she remember this special kind of terror – the fear of being trampled underfoot. Somehow they reached an open space where a stationary tram was surrounded by thousands of miners. Here the crowd stopped, pressed so tightly together that she could hardly breathe, and again and again came the distant crackle of gunfire.

Her ears rang with hoarse voices, all shouting together in a mixture of angry, defiant phrases. She was transfixed with fear in the midst of that violent mob, bent on what they considered to be justice for their cause as their leaders, shouting even louder from the tram, declared a General Strike. Then several armed men started to fire at the soldiers. Someone screamed as a man went down, and there was sudden panic as the crowd heaved together, trying to get out of the way.

Arabella was badly shaken to see a stray bullet come whizzing past, to strike a man behind her. Another bullet zinged and she ducked just in time to see it embedded in a nearby cart. She felt deeply shocked by this mob savagery, for she had always thought of strikes in terms of sporadic and passive resistance, of downing tools, and a dignified exchange of demands.

Then somehow she was out of it and making her trembling way back to where she had last seen Oubaas thrown from the landau. She passed a dead body lying on a cart, covered by a blood-soaked blanket. Turning her head away, she hurried to where the landau lay on its side, her heart thumping wildly with shock.

The crowds had thinned here as she crept along the walls of the shops under the awnings, inching her way towards the overturned carriage. Her straw boater had been lost, and her string of amber beads broken. Her coat hung about her shoulders, torn in places, and she was very pale but unhurt. As she left the sound of shouting and the echoes of the disturbance, she began to fear for Oubaas's safety. With these thoughts ringing in her mind, she reached the smashed carriage. The vehicle, for all its damaged condition, was a refuge, and with great relief she saw Oubaas moaning and sitting in the shelter, of the overturned seats, nursing a wound on his forehead.

'Thank God you're all right, Oubaas,' she whispered breathlessly, creeping up to him as he sat there, almost sick with pain.

'The missus she be very cross, Missy Allen,' he moaned, looking at her from two old, world-weary dark eyes, and shaking the long polished ebony of his face, with its tiny thread of grey moustache. 'The missus she be very cross. She say, "Oubaas, you go! You no good, you go back to the eight children, back on the farm with so very hungry mouths to feed"'.

'It will be all right, Oubaas. I'll take the blame. After all, it was my idea to come out today, and knowing Mrs Rigby, she'll be far more concerned with how you are than the damaged carriage.'

In a businesslike manner, she mopped up the blood from his wrinkled forehead with a lace-edged handkerchief, then bound the wound firmly. It was not long before a party of soldiers found them, and escorted them back to the Villa Valencia in an open cart.

'Hundreds of them strikers are marching to Pretoria, ma'am, to press their claims on the authorities.' The sergeant who was driving the cart turned his head from the road to address her, and narrowly missed a dog. 'Two British regiments have been called out at General Smuts' request to patrol the Rand.'

Suddenly the comfort and warmth of a family, the male strength of a husband, seemed to beckon to Arabella. She hated being alone, feeling so insecure and afraid ... suddenly she wanted someone to share her life with, someone she loved.

The shock of the day's experience had till then overwhelmed her almost completely, but just as circulation returns to deadened limbs with sharp pinpricks of pain, so now the memory of Deneys and what she had lost invaded her mind, and she was acutely conscious of her heart, where a stabbing ache, a conscience, had suddenly come to life.

She was remembering the hurt, bewildered expression on his face after the picnic. She recalled how he had clenched his fists with pain ... those powerful hands that had held her so securely, so lovingly, and she thought of what could have been ...

All during that week and the next, the newspapers screamed with headlines that three hundred strikers had marched to Pretoria, and that the two British regiments called out to deal with them had met with several vicious counter-attacks. For a while it became a common sight once more to see soldiers on horseback patrolling the streets. But even more than this, another development had occurred that affected Arabella personally – and with particular force. Her old enemy Sean O'Shea had not been idle. Cheated of his German heiress, he had been drinking too much and began circulating scandalous rumours about Arabella, resurrecting the attempted seduction in the Heinz mansion until once more, the sordid tale reached the more gossip-hungry newspapers, and was rehashed, all over again.

It was late one Friday afternoon, at the Crossroads Bar – a pub in the seedier part of town owned by former Irish boxer Tom O'Callahan – that Deneys du Rand found O'Shea. Deneys stood in the doorway with the blue-bronze light behind him, the smoke and noise hitting him like a solid curtain. The place was crammed with men, mostly striking miners, sitting at baize-covered tables or leaning against a long wooden counter, behind which hung a picture of a scantily dressed woman.

No one stopped drinking, talking, or slapping down brandy-soaked cards, but there was a sudden stillness, a tension of waiting, as he looked around the room. Then, pulling off his hat, he threaded his way through the groups to the wooden counter where O'Shea was sitting.

'We finally meet again, O'Shea.' The voice was deep and low, but it carried, and the pub fell silent.

O'Shea looked at him with unnaturally bright eyes, the fingers of one hand curled around a glass beside a half-empty green bottle. He fumbled a few coins from a pocket, dropping one into the ready hand of fat Tom O'Callahan, standing behind the shining silver beer-pumps.

'There's nothing you and I have to say to each other, du Rand. Go back to the veld where you belong.' He stood up, leaving his empty glass on the counter. 'I have nothing to say to you, ever – and I spit on the memory of your brother Christiaan,' he hissed bitterly, moving away. ''Twas he who ruined my life – getting us caught and sent to St Helena to starve under the eyes of the stinking English!'

Then Deneys' hand was on his shoulder, hard and sudden, spinning him round so fast that he knocked against the bar and his glass fell over and smashed.

'We've plenty to talk about, you cheating, lying Irishman. An apology is due to Miss Arabella Allen, for a start, right here, before all these men. Go on, tell them how you've lied about her, dragged her name into the filth – and all because she defended her own virtue and stopped you marrying the Heinz girl. She showed you up for what you are!'

'You take your hands off me, du Rand! All your kind is good for is to take the places of the striking miners at lower pay – putting them out of work, so their strike fails! That's the low-down kind you are!' O'Shea suddenly swivelled cunning eyes from Deneys to the men around him. 'Hey, boyos – here's one o'them who takes your jobs then walks in here as cool as you please, accusing *me* of cheating and lying.' More sure of his support, he turned glinting eyes to Deneys. 'Arabella bloody Allen is nothing but an English whore, hiding under those prim and proper airs o' hers. She's a slut, no less.'

'You swine! You come outside right now and clear the name of Miss Allen forever.' Deneys hand stabbed out again, the heel jarring against O'Shea's shoulder, while behind the bar, Tom O'Callahan shifted the bottles and glasses. There was a low, ominous murmuring among the men.

'Attempting to defend that cousin of Milner's right-hand skivvy, Saville? You're wasting your time. There's nothing to defend beneath that degraded little piece o'skirt!'

Before he could turn his back again, Deney's fist caught him high on the chest, staggering him. Tom rapped with a cane on the counter, almost knocking over a soda-siphon.

'Enough, gentlemen, enough. In the name of the Holy Mother, ye know there's t'be no fightin' in here.'

Around Deneys the hostile customers were moving in closer, blocking the way to the door, pushing and urging. 'C'mon Paddy – show this Dutchman where he belongs. Sort him out for good!' rumbled a bewhiskered miner, breathing potent whisky fumes.

A fellow with a hat pulled over his brow jostled him without an apology, and said bluntly, 'Refusing to give us our rights, now are ye! Sneaking in and taking our jobs at lower pay – what a nerve! Send this man to hell!'

Deneys cooled off for a moment, realising that he stood alone in enemy territory. Then he nodded sharply to the bar tender. 'All right then – I'll teach him a lesson outside.' He shrugged off his coat and turned to go.

Everyone was shoving suddenly to the door in a swell of sound. Deneys was already rolling up his sleeves, and O'Shea, caught in the moment, saw that he would have to go along with it. Then they were all out in the dusty street, in a rough ring, with a crowd of onlookers gathering around them. Deneys, to one side, stood strong and easily across the shifting circle of dust where O'Shea carefully folded his coat, put down his smart straw boater, and folded back the cuffs of his expensive white shirt to just below the elbow. There was a second of silence as Deneys placed himself directly in front of the sneering Irishman, who stood regarding him through slit eyes and a thin, humourless smile.

'Come on, Dutchman – let's show the world just how inferior you really are!'

The crowd roared as Deneys jumped forward. Charging like a wild animal, he lunged at O'Shea. Hooking with his left, he drove for the midriff with his right. Both punches landed, but O'Shea stepped back and kicked with the heavy soles of his boots, right in Deneys' groin. The pain was agonising. Deneys let out a grunt of anguish, hands clutching at the tearing pain. Before he could recover, though, he felt himself being lifted up and slammed against the wall, where his head struck a brick.

'No wonder you lost the war, you scum. You got no brains!' O'Shea taunted, and Deneys felt the man's boot sink into his stomach. 'See, my boys, these stupid Dutchmen are all talk – nothing between their great clodhopping ears! We must have been dog-crazy to come and help them fight!'

'Two can play your filthy game, O'Shea!' Deneys shouted hoarsely, as he recovered himself.

'Are you coming back for more of the same? God help us but you're more stupid than Paddy's mule!' O'Shea cried, his face twisted into a contemptuous grin.

The crowd shouted encouragement as Deneys staggered upright and went in close. Before the Irishman had time to think, Deneys jerked a savage knee into his chest, and O'Shea toppled sideways into the dust. Deneys measured his distance carefully as O'Shea staggered up, swinging his foot heavily, deliberately aiming again for Deneys' groin. This time, however, the other man was ready for it. Deneys shifted his stance and lined himself up for a final punch to the head. As his fist shot out, O'Shea heaved and the punishing blow took him just where his neck and shoulder joined.

O'Shea went down before he knew what had hit him, his face smacking the dirt, and even the shouting could not hide the dull, cracking sound as his collarbone broke. Breathing heavily, and with a grunt of satisfaction, Deneys wiped his hands and slowly walked away. As he reached the outer circle, he turned and faced the quiet crowd.

'O'Shea is the biggest liar in this town. He tried to have his way with Miss Allen and she fought like a tigress to defend her honour – and her life! And if I ever hear anything to the contrary, *ever*, there'll be the biggest court case this town has ever seen.'

With that, he picked up his coat and hat and, swinging the coat over his shoulder, he walked away, the silence following him like a shadow.

9

The dim gaslight from the crystal chandelier in the guest room of Isaac's small, expensive house shone on Deneys, where he lay on his side on the bed. His open shirt revealed a dark patch, where the skin and bone had been deeply bruised by O'Shea's boot. When he moved, his face creased in pain and he groaned. Then he rolled over, and stared at Arabella, who had been called urgently by Rachel, and was now looming over him, her pinafore a blur in the gloom, as the under-curtains at the window billowed out in pale-lilac silk.

'You were unwise to fight O'Shea, Deneys,' she said with deep embarrassment. 'He doesn't fight fair – he never has.'

Deneys frowned, then his eyes cleared. 'I know him all too well. We fought side by side for some months, and it was because of him that my brother Christiaan was caught after his escape from Ladysmith, and sent as a prisoner to St Helena for the remainder of the war.' His voice hardened. 'But I had to do it – I owed him a big lesson and he will leave you alone now, for good.'

He tried to prop himself up on his elbow, on the ivory-coloured hand-crocheted bedspread that was generations old, but the pain stopped him halfway. Arabella winced, seeing his discomfort. From a small silver tray on the polished mahogany dressing table, she picked up a steaming bowl of Rachel's special chicken soup, and gave it to him.

'But you didn't have to do it for me. After the way –' she stammered, as he sipped the soup and sank back against the propped-up pillows.

'After the way you dropped me like a hot brick?' he finished for her, trying to glare without flinching. Then suddenly his face fell into lines of weary deliberation. 'I wouldn't worry about it if I was you. I did it for my brother – he nearly died because of O'Shea.'

'Well, I want to thank you, anyway. It was a courageous thing to do.'

She watched as he spooned up the soup, noticing how quickly the hot liquid was reviving him. His brown eyes appraised her over the bowl, held close to his mouth, his golden hair tousled and falling over his forehead, and she could feel the ache of loneliness and longing building up deep inside her. Then he leaned back against the wall as she took the empty soup bowl, and watched the shadows moving along the ornately decorated cornices.

He had such an extraordinary inner strength, she thought, with just a hint of vulnerability. It was a potentially explosive mixture, and suddenly in that silent room, she felt strangely humbled that he should have asked her to marry him.

'Would you like some freshly baked kitke and roast chicken, Deneys?'

A shadow fell across the threshold and Arabella turned to see Rachel enter the cool room, dark-haired, red-lipped, her lovely eyes shining like closed sea anemones. 'You really need someone to look after you, and that's a fact.' Without looking at Arabella, her long, full-breasted body crossed the light-grey fluffy carpet, accompanied by the delicious smell of bread and chicken on a large silver tray. 'Isaac would land up in a dreadful mess without me to look after him like a baby.'

Ignoring Rachel's remark, Arabella continued to surreptitiously study the man on the bed, a familiar sense of despair washing over her. Would she ever be able to reach him again? Would that barrier between them never be lifted?

Deneys shrugged his shoulders and grimaced. 'Isaac happens to be a very fortunate man.'

Rachel laughed, and as she took the empty soup bowl from Arabella, she gave her a meaningful look and left the room.

'Deneys,' Arabella said suddenly, taking a step closer to the large canopied bed. Deep within her came a brief trembling trepidation that he would no longer want her. She sat down on the bed, a hesitant smile on her lips. 'Deneys, can you ever forgive me for what I did? I'm so sorry,' she hurried on before he could speak, afraid that she would lose the courage to continue. 'I was wrong, Deneys, so very wrong to refuse you.'

He lowered his head momentarily, his eyes hidden from her, then, raising it once more, with a wooden expression, he said quietly, 'What has happened to make you change your mind like this?'

She refused to be upset by his reaction, as his nearness went spiralling through her with intoxicating effect, snaring her mind and her emotions and blending them with past memories.

'Deneys.' She moved her head, the light making a shining aureole of her brown hair. 'I love you and I've missed you, and if your offer of marriage still stands –'

'You never cease to amaze me.' He stared at her for a moment or two and then a slow mocking smile bloomed faintly around his lips. 'Are you sure it's not pity for my condition – and a little gratitude, perhaps?'

She shook her head. 'I thought I had a commitment to Althea – she's done so much for me – and you're right, she didn't want me to marry you ... but I've been thinking. I've decided never to make compromises with myself again. I shall live the way that is right for *me* from now on. And I want to marry you – desperately.'

Although she was sitting beside him, he made no move to touch her. He took up a piece of the plaited bread, broke off a portion and ate it. The light from the chandelier lay across his bare chest, the blond matted curls gleaming like polished bronze. He waited for her to continue as she rose restlessly from the bed. She was nearly twenty-nine and her body had lost some of the slender suppleness of a young girl, but it had found the beginning of the dignity and maturity of a woman. He watched her pace to and fro for a while, her long hair worked into a knot on top of her small, proud head. She stood in profile to him, beside carved mahogany chest with a marble top. She had always been attractive, never pretty, but now with the light falling on her face, and lying in a pool of soft gold in the hollow of her throat, she was beautiful.

Then she faced him, searching his face before vehemently shaking her head. 'I could never pity you, Deneys – you're far too strong for that.'

He finished the bread and chicken and then laughed painfully and said, 'Come, sit down. We have much to talk about, you and I.' Then he slowly pulled her down on to the bed beside him, and the warmth of his breath fanned her cheek. It set her pulse leaping uncontrollably for a second, as a warm glow crept into the brown depths of his eyes. 'I've always thought you'd make a fitting wife for a renegade Boer, my dear.'

Her spirits responded to his humour, and in a half-teasing manner, she retorted, 'You'll really be letting the side down with a rooinek wife.'

For a moment he hesitated, then he released her wrist and sat back against the pillows. In an almost careworn voice, he said, 'Arabella, I wrote to my father about you long ago. As it happens, he and my brothers do *not* approve of my marrying an Englishwoman – especially the cousin of Benjamin Saville. They tried to dissuade me before I proposed to you.' A grin flashed briefly across his weary, handsome face. 'But then, when all's said and done, I don't think your cousin and his wife would welcome me into their fold too warmly, and nor will Mrs Rigby.'

'They won't. But then I never see my relatives – it's as if they're dead. And Althea will be extremely upset ...' She would miss Althea, her beautiful home, the loyal and reliable servants, all her friends ... The room swam before her and for a moment she thought she would burst into tears. Then she swallowed, and tried to speak calmly. 'She definitely won't come to the wedding. In fact, very few people will come. But it isn't important any more, Deneys.' Her eyes, so brilliantly intelligent, so alive, were suddenly full of determination, the green a little more intense. 'We love each other, and that's all that matters.'

She straightened her small shoulders proudly, her mind host to one surprising truth – this man had made it clear that she meant so much to him because he knew that there was a bond between them – one that had sprung up since the very beginning. And physically, Arabella knew a violence of response which she no longer wanted to suppress – an unbridled, passionate hunger for him.

She said, as evenly as she could, 'I think we should marry as soon as possible, my dearest Deneys. If you agree, Rachel and Isaac have suggested having the ceremony in their house. I informed them of my decision when I arrived this evening.'

For a long moment, Deneys eyed her. 'I see you have it all planned.' He smiled and drew her awkwardly to him. His arms painfully encircled her and his lips came down to hers and took them. Then, kissing her eyelids gently, he said, 'I think I had better arrange for a minister who will marry us right away, before you change your mind again.'

10

Samson met them in a horse-drawn cart at Heideville station in the grassy plains of the eastern Transvaal, towards the end of a blazing hot summer's day. He had not changed very much since Arabella had last seen him during the war. His small face was a bit more wizened and his stubble of hair more grey, but his small body was as wiry and strong as ever. After a sharp, dubious glance at his master's new wife, he climbed back on to the driver's seat, and the cart, scrubbed and polished for the occasion, jolted away towards the rambling village as the last sunlight touched the tops of the high old trees along the way, and rippled faintly across the mealie fields on either side of the dusty road.

Arabella was dressed in a grey linen suit, which brought out the extraordinary green of her eyes. The jacket fell open on a soft white blouse, which was not boned to the jawline but which revealed her pale throat and the glistening pearls around it. She wore a smart straw boater, banded by a wide grey ribbon. A grey handbag lay on her knees, and she crossed her hands over it as she studied the surroundings with gentle candour.

Heideville, nestling beneath its fold of hills to the east, with its backdrop of dark rugged mountains to the west, had for her the unreality of a feverish dream. A wild beauty lay on those lands, and a remoteness that hit her at first sight. The fierce lines of the hills marched along beside them, and even when she could make out the scattered farms, and the few wide, dusty streets of houses with kitchen fires sending up trails of smoke as they clustered about three small churches, the impression of wildness persisted.

Out of this uncompromising small world had come the gritty opposition of the Transvaal Boers to British imperialism. Their presence still lay irrevocably across the land. It was seven years now since they had died or returned from exile and surrendered to their enemies, but something of their fierce, indomitable energy still lingered about the countryside. Hidden fires might even be smouldering yet, under the jagged hills and open pasturelands, to suddenly erupt into full flame against General Botha.

They jolted up into the main street, where Samson pulled the reins sharply as a covey of guineafowl ran high-headed across their path. Arabella looked at the straggling village with interest, catching a glimpse of a few more streets winding off from this one, the houses already bright with light behind their heavy lace curtains. The mare quickened her pace from a jog to a spirited trot and they finally came within sight of Deney's house, situated opposite the school.

His house was almost exactly like the neighbouring ones, except that it was a little bigger than those nearer the centre, and smaller than those further out. Built of red brick, it had a corrugated-iron roof, dull green shutters, high steps leading to a small verandah running the whole length of the front of the house, and an untidy garden both back and front, with a chicken coop and a stable for three horses.

A small group of dark-coated bearded men, and women in plain black dresses stood on the verandah, waiting with expectant silence as the cart jerked to a halt.

'Ah, we have the mayor, the doctor, the magistrate and their wives to welcome us, Arabella, and there is even Marietjie de Villiers, the magistrate's daughter,' Deneys announced as the small group came forward. 'They're all good friends of mine, and have been curious to meet you.'

Arabella's mind suddenly groped. Before and after the small wedding ceremony in Isaac's house and during the train journey, in the beauty and sense of complete happiness that had taken possession of her as she and Deneys travelled all those miles together, she had forgotten all doubts and fears of her place in a closely-knit Dutch dominated village, with its deeply-rooted religious fervour and bitter Anglophobia. Now they rose to engulf her as she faced this first meeting with the most important people in her new life. She felt suddenly alien in her light-coloured clothes and pearl necklace beside the solemn, dark-clad figures who confronted them, as the matter of feminine adornment played little part in the lives of the women, whose hair was severely drawn back into buns, wide wedding bands their only jewelry.

Arabella stared at this reception committee but hardly saw them. She was too aware of a young woman standing near the edge of the group, her face strained, her eyes too bright as they watched Deneys agilely jump down from the cart.

The girl could not have been more than nineteen or twenty. Plainly dressed in grey and white, she was tall and big-boned, with good features – large hazel eyes with sweeping lashes, a beautiful if somewhat narrow mouth, and a perfect nose. Her glossy, dark-brown hair was swept high, and coiled at the back. As their eyes met, the young woman's dark brows contracted and a cold expression settled on her face.

The sense of alienation increased in Arabella, as Deneys helped her down from the cart and led her forward. She straightened her shoulders and looked up at the small group of leading villagers, trying not to tremble.

Petrus Viljoen the mayor, Tiaan Malherbe the doctor, and Ernst de Villiers the magistrate were big men, all three, their faces as rugged as the hills which lay beyond. On introduction, they stared at Arabella curiously, their eyes softening a little when she attempted to greet them in Dutch. She glanced towards Marietjie de Villiers once, then turned back to the other women – all tall and raw-boned like their men, who bestowed respectful but affectionate smiles upon Deneys.

It was then that Alida Viljoen, the mayor's wife and a woman of large proportions, gazed at Arabella through ice-blue eyes, and suddenly said, in Dutch, which was quickly translated by Deneys: 'We must welcome this little English lady into our community, especially since she was so brave and kind to our women and children, even going against her own family during the war, that terrible war in which our own Mr du Rand was such a hero to his people. She and that wonderful lady Miss Emily Hobhouse did such great good, and but for them, many more of us would have perished.' She then came forward, and placing her large hands on Arabella's diminutive shoulders, kissed her soundly on both cheeks.

There was a moment's silence as a wagon crunched along on the gravel, and one rooster then another and another crowed, their high-pitched cries thrown triumphantly into the dying sky. The faces of the men and women subtly changed. They all stepped forward to take her hands, and welcome her, all except Marietjie, whose hazel eyes shone with sudden hatred.

The front door was thrown open, and lamplight streamed out like loving arms to embrace them, and they were ushered into the small dining room, where the women had laid a tureen of steaming lentil soup, dishes of sliced biltong, platters of mutton and brawn, wild dassie stew, frikkadels and rice, salt ribitjies done on the gridiron, hot boiled sweet potatoes, sousboontjies, buttermilk rusks, golden-brown vetkoeks, a melktert, jam and coconut tarts and a selection of preserved peaches and apricots and figs. A coffee pot stood on the solid dark sideboard filled with bitter black coffee, beside a full sugar bowl and a large jug of fresh milk. The few black servants watched the proceedings curiously from behind their masters and mistresses.

Arabella forgot her fears for a moment as she gazed at these delights, aware that the small front room was crowded with people, and that more were coming as word spread that the distinguished lawyer Deneys du Rand had returned with his new English wife, the one who had worked in the concentration camps with Emily Hobhouse.

After the last guest had gone, Deneys carried Arabella into the small square bedroom, kicking the door closed and frightening a lizard flicking across the wall. A bright yellow leaf-nosed bat jinked and dodged past them through the open window in slow flight, as he set her on her feet.

'This may not be the Villa Valencia, Mevrou du Rand, but it is our home, complete with Thor, our loyal wolfhound who stands guard beyond the door.'

'It is indeed a man's house, my dear Deneys,' she replied pertly. 'I think a few feminine touches will not go amiss.'

A breeze rippled through the windows, but it could not blow away the lingering scent of Arabella's Crab Apple Blossom perfume. It was in the room like a sweet and subtle presence, just as she was, with her green eyes and charming, sensitive mouth. He watched her for a second as she stood there facing him. The lace at her throat had parted a little more, and he could see the hollow of her throat, filled with soft shadow.

'I think they liked you – and they've already put you on a pedestal,' he teased. 'I saw hero-worship in the eyes of some of the old ooms, but I'm not so sure I like it. And Alida Viljoen has you marked down for her ladies' committee for sure – most probably to make watermelon konfyt.'

'You can't be serious! Me – making whatever you call it?' Then she laughed. 'I shall have to be very firm about my commitments, I can see that. And I do loathe pedestals – it's so beastly draughty up there.'

'Come down then and join me in bed. I love you and I want you, and I cannot wait any longer. Just looking at you makes me lustful.' His white teeth gleamed beneath a widening grin. 'But I promise to be a gentleman.'

It was her turn to cock a brow at him. 'No doubt a married gentleman who takes his liberties seriously.'

'Naturally!' he chuckled, drawing her close into his arms. 'How else should I take them?'

He began to struggle with the tiny fastenings of her clothes then moments later he sobered as the back of her chemise fell apart, revealing her breasts and shoulders down to the waist. 'Oh Arabella,' he murmured, kissing her neck and shoulders. 'You're so beautiful. More beautiful than I ever imagined.'

He unpinned her hair, and ran the smooth brown locks between his fingers, and then she drowned as his mouth found hers, and she could feel the quickening thud of her heart. His open mouth moved on hers and passion sparked in her suddenly, turning her mind inside-out. Then he let her go, and breathing hard, he said in a deep and husky voice, 'I love you so, I can't wait to make you mine.'

She felt her heart lurch again with a raging desire for him, breathlessly aware of the rugged swell of his muscles as he undressed swiftly, his short golden hair gleaming in the lamplight. Oh, how wonderful he looked, standing there, everything she had ever admired and wanted to love.

Trembling, she tugged the ties of her petticoats free and pushing the billowing folds down, she said softly, 'I think you have the heart of a rake, Mr du Rand.'

Emotion played like lightning between them as he stood before her naked, his strong athletic body glimmering in the light. He caught her in his arms. 'Then I'll make love to you like a rake, my darling, but I'll love you like a husband.'

Imprisoned within the tight, hard circle of his arms, she felt the warm demand of his lips once more and was eclipsed by an upsurge of pure joy. She wanted him, now, with a violent passion she no longer needed to deny, as he carried her to the bedstead that was no more than a wooden frame with riempies stretched across it, and laid her on the large feather mattress. He buried his face in the scented mass of her hair, his lips exploring the long line of her neck and the tightly pointed nipples. She clasped him to her fiercely, her breasts pressing on his strong and powerful chest. Time, place, everything except the joy they shared, was forgotten as Deneys took her.

Her body tensed, she was gasping for breath, but she clung to him fiercely through the first, sharp pain to a crescendo, which all but threw them off the bed in its violence. Then the whole world seemed to explode as she soared with him into supreme fulfilment. The piercing sweetness of him made it an agony to hold on to safety. She let herself fall into the void and as she fell, she called his name. And when the tremors that shook her stilled, she found that he had never let her go, that his arms had held her safe all the time.

Afterwards, while he lay across her, his heart thudding against hers, her hand moved gently, caressing his back with an odd timidity, as though she was suddenly hesitant of his reaction. She drew a fingertip from his eyebrow, down to his throat, and he opened his eyes. Then, his mouth pressed very softly against hers.

'Arabella,' he whispered, his deep, musical voice and the softly rounded accent giving an exquisite inflection to her name. 'I hope I didn't hurt you too much.'

'No, dearest one – the pain was worth the pleasure. I love you now, Deneys, my darling, more than ever,' she murmured as he kissed her gently on her eyelids, her breasts, which brought her eagerly into his arms once more. She let him caress her, as she drew strength and confidence from the physical contact.

Then their bodies fused again in mutual passion, first one then the other igniting the flames of fiery love between them, and they rose again, forgetting the outside world, to the very highest peak of ecstasy and then slowly, and reluctantly, they came back to consciousness.

Later, as Arabella lay back on the pillows, her head nestling on Deneys' shoulder, she thought about her emotions. She had never in her dreams imagined a more glorious moment – the reality had far exceeded her dearest hopes, and Deneys du Rand was hers. She came to the conclusion that love was an essence, an atmosphere which defied analysis, as did life itself. She loved and was beloved. Disaster and humiliation were behind her. She had come to a strange world determined to make the best of it, and suddenly the best of life had come to her. She now had so much, where once there had been so little.

She gazed around the room, which was filtered now with early morning light, at the old riempie-backed chair, worn and split in places, and her own elderly portmanteau, standing against the wall beneath the window and reminding her of the scent of English roses in this vast, dark-bright land. The sight of the large cracked water jug and basin heartened her. There was no electric light here, nor running water, and they did not have all that much money between them, but in those private, precious moments, with Deneys' arms about her, she felt as rich as a queen.

II

At first Samson did not take easily to the fact that as Arabella was now mistress of the house, he had to take his orders from her; but as she deplored anything dictatorial and her way was conciliatory, they managed over the following days to come to some sort of amicable agreement on what she would do, and what he would do.

She was extraordinarily happy as the weeks passed into autumn, even though a small group of the younger women would allow her no place in their lives. It was Marietjie de Villiers who was the unchallenged social leader and high priestess of this corps of young women, the daughters of the most prominent local families. She and the Dutch Reformed Minister's niece, Elsabe van Niekerk, had apparently fought for Deneys' affections before his marriage, but their intense rivalry had ceased on the arrival of Arabella. They both hated the small, clever Englishwoman with an intensity bordering on fanaticism, and it was they who incited a group of outraged older women from the Dominee's church to confront Deneys with the charge that his wife riding a bicycle in a divided skirt and tam-o-shanter was an affront to the whole community. He spent time calming them down. His wife was a foreigner, he explained. They must not take offence if she brought strange ways with her. The appeal in his voice and the charm of his smile helped to appease their grievance but Arabella was never quite able to escape the sharp criticism of either Marietjie or Elsabe.

However, even these difficulties could not dim the bliss of their first months together, as she and Deneys turned to each other, discovering new releases, and a deepening absorption. She had a genius for arranging the furniture into the perfect combination. She could make a room take on unsuspected beauty by the addition of a picture or a mirror, a lamp or a bright square of cloth laid on the table. She turned the cheerless bedroom into a haven of peace and comfort and one of the two spare rooms into Deneys' study, which became a wonder to callers, with its chic yet comfortable atmosphere.

These were challenging times for Arabella as Heideville opened up to her, revealing its pitfalls, its multiple crossroads. She was accepted by a large part of the community, but appeared highly eccentric to many because of her ignorance in regard to making sausages and butter and candles, slaughtering pigs and poultry – and her complete lack of interest in local gossip. Instead, she caught up with news from the outside world through her regular correspondence with Rachel, who had given birth to a son, Mark, and by reading newspapers that were weeks old. From Althea there was no word; she had refused to speak to Arabella after she announced her marriage to Deneys.

As the bitter Transvaal winter turned to spring, and then to summer, the four new provinces, led by the Cape, sent representatives to a National Convention to decide on the new form of government for the country. Ben Saville was the leading representative for Natal. What interested Arabella most was the move in one of the parliaments to give women of European descent the vote ... but this was the extent of the debate on women's suffrage, and it was shelved until the question could be submitted to the new Parliament.

Yet not even this delay could mar her happiness, with the exciting knowledge that she carried Deneys' child. As the brown dry veld sprang into a carpet of glorious white, pink and maroon cosmos, and the fresh young green of the mealies began to show through the red soil, the garden under her hands became a skilfully controlled riot of plants and shrubs. She laid out a vegetable garden along the back fence, beyond which spread miles of virgin veld, hiding a host of snakes and small mammals, which always seemed to threaten her recently cultivated beds. Near the vegetable garden, more White Leghorns and Rhode Island Red chickens were added to those already in the coop. Her constant companions were Thor, the big grey wolfhound, his body power-packed with solid sinew, who had killed warthogs and porcupines and once, a hyena, and a new addition to the family – Wasp, a stumpy wire-haired dog with long red furry ears.

Now and then the old panic would seize Arabella at casual gossip that Marietjie de Villiers and Elsabe van Niekerk still had an eye on her husband ... then the feeling would pass. She was sure of Deneys and his love, as she had been sure of so few things in her life until now. Nothing would ever come between them – certainly not the past, which she had put aside like a worn garment – and certainly not two jealous young women.

The sun was shining, the sky was blue and white, billowing clouds sailing along its vastness as Arabella returned after collecting baby's clothes from a farmer's wife nearby. She was in her eighth month of pregnancy, heavy and uncomfortable, but not even Samson's most vigorous pleas that he accompany her had made her change her mind.

Her thoughts were busy as she guided the mare over the shallow river crossing. As she clucked the horse on, flipping the reins lightly across its back, she looked up the rutted road to where the village rose in the distance. Children's happy, eager voices drifted across from the schoolhouse and she thought with excited anticipation of her own child, nearly grown to full-size within her womb. At the far end of the wide main thoroughfare, the slim white tip of the Dutch Reformed Church steeple rose above some trees. Overhead, a flock of small brown sparrows whirled suddenly on swift wings as a dassie scurried across the road. Startled, the mare shied with a sudden jerk, and dashed in fright down into a ditch at the side of the road.

What happened next was like a nightmare. Arabella tried to draw in the reins sharply to force the horse to stop, but the cart slewed over the grassy verge and crashed upside down in the ditch; she was thrown roughly on to the ground.

With her one free hand, she tried to push up the side of the cart that was pinning down her leg, and as she thought of the unborn child within her, terror such as she had never known before engulfed her and she screamed like a madwoman.

She did not know how long she had been screaming when she heard voices and the sound of horses' hooves somewhere on the other side of the cart. Through her terror she was conscious of the sound of heavy booted feet and the feel of the cart being lifted from her leg.

A voice said in Dutch: 'Mevrou du Rand! It is Meneer the lawyer's wife.'

A sallow malarial face came down to hers, crowned by a thatch of dull fair hair, and she vaguely recognised Anton Meyer, the mayor's clerk. She remembered him; he had lost one leg at the knee during the war, and now skilfully hopped around on a roughly whittled wooden leg. She fainted, but not before she was dimly aware of being picked up and placed on something hard, then she knew nothing more.

Someone groaned. She was aware of the long, shuddering sound of distress before realising that it came from herself. She strained to raise her eyelids, but a blinding light and a blur of faces turned her dizzy again. Nausea overcame the blackness, and sharp smells and still sharper pangs made her conscious once more.

'There now!' she heard a woman's voice say in Dutch. 'She's over the worst of it, and thank God the child is still moving inside her. We need not send for Doctor Malherbe again.'

Another spasm shook Arabella and when it passed she was able to fix her attention on nearer objects. She saw she was in her bedroom. Late afternoon was at the window, its light mingling with that of a lamp beside the bed.

'What happened?' she whispered, in Dutch, 'How long have I been here? Where's Deneys? The baby –'

'Now don't you worry yourself, Mevrou du Rand. You have had a shock, and the baby is all right, thanks be to the Lord.' The words came short and abrupt as Tienie Meyer, the wife of Anton, a large-boned young woman with brown hair and small but pretty brown eyes, pressed smelling salts to her nostrils. 'Your husband has been here all the time. He's in the kitchen having a cup of hot coffee with Meneer Viljoen, the mayor.'

Arabella lay exhausted, scarcely aware of who came and went, though she knew that there were those who took turns sitting by the bed, urging her to eat the food they brought, and fanning her to keep away the flies. Towards evening she felt a lot better, and the air freshened as a summer shower cooled the streets.

And then, as she suddenly went into premature labour, Deneys was there, and she was in his arms, weeping as if her heart would break.

It was a long and difficult birth, and Dr Malherbe when he returned showed a businesslike dismissal of her pain. He explained briskly that the 'discomfort' experienced by a mother was considered to be an integral part of childbearing. A process as natural as giving birth required no anaesthetic – for which she begged – and most women gloried in bringing forth their young without any aids.

Arabella lost count of the hours as she lay wracked by pain and drenched with sweat, trying not to scream or to beg for drugs. Excruciating spasms took over her entire body and mind, and she longed for it to be done with. The whole world was compressed into her small bedroom, its curtains and shutters closed against the bright glare of the sunshine outside. Somehow she got through the next few hours, moving in and out of consciousness as first Deneys, then the midwife came, but always in silence. Still swimming in pain, the child, a boy, was born.

'How are you, my darling?' Deneys was bending over her, his haggard face, his blond hair tousled and damp.

She tried to smile, not able to speak, her whole body bruised and weak. The experience had been shattering. Although, as a nurse, she had witnessed many a birth, she recoiled from her own personal torment. She did not know how long she had lain there, as the street outside took on a mid-afternoon tranquillity, and the children's voices from the schoolhouse died away. Her eyes fell on the chest of drawers, where someone had taken pains to arrange a glass vase of flowers, and she felt a moment of gratitude. Then it passed as she met the weary gaze of her husband's eyes, and saw the rigid muscles in his jaw.

'I never want you to go through that agony again, Arabella.' He sat down on the bed, taking her limp hand in his strong ones, his clothes crumpled as if he had slept in them. 'I never want you to suffer so – not even a child is worth it.'

'What do you mean, not worth it?' She stared at him in a rising panic, wondering which of them was mad. His familiar, handsome face should have stirred warm feelings in her but, inexplicably, there was something about him that sent a shiver of dreadful foreboding through her.

'Tiaan Malherbe should have given you something for the pain –'

'He wasn't very sympathetic, but it's over now, Deneys. We have a son and we must think of a name for him as soon as possible. A child must have the right name –'

'Don't, Arabella!' he hissed in the silence of the dim room. 'Hush. It's over, as you say – and you're all right.' He pressed her hand. 'You must rest and recover your strength, then later we'll talk about the child.'

'What is it, Deneys?' she managed to whisper hoarsely. 'I've never seen you like this before.'

'We'll talk later, my dear. First I'll bring you something to eat,' he said, gently smoothing back the damp tendrils of hair from her forehead. 'Tienie Meyer left a pot of bean soup and some of her famous meat turnovers which we call "old lady under the blankets."' A slow, painful smile loomed faintly around his lips. 'My stepmother used to make them when I was a youngster. And there's a buttermilk pudding from Mevrou Marais, the butcher's wife.'

'Deneys, you're hiding something. The baby – he's all right, isn't he? I haven't seen him yet – they said I was too weak. Deneys, please let me see the child!'

She plucked at him with a shaking hand and he took it. Then he gently brushed away the tears that stole down her cheeks, and which she did not have the strength to wipe away herself.

'You look so young, lying there,' he said, trying to hide a glimmer of anger that lit his eyes for a brief instant. 'I'll see to it that you never go through that again.'

She feebly tried to rise. 'Where is the baby, Deneys? Something has happened to him and you won't tell me! Is he deformed in some way, or is he – dead?' She began to cry uncontrollably, and he took her into his arms as if he was comforting a small child.

'Now don't upset yourself, darling. You're still in no state to –'

'To what?' She pushed him away with all the strength she had left. 'I demand to know what has happened to the child, Deneys. I have a right to know – I'm his mother.' Her green eyes were accusing in an ashen face.

He rose and stood beside the bed, his posture withdrawn, as if a burden that was too heavy hung about him, weighing him down. When he spoke his voice was very low, without emotion; somewhere inside him he had put the brakes on his feelings. 'Arabella, I wasn't going to tell you until you were stronger.'

'Stronger? I may be exhausted, but otherwise I am perfectly all right, and I demand to be told about the child I bore for nearly nine long months, and gave birth to in such pain!' she almost shouted, knowing now that something was terribly wrong. 'What gives you the right, Deneys, to decide what I must know regarding our baby? What makes you so much wiser than I?'

'Men are better able to take these things, Arabella. They've been schooled since birth for the crises of life. And our nature is more –'

'More what? You've never given birth to a child! How can you possibly know what I may be feeling? How can you stand there, and arrogantly tell me you know whether I'm strong enough to take the news, whatever it is, or not? What gives you that right to decide for me?'

'The child – our son – was stillborn.' In the deathly silence of the room, his voice was barely audible. 'How could I tell you, after you had gone through so much?'

Utterly numbed, Arabella fell back against the pillows, unmindful that she had swept off the multi-coloured counterpane. Her skin was drenched with perspiration; it seeped through her cotton gown, which clung to her clammy skin as her brain tried to take in what he had said. Slowly, her eyes flicked to the figure now standing at the foot of the bed, and suddenly the man with the broad shoulders in the finely tailored white shirt was like a stranger to her, telling her something she did not want to believe.

'It isn't true. You're lying to me! I will not believe it.'

'It's true, my dear. He could not have survived, not after –'

'After I went out alone and had that stupid accident – is that what you're saying?'

The awful realisation crept over her with sinuous, stealthy fingers: all those months of pleasure and planning as the little boy grew inside her, then the accident – and the most terrible agony – all for nothing!

'Are you blaming me, Deneys?' she sobbed. 'If he is dead, then I want to die myself!'

'No one is blaming you, Arabella. It happened, that's all.'

'Then let me see him, please. I want to see my child!'

'Tiaan took him away, my dear. He and I thought it better that you didn't see him.'

'You and he thought it better!' she screamed at him, her eyes wide and demented. 'How dare you decide that without asking me! Did I have nothing to do with it, Deneys? Am I so unimportant that I have no say in anything regarding the child, dead or alive? I gave birth to that baby – I had a right to see him.'

She searched her husband's face, but found in it no consolation. It was drawn into lines of bitter sadness, but she hardly noticed in her own overriding shock.

For a moment he hesitated, then gave a deep, weary sigh, as if he had gone over this ground before in his own mind. 'I wanted to protect you, Arabella – that is a man's duty and responsibility. Tiaan and I thought it best in the circumstances. After enduring so much, we thought it might kill you to see him – like that.'

'But *you* could see him! It was a cruel and selfish thing to do, not to let me see the child I gave birth to – not to let me say goodbye to him . . . Leave me alone. I don't want you near me!'

She flung her words out as if she were flinging some dangerous explosive into the open space between them, then tearfully flinched back against the pillows, waiting to hear it go off.

Deneys stared at her, the angry power of his body concealed by his clothes. Then he picked up his jacket from the worn riempie-backed chair. 'As you wish, Arabella. I shall be in the study if you need me. I'm sure you'll feel different after a good sleep.'

Rage forked behind Arabella's eyes. 'I won't feel any different after a sleep, believe me. I shall never forgive you or Tiaan Malherbe, ever!'

'Forgive me?' His control deserted him, and his grief welled up. 'Forgive me? What have you got to forgive *me* for? Perhaps if you hadn't been fool enough to go driving alone in your eighth month, we would have a living child today!' With that, he turned abruptly on his heel and strode from the room, closing the door behind him with a resounding crash.

The heat in the room seemed to be coming at her in scorching waves. Everything, including the spot where they had taken away the cradle, seemed to waver a little. That empty space and Deneys' parting words were the last cruel straws. She realised she was crying as if her heart would break. Everything that had seemed so beautiful and exciting had been crushed by some unknown evil, forcing life out of their helpless little son.

She wanted Deneys, but she did not want him, and he was the only one at whom she could hit back with all her anger and confusion. When he came in to see her later, she refused to speak to him, and kept her head turned away.

The house grew quiet and subdued after the last caller had left

Deneys, and the last flickering flame was snuffed. In her lonely bed, Arabella stared into the darkness. Her body was clammy beneath the sheet and she pushed it away, to let the cool air dry the mist of sweat. And in those moments, she intensely wished she could die, because the most precious gift she had ever been given had been so cruelly taken from her.

12

Arabella returned to her house duties, a haggard and grief-stricken woman. Nothing was the same as before: something had gone out of it. The baby's room, which had for so many months been the heart of the house, was now empty, except for a table, chair and a couch, and here she sat hour upon hour, trying to come to terms with her loss, but only feeling frozen and empty. Of all the trials and misfortunes in her life, this was the one that had grieved her the most – *and it was all her fault.* She was still angry with Deneys and Tiaan Malherbe for high-handedly making a decision without consulting her, but her feeling of guilt overrode all of this.

For days she secluded herself in the baby's room, even sleeping there, and saw nobody. She even gave up writing to Rachel, who was expecting her second child, as she mourned the loss of her own intensely and privately.

It was late one night when the sound of fists battering at the nursery door shocked Arabella out of a restless sleep. She cowered on the couch for a few moments before lighting the oil lamp beside her.

'Open this door at once, Arabella! You've locked me out of your bed for too long! I'm sick to death of your unnatural attitude!' The usual musical timbre of Deneys' voice was lost in harsh, angry tones. Arabella dragged a trembling hand across her brow, and sank back into the pillows. 'Are you going to open this door?'

She shrank back further as the battering continued. 'Go away and leave me alone.'

'Arabella – if you don't open this door, I'll break it down!'

Unable to bear it any longer, and with a growing fear that he would do as he threatened, she cautiously went to the door, and opened it.

Deneys was standing in the passage, a fireplace poker in his hand. Fear ran through her and she froze even before she saw his face. In the lamplight, he was unrecognisable, except for the burnished gold hair, and the blue silk dressing gown.

'What do you want, Deneys? I told you to leave me alone.'

'You've no right to lock me out of your bedroom or your life,' he said, staring at her through enraged brown eyes. 'Under the law we are married and you owe me –'

'I owe you nothing! We may be married under the law, but that gives you no right to barge into my room and demand rights which I have no desire to give you. You make decisions over my head and then bully me when I make decisions of my own.'

The muscles beneath his handsome face had tensed, and Arabella's heart set up a frantic beating as she feared he would touch her. 'Now leave me alone, Deneys. It's not fair that you torment me so. I've made my decision and I don't ever want you to touch me again!' The words echoed hollowly between them as she watched him gripping the poker with white-knuckled strength.

'You are damaging our marriage, Arabella. Things cannot go on like this – it's unnatural and selfish of you. I'm a man and I have a desire to sleep with my wife. And I will sleep with you – tonight!'

Arabella shook her head, though her heart thudded heavily in her breast. 'And I am a woman with a desire to be left alone. What will you do to change it – rape me? Are you so bestial that you will take your desires in whatever way you can?'

As he stared at her, she saw a sudden wave of unfamiliar defeat on his face. 'Why do you taunt me, why? You know what I want, and yet you bait me. I have never forced a woman to my bidding, and I don't intend to start now,' he said bitterly, throwing down the poker with intense disgust. 'But you knew that all along, and you don't care a damn! Not one solitary damn!'

He stood before her, his anger at her suddenly weakening in the soft, appealing vividness of her presence in the lamplight. She was changed. No longer innocent, but a woman who had known his love, his body and the fulfilment of her own passions. But now, she had turned from him, shut him out of her life. He had not seen her in her nightclothes for many weeks, and the sight of her face suffused with warm colour filled him with a longing to take her in his arms and crush her close against him.

A long moment passed as his gaze intensified. She raised a shaking hand to cover her face and banish him from her sight, as he said fiercely, 'I'm living with a ghost, do you understand that? Do you know what it's like, to live with a shell that does not care whether you exist or not? I can see that it means nothing to you.' He let out a deep, rasping breath. 'I shall not trouble you again!'

Arabella experienced a rising panic. How could she continue to endure the most terrible loneliness of her life, separated emotionally from this man she had married? But still she could not make him understand. Didn't he see she was still mourning the little one? Did he not love her enough to suppress for a while his own selfish masculine desires?

Averting her face, she wept inwardly as she heard him turn and stride away towards their bedroom, where he slammed the door shut.

Deneys did not see the translucent green eyes follow his departing back. Once in the bedroom, he braced an elbow high on the wall and, pressing his brow against his forearm, struggled to subdue the thunderous beating of his heart, and the angry, frustrated tears that threatened to flow and undo his deep masculine pride.

Christmas was a quiet, religious day in the Dutch community, while New Year was celebrated by a large gathering in the hills outside the village. From early morning, wagons and carts had passed the du Rand house, trailing down the dusty, street loaded with sucking pigs to roast over the coals, chicken pie, pickled eggs, beetroot, sour beans, potatoes to bake over the ashes, breads of all sorts, custards, cakes, pies and preserves, and to drink, ginger beer, pineapple beer and peach brandy.

'Are you coming, Arabella?' Deneys' head appeared around the nursery door, gleaming and freshly washed. 'You should come – it's expected, especially from the important members of the community.'

Arabella turned her tired, strained face from staring out of the window, and looked at him, a strange confusion pervading her mind. But for some time, she only waited.

'It'll do you good to get out into the fresh air and eat properly for a change,' he said at last.

She sat down on the chair beside the bed, and let herself lean back, very stiffly, then she determinedly adjusted her skirt. 'I cannot go – I'm not in any state for festivities.' She paused. 'But don't let that stop you. Go – as you say, it's expected of you.'

'You can't go on mourning forever, Arabella,' Deneys said abruptly. 'It is madness to lock yourself away. What is done, is done. You must start to live again.'

She shook her head violently. 'That will be my decision,' she replied. 'I'm not ready yet.'

'But you're not trying!' Deneys exploded. He came a pace nearer into the room, his eyes a brown flash of exasperation in his face. 'You're wallowing in self-pity.'

'Leave me be, Deneys. You'll never understand how I feel,' Arabella said with muddled anger. She stood up, and they faced each other across the small space. She wanted to smile, say something light and sensible. But she could not. She could only stand there and wait.

Deneys shrugged with frustrated eloquence. 'You're being stubborn and pig-headed, my dear, and there seems to be nothing I or anyone else can do to change it.'

Arabella could only fold her shaking arms and say nothing. But furtively, she glanced at his departing back, clad in his best dark suit. She had few memories of him which were not strong, controlled, reassuring – until recently. He was now often restless, impatient, even unreasonable.

As he reached the door, he stopped and looked back at her. 'You do realise that this is no marriage, and that soon there'll be nothing left of it? I will go once more to a gathering as one of the men whose wives are dead.'

She turned back to the window after he had left, staring out over the neglected garden that was becoming untidy. She could control nothing in her life, no matter what Deneys said, no matter how much he bullied her – not even her own thoughts. Some centre in her life had disintegrated. Everything, until the fateful accident and the baby's death, had proceeded so well and so happily, but now, everything was in disorder like the garden outside. People talked about her, she knew. Marietjie de Villiers and Elsabe van Niekerk were behind the malicious rumours about her madness. She struggled with herself. Her mind, always so disciplined, was in such a wordless panic, that everything seemed to have become dangerous and sinister.

Deneys stepped into the bright sunshine and climbed into the cart, all scrubbed and cleaned for the day. Marietjie de Villiers, her shining dark hair coiled artfully under an elaborate and exquisitely stitched bonnet, stopped beside him in another cart driven by her young brother Kobus. From a box in her hands she took a piece of watermelon preserve and offered it to Deneys with a knowing smile, the movement of her young body throwing into bold prominence her firm, well-formed breasts, which even the demure line of her white dress could not hide. But more than the allure of her young body, was the beauty of her face.

From the shaded depths of the verandah, hidden by the profuse leaves of the Catawba grapevine, Arabella silently watched them. She saw Marietjie laugh and tug playfully at the loop of rein that curved between the mare and his hand, before Thor the grey wolfhound barked and leapt around them, making mock savage attacks at first one and then another. A small group crowded around both carts, laughing and chatting, carrying baskets and platters, pots and bowls filled with food and drink. Then the carts rumbled away in clouds of red dust, as Thor raced after Deneys. Behind them some noisy youths rode on horseback, joking and whistling and trying to catch Marietjie's attention, which was determinedly fixed on the handsome man in the conveyance ahead.

Arabella turned away slowly and painfully, feeling the dryness of Wasp's nose as it investigated her hand. The brown eyes looked up at her and she stretched out a pale, thin hand and patted his furry red ears. But as she walked back through the front door, with Wasp at her heels, she knew that everything had moved, shifted. She could feel it. All about the house was sunshine, and happy people enjoying themselves, but it was like looking on the brightly coloured façade of a nightmare, knowing that something horrible was shaping behind it. And as she closed the door, shutting the bright world out, she felt that she had no power whatsoever to exorcise the shapeless fear inside her.

13

Autumn was on the land, and here and there the small Burning Bush bearing its striking four-winged russet and green fruits flashed like little flames while the attractive red trumpets of the Cape honeysuckle bloomed for the last time that season in informal hedges. It was the quarterly *Nagmaal* or Holy Communion – a great social and religious event in the lives of the Boers, when farmers and their families travelled to the village, some to the houses they kept especially for the occasion, others to stay with friends, yet others to camp in tents near the Dutch Reformed Church for the coming weekend. Now everywhere there was movement in the streets, and the hum of a serious intent.

It was late one Friday morning, and Arabella, uncaring of the bustle outside, sat at the well-scrubbed kitchen table, a month-old newspaper before her. The kitchen was a fairly big, light room, and now it was flooded with bright sunshine. She read on, oblivious of Samson energetically stoking up the fire in the stove and looking anxiously at her from time to time. She had not finished her late breakfast, only pushed a piece of toast around her plate, then dropped it. There was no use ignoring any longer what was happening in the country at large, including Ben Saville's not inconsiderable part in leading the Natal delegation in their lonely fight for federation. Small snatches of articles in newspapers over the months came back to her as the delegates of the National Convention moved from the humidity of Durban to the more temperate climate of Cape Town. Now the latest developments were in all the newspapers – small but significant winds of change.

All of a sudden, the room seemed very hot. Sweat broke out on her forehead, and under the high neck of her muslin blouse. Ominous fragments began to drift through her mind. Isaac's *Southern Herald* had recently reported that the political gamble taken in the Draft Bill for Union had been enormous, but that it had completely shelved the issues of the so-called Non-Europeans and women's emancipation. It was all very subtle – but they were there: little prickling disturbances, little dancing points of flame, in a great quiet forest.

Something was happening in the country that would affect all their lives, changing the face of South Africa forever. She remembered the articles she had read recently – with their talk of 'Union or Federation'. She had not focused on any of it for months, and now the Draft Bill had been passed and taken by an official delegation to the Westminster Parliament. Ben Saville had been hailed as a hero in Natal on his return from England, for his unsuccessful fight for a loose federation, while his fellow delegates were denounced in a storm of protest as traitors for agreeing to Union.

She began to think about it confusedly, and when there was a knock on the front door, did not move or even appear to hear it. Samson looked up, frowning, then went to answer it. Seconds later he returned and announced Tienie Meyer in his high, singsong voice.

There was a deep and affronted silence on the part of Arabella, as Tienie's broad cheerful face stared down at her, a plate of golden-brown biscuits in one hand, slices of snow-white bread in the other.

'I am sorry to trouble you, Mevrou, but I was baking for the Nagmaal, and I brought you something to eat.' The woman placed both plates on the table, a hesitant pride shining in her homely face. 'You must try my kaiing biscuits, Mevrou. They are made from the remains of rendered fat, which we call kaiings, with ground cinnamon and ground ginger – you will like them. And the bread, Mevrou, it is salt-rising bread spread with yellow butter from Meneer Hennie Venter's farm, with fresh slices of biltong on top.'

Arabella's lips tightened in resistance at the rather overpowering physical presence of the young woman, but Tienie seemed undeterred. She pulled out a wooden chair and sat down, then turned to Samson.

'We will have coffee, Samson, Mevrou du Rand and me. And plates. The Mevrou looks as if she has not eaten for all of six months.'

Samson nodded his head vigorously, almost in relief, and hurried into the pantry, as Arabella drew in a sharp breath of angry protest. 'Thank you, Mevrou Meyer, but I'm not hungry and in no condition to receive visitors.'

Tienie's pretty brown eyes followed the agitation of Arabella's fingers as they crumpled the newspaper in her hands.

'Mevrou du Rand,' she said suddenly, in a brusque but compassionate voice, 'I know what it is like to lose a child – I myself have lost two little ones. I also know what it is like to be closed to one's man – but you are one of the lucky ones. Your man cares about you and he worries about your suffering. I know Meneer du Rand, our esteemed lawyer. I see it in his eyes.'

When Samson brought in the coffee-pot and two cups, Tienie settled herself to pour and to hand out the food she had brought.

Soon the kitchen was filled with delicious aromas, subtly awakening a stirring to life in Arabella, as she sat looking across at Tienie. For a second, her green eyes gleamed.

'What right have you to come here and talk about things that are none of your business?' she hissed, as if some spark of fire deep inside had been ignited.

A worried look creased Tienie's brow for a second, then it smoothed out. 'I hear what you say, Mevrou du Rand, but I worry for you and your husband. I see what is happening and I know it mustn't go on.' She looked down at her large, capable hands nervously folded in her lap. 'My cousin, Marta van Wyk, she was in Leeukop concentration camp, Mevrou. Her baby died there, from measles, and it was you who helped her through that sad time. You, the English rooinek nurse who fought to give those people more comforts and better treatment, who wrote to Mejuffrou Hobhouse so that the rest of the world would know. I, too, was in a concentration camp, near Middelburg, and we did not have such a nurse as you.'

She raised her cup and drank slowly, urging Arabella to do the same. After a while, Arabella copied her. She was thirsty, after all, and glad of the dark hot drink. As she put the cup down, she raised an ironical eyebrow. 'So? Those days are gone, Mevrou, and no one can bring my baby back.'

'Eat – it will do you good,' Tienie persisted, pushing a plate of food closer.

Arabella succumbed and allowed herself to eat the bread offered, feeling for the first time in months, a warmth and a strange comfort spreading through her. She managed a wan smile. 'It's very kind of you, Mevrou – Tienie – to bother about a madwoman like me.'

Tienie looked at her thoughtfully. 'Not mad, Mevrou, only one who is in deep suffering. *Liewe Hemel*! But it is hard to be a woman, and the menfolk they do not understand.'

There was a silence and Arabella cleared her throat. 'I caused the death of my child, Tienie. It's hard for me to talk of these things –' She bit her lip furiously. 'Deneys doesn't understand. He gets impatient with me, you see – then he goes out for hours and comes home very late. I think he blames me for what happened. I don't know if I can have any more children, and he won't like that, not deep down.'

Tienie took a breath and stared straight ahead. Arabella could see she was embarrassed and was wishing she had not spoken, when the other woman said suddenly, 'Yes, it is good to talk of these deep things, Mevrou – Arabella – these women's things which we bury so deep inside our hearts. I have had four daughters and two stillborn sons, and Anton my husband has never forgiven me for not giving him a boy.' Her lips quivered for an instant. 'Sons are so important to us Boer people – from long ago, when the father's lands were divided between his sons and as they became men, he gave them their own cattle in preparation for marriage. It is deep in our race, the continuing of sons for the family, and I have failed him.'

Arabella's brows soared in disbelief, and that gesture mysteriously changed her appearance. Her lethargy vanished, and her small face became alive. '*Failed* him? But you have four healthy daughters, Tienie! I would have given anything to have *one* healthy child, boy or girl!' Tienie watched her take a kaiing biscuit and break it with quick, nervous movements in her trembling fingers.

Tienie glanced away, her lips working. 'I know this, but Anton, he is still in the old ways. He is like a child himself sometimes, so I suppose the Lord has seen fit to give me a son after all, in a man's body.' She smiled dejectedly, then her eyes met Arabella's, which were sparkling with suppressed mirth, and soon they were both struggling to stem the great tide of their humour.

Arabella gasped for breath, as her laughter finally subsided, and she said rather diffidently, 'I suppose all woman inherit a ready-made son. Men have always wanted sons, no matter their race, and a lot of women too. They don't realise the tremendous value of daughters, but it's up to us to make them understand these things.' Her eyes had lost their dull, shadowed expression as anger suddenly burned in them. 'We have to stand up for ourselves in this man's world, Tienie, or we'll go on being trampled underfoot. I resented Doctor Malherbe's attitude while I was in labour – many male doctors have this arrogant, unsympathetic idea that we are some kind of animal bringing forth young without any feelings whatsoever. This must be changed!' Her hands locked themselves together in a tight, agonised clasp. 'There are women we must help in this community, Tienie, if only we can reach them.'

The other woman stuck a biscuit into her mouth and chewed it vigorously. 'But first, Arabella, you must get your husband back.'

'Back? What do you mean?' She was confused.

Tienie sighed, hunched over her plate, then she spoke rapidly, the words hurrying over each other. '*A-le-magtig*! but there is such sinfulness in this world. There is much talk in this dorp, Arabella, about the wickedness of that Marietjie de Villiers and that Elsabe van Niekerk, and she the niece of Dominee Conradie himself!' She took a deep breath, her face suddenly flushed. 'My God, but that Marietjie de Villiers is evil, Arabella. It is she who has spread the gossip that you hate Meneer du Rand and close him out because he is a Boer. It is all over the place. She wishes you harm, that one. I think she wants

280

to make it so bad for you here that you leave and go back to Johannesburg, so that Meneer du Rand will divorce you and marry her. And, my God, she doesn't even care that divorce is a mortal sin in our community! But she has a great fear of you, nevertheless, because she is not really sure of your power over your husband.'

Arabella went cold as she remembered New Year's Day, and saw again all too clearly the way that beautiful young woman had plucked the rein in Deneys' hand . . .

'*Liewe Vader!* But you must do something to stop that Marietjie, Arabella. Your husband he is a handsome man, and clever. He is well-liked and respected, and those two they work hard to send you away, so that they can step, how you say – step in your boots.'

Arabella sighed with suppressed rage. 'But what can I do if he doesn't love me? I've already lost him.'

'No, Arabella, that is not true,' Tienie ventured. 'It is not too late. Why do you think those two go on with their spiteful games – because they think it's *not* over for you! So do it – and stop them before it *is* too late.'

Arabella stood up, feeling old and tired as Tienie rose with her, waiting for her reply. 'I will try, Tienie, though for the life of me, I don't know how.'

Tienie smiled, pleased, and picked up the empty plates. 'I will come again, Arabella, and bring one of my orange cakes. You will like the recipe, perhaps – it's an old one from my grandmother who lived a large part of her life in the Western Cape. She used to make brandied grapes too, before pressing time, and wonderful grape jam. Well,' she turned to leave, 'I can tell you such stories that will fill up a year.'

Then she was gone, and Arabella felt a deep foreboding as Samson stood for a moment looking at her, before depositing a basket of freshly laid eggs on the table. There was an awkward silence, then she quickly turned away, but not before she had seen the pained accusation in his eyes, for he knew what had happened between her and his master . . .

14

The rains came early, in that year of 1910. The last remnants of the cold season had hardly disappeared before buds swelled on trees and shrubs and the veld began to reveal its mysterious and haunting beauty once more. Then the river came down in flood, missing the village by a few miles, but the rushing of the muddy water could be heard everywhere as a deep, ominous swell. Trees were uprooted, and even rocks and boulders from the craggy foothills loosened and came tumbling down the river banks.

November, blossomed in summer heat as the Act of Union was carried on a wave of good feeling, but as the celebration pageant in Cape Town faded, the opening of the first Union Parliament by the Duke of Connaught brought the country back to solid, hard reality. The representatives of the two British colonies and the two former Boer republics now merged into one country, under their first Prime Minister, Louis Botha, were now faced with many extraordinarily complicated issues.

It was two o'clock one afternoon when Samson came running up the garden path, gesticulating wildly. Arabella hurried from the verandah and managed to calm him down sufficiently to learn that Anton Meyer, Tienie's husband, had returned home early from the mayor's office, and gone with his black servant Hosea, to chop firewood near the river, where it had flooded in the rains. A large rock had dislocated and fallen on them: Hosea had been killed outright, but Anton was still pinned beneath it.

'Go, Missus! You nurse – you help Baas du Rand in the war. You go now and work good medicine on Baas Meyer.'

Arabella struggled with a sudden nausea, and heard herself say: 'Yes, yes, Samson. I'll go to Mr Meyer, but we need big strong men if he's under a rock. Go and tell the Master and get Doctor Malherbe right away.'

Samson nodded and raced off on his spindly, sinewy legs, while Arabella ran back inside and rummaged frantically for her old medical box. Then she was out and down the front path. The afternoon air vibrated with the shouts of people calling for help. Doors opened and householders emerged, scenting disaster.

The school doors were ajar as Arabella hurried by, and she could hear the boisterous voices of the children. She forgot Anton for a brief instant, and stared emptily before her, her face a ruin of agony. She knew it would be that way for a long time. Then she was past, and the voices of the children fell behind, becoming fainter and fainter. She ran alongside the larger houses and into the open veld, making for the rocky outcrop where Anton and Hosea had chopped the wood. It lay in a wild stretch of land near the river, within easy walking distance of the village but dangerous and open to rock-slides. She thought she would never reach the spot, so tortuous was the path, so dark between the shadowing bushes, as she struggled over rock and shale, where in one place, a long black snake slept on a nearby stone. She followed the sound of agitated voices which gradually became louder, and for a moment she recoiled, for it seemed that the whole village was there. But she had to go on, for after Dr. Malherbe, she had the most medical knowledge.

Then she saw Alida Viljoen, who ran up to her, her face as white as chalk. 'Ach, Arabella – thank God you've come. No one knows what to do with Anton. The rock is too heavy and he is in great pain. Poor Hosea – he had no chance. It was too quick.'

Arabella followed Alida's pointing finger to the body of Hosea – a young man with four children – lying under a blanket. She struggled through the praying, weeping women, the frantic to and froing of the men, and shouted in Dutch; 'For heaven's sake move back and let me get to Mr Meyer! I am a trained nurse!'

But she still had to fight her way through the mass of excited humanity to where Anton lay, a mighty rock wedged across his chest and abdomen; she could see that the huddled shape of his body was unnaturally twisted. Beside him, a woman and two little girls were kneeling and quietly sobbing. It was Tienie, with two of her daughters. With horror, Arabella saw that Anton Meyer's torn clothing was one tattered mass of red rags; even his wooden leg was smashed.

She knelt down and immediately felt his pulse; it was fluttering but still present. His breathing was ominously shallow, however, and he was restless and sweating profusely – all signs which caused her great alarm. But there was still time to save him – if luck held and they could lift the rock away. She knew that he would be losing a great deal of blood, for his pelvis and lung were crushed.

At that point, Anton raised his head, groaning, *'My vrou! My kinders! My liewe kinders!'* then closed his eyes, in a fresh onslaught of pain.

Arabella's small face was running with sweat, as she undid her medical box and gave him a few drops of laudanum. Then he lapsed into unconsciousness and Tienie wept, her arms about her daughters.

Arabella pulled off her shawl and tucked it around the wounded man to keep him warm, her hand automatically smoothing the dirtied fair hair from his forehead. There was nothing else she could do until the rock was removed.

'There's still hope, Tienie,' she said, as she settled down to wait, 'if Doctor Malherbe gets here soon and the men can work out a way to lift the rock without much more delay.' Oh, how she wished Deneys were here. He would know what to do. And where was Samson? If only they'd hurry.

She turned to a man kneeling beside her. 'Please get a stretcher or a board or something we can tie Mr Meyer on to when the rock is removed, and fetch some blankets.'

The man, wearing rough trousers and shirt-sleeves rolled up at the elbow, nodded and rose, shouting orders to those pressing in behind him. Then Anton opened his eyes again, his face twisted with pain. He tried to mouth some words but could not.

'Oh, Arabella,' Tienie whispered in anguish. 'What will I do if –'

'Hush, Tienie. During the war I saw men survive worse injuries than this. We must keep hoping, that's all we can do.'

She could hear the insistent shuffle of boots as men and women still gathered around, some with advice, some with comfort, others shocked into numbed silence, but the weeping and confusion had stopped in the presence of this small Englishwoman who, just by her quiet authority, had taken charge.

Then, miraculously, Deneys was there with Samson, announcing that Dr Malherbe was on a farm some miles away, delivering a baby. There was a moment's silence in which he and Arabella glanced at each other, then he took over, ordering the men to lever the boulder slowly from Anton's chest and abdomen. He threw off his coat, rolled up his sleeves and started to heave slowly with the men.

From that moment on, Deneys was continually on the move. He directed the proceedings, careful to see that no further damage was caused to Anton, gave orders to some, turned to answer enquiries from others, stooped every now and then to give Anton encouragement, and to check with Arabella on his condition. As time passed, other men came to bend their backs to the labour.

Arabella scarcely breathed, yielding to a surge of hope. Her anxious eyes followed her husband's every move, and she became the silent sharer of his actions as never before. Beyond them, others headed back and forth from the village to the koppie.

Some of the women, carrying water, bandages and brandy, drew up beside her as the men strained at the huge boulder that crushed Anton. Suddenly, it lifted; rolled, and fell away. Once he was clear, Anton screamed in agony, while there was an audible gasp of relief from those gathered about. Arabella administered a few more drops of laudanum, bandaged the external wounds and supervised the placing of him on the rough stretcher that lay ready nearby. Deneys was there beside her, helping to stabilise the injured man by tieing him to the stretcher, then he stepped back as she laid a blanket over Anton, who was carefully carried back to the village, with Tienie walking tragically beside him.

Arabella stood at Anton's bedside with an arm about Tienie, who sobbed desperately. Then, as the house expanded with the arrival of more family and friends, she realised that Deneys was not among them. He had disappeared somewhere during the afternoon, and she had not even noticed. She was completely exhausted and wanted her bed. Her tired heart was pounding uncomfortably as she thought of Deneys and the way he had helped Anton earlier. And as the minutes passed, his face did not fade in her memory. It became clearer, more urgent. Suddenly she wanted him near her; she wanted to tell him what had frightened her for so long. She had shut him out when he had needed her in his own time of grief. He was part of her life, her family. She wanted him. Tienie had been right – *she had to get him back* ...

Her heart was pounding even faster as she excused herself and walked quickly out of Tienie's small house halfway down the hill. Her need for Deneys became almost passionate. There was a hunger in her, divorced from any physical desire. Deneys would understand. He was her friend. She put a hand to her throbbing head, and began to run up the hill. I need my husband, she thought. I need to be an intelligent and understanding wife. I am so lonely. I need Deneys.

Her new conviction became crystal clear as she ran faster towards the house, past the unpretentious dwellings set about small, enclosed plots of grass and trees and vines, where mothers and their children watched her with curious stares. She could see the mountains in the distance. They were a brilliant mauve against the glaring sunset sky, their serrated tops rising high beyond the village. She paused for a moment as she reached home, then hurried towards the verandah, now in deep shadow, where the hall lamp filtered on to it through a pattern of dark vine leaves. She looked at the house critically. It had once had an attractive appearance, but was now blistered and peeling. The wooden verandah posts had faded and cracked in places, and the shutters had been neglected. The windows had started to look grimy, the lank curtains behind them noticeably dirty.

It was all her fault. She had neglected the place for months. She had failed to make it attractive and inviting. No wonder Deneys was away so often. How he must hate it, every much as she did, in that moment. As he must hate her ... she became aware that her hair was untidily held up by a series of very visible hairpins, and that it straggled down her neck, that her apron was conspicuously soiled, and her black buttoned boots had scuffed toes. Then her thoughts blurred, became a chaos in her mind. She ran quickly up the steps, and opened the front door. She had to find him. He must know how she felt. She had left it too long – a winter and a spring too long.

But there were only the dogs to welcome her, and Samson in the dining room.

'Where's the Master, Samson? I thought he'd be home for dinner. Why are you setting only one place?' she blurted out, her heart thumping in her chest.

Samson looked up from laying a set of cutlery beside a plate, and quickly adjusted his dark-blue waistcoat over a spotless white shirt. He frowned, disturbed. 'The Baas he gone to dinner at Baas de Villiers house, Missus. He back very late.'

A suffocating sensation tightened Arabella's throat as she stared at him, then she turned and walked quickly out of the room. In the gloomy passage she closed her eyes, but saw only confusion behind her lids. She opened them again, and went into the nursery where she fumbled for the chair she knew was nearby. She sat down, rested her elbows on her knees and covered her face with her hands. She felt so threatened. So terribly afraid! And her mind was filled with images of the beautiful, taunting face of Marietjie de Villiers ...

15

The following morning she awoke, determined to start again, and to put the past behind her. Deneys had already left for his office as she gave Samson the day off and set to work. In the morning's oppressive heat, the White Leghorns and Rhode Island Reds *car-r-rkhed* lazily as they dusted themselves in the powdery dirt of the chicken coop, the hot air smelling of steaming plant-growth. She opened the front of the black cast-iron stove in the sunny kitchen where Samson had placed sticks of wood and a shovelful of coal in the firebox, and set it going. The stove gave out a companionable roar, and she found that to be doing things was a comfort. It helped keep her mind off her problems and to pass the time until Deneys returned. She put the kettle on to heat, and afterwards she took down the lace curtains and did the washing, then hung it out in the hot, still air, near the barbed-wire fence on which small grasshoppers were impaled by fiscal shrikes and where a buff-coloured scrub hare, finely speckled with black, rested in the mysterious, sinister long grasses of the veld that seemed to encroach ever nearer with its silent wildness.

She cleaned and swept the house from top to bottom, and polished the copper baking pots and pans taken down from the wooden rack above the row of lidded jam-pots. She scoured the table and shelves, and cleaned the windows until they shone. Then she went into the pantry with its single window leading off the kitchen and dusted every canister on the shelves. She looked around the dining room, at the well-cleaned and polished yellow-wood table in the middle of the room; the six stinkwood chairs strung with leather thongs around it. From the wall-cupboard she took down the cups and saucers ranged for daily use, and cleaned them, remembering the happy meals eaten in this room so many months ago. The noisy ticking of the clock on the cupboard shelf was the only sound which broke the stillness as she worked with almost desperate urgency.

All through that day she tried to turn her thoughts elsewhere, but they always returned to Deneys, and the image of him and Marietjie together. For the first time she understood what Rosamunde had suffered when she, Arabella, had caused her such torment. Now she knew that no one was invulnerable. Her world had been shattered. She had become vulnerable because she had suddenly become perceptive.

Dinner was ready – a savoury pot bubbling contentedly on the stove – when she tended the chickens and gathered in the dry, sun-smelling washing, taking it into the cool shadows of the house.

The sun was fingering the opposite wall of the kitchen as she piled up the clean clothes and curtains to be ironed. The waiting was so hard and she shivered suddenly, for although the house was still warm from the afternoon's heat, it was lonely in the gathering darkness, even with the dogs cuddled close for company. To keep her spirits up she lighted the oil lamps, but the dim golden glow only made the house seem more empty, more forsaken. And still there was no sight or sound of Deneys. She peered out into the darkness, listening. The moon was up, an enormous yellow eye under which the countryside looked strange and hauntingly beautiful.

With the silence deepening about the house, she damped the dry, clean clothes, prior to ironing them. Bitter defeat shone in her eyes. Nothing would ever be the same again; Deneys was a stranger living in another world, all their first wonderful months buried and forgotten ... When the irons sizzled at the touch of her wet finger she began to press the clothes and the curtains. Nothing comforted her any more, not even the presence of the dogs lying near the door, snoring softly in their sleep.

Later, pulling her shawl closely about her shoulders, she waited while the hours ticked by, the multi-coloured tea tin at her elbow as she sat at the kitchen table, drinking cups of Mazawattee tea, the dinner keeping warm on the stove. She thought about Marietjie de Villiers. Now she began to see her as an over-eager girl who needed to be pitied. Marietjie was young, inexperienced in the real pain of being a woman, as she herself had been not so long ago. Marietjie, Arabella decided by some obscure intuition, thought she was in love with a dashing, handsome, older man, just as she had once been with Ben. Marietjie was infatuated with Deneys; he was so different from the other men in the village – widely travelled, educated, sophisticated ... She knew she was young and that he had chosen to marry someone else ... and this made her jealous and spiteful. Now Arabella was full of understanding for Marietjie, and yet she was still so very afraid, for there was an untried and bold power about the beautiful young woman. At this thought, panic again overwhelmed her. As she sat in the gloom, the prospect of losing Deneys swept through her heart with so sharp a sense of desolation that her torment became unbearable.

She rose quickly to make for the comfort of her bed. How could she go on? Was there to be no end to her pain? She could hear the paraffin sloshing around the bowl of the lamp in her hand as she stopped outside the room she had once shared with Deneys. How could she bear to lose him? She could *not* bear it! Never again to feel his hands upon her, to hear the steady beat of his heart as she lay in his arms – to lose forever the special companionship which he alone had brought her. She must surely die if he left her. But it was too late ... she had been a fool and now she had to suffer the consequences.

Slowly, as she stood in the darkness, she mastered her emotion and faced her fear. Another door had closed in her life – one she would have done anything to keep open. Then, with the harsh wailing of a distant bushbaby in her ears, she turned away and went to the nursery. And there she lay, fully clothed on the couch, crying bitterly.

As Dominee Conradie was mounting the pulpit with the big Bible, Arabella stood for a second alone in the entrance of the overflowing square white Dutch Reformed Church. He gazed down at her as she slipped into the back pew, looking neither to right nor left from under the brim of her black mourning bonnet, on that strange quiet day of Anton Meyer's funeral. Something of the shock of his sudden death seemed to be brooding over the quiet world outside, as the congregation stood to sing a psalm. The church was clean and bright, with the long wooden coffin covered with wreaths at the further end, a little way from the pulpit. Seats were placed at either side of the coffin, and in the middle, facing the congregation, stood a black chair, evidently the seat for Dominee Conradie.

She saw Deney's strong, athletic figure standing some way in front, beside Ernst de Villiers, his large, stout wife, Petra, Marietjie and her brothers. To the prayer, the psalm, and the opening of the Dominee's service, she listened as one might to an unknown language spoken in a dream. But suddenly she realised, from the quick, surreptitious glances cast at her by the men and women on either side of the pew, that something quite apart from the service was taking place. It was then that she saw Marietjie turn her beautiful head in her full black bonnet and stare at her for a long, penetrating moment. Arabella felt the young woman's triumph and she knew she was right when she saw the swift and secret glance between Marietjie and one of the other girls standing close by. She cursed herself for coming alone, without Deneys, but it had been a last-minute decision on her part, a decision to support Tienie in her grief. She was suddenly terribly afraid again, knowing how she would diminish beside the tall, beautiful younger woman with the influential father and the village youths grovelling at

289

her feet. She looked away. She had handled this all wrong, and now Marietjie and the other girls were making her feel stupid and out of place. And she was well aware that this was their intention.

She lowered her head, afraid of what she had seen. Everything she had done since her son died had been wrong, all wrong. And Marietjie knew it, and had taken advantage of her glaring mistakes. Again that oblique glance ran between the two young woman, and Arabella felt increasingly awkward. But she would stay until the service ended. They would not drive her away so quickly.

Then the last hymn was sung, and the service was over. In the brilliant sunshine in front of the church door, men and women greeted each other and spoke kindly to the bereaved family. Arabella joined them with all the pride and courage she could muster. Standing beside Tienie and her daughters, she listened to the talk around her but took no part in it. Soon the group in the doorway was joined by the magistrate and his wife and family, and she saw a peculiar flash pass between Marietjie and the golden-haired Elsabe van Niekerk.

They are puzzled, she thought with sudden surprise. They could not understand why she stood with the others without any apparent embarrassment, and without Deneys, who had not yet noticed her, as he stood chatting beside Petrus Viljoen, the mayor.

It was as she was turning to leave, that Deneys spotted her. She said goodbye to those around her, forcing herself to appear indifferent, and as his brows shot up with surprise and bewilderment, she moved away, not daring to look back.

She walked quickly by the whitewashed graves towards the commercial centre, past the store run by the old Polish Jew, Paul Slowoski, and his wife Rebecca – a small bent woman, wrinkled by age, who told many horrifying stories of how she and her husband and son fled from the terrible things happening in the old country. Arabella went by Mevrou Sannie Venter's small coffee-house, where Marietjie de Villiers liked to meet her friends, and the post office run mostly by the Widow Hendricks, whose husband had been killed in the war. She was a lively, generous woman who knew the business of everyone in the village. No one married or died without her knowledge, which was good naturedly spread to everyone. The post-cart arrived, filled with the mailbags from the train; it was drawn by two small sturdy Boer horses and driven by Samuel, the handsome young black man with magnificent white teeth. She hurried by Deneys' office and on up the rise to the row of small houses fanning out northwards, quiet against the ever-changing pinks and purples and greys of the mountains to the west and the curving arm of the hills, which in her first months here had amazed her with their miraculous wealth of colour, light and shade. But today the clear, invigorating air failed to fill her with the usual exhilaration.

At the top of the rise stood an old acacia tree, its branches blasted years ago by lightning, and it was here that Deneys caught up with her, reining in his horse sharply as he drew alongside, the sweat of horse-hide strong in her nostrils.

'Arabella, wait! Why did you go off in such a hurry?' he called down leaning forward on the pommel, oblivious to the passing creak and rumble of carts.

'I don't want to talk to you,' she said bitterly, averting her head as she marched on. 'I don't want to talk to anyone! I've just made myself the laughing stock of the entire village.'

'No, you haven't,' he said, his horse keeping easy pace with her rapid, angry steps. 'Hop up on the back – I'll lift you home.'

'No.' She stopped and stared up at him, his golden head and shoulders framed in sunlight. 'It won't do any good to pity me. And anyway, shouldn't you be with Marietjie de Villiers?'

For a moment or two, he watched her fold her small arms defiantly, and then turn and march on. Easing his horse up to keep pace with her once more, he said, 'What's Marietjie got to do with it?' That he gave no sign of embarrassment did not deceive her, and she guessed that his numerous evenings at the magistrate's large and comfortable home must have held more than discussions on politics and the law.

'She's in love with you – it's plain for all the world to see! And she thinks I'm just an old, stupid fool – a woman who can never have another child. Barren, to be pitied –'

'Come now, Arabella, that's not true.'

When she slowed down a fraction to glance at him, his face showed nothing except a slight tightening of the lips. He said, 'She's attentive because her father is a friend of mine, nothing more. Let's stop this nonsense, it's a waste of time. Besides, I thought you were very courageous to attend the funeral alone. Only you would have that kind of bloody-minded courage.' He smiled, his brown eyes warm. 'And you kept Anton Meyer alive until Tiaan Malherbe could arrive.' He went on soberly, 'It was all due to you, Arabella, that he could die in his own bed. Everyone knows that, and they respect you for it.'

Arabella said quietly, 'If it hadn't been for you, the rock would not have been lifted and he would have died in that lonely, wild place.'

They passed Tienie's small house where already mourners were beginning to gather. Deneys raised his hat in greeting, then proceeded to follow Arabella's path towards the larger dwellings opposite the schoolhouse. From high above them, a small grey and white black-shouldered kite hovered in the sky, before dropping on its prey further out in the veld. At the heels of Deney's horse, Thor, who had waited for him outside the church, loped along, sniffing at the ground.

Deneys was silent for a moment or two and then with something like a sigh he shrugged his shoulders and remarked, 'I noticed you'd been busy in the house. It looks nice again.'

Arabella's face muscles tightened. 'Yes. It looked terrible – I hadn't realised . . .'

'Arabella, stop this nonsense now. It's not right for you to be walking while I ride. And it's damned awkward for me and Kitchener to walk with you.'

'Well go away, then,' she snapped, starting to run towards the house. 'Go back to Marietjie – that young lady will be overjoyed to see you.'

She flung open the creaking gate, raced up the path and threw herself inside the door, but footsteps sounded behind her and she was caught in a steel grip and spun round.

'Arabella, you mad little fool! We can't go on like this, and you know it.' Deneys' eyes were blazing so fiercely that she thought he was going to shake her. 'It's been a long time,' he said roughly, 'and this house has been the saddest place this side of hell!'

Her body started to heat under his intense gaze, then her eyes glazed with quick, hot tears, and she started to cry. He hugged her close for a moment, and then gently but forcefully held her face in his cupped hands. Her eyes remained tightly closed, but the tears seeped through her lashes.

'Don't cry, Arabella – there's no need.'

His strong arms enclosed her so tightly that she expected her lungs to burst. Unable to contain herself any longer, she buried her face in his chest and wept.

'I've been so selfish, and so cruel to you, Deneys, and now there's Marietjie and –'

'Marietjie de Villiers means nothing to me,' he said huskily. 'I was lonely and her family were kind. Besides, she's still a girl, and I like older woman.' She felt his hand seek hers and clasp it, and looked up to meet his hungry brown eyes. 'But you have to choose, Bella,' His voice was suddenly rough again, as he loomed over her, his hair ruffled and his tie crooked. He placed her arms about his neck and she was acutely conscious of the brush of his hardened thighs against her own. There came then a brief flash of understanding as her eyes met his and for the first time in months, some real truth was communicated and shared.

'I've missed you, Deneys – you'll never know how much,' she said, her heart beating rapidly, her lips and mouth drying with mounting excitement.

'And I want you, Bella, as I've never wanted you before. I knew you'd come back to me when I saw you at the church.' The impatience in him matching hers, he picked her up and strode into the bedroom, lowering her on to the riempie-thonged bed.

'But what about your work? Your clients –' Then she stopped as he undid the buttons of her bodice and pulled down the chemise which hid her cool, smooth, round breasts.

'The clients are all at Tienie Meyer's house,' he whispered passionately, 'And not giving me a thought ...' His fingers moved to the buttons of his shirt, and in a moment his strong shoulders glimmered in the light filtering through the open shutters. Then his open mouth captured hers, and passion sparked, turning her emotions inside-out in the old familiar way. With a moan, she moulded herself to his body, inviting him to caress her. And as he took her after all the months of emptiness and deepest loneliness, he slowly and deliberately stressed his next words. 'I love you, Bella, and only you. You'll never know the weeks, the months of hell I've been through.'

With a rush of acute insight, she suddenly realised just how terribly he had suffered. Now the pressure of his lips, his arms and his body told her that he needed her as she had despaired of ever being needed again. And in those stolen, ecstatic moments, the recent period of desolation fell away in the miracle of new life. With blessed relief, Arabella knew that their earlier love had not been killed, but only postponed into its full blossoming.

16

The next day she sat in the small nursery and looked around, striving to keep back the tears. How could she explain the emotion she had felt yesterday, transcending any she had ever experienced ... In that delirious, deepest moment of love, she knew she had conceived again.

Arabella decided not to tell Deneys yet of her conviction about the child. She was afraid of losing it, and that fear took away much of her joy. She wanted Deneys to be near all the time, as thoughts of the baby nestling within her womb became more and more the focal point of her life. She longed to talk at length to him about it, but she could not bring herself to do it – not then.

It was on the hottest day in February that she collected the mail at the post office where the Widow Hendricks was holding forth on the latest good-natured gossip as she sorted the letters into the pigeon-holes behind her. She handed Arabella a small packet containing a two-week-old newspaper, a letter from Rachel and one from Natal, marked Urgent. The envelope was addressed in Ben's precise and flowing handwriting, and suddenly across her happiness and contentment there ran a deep unease. Once outside, she tore it open with trembling hands and read its contents under the shade of her parasol.

The news was the worst she could have expected. Rosamunde had fallen pregnant and given birth to a stillborn son. Ten days afterwards, she had developed a condition diagnosed as child-bed fever. Now she was in a sanatorium in Pietermaritzburg, where the prognosis was not good. Rosamunde had urgently asked to see her again, Ben wrote. He would not have worried her, had the situation not been of the gravest importance.

Standing alone in that street, her body immobile with shock and sorrow, Arabella acknowledged through her anguish that this was the beginning of more pain ... one which she had dared to hope was over. Rosamunde was dying ... Rosamunde, whom she had once loved like a sister and then turned from in bitterness and hate, and who was now calling her back ... back into those wretched years of emotional conflict.

Arabella walked slowly back to the house, her thoughts both alarmed and confused. She knew that Rosamunde's condition usually had fatal consequences, but she had not seen her cousin for so long ... and then there was Ben. He had been so cruel, and she had hated him for it. But even in her reawakened anguish over the past situation, her heart now cried out to Rosamunde. It was not in injustice that Rosamunde had railed at her so long ago; it was not in perverse cruelty and capriciousness, as Arabella had once believed. It was she who had failed to comprehend the depths of her cousin's fear and panic. Rosamunde was no more to blame for her reactions than she herself had been, over Deneys and Marietjie de Villiers.

Later that evening, as Deneys worked on a case in the study, she turned up the lamp and stared about the small bedroom where great ghost-like moths fluttered around the new bed. She thought about the farm in Natal and the day that Luke had brought Deneys into her life.

The soft drapes had been drawn, and the covers of the bed turned back. The mirror's curves gleamed on the chest below as she recalled little Luke and Cynthia running up to the mirror in her room, pulling faces at their reflections. The grandfather clock in the silence of the passage struck ten, and the whole past suddenly rose up, as though it had been lying in wait to close over and submerge her. Tears gathered in her eyes, and she was instantly afraid. For all her present compassion for Rosamunde, she had been terribly betrayed by Ben – and feared to suffer at his hands again.

As the subtle fragrances of late summer roses filtered through the open shutters, she decided not to brood too much. She was pregnant, with six months to go before the birth of her own child. Then she heard Deneys whistling down the passage, and her heart started racing in turmoil. She knew instinctively, that if she told him about the child she carried, he would forcefully prevent her from going to see Rosamunde. The last thing she wanted was a scene, anything to mar their re-found happiness. But, if he did *not* know? Then the door opened, and she saw him in his blue dressing gown.

'Oh, Deneys! Deneys!' she cried as she flew into his widespread and welcoming arms.

'Bella! What is it, my darling?' He clasped her close, and she felt his lips brush her hair, his pronunciation of the endearment deepening her sense of that wonderful and deep intimacy which now filled her heart with such joy and such fear. His arms were around her, his kisses on her neck, her ears. She stood safe in his embrace, listening to the steady beat of his heart and feeling that sense of security in his presence which was one of the most precious miracles of their love. In the quietness of that half-darkened room, in the peace that enveloped the house and the street outside, she felt she could listen to its rhythm for ever ... if it had not been for Ben's letter. The thought of it now sent her body into a new panic – that Deneys had felt it, she did not realise.

'Tell me,' he whispered against her ear. 'Whatever is the matter?'

Arabella's hand slipped from his arm, and her face grew pale and drawn. She knew she must tell him at once. Something terrible was happening to Rosamunde, and she had to go to her – she was compelled to answer her call for help! There was no other way. She must speak before she lost her courage completely.

Turning to face him, she clasped and unclasped her small hands together in a state of heightened agitation. 'Oh, my dearest one, I received a letter today – a letter I would never have chosen to receive, but it came out of the blue from Ben Saville, begging me to go to Rosamunde's bedside. She is dying of puerperal fever, and is asking for me. I think I should go, for it will be for the last time.'

Deneys watched her from beneath his brows with the quizzical expression that was so much a part of him. Then his face closed grimly.

'No!' The word was fierce. 'You have been through enough because of them – because of Benjamin Saville! I will not let you go. He still has so much to answer for!'

'But Deneys, Rosamunde needs me as she has never needed me before.' Arabella's voice was desperate. 'There is nothing more she can do to hurt me – she is dying! Let me do this one thing for her, or I shall never forgive myself,' she cried imploringly as he folded his arms across his chest.

'And he? Is there nothing more *he* can do to hurt you? Has he been rendered harmless after so long? I am not so sure. What he has done once, he'll do again and again. I know his type,' he said sharply, taking a deep, angry breath. 'He uses you as he has always done, but you fail to see it!'

In a bitter desolation of spirit, she went to him and took down his arms, and covered them with the urgent, gentle pressure of her own. 'Deneys, my darling, please understand. Ben means nothing to me. What happened, happened a long time ago when I was still young and innocent. I am changed – you have changed me. I want to go to Rosamunde, for it will be the last thing I do for her. It is not for Ben's sake, but *in spite* of him. I shall be strong against him, you will see.'

'Perhaps you are right, I don't know anymore. I just don't trust such men. But we will talk about it in the morning.'

Relief flooding over her, she entwined his strong, capable fingers with hers. 'Yes, yes, let's forget about them now. I want you and that's all my heart listens to tonight.' She rose on tiptoe to whisper in his ear, disturbing the sudden silence in the room.

Suddenly his good humour, his buoyancy rapidly returned, and she was lifted from her feet and brought firmly against his body, his eager lips covering hers. Miraculously for her, the immediate ordeal was over. Deneys, incomprehensible man that he was, seemed to be taking a fairly reasonable attitude. Relief now was uppermost in her feelings, as the present, not the past or the future claimed her thoughts.

'Deneys, behave,' she pleaded breathlessly as his mouth sank to her throat and her world tilted in a mad spiral.

It was not tenderness that he aroused in her now, but an overwhelming, primitive desire to minister to his needs. And in service to him, there was no separation between the joy of her body and the joy of her spirit. Together, they created for her a sudden glory that had no holding back.

17

Removing her gloves in the small, neat sanatorium room, Arabella gazed down at her cousin. Rosamunde's eyes were fever-bright, her cheeks deeply flushed, lending an even more remarkable beauty to her face.

'Oh, Bella.' Rosamunde's voice trembled as she tried to smile. 'Bella – I need you so much.' Tears glistened in her hazel eyes. 'Ben said you would never come. There's so much to forgive ... on all sides ...'

Arabella picked up her cousin's hot feeble hand and pressed it to her lips. She thought with terror, the fever's spread throughout her body. She's terribly, terribly ill.

'I had to come, Rose,' she told her softly. 'Under the circumstances, I had to.' Then she let herself drop into the chair beside the bed, her heart pounding in her ears.

'Dear, dear Bella,' Rosamunde whispered. 'You were the strong one, after all. It's strange, when we were young I never valued your qualities.' She leaned back wearily against the pillows, fluttering her hand restlessly. 'We've been apart for such long, foolish years. So much wasted time. If I had known what I know now, Bella, how different it would all have been.' She smiled without the slightest trace of bitterness. 'So glad you're here, my dear, dear sister.' Then her hand, which had been lying on the blanket, slowly stretched out again towards Arabella and gripped hers hard, holding on with surprising fierceness, seeking, it seemed, support and comfort and reassurance.

'Belle – I saw Papa in a dream last night. He came to fetch me on a beautiful white horse.'

A cold shiver sped down Arabella's spine. She looked at the woman she had loved, and felt utterly desolate. Her eyes brimmed with unshed tears, as she smiled comfortingly at this poor, suffering woman. 'Don't upset yourself, my dear Rose. We're together now, and that's all that matters. Is there anything at all I can do for you?'

Rosamunde did not answer. The spirit of need ebbed in her after a while, and she let go of Arabella's hand. She dozed while Arabella's mouth moved in silent prayer. She closed her own eyes, and dimly heard the door open and then shut. She turned her head to see who had arrived, and saw it was Ben.

He stood in the doorway, removing his smart black top hat. He was wearing a dark-brown coat and trousers, and she was struck again by the nobility of his features. There was silver in the smooth dark hair, and deep lines at the side of his mouth where the dark moustache stood out in deep contrast to his tanned skin, but he had a weariness about his eyes that made him look all of his forty-three years.

'Arabella!' he exclaimed, and he was young again. He limped towards her with the aid of crutches, his hands extended, and she rose and stepped back.

She remained at a distance, rigid and white, looking at him with cold and terrible denunciation. 'Don't touch me, Ben,' she said. 'Don't ever touch me again.'

His hand dropped. Her triumph – so different from the triumph she had once envisaged – was complete. She was paying him back in pain at last for all that she had suffered at his hands.

'I have only come to comfort Rosamunde – and possibly the children, but I believe that Luke is in England pursuing further studies while Cynthia is at boarding school in Cape Town. I hope she will arrive soon,' she said, deliberately moving away from him.

As they stood and stared at each other, all at once she felt that something had changed. She was sick with her anger and hatred of him, but still she knew that something was different. Ben seemed mysteriously altered, and emotionally moved. But it was only her imagination, she told herself. This was Ben Saville, Deneys' enemy, *her* enemy – the enemy of everyone of honour and decency. She clenched her ungloved hands together and told herself that she hated him.

'How long have you been here? Arabella, when did you arrive? What is wrong?' Ben asked her hesitantly. 'What is the matter? Arabella, speak to me – it was good of you to come.'

She did not answer for a moment, for suddenly she saw how vulnerable he was, how bitterly hurt, and her heart stirred with pity. She looked from him to Rosamunde, and back again, aware of the mute agony in his grey eyes. And then tears smarted her eyelids, and she thought involuntarily, I am standing with him, as I did so long ago.

She could not take her eyes from him now. He's older, she thought vaguely. He's suddenly much older. He's not formidable any more, I just though he was. She swallowed the huge lump in her throat, and forced her thoughts back to Rosamunde.

That evening, the lights were turned down low as she and Ben continued their vigil with the dying woman. A nun sat in a corner, reading, but alert for any movement or sign from the patient. Arabella, seated near the bed, facing Ben, could feel no more anger against him, but only compassion. This was a man who suffered, and had suffered, cursed by his own pride and stubborn nature; a man incapable of accepting love simply and of giving it as simply. Everything was always so complicated and tortuous for him.

Her eyes dropped to Rosamunde lying immobile on her pillows, breathing audibly and uneasily, her face still a radiant fever-pink, and she felt suddenly suspicious. Something was wrong. Although infections during and after the birth of babies were common, something did not fit in here ... Then she told herself that these suspicions were too big a burden for her to carry alone. She must find someone to talk to about it – someone she could trust.

She asked permission to stay that night in the room, and questioned Dr Holland about the birth. It had been a surprisingly easy one, he said, despite the stillborn child, and nothing had seemed amiss. He could not understand why Rosamunde should have come down with the fever.

It was in the grey dawn that Bishop Sebastian arrived in answer to Rosamunde's request, even though she was not Catholic. Arabella's old friend was dressed in dignified black vestments, his white collar shimmering over the dark broadcloth. There was a deep silence in the room as he entered, broken only by a horse-drawn carriage clopping down the street and soft voices rising and falling in the passage outside the room. Arabella bent forward, looking at Rosamunde's still face, her hands holding Rosamunde's tightly in protection and comfort, as she and the Irishman met again after so long.

Much later, they walked down through the green lawns of the sanatorium, and into the wide, dusty streets of Pietermaritzburg, with its attractive shops, red-brick buildings and small green parks. They were to have breakfast at Bishop Cleaver's residence, where Bishop Sebastian was staying. The other clergyman was already at work, so they ate alone, in the wood-panelled dining room, served by soft-footed Zulu servants. And as they were offered the very best, blackest coffee with thick cream, hot wheaten bread and cold white bread, eggs and bacon, and a huge ham and enormous sirloin from the previous evening, Bishop Sebastian revealed that the midwife, a Mrs Daniels, had told him she had recently returned from a serious case of measles when she went to attend Lady Stradcombe during the last stages of her pregnancy and during the actual labour and birth of her child.

Arabella's face was as pale as the white, frothy lace blouse she wore beneath the tailored grey bolero. The whispers of doubt and suspicion she had recently begun to harbour about her cousin's condition became a shout in her mind, one that echoed with madness and evil and menace, of the injustices to vulnerable women.

'Are you saying that Rosamunde was infected by that woman? That she and the child would have thrived, had this not been the case, my lord?'

The Bishop took off his glasses and polished them, then replaced them on his nose. 'That is so, Arabella. It was gross negligence on the part of the midwife that has led to this deplorable and tragic situation.'

Arabella bent her head, the grey hat with its spray of black ostrich feathers hiding her face. Then she looked up, her fingers playing with the huge white napkin on her lap.

'This has to be brought to the attention of Dr Holland at once. That woman should never be allowed to practise as a midwife ever again! Does Ben know? I thought not. We'll have to tell him as soon as possible.'

They could hear the sound of the traffic from the street below and the carillon of twelve bells from the imposing town hall, reputed to be the largest all-brick construction in the southern hemisphere, soaring above all hatreds, angers and terrors, as the Bishop looked up from his plate.

'Women – mothers such as you and Rosamunde – will never be free until the women's movement has done its work for the good of all. I hear you have given up your suffrage work, Arabella.' He sighed, and made a helpless gesture with his long, lean, scholar's hands. 'God gave you genius, my dear child, and the ability to help your fellow men and women. You have been stopped, partly by circumstances and partly by yourself, because you are a woman, and not always strong enough to defy the world of men. This I understand only too well.'

He looked intently at her, as she listened painfully. Her head was bent unconsciously to one side, the black feathers on her hat gleaming iridescently in the strong sunlight flooding through the long, open sash-windows.

'But if you give up your work, you won't just be smothering yourself, you'll be smothering every woman and child with your timidity. And you'll have killed all faith in the cause of women everywhere. Is it a priest's duty to keep silent when his people continually suffer?'

Arabella wiped her face as simply as a child with the palms of her hands, and looked up at him with suddenly wet eyes. 'I hear what you say, my lord, but it is not the time for me to take up the fight again.'

'That can be said for any time, my dear, but to put it off is to lose your integrity, your own identity.'

She looked up at his face and spoke with conviction. 'But I will stand up for Rosamunde, my lord. I will see that justice is done.' Terrible anger swept through her then as she plucked distraughtly at the lace-edged cuffs of her blouse. She was a young inexperienced mother again, losing her first child ... decisions had been made for her without her consent. She had been so helpless, so defenceless against them all, just as Rosamunde was now. Something would be done this time, and she would not rest until it was completed.

It was too late to save Rosamunde, but she could help to protect other women from the same carelessness. Within days her cousin would be gone, and it would be a long time before the sharpness of her grief lessened; many months before she stopped asking why. She suddenly felt exhausted by the knowledge that she had always possessed, but now acknowledged so much more poignantly, that until all women received their full rights before the law, they would be forced to suffer in these cruel and senseless ways ...

If we think of ourselves as victims, we become victims, she thought grimly as she parted from the Bishop, and her vocation stirred in her again, deep and urgent – the will to help that silent, frustrated, unemancipated mass of womankind.

That night, her cousin went into a crisis. Gangrene had set in, and her condition worsened. A nun sat watching near her head, her fingers never leaving the patient's pulse. Ben, who now knew of the midwife's carelessness, stood in the shadows cast by the lamps. Bishop Sebastian, in his vestments, knelt down beside the bed, crossed himself and said the prayers for the dying, tears streaming down his cheeks.

Rosamunde lay with her eyes half-closed and glazed, then suddenly opened them wide as if she could see clearly and turned her face to look at the three people standing nearby, then she lifted her head.

'Rose – it's me, Bella,' Arabella said, bending urgently forward. 'See – I'm here, darling.'

Rosamunde panted and moaned. Then, suddenly, her face flooded with light and joyful recognition and very clearly in that silent room, she said: '*Papa.*'

The smile remained, though she died in that instant, and Arabella closed the hazel eyes. She rested her head for a moment on the bed, overcome with the shock of grief. Then she stood up to give Dr Holland her place. He had dressed hastily, and his reddish hair was rumpled. He took Rosamunde's wrist in surprisingly gentle fingers then very slowly he withdrew.

Arabella, sobbing silently at the window, heard a slight movement near her and lifted her tear-disfigured face. Ben was standing very close to her, and she began to tremble, for his eyes were not the eyes she had seen since she had arrived. He was a man of vengeance now, a man of hatred. Dimly, she looked beyond him at the Bishop, but he was still praying. And when she looked back at Ben, she knew that between them, something would be done about Mrs Daniels.

Every available space in the big stone church spilled over with white, and pale yellow flowers, delicately scented, in baskets, pots, in wreaths and bouquets. Arabella could see that the church was overflowing. People sat and stood crowded together and there were many unfamiliar faces. The ushers were sweating profusely, scurrying to get extra folding seats from the store-room; these were hastily dusted and placed at the rear and in the side aisles. The church was alive with moving black hats and heads; the heat was so great that the perfume of the roses set in vases near the altar pervaded the whole atmosphere, and palm-leaf fans held in gloved hands made a soft rustling in the low murmurous quiet and could be heard above the first soft chords of the organ.

Arabella was numb with fatigue. Earlier, she and Ben had gone to see Dr Holland, and after a lengthy period of fierce argument, he had agreed to dismiss Mrs Daniels. He promised to see that she never worked as a midwife again, but more than that he could not do. He could not prove that his midwives were infected, unless they told him. Now there were no more tears left in Arabella. It was an effort to breathe, to hold up her head. She wore a thin black dress, but the day was so hot that the light fabric clung to her shoulders and breasts.

Fifteen-year-old Cynthia had arrived some hours before, distraught at the knowledge that she had not seen her mother at the last, and Luke had sent a telegram from England. As the last hymn was sung and the music died away, she looked up at Ben standing beside her, and for the first time in her life, she saw real tears in his eyes. Impulsively she placed her gloved hand on his, and felt the strong pressure of his fingers encircling hers. The words she wanted to say would not come, so all she could do was to hold his hand in silence. Cynthia, now tall and blonde like her mother, saw it.

Arabella noticed that the young girl's eyes were sliding back and forth between her and Ben, and she felt intensely irritated, for the sliding look was very quick and knowing. She noticed that Cynthia had been crying, and as she caught Arabella's eye, her arms dropped to her sides, and she gave a dry, gulping sob and dropped her head on her breast.

She had been reserved with Arabella from their first meeting in Lady Clare Mortimer's house, where the coffin had rested, and Arabella knew that the influence of her parents in the past, particularly of Rosamunde, to whom she had been devoted, was still too strong in the young girl to overcome her resistance.

And then it was over, and she was saying goodbye to Ben on the busy platform of Pietermaritzburg station, where she had first arrived with him so many long years ago.

He looked at her intently as he leaned on his crutches at the window of her carriage. 'Your Boer husband is indeed fortunate, my dear.'

She stared at him from under the straw brim of her hat, biting her lips to keep them from trembling. 'Go well, Ben,' she whispered, as the train whistle blew, and a man near her spoke to a woman passenger.

'It's hard to think of you miles away buried in the bush,' he said, not looking at her now but gazing at a point above her head. 'You should come back to Natal, you know.'

Seldom had she heard him speak so wistfully, and she missed the old rebellious spirit in him, but she found herself deeply and strangely moved by his words. Then, mastering her emotion, she leaned a little out of the window and touched his arm. 'It's right for me to be there, Ben. I'm not ready for anything else yet.'

'Perhaps,' he reluctantly agreed. 'But is he good to you? Does he treat you well? I know the Boers – they are not like us, their values are different.'

She did not answer. For an instant, she turned her head away. From all around them came the noise of bustle and conversation, steam and the hooting and hissing of the train. Then she looked up. 'Yes, Deneys treats me well, Ben,' she whispered . . .

And even as she said it, he was gone.

18

Mimi was born that August, a strong, healthy little girl, and Arabella, after the deep depression caused by Rosamunde's death, began to feel renewed as she watched the baby grow, seeing in the child her own green eyes, Deneys' golden hair, and small cleft chin. No moments throughout the day were as precious as those she spent with her child. She was vividly aware, as she fed the baby with a strangely selfless passion of tenderness, of the smells and sounds of the countryside, of the sharp clearness of the invigorating air.

But with this contentment, something else had stirred during her visit to Natal. Rosamunde's untimely death and Bishop Sebastian's words crept up at odd moments which were becoming more regular, and a letter from Rachel only deepened that feeling within her. Rachel had given birth to a second son, Louis, the year before, but still kept her contact with the enfranchisement league. Her letter was full of the fact that the Johannesburg League wanted a link-up of all the women's suffrage movements, believing that only when there was a national movement would their cause, which they wanted to present to the new, all-male, Parliament, gain more power. One significant obstacle to unity was the hesitancy of the Afrikaans-speaking women to join, because of the strong influence of their church. Rachel wondered if Arabella could try to influence these women, and set up a local league in Heideville. Arabella knew that it would be difficult to do this in the predominantly patriarchal community in which she now lived, but she let the idea slowly take root.

Close upon the receipt of Rachel's letter came a bitterly cruel event that was to shock the entire community of Heideville for months to come.

Tienie arrived with the news that Annetjie du Preez, the fifteen-year-old daughter of Jacobus du Preez, had been raped by one of François Louw's sons in the veld behind old Paul Slowoski's shop. Everyone was condemning Annetjie, while nothing was said about the boy.

Oh God, what am I hearing? thought Arabella, when Tienie left. It could not be true. Suddenly that terrible experience with Sean O'Shea came back to her, with all its terror, humiliation and degradation. She felt again her defencelessness against his brute strength, her deep feelings of utter loathing and repulsion. Intuitively, she knew what Annetjie du Preez had felt, must be feeling now ...

There was talk that Jacobus du Preez felt so disgraced that he planned to send Annetjie away to his brother on the borders of Mozambique in the bush country, where she would stay for the rest of her days. Arabella felt intensely that this was a time when a father should support his daughter, and find out the truth behind the sneers and rumours. It was also a time for the women of Heideville to stand together and speak up, and possibly save other young women from the same fate.

Deneys came into the kitchen in the late afternoon, pulling off his hat, all buoyancy and expectation, and Arabella could not help smiling as she went to greet him, three-month-old Mimi nestled in the crook of her arm.

'All they can talk about downtown is the du Preez affair,' he said, tickling Mimi's nose, and making her crow with pleasure. 'It's best that it blows over soon.'

'But we are going to do something about it, Deneys,' Arabella said. She handed Mimi to Maisie, the new nanny, a tall, stately black woman in a spotless white pinafore. 'Tienie and I are holding a meeting here in this house, to decide how to approach Jacobus du Preez.'

Deneys was astonished. 'You're *what*?' Then he narrowed his eyes. 'Has this anything to do with your suffrage nonsense, Arabella? You know I won't have it.' He was not smiling any more.

Arabella kept her face expressionless. Only days ago she had suppressed all other thoughts except those regarding her husband and her daughter and their safe, orderly life in this small God-fearing village. And now it was all gone. Something ugly and menacing had entered it, and she was not going to sit back and ignore it.

She repeated: 'We're holding the meeting, Deneys, to demonstrate that women are not playthings, that they too, have feelings and desires that must be accepted. I cannot turn my back on it.'

Deneys was stunned. His cosy, happy home, built on safe old traditions where everyone knew his and her place, was all set to fall apart. His face darkened. 'You will hold no such meeting in this house where your daughter sleeps in peace. She will not be touched by this obsession of yours, do you hear me? Stay out of it, Arabella! It is none of your business what Jacobus du Preez decides to do with his own daughter.'

'You mean,' said Arabella incredulously, 'that you can decide what I may and may not do in this house – my own home? I cannot believe it.'

His eyes were cold and proud as he faced her across the table. 'That is just what I do mean, Mevrou du Rand. No meeting of such a kind will ever be held in this house, and that is final.'

'No, Deneys, this is a very serious matter – just what the Women's League is fighting against. I will not turn my back on it,' she called after him, as he turned on his heel and left the room. 'There is very little time for us or for Annetjie du Preez if she is to be allowed to stay with her family and friends in this village, her reputation restored.'

One clear afternoon a few days later, Tienie's small house was thrown open for the meeting. She and Arabella had canvassed the whole village, and there promised to be a good attendance. By that time the news of Annetjie had spread quickly from house to house, from farmstead to farmstead throughout the valley, and with it the young girl was scorned and shamed, and ostracised from the community.

And back in the du Rand home, while little Mimi slept peacefully in her cot under the watchful eye of Maisie, Samson knew that Arabella had taken command.

By the time his master had left, she was moving from woodshed to stove, from pantry to table with the precision of a general marshalling his resources in preparation for the meeting. She had already made the flaky pastry for the melk terts the night before, hung it up in a cloth and rolled it out at dawn. Now, orders issued from her lips as she sifted flour, broke eggs and measured sugar into mixing-bowls, and Samson, astonished, found himself following directions without further questions. As the spiciness of the baking cakes and tarts filled the kitchen, he recognised the creative fire in his mistress' eyes, and felt awed by the power that emanated from her willing the fire to burn, the cake batter to assume golden smoothness and hidden stores of preserved peaches and apricots to appear from dark corners.

She went to the bedroom to dress and marvelled anew at Tienie, who had suggested they bake a good spread for the ladies who expected it at every gathering. It also, she said, softened hard hearts, and made them more sympathetic to one's wishes. Alida Viljoen and the other important wives had refused to attend, but there was a group who were either interested or curious.

The meeting started without mishap in Tienie's small sitting room, where the wooden shutters were wide open and the curtains drawn back to let in the light of the afternoon sun through the heavy lace. As the small, formidable group of women in their starched calico bonnets sipped coffee and sampled the variety of English and Dutch cakes and pies, the tarts and biscuits, Arabella threw herself into the spirit of the occasion. The women were decidedly impressed with the spread, as they settled down to discuss the matter of Annetjie du Preez.

Arabella knew most of them, if not personally, then by sight – widows, wives, grandmothers, but no spinsters or unmarried daughters, as she explained the situation and how she felt they must stand up and ask Jacobus du Preez and the rest of the community to consider the matter more carefully. Annetjie had suffered irreparable emotional damage from the encounter, and it was cruel to banish her from everything and everyone she knew for the rest of her life.

'But it *is* a disgrace for such a thing to happen to a young woman – she must suffer for her wicked ways. She must be punished.' Old Mrs Vlokman, the grocer's wife, faced her from her chair in one corner, cold, deliberate, and righteous. 'The sinner must suffer, Mevrou du Rand. It has always been the way of the Lord, and no man can change it.' Arabella's gaze met hers and was answered by a slow and ironic twist of Mrs Vlokman's grim lips.

'But Tante Martie, surely our God is not full of vengeance, but full of love and forgiveness?' Tienie spoke up from the chair beside Arabella. 'Did not Christ Himself say to His disciples that He would not leave them without comfort? Surely Annetjie is without comfort this day ... without friends ... with no safe arms to gather her in? Surely it is for us to forget our own bitter condemnation of this child and to welcome her back?' Her voice was at once so compassionate and so full of tender sorrow that tears started in several eyes.

'But her sin is too great for us to forgive. It is for the Lord to forgive, and that He will not! The daughter of Jacobus du Preez has committed the most shameful sin.' Old Mrs Vlokman would not remain silent, and her voice was hard and final.

'But Mevrou,' a shy, hesitant voice began in one of the corners of the room. It belonged to Maryna de Lange, a thin withered widow, perched on her chair like a small black-eyed sparrow. All eyes turned to her. 'Surely Mevrou, sin as I understand it, is the passing weakness of God's children who must learn to love one another and who, even in sin, are safe in the keeping of the loving Father. Sin passes, and so with it will Annetjie du Preez' moment of weakness, but it is the compassion of the Lord Himself that will never pass, He who was sent into this world to forgive and heal. Is it not then for us to show Jacobus du Preez the way of forgiveness for his daughter?'

There was a low, steady murmur in the room, as the women debated among themselves, for and against the issue. Then Sannie Venter from the coffee-house, a big, impressive woman in a large black calico bonnet spoke, and immediately silence fell.

'You have spoken well, Maryna de Lange, and with courage. Surely the wife of Jacobus du Preez himself, Tante Betje, is suffering in deep sorrow for her daughter – and the grandmother and the sisters ... But what right have we, here in this room, to interfere with this family matter? Would we want others to interfere in our pain? Surely not. We must have compassion for this family at this time, yes, but only Annetjie du Preez knows in her deepest heart what really happened that day in the veld and it is not for us to tell her father what to do.'

Arabella's eyes followed the movements of a fly that buzzed at the window, and a sickening tremor ran along her nerves as the thought of Sean O'Shea came back with full force. Her face flushed with sudden emotion, she interrupted: 'But who else does Annetjie have to support her? That girl has had to suffer her fear and her sorrow in silence. There has been no consolation for her. She was vulnerable, she screamed for help, no matter if she had encouraged the boy up to that point. She screamed for him to stop – and it was her right that should have been respected. She has been unjustly shunned like a leper. We can't just sit back and let this happen. There have got to be laws passed against this kind of abuse.'

The following day, having collected the signatures of those women who were against Jacobus du Preez' decision to banish his daughter, and who wanted to see the Louw boy answer for his actions, Arabella and Tienie set off for the du Preez house with a small group of women. It was a hot day, so sultry that they could hardly breathe, and with a blazing sky ominously piled with thunderheads as they walked defiantly down the wide, dusty road, the valley of hills lying around them to the east shimmering for miles like a green lake, and behind to the west, towering in blue and paler blue, the majestic outline of the mountains. The du Preez house was one of the larger residences on the outskirts of the village, with a straggling large garden, a fair-sized orchard where the fruit trees were heavy with ripening fruit, and a stable for six horses.

As the women stood before the front door, it was pulled open by Jacobus himself, a man in his late forties, dark-haired, with a beard and dark eyebrows that merged with one another over the high bridge of his hawk-like nose. He stood on the stoep, pipe in hand, in his shirt-sleeves, his dark waistcoat open to expose the leather braces of his cord trousers. Two of his sons, one in his early twenties, and the other a lad of sixteen, had joined him and now stood silently behind him, their fierce eyes glaring at the band of women. Someone had pulled a lace curtain aside, and a shadowy figure stood behind it.

Arabella took her place in front of the women, the signed petition in her hand. A silence fell, except for the piping of a *piet-my-vrou* bird in a nearby tree, as she spoke: 'Mr du Preez, we have come to ask you not to send Annetjie away from all her loved ones, but to help her restore her reputation as your honourable daughter in the eyes of the community, and to request that Mr Louw's son, Bertus, be forced to answer for his actions.'

For a minute, Jacobus du Preez looked incredulous and there was a flutter of calico dresses rustling behind Arabella's back. Then, his dark brows lowering, he said angrily, 'This matter is none of your business, Mevrou du Rand – or any of you women. I am the master in my household and I do not answer to anyone about what goes on there. I have nothing to say to you.'

For a moment before he turned away, Arabella had an almost irresistible urge to hit his inflexible face and grind his pipe into the dust. Then, controlling herself with a great effort of will as he stalked inside, followed by his sons, and banged the flyscreen closed, she turned away, her eyes narrowed to two small points of light as a murmur of indignation amongst the women grew more heated.

'There is nothing more we can do,' Maryna de Lange hesitantly ventured, wiping a shaking, worn hand on her dark calico dress. 'Jacobus du Preez is the law of his household.'

'But what about his wife, Annetjie's mother? Does she not feel her daughter's pain?' Arabella answered stiffly.

Sun filtered down through the branches of a nearby tree and lay in bright streaks on her olive-green hat. Her proud, clear profile was sharply defined as she turned to look at the women facing her, unaware of the horses suddenly cantering from the back of the du Preez house in the direction of the village centre.

'Tante Betje du Preez listens to her husband, as do most of the women. She will not go against him,' a tired young woman in a large white sunbonnet said. 'And it is so, Mevrou du Rand, that many of the women agree with Jacobus du Preez that Annetjie has shamed her family and the whole community. It is said that she has even shamed God.'

Arabella lifted her chin defiantly. 'Jacobus du Preez can turn away, but neither he nor his family have heard the last of this matter. I shall send this petition to a friend of mine in Johannesburg and ask that other women put their names to it, and eventually we shall present it to Parliament as a cruel example of what we women are made to suffer.'

Just then a small boy in shirt-sleeves and braces ran up and shook her skirt. 'Mevrou, mevrou, there are people at your house! It is Coen du Preez and his brother Dirkie. They go with sticks and stones!' his young voice piped, and Arabella heard a strangled gasp from one of the women behind her.

Then she and Tienie were running up the street towards her house. There they saw a crowd of men, youths and boys, converging on the house and its garden. They were shouting and carrying all manner of makeshift weapons, and there was a peculiar, almost animal note in those hoarse male voices – something menacing and unrecognisable.

Oh God, bloodlust is in their voices, Arabella thought, as she stopped for a moment beside Tienie to regain her breath. And what about little Mimi inside with Maisie and Samson?

'Tienie!' she breathed. 'Go and fetch Deneys. He is needed urgently.'

Then she was running across the street, out of the way of a jolting cart and a barking dog, until she arrived at the open front gate. Pushing her way through the jostling crowd, she arrived at the top of the verandah steps, where far above her, the catawba vine stretched its tentacles. From inside she heard the dogs barking, and then Samson was there, hovering behind her at the front door. Gasping painfully, she stood before them and threw out her arms.

'You cannot trespass on this property! You leave this house alone, do you understand me?' She shouted the words in Dutch over and over as the dangerously jeering crowd shouted back, doubling their great fists at her.

'Leave Jacobus du Preez and his family to themselves! You are a wicked meddling woman! Annetjie du Preez deserves to suffer!'

Arabella could see that the mob, by now in a highly charged and vengeful state, was determined to destroy both the house and the garden, and her terror was for those inside, especially her helpless child, for she feared that once in this mood, the men and boys she had known, many of whom she liked, would show very little mercy.

'Violence is not the answer to your anger – it only creates more violence! We women bear your children and educate them, look after them and yourselves when you are sick, we tend your homes – we deserve to be heard, as Annetjie du Preez deserves to be heard. There are two sides to every story, and Annetjie du Preez has hers.'

'Get out of our way, Mevrou, or you'll get hurt!' Coen du Preez, the oldest of the brothers, a thickset young man with dark hair and a beard, shouted with rage, lifting a dangerous-looking knobkerrie in his hand as he advanced towards her followed by the yelling, menacing crowd. She could hear a deep-throated growl from Thor behind the door, where Samson had beat a hasty retreat, and the nervous, high-pitched barking from Wasp. 'You are causing great trouble in our village – you are interfering with our lives! And that we will not allow!'

'You are sowing the seeds of destruction in our community! You lead our sisters and daughters into the paths of great wickedness – you shame us and our church!' someone else roared.

A black fury suddenly welled up inside Arabella. She drew breath and shouted angrily, 'But what good will it do to destroy this house? It is Deneys du Rand's house.'

There was a slight pause in the yelling as Coen du Preez stopped, his dark eyes still flashing with insult and outrage. He lowered his knobkerrie, and said harshly, 'Then our worthy lawyer must teach his wife obedience.'

'Must he?' Arabella placed her hands on her hips and stared at him, presenting an unconsciously arresting sight. Her hat had been pushed to an unwittingly rakish angle, and her anger and terror for those inside the house, filled her cheeks with colour and brightened her eyes. The little light-brown ringlets, curled on her forehead, and on her nape, were moist and soft. Her olive-green skirt and bolero clung to her figure and outlined her waist and arms. Her throat was bare, but there was a froth of an airy lace blouse under the bolero which did much to compliment her fair skin.

'Surely it won't harm you to forgive Annetjie as Bertus Louw has been forgiven, even though he was a part of it? Why is Bertus Louw freed from all guilt and not Annetjie? Is it because she is a woman?'

'You are turning the community against God and the Bible, you heathen woman!' Another man whom she recognised but could not place, pushed himself forward through the shouting crowd, now pressed thick in front of her. 'You do the Devil's work in this village and you must be punished!'

The late afternoon sunlight revealed the flash of furious eyes, as the hostile crowd began to advance towards her. Helplessly she watched them, then suddenly called Thor. She heard Samson open the door, and from the verandah behind her came the greyhound, like a great shadow, swift and true, starting to rise in a long curve from the ground to take the first man at his throat. She called to him sharply, and with both hands grabbing his lead with all her strength she pulled him down, to sit guard beside her. She stood facing the crowd, like a small defiant tree holding the earth in its place against the threatening storm, and clinging tenaciously to the soil.

'I will not let you lay a finger on the house of Deneys du Rand –'

There was a sudden stillness, except for the incessant barking of Wasp inside and the low excited growl from Thor, as a voice raised itself above the fierce, angry murmurings of the crowd. 'And what goes on here?'

Arabella's thickly-lashed eyelids opened wide as the familiar resonant voice filled her brain, and the deep pools of green moved beyond the angry crowd to the man who was striding towards them, and shouldering them out of the way. Then Deneys was there, hardly more than a heartbeat away, ready to protect her. He reached for Thor's head and briefly fondled and teased the dog's ears. Then he turned to the restless crowd still waving their weapons, put up his hand and eventually silenced them.

'We've had enough fighting in this country, my friends. It has to end somewhere, and today, it will end here. Go home to your families and we will talk of this matter tomorrow.'

A hush hung over the crowd, then Coen du Preez turned to Deneys, breathing heavily. 'We have no quarrel with you, Meneer du Rand, but with your rooinek vrou! She sets the women at our throats and encourages them to wickedness. She shames us all as my sister has shamed her family. She speaks with the tongue of the Devil, Meneer. Either take her away from here, or lock her up and shut her wicked mouth before she causes more mischief in this dorp!'

Somewhere in the mass of people, a word was spoken, and a bitter oath answered, and then Deneys replied, 'I will talk with my wife, Coen du Preez, and now you must go home to your father. One does not take the law into his own hands, for even a murderer is allowed protection before he is hanged. If my wife is wrong, she will take back what she has said, but until that time, you must leave her be.'

Unobtrusively, Arabella regarded him, admiring the fine figure he presented in his beige tussore suit. The sunshine had tanned his skin until the brown eyes seemed to sparkle with a light of their own. In contrast to the men present he seemed quick and vivid, with a more worldly and subtle sophistication about him, standing a little apart from these others, who retained so strongly their own direct Biblical interpretation of life, as had their forebears for centuries when the Bible had been their only book during past suffering and sacrifices on their long, hazardous treks through unexplored desert and veld.

As the group, now grown appreciably smaller at his appearance, but still sullen, listened to him, Arabella knew how much she loved this man, as the memories of the past were being overshadowed by the more recent ones they were making together.

Then the crowd turned away, muttering angrily, and trooped out of the garden. When the strength had come back to her knees, Arabella turned to her husband.

'Thank you, Deneys,' she murmured, and cast an anxious glance at him as his brown eyes hardened and became cold.

'You have no right, no right at all, to meddle in the affairs of others, Arabella.'

'Meddle?' she burst out, the blood draining from her face. She tipped her head to look him in the eye. 'Do you know how much Annetjie du Preez has suffered because of this crime? She stands unjustly accused of being a whore! Yet nothing is said about the perpetrator of the whole shoddy business. Where is the justice in that?'

Deneys stared down at her sternly. 'You are using that girl's suffering to promote your own cause, Arabella, and you have paraded that family's misfortune in public when it is a very private affair. What gives you the right to use their pain as an example? Who says you're right? Haven't you, in fact, done Annetjie more harm than good?'

'Good God, Deneys!' She could see that he was tempted to pick her up and shake her, but she faced him bravely. 'Don't you see that this is the only way to prevent other girls in this community from suffering the same fate? If it has happened once and the perpetrator is allowed complete freedom to act as he will, it will happen again and again. We are just making it safe for other young men to do the same thing because we don't dare to punish them. Annetjie is an innocent girl whose life has been ruined forever when it needn't be.'

'By what right do you set yourself up as a judge in this matter, Arabella?' His voice was hard and clipped. 'It is none of your damned business!'

She placed her hands angrily on her hips, her head tilted challengingly up at him, unaware of the small collection of children at the gate, watching with amusement and curiosity.

'The discovery of what happened to his daughter was a vicious blow to Jacobus du Preez' pride, Deneys, as it is for all fathers. It has very little to do with Annetjie herself but with her father's image. Annetjie was one being whom he completely dominated, and he is afraid that if he doesn't punish her he will be seen as weak by his fellow men, by his community and in the eyes of his God.'

Deneys gestured to the children at the gate to go away, and they fled, giggling. 'It's no use carrying on this senseless argument in full view of our neighbours,' he said sharply, as he angrily pulled open the door. Bracing it with a shoulder, he let her pass, then banged it closed.

They faced each other in the hallway, both tense and ready to spring. A deep scowl drew Deneys' brows down sharply and the muscles of his cheeks on either side of his golden moustache twitched in outrage. 'You will do no such thing again. I completely forbid it, do you hear me?' he commanded. 'And you are to give up this women's suffrage nonsense for good – do I make myself perfectly clear?'

'Give it up?' A shocked expression contorted her face, and she sucked in her breath. 'You have no right to make that decision for me, Deneys.' She stepped very close to him, her sweet lavender perfume swirling tantalisingly between them. 'You knew when you married me that it was an important part of my life. I gave it up to be a wife to you, and to have your children, but it has surfaced again in a most terrible way, and I will stand by my convictions.'

'You will do as I say,' he growled, catching her wrists and holding them away as she jerked forward with anger. 'What you did before our marriage was your own affair, but now you are my wife and Mimi's mother. No wife of mine works, Arabella! Your place is in the home.'

A strangled gasp came from Arabella's throat, and there was a swish of olive-green skirts as she jerked away. With quick, angry movements she pulled off her hat. Then, she stated, with deliberate contempt, 'Because I'm your wife changes nothing! It does not alter my ideals. I am still committed to the cause for women's rights in a selfish, male-dominated world. If you don't like it, Deneys, you'll just have to learn to live with it.'

Then she hurried away to their bedroom. A moment later, the front door was slammed shut as Deneys left the house in an angry mood. A sombre silence settled over the place as Mimi was put to bed and Arabella sat down to eat alone, ignoring Samson's curious eyes as he stood beside her for a moment, his open blue waistcoat bright in the light of the lamp on the table.

The resentment in her against Deneys was smouldering still. Althea had been right: he did not understand. She felt trapped, torn between her marriage and her desire to help women. All at once she was seized by claustrophobia. She couldn't breathe. The walls appeared to crowd in on her. She rose quickly, her voice almost a whisper as Samson appeared with the strong, black coffee.

'No coffee for me, Samson. You may clear the table. Thank you.'

And then, before he could answer her, she almost bolted from the room.

19

During the night, a violent storm broke out over the mountains, and Arabella was awakened by a crash as the curtains blew wildly. Lightning more vivid than she had seen in a long while was followed by a tremendous crack of thunder and then a roar which seemed to shake the earth. As the thunder stilled, and the sheets of rain poured down, she could hear the joyful croak of hundreds of frogs. With a start of dismay she realised that Deneys had not come to bed; frowning worriedly she ran from the bedroom with an oil lamp sloshing in her hand.

She found him, fully dressed and fast asleep on the couch in the sitting room. The sight of his dishevelled appearance and familiar face reposed in sleep, aroused all the deepest feelings of longing in her.

'Deneys?' she whispered, hearing the rain clatter down on the corrugated-iron roof as she knelt at his side. 'Deneys – you can't sleep here all night. Come to bed.'

But he did not answer, and with sudden compassion she bent and tugged the boots off his feet, then, fetching a blanket, gently pulled it over him. For a moment, remembering Althea's anxious words to her before her marriage, fear swept through her heart. Could her dedication to help all women cause the end of her marriage? Would it kill Deneys' love for her? Surely it could not be so. They had so much together. Her love for him and his for her had turned the very fabric of her life to richness, and through this love had come Mimi, that darling, beautiful child, a miracle of life. All that had been in her power to give, she had given to this man, and to her child. But day by day so much more was being demanded of her, so much that she could not quite understand yet, but give she must.

Regretfully, she stared down at the sleeping figure, huddled in the blanket like a child instinctively seeking comfort – the comfort she felt helpless to give him, then she went back to the lonely bedroom where she lay back on the pillows.

The soft pink and mauve shades of the breaking dawn swept across the sky in undulating waves from the eastern horizon. A cock crowed triumphantly nearby, and the small clock on the dressing table struck the early hour in dulcet tones, as she woke to hear movements in the kitchen. Grabbing her dressing gown, she looked in on Mimi who was still sleeping peacefully, then headed for the kitchen. An oil lamp stood on the table, and the back door and fly-screen were wide open. She saw Deneys standing before it, a towel flung across a naked shoulder. His hair was wildly tousled, and his feet were bare against the wooden flooring.

He turned when he heard her footsteps and their eyes met briefly.

'I missed you last night, Deneys,' she said as simply and directly as she could, giving in to the pleasure and relief of seeing him.

He nodded curtly. 'Thank you for the blanket.'

'Deneys, I don't want you sleeping on the couch – it isn't right. Come back to our room, as if nothing has happened,' she pleaded, and he let his gaze sweep over her. Then the brown eyes hardened, the muscles in his cheeks flexing angrily.

'But dammit, something has happened! Nothing will ever be the same – you've seen to that. It's all over the dorp about your meeting in Tienie Meyer's house. Everyone is up in arms about it – Alida Viljoen is calling her own meeting to stop you spreading your dangerous ideas. And, as if that is not enough, you have to go and see Jacobus du Preez. He is furious enough to murder both you and Tienie! You went against me, Arabella – you deliberately defied me and you have upset the entire community by indulging your conscience at the expense of the suffering of others!'

Her heart was pounding loudly now. 'Let's try to adjust, Deneys. We have before and we can do so again. Things change and we have to change with them. Please.'

He stood holding his shaving knife, measuring it in his hands, his face stiff with anger. 'It is you who must change, Arabella. You are not living with Althea Rigby now – you are in a Boer community that has its own rules and customs, its own way of life. You can't just come in and stir things up because you are dissatisfied with the way they are.'

The birdsong outside rose, and the rooster in the yard crowed into the growing light. Arabella stared at her husband, emotion playing within her like summer lightning. She was about to reply when the expression on his face silenced her. Deneys meant every word he said.

Despair possessed her. He did not understand her and the way she thought. His outlook to women was strangely simple. All that was most selfish and possessive in him was excited by her as a woman – by her body, by the way she ran his home and provided comforts, by her bearing his children ... but he failed to grasp the depths of her soul, of her inner yearnings. Somehow, she had expected more from him. With a feeling of intense disappointment, she watched him begin shaving at the dresser, knowing that this was one important area they would never share.

Deneys knew her green eyes were watching him. Holding down a sudden movement of bitterness, he said abruptly, 'I'll be late this evening – there is an important case in one of the outlying districts. Don't wait up for me.'

Arabella's eyes flickered hurriedly downward, and she stared in abstracted attention at his firmly muscled, matted chest. She felt so sensitive to his nearness, and knew that this was how she existed for him – the giving of herself in the passion and comfort of her body, the selfless giving in the home, but nothing else.

He finished shaving as Samson appeared to light the stove, and slowly she walked away down the small entrance hall to the front door, and opened it. She stood in the sheltering shadow of the verandah, breathing deeply the crisp, fresh air. Smoke rose from the houses on either side, a skein of Egyptian geese came in noisy flight from the river and rock pigeons called *doo-doo-doo* over the veld.

Everything was profoundly still in that moment as the post-cart drawn by two Boer ponies suddenly came into view, rattling down the street. Its appearance was unusual at that early hour of the day. It was driven by old Klokkie, the coloured man who helped out in the Post Office, and not the handsome young black driver. Then she saw why – for sitting beside him, huddled in a grey blanket, was Annetjie du Preez, her pale young face hidden in the brim of a black sunbonnet. She sat like a stone statue, looking neither to right nor left as the cart jolted past on its way to the station.

Arabella was about to cry out, when something stopped her; the silence of the street and the houses closed in upon her, isolating her. A father's right, backed by the community, had been dealt out, and there was nothing she could do about it; to acknowledge Annetjie would only make it that much worse for the girl. Her hands were tied, and with quiet desperation, she knew it.

Deneys came out on to the verandah, his hat in his hand. Fleetingly, his eyes followed the cart and its occupants in the street which was hazed with the dust kicked up by the cart ponies, then he saw his wife. Her pale-yellow dressing gown was very vivid in the green and sunless quiet, where the catawba creeper closed them in, except for one break in the leaves which exposed a sliver of brightening sky. The slightest wind fluttered the leaves above them, turned them silver for a moment or two as a bird cried far out in the veld.

Something flashed into his eyes, deep and brilliant. All at once the silence on the verandah was portentous, meaningful, as Arabella stood near the steps, quite unable to say anything with Deneys looking at her. For a long time, he seemed about to say something, and then he collected himself, pulled on his hat and strode by her, leaving her staring emptily before her, her face suddenly mournful and still.

But the matter did not rest there. It was taken up by almost the entire community. Alida Viljoen held her meeting, denouncing Arabella and Tienie. She even went as far as visiting Dominee Conradie to register her deepest disapproval. The Dominee began to lecture from the pulpit on the evils that certain members of the community were perpetrating against the rest. And since country people are always hungry for gossip and something new, the matter was discussed all over the locality until it blazed like a summer fire through dry grasslands, splitting the inhabitants down the middle. When a small rock was thrown at the sitting-room window, smashing it and arousing Deneys' intense fury, Arabella decided that matters had gone far enough.

Shaking her divided cycling skirts free of dust from the bicycle ride to the Dominee's house near the Dutch Reformed Church, she paused to steady herself before knocking on the door. It was not a visit she anticipated with any pleasure, but she was determined to carry off her side of it to the best of her ability. She followed a maid to the Dominee's study, where she greeted his wife, a tall thin woman in severe black calico, with grey hair pulled tightly back into a bun, and spectacles pinched on the edge of her nose. Elsa Conradie excused herself, sniffing with intense disapproval, and Arabella was left with the Dominee, an elderly bearded man, tall as a stork, with still vigorous iron-grey hair. Blotched freckles of age showed brown on a strong stubborn face, with lines of censure cut deep around the mouth.

'How do you do, Mevrou du Rand,' he said stiffly, shuffling back to his chair by the fireplace and waving a long, veined hand towards a heap of papers, letters, and pens that crowded a nearby table to overflowing. 'A minister's work is never done, mevrou. He looks after his flock from morning to night.' He paused and shot her a penetrating look from two faded blue eyes. 'I knew you would come to visit me some day, so I am not surprised to see you.'

Arabella felt a sudden chill at his words, and resentment attacked her fiercely at his obvious triumph. 'Yes, Dominee Conradie, I have come to speak to you about Annetjie du Preez.'

'And you think that what you did was right, mevrou?'

'Yes, I do. Annetjie du Preez is only a child, helpless against the bitterness and prejudice of the whole community. What chance did she have to speak up for herself? She deserved a hearing.'

'So you decided to speak up for her! And in so doing you have violated the divine laws of God, mevrou. You will be punished, just as Annetjie du Preez has been punished, and it will be divine justice. At your age, mevrou, you should have more sense.'

Arabella flushed at his words. 'I'm old enough to know what I'm doing, Dominee, and believe me, I know that what I attempted to do was morally right,' she answered forcefully. Pearls glimmered in her ears, the light-brown hair rising in a high wave above her forehead, which was now puckered with growing annoyance. Her eyes, so brilliantly intelligent, so responsive, were now fixed on the elderly man in a direct challenge as she stood near the cluttered desk, her pale hands clasped tightly before her.

'It is wrong for you to poison the minds of your congregation against the truth,' she said steadily, 'and to keep them in bondage to old-fashioned customs and ways of thinking when there is change everywhere else in this world. You are keeping them prisoners of your own concepts and beliefs, and that is not fair.'

The denial was instant. 'I have *every* right to look after my people, mevrou – otherwise I would be failing in my duty, and I know that duty as well as I know my own skin. I look after their spiritual needs according to the Great Book. I bring them to the Father's feet in grace and forgiveness, mevrou. But you – you are the Devil's child. You turn them away from their own salvation.'

'Dominee Conradie!' Arabella leaned forward, bridling. 'I have done no such thing! You talk of forgiveness when there is none in your heart for one poor innocent girl in your congregation. You do not understand the first thing about your women – you know nothing of their sorrows, their pain, their humiliation, and yet you talk of leading them in grace!'

Dominee Conradie stared at her for a while from half-hooded eyes, then taking a slow breath to calm the suppressed rage in him, said, 'You do not understand these people, Mevrou du Rand, while I have lived in this place for many years. My father was one of the first ministers in the Transvaal – it was he and his family who trekked with Paul Kruger to make our republic, before it was taken away from us by force!'

Involuntarily his eyes turned to reminders of those days: a large picture of President Kruger beside the red, white, blue and green flag of the former South African Republic hanging like a ghost in the corner, and a framed letter from General de Wet.

As he regarded each symbol of the lost cause to which he would always cling, his voice took on a note of fierce pride, mingled with bitterness. 'First your people took away our country, humiliating and betraying us, mevrou – but that is not enough for your rapacious heart. No, you must now come and cause mischief in my community, turning wives against husbands, daughters against fathers. You condone Annetjie du Preez' actions and those of like-minded girls – you say they must be free to seduce the men and the boys and then, when they scream that they were forced into it, you forgive them, and encourage them to repeat their wickedness again and again. What kind of a society would we live in, if we were all free to do as we pleased? People are only saved by their sense of sin. If you take that away, then they are damned by their own weaknesses.'

Arabella answered his accusation calmly, but her colour deepened. 'I think you know very well that I'm not condoning any mischievous and harmful behaviour, Dominee Conradie. More to the point is the fact that *you* know nothing of the suffering of Annetjie du Preez and yet you would prescribe for her!'

The hostile eyes assessed her shrewdly. 'And do you, mevrou?'

Arabella sighed, her face suddenly ashen. 'Yes, I do.' Her voice had grown low as she forced herself to say the words, but it vibrated with the intensity of her emotion.

The Dominee's mouth fell open in astonishment for a full five seconds, then it snapped shut and he stared at her darkly in a forbidding mixture of ferocity and contempt. She saw in that expression, what poor Annetjie du Preez and the rest of his congregation had to face, and felt a sudden uprush of sympathy for them.

When he spoke at last, his voice was harsh and accusing. 'So! You yourself have been in such a position, mevrou! And you would encourage the younger women to do as you have done. Your own life since you have lived here in this dorp is no example to the women in my community. You cast out your own husband for long bitter months after the death of your first child, and yet you have the shamelessness to stand up and tell my people – the good, obedient wives and daughters of my village – how to behave!'

Arabella scarcely heard the acid words, but felt only a thrust of shock. No one had spoken to her so openly, except Tienie, of what lay between herself and Deneys, and this man was virtually a stranger to her. She felt a stinging resentment that he had mentioned it.

'The past is dead, Dominee Conradie. While I honour your loyalty to your past and to your people, I know that the old way of life is going. I myself cannot afford the luxury of living in that past and I must do what I think is right for the good of the future.'

'I see.' The old man reached for his spectacles with a shaking hand.

'You will persist until you have broken up the whole community into chaos and confusion! You are an evil woman, Mevrou du Rand, and so is this women's cause you lead. I will do everything in my power to stop you!'

Arabella stiffened, and a horrible despondency clutched her, but she faced him squarely across the table with its green-shaded oil lamp. 'You may think you can stop me, Dominee, but you will never stop the women's suffrage movement. Already, with the help of the International Suffrage Alliance, the Women's Enfranchisement Alliance Union has been established, linking the women's leagues throughout the country, except Cape Town. This is a most significant step forward for the movement, which will strengthen it against all parliamentary tactics of delay and evasion. You will never stop it, Dominee – it's too strong an urge throughout the world. It's like trying to hold back the tides.'

The Dominee leaned forward, his expression hostile, malignant even. 'Then may God forgive you and all the women in this work, mevrou, for sowing the seeds of chaos everywhere among ignorant women who turn against the salvation of their church. Stop you I will – if only in this one small place among my God-fearing and upright people.'

Arabella brushed down her skirt and gathered up her handbag. Her face took on a pallor from the green lamplight of the dull room, which lent it sudden strength, and the colour of a marble bust. 'You can only speak for yourself, Dominee Conradie, and I can only answer for myself,' she stated quietly, before she left his study and made her way out of his unwelcoming house.

20

The sun was setting behind the hills in a blaze of orange glory and the clock was striking six. Arabella shifted her position beside Deneys on the long wooden platform of the station. It was splintered here and there, and covered with powdery black dust – the same gritty dust that darkened the windows of the small ticket-office, as the train bringing Sarel du Rand on his first visit for Christmas since his return from America, pulled in with smoke and cinders pouring in at the open windows.

Arabella unfastened the ribbons of her straw boater and wished she could discard her smart grey coat and gloves. Her head ached with the throbbing vibrations of the engine and her own anxiety. She dreaded meeting Deneys' father as much as she had dreaded anything. She had heard his name ever since she had arrived in this country, and long ago she had built up a deep dislike of him, although they had never come face to face.

Yet it was hardly the end of the world, she reproved herself. Even though Sarel du Rand had been elected to the Union Senate, he was simply an old man, a father who loved nis children, a man who had buried two wives and lost two sons ... But these reflections did not comfort her. The path of her marriage was rough and uneven, but she still loved Deneys almost desperately and in order to save it, she was not sure whether it would be enough to overcome the prejudice of his father towards her.

Sarel du Rand alighted near a pile of wooden crates and boxes, and stood before them. He was not at all what she had expected. He was a small man, far shorter than his son, and about seventy years old, but for all his lack of height, his presence was imbued with immense dignity. Deneys shook his hand and they embraced like two Old Testament Israelites, then Arabella was introduced.

Looking at him more closely, she was struck by his erect bearing, and by the beauty of his sharp features above the neat silver moustache and goatee beard. The silver-white hair was thinning and the eyes were deep-set and searching under jutting grey brows. An intangible

323

aura of austerity emanated from him which commanded instant respect, and behind that stern old face the flame of his spirit was almost visible.

And as Deneys stowed away his father's luggage in the cart and helped Arabella up behind the old man, she tried to banish the feeling that Sarel's presence was like a shadow, subtly darkening the sunny greenness of the dying day ...

After Mimi was tucked in her cot, they led Sarel into the dining room, which was already beaming with lamplight. The best silver was on display, beside dishes filled with soup and home-made milk noodles, dark brown bread, pumpkin fritters, sliced biltong, sosaties and creamy melk tert, with golden, flaky puff pastry. They stood with bowed heads as Sarel said Grace before the meal. He seemed, Arabella thought, to be speaking sincerely and intimately with an unseen Presence as naturally as he breathed.

As the meal progressed, Arabella noticed that between Deneys and his father there existed a deep bond; the old man rarely argued with his son, but listened with absorbed interest to what Deneys said, while watching him with great affection. He only spoke to Arabella about her country once, and she was surprised by his reference to it.

'I found England to be a beautiful country,' he remarked, referring to the time when he had visited Europe as President of the Orange Free State, 'but I especially liked the ruggedness of Scotland. The Scots impressed me with their thrift and hard work.'

'Pa – comparisons are odious.' Deneys said it teasingly, but the lamplight marked a familiar ironic smile.

Prompted by a wry sense of humour, his father returned, 'True, my son – and are we not the very ones to resent any kind of comparisons?'

Arabella thought that such a remarkable old man would have awed anybody into respectable silence, even a hard-headed Scot or Englishman. Not for the first time she felt a tremor of apprehension lest she be found wanting in his eyes. She wondered what his reaction would be, when he heard about her from Dominee Conradie and the others. He would have no mercy, of that she was certain.

Their conversation ended as Samson came in to set another oil lamp on the cleared-away table for the evening reading, which Deneys had never insisted upon until his father's visit. He brought in the large family Bible which he laid on the table as they took their places and from the kitchen came Samson and Maisie, to stand in the doorway as the chapter was read.

The lamp on the table threw a warm, intimate circle about the small group, as Sarel read the chosen passage from Proverbs about the virtuous woman. As the full fragrance of summer flowers from the garden floated in through the open window, along with the deep guttural song of bullfrogs in the veld, Arabella kept her eyes fixed on her hands which were clasped in the lap of her mauve silk dress. Blood began to throb in her temples in the silent knowledge that Sarel was reading only to her. He was asking her if she was the right woman for his son ...

The old man's voice never faltered in his fierce conviction about the virtues of the righteous woman, who supervised her household with such wisdom and kindness that her husband and children would praise her. Arabella raised her head for a moment, just in time to see Sarel's long forefinger brush away a flying ant that had alighted on the page, and in an instant she was forcibly reminded of the solemnly pointed steeple of the Dutch Reformed Church.

Yes, she thought, her sadness like the evening shadow outside. A man ought to have a good, understanding wife, a wife of tenderness and compassion and obedience ... but she doubted her ability to give that complete obedience.

On the first Sunday after his arrival, Sarel went to church, and later was invited to coffee and dinner at the most important houses in the village – invitations which Deneys declined because Arabella's isolation from the community was almost complete. But when Sarel returned, he remained silent. Every night Arabella would lie awake, tossing and turning, the old man's silence too much for her.

Christmas came and went, followed by New Year. On the last Saturday of his visit, when the sun brightened in the eastern sky, Arabella quickly rose and dressed, yearning to paint once more, to relax her confused and apprehensive spirit in the pure joy of texture and colour and shape. Equipped with crayons and a sketchbook, she stole outside and pedalled on her bicycle up towards the nearest koppie, where there was a beautiful view of the village.

Only a few noisy plovers, stalking through the long grass with their bright red legs noticed her appearance as she spread out her work under a tree which grew with stubborn vigour in a deep cleft of a boulder. There was a very heavy dewfall, and red cows cast long, early-morning shadows as they streamed towards the open veld from a nearby farm. Arabella's hands began moving with swift skill, outlining and blocking in flat colour masses, in preparation for shading. She had been busy for some time when she heard the village clock strike six. A sakabula bird with its long, beautiful tail flew low over its territory and the loud *kree-kree-kree* of a crowned plover filled the air as the nearest farmhouse sent up fresh blue feathers of smoke. The sun grew warmer on her shoulder and she knew that she would soon have to return to the house.

Just then a figure emerged from further up the hillside, and with surprise, Arabella recognised the spare frame and white hair of Sarel, spryly climbing down the rocky grass path with the aid of a stout stick. She felt a heaviness in her heart. Now that the moment was on her for a private confrontation, she suddenly felt helpless and undecided. So far, she had no idea what he thought of her. She only knew that he could not be pleased with what he had heard.

He was almost at her side before he spoke. 'A beautiful day,' he said in answer to her greeting. 'I have just thanked the Lord for it. I see you are using the talent He gave you. That is good.'

'Do you often climb the hillsides so early, Mr du Rand?'

'I find it is the best time to think,' he explained. 'One's mind then seems clear after a good night's rest, and in these hills as in all hills, the Lord seems very close.'

She watched a rock kestrel hovering above, a motionless speck looking for its prey, then she laid down her work and looked up into her father-in-law's eyes with sudden directness. 'Mr du Rand — you've heard the sermons preached by Dominee Conradie as you have heard the talk in the village about me. Does this mean that you believe I'm not all that a woman for your son should be?'

'Why do you ask me what only your conscience can answer?'

'Because, Mr du Rand, that is not enough. I never want to separate you from your son, for that would be striking at the deepest bond. But I would like you to be reconciled to our marriage, if not for my sake, for Deneys'.'

'I know you have undergone great suffering, Arabella.' He seated himself on the rock beside her. 'I know of your work in the camps, of the imprisonment for your beliefs. I also sense my son is not happy with your actions against Jacobus du Preez and your dedication to the cause of women, though he has not spoken of it.'

'I am unacceptable in your eyes, Mr du Rand, and Dominee Conradie's attitude and those in the village who support him, have strengthened it.'

He flicked his hand at a horsefly which buzzed above his head. 'I see that you think me a harsh and uncompassionate man, Arabella.' His eyes searched her keenly from their deep sockets. 'Perhaps in some ways I am, yet I continually remind myself: "Judge not, lest ye be judged."'

A long silence fell between them, broken only by the call of birds and the distant lustiness of a rooster.

'I have had to wrestle with my conscience every night I've been here, like Jacob and the Angel, and it has come to me that though Dominee Conradie is a sincere and devout man who believes implicitly in what he says, and though there is great reaction against what you have done, there is a place for women such as yourself in this fast-changing modern world. You may be surprised to learn that I myself voted for the motion calling for women's voting rights, but was defeated by an overwhelming majority in the last session of Parliament.'

Arabella folded her hands and looked into the distance, hearing his voice as if it had become part of the summer morning, her mood changing, for now with the old man's unexpected response, relief welled up inside her like the sudden sweep of light from the sun breaking free of dark clouds.

'There is so much to put right in our imperfect world, my dear – and we would be foolish to overlook it. But perhaps Heideville is not yet ready for your message and Dominee Conradie understands that. He understands our people intimately.' He gave her a peculiarly penetrating look. 'We Boer folk are unique: we became insular because of our history of trekking into the isolation of the veld and the bush, and God-fearing with only the Bible as our handbook to life which we have always used for every and all occasions.'

'But your son – he does not think as you do, Mr du Rand. Will you not speak to him as you have spoken to me?'

Sarel frowned, an enigmatic expression in his eyes. 'That is not my place – it is for you to show him the way. Deneys is from a family of men, Arabella. His mother, who was the most beautiful of women, with hair the colour of cornsilk, and eyes as blue as the summer sky, died when he was six years old.' He paused, as if it was hard to continue, then he said, 'My second wife, a good, solid woman and the mother of Johan, my youngest son, died when Deneys was but thirteen. From then on, it was a male household, with stern and proud male values. Deneys has to learn to give you a place beside him – but there, you must gently lead him. You see, I have learned much in my old age.' A faint smile flitted over his lined and noble features, before it vanished, and a trace of shyness was left in its place.

He rose, but still lingered by the rock, obviously struggling to say something more. It was far easier, Arabella guessed, for him to talk to his son or another man than to her.

'For all my feminist leanings, Mr du Rand, I do love your son and I should like to feel that I have your acceptance,' she ventured, moved by his words.

For a moment or two Sarel gave no response, his eyes hooded with thought, then slowly the corners of his solemn mouth moved to a smile. 'You have it, my daughter.' He took the hand she held out to him, then added, 'I think you are strong enough to deal with my adventurous and proud son, but take your time and be patient.' His eyes were surprisingly gentle as they met hers. 'I hope that we will come to a better understanding as time passes,' he said, as he turned to go back down the rough trail. 'The one thing that I have learned during my visit is that you do sincerely love my son, and what more has a father the right to ask?'

The Dutch Reformed Church was crowded that Sunday when Dominee Conradie made his strongest denunciation of Arabella. Everyone was excited because they knew that Sarel was present, and they crowded up against their neighbours. The service had begun in the usual way, and then the Dominee had broken out into a tirade, thundering harshly from the pulpit, almost unable to control the tremors in his voice. But this only seemed to add to the intensity of the occasion, as the congregation sat down, rustling, the brittle sound of the prayer-books like the sound of a summer wind.

'My people,' he bawled, banging his fist on the pulpit. 'Let each one of us seek out the evil in his heart, for are we not all born in sin? Evil lives in this community, my good people, though we would have it not. The disciples of the Devil live among us, though we would know them not!' He lifted up his hands in a gesture of simple but terrible warning: 'They disguise themselves in the robes of angels and good-doers, but they speak with the forked tongue of the Devil, that eats away at the very heart of our community!'

Tienie, sitting with her daughters, listened, and then her small brown eyes became defiant, and she set her head at an arrogant angle. The congregation rose to sing a psalm. Only Sarel did not open his psalm book, nor did he rise with the others but just sat there, arms folded across his black waistcoat, staring at the Dominee. Those around him shot him sharp glances, or stared with round-eyed disbelief.

Then all at once, as the last chords of the organ died away and everyone sat down, he rose and stood in the aisle. Now there was a great hush in the church as everyone craned their necks to see him. He looked up at the Dominee in his pulpit for a long moment and the feeling of drama grew into an almost unbearable tension.

'Dominee Conradie!' His voice rang fiercely through the quietness. 'We have heard in your sermon this morning about hatred – hatred for some of our fellow men, or fellow women. You have spoken about the evil in our midst, and you are right. There *is* evil living in this community – but it is the evil of bitterness and hatred that judges our neighbours.'

Dominee Conradie's hands gripped the edge of the pulpit, and he leaned forward on them heavily, his eyes fixed on Sarel's face.

'It is not for us to judge, Dominee Conradie! It is for each one of us to seek forgiveness for our own sin, and to understand the sins of others,' Sarel said, and now his voice began to mount. 'As the Father Himself taught us, only he who hath no sin may cast the first stone! He did not judge Mary Magdalene – He drew her to Him in forgiveness and understanding. You are good people, reasonable people, but you have listened to the voice of hate, which destroys the human spirit. Not one single word of the Father's eternal and unchanging love has been spoken of this day.'

Very slowly and carefully he turned his head and scanned the frozen rows of people, seeing faces thoughtful and concerned, faces full of sternness and disgust, confused faces, embarrassed faces, and here and there faces full of hate and defiance.

Dominee Conradie reared up in the pulpit, shaken and white, but still indomitable, his eyes as unrelenting as before when they met those of Sarel. 'We are all here to search our hearts and to do the will of God, Meneer du Rand,' he said bitterly. 'God will never forgive evil, for in evil there is no mercy. You speak, Meneer, as an enemy of God. You blaspheme in this church, and may God have mercy upon your soul.'

It was so quiet that everyone could hear the long, agonised breath that came from Jacobus du Preez, sitting near the back. Slowly, Sarel lifted his eyes up to the man in the pulpit.

'Those who hate, Dominee Conradie,' he proclaimed, his voice ringing from the walls, 'are not governed by God. It is they who are the enemies of God, not I.' Then he swung round in the aisle and left the church.

Deneys pulled off his hat, and threw it angrily, to land on the hatstand in the entrance hall, after saying goodbye to Sarel at the station the following day.

'Arabella, why did you have to do it? Why did you have to push the old man to drive a wedge between the people of this community! Now you have the Dominee and my father at each other's throats, and everyone else in an uproar!'

Arabella stared up at him beneath the straw brim of her hat, her green eyes flashing suddenly in an otherwise quiet and pale face. 'I never drove your father to do anything. He had his own strong convictions that it was the morally right thing to do.'

Deneys' expressive masculine mouth curled scornfully at the corners. 'You know perfectly well that it's not a matter of right and wrong any more! My law practice depends on the goodwill of this community and you know it. I really do not understand you at all!' He spoke in a low voice, but Arabella could feel his rage which he had suppressed during his father's visit. Sarel's outburst in the church the day before had caused an uproar such as the community had never known. It had angered and confused Deneys, even though Sarel had not referred to the incident afterwards. Until he had left on the train no one spoke of it, but it stood like a spectre between them.

Arabella bristled, but controlled herself behind a mask of cool composure as the battle lines were now made all too clear, then Deneys turned and strode towards the bedroom, slamming the door behind him.

As an early autumn crept across the countryside bringing frost and the hint of crisp, cooler weather, and the northern visiting birds began to collect for the long migration back, Arabella lay beside Deneys, listening to the steady beat of his heart in the darkness. There had been an uneasy truce between them for some weeks, but always the women's cause divided them, like a grey menacing shadow waiting to spring. She longed to break away and be free from all that restricted her in this isolated place, in her marriage. She ached for that larger world outside, beyond the hills and the mountains, unhampered by Deneys' prejudice, his narrow, unreasonable vision which distorted his potential greatness, and the prejudices of those in the village who thought as he did.

This frustration clouded the secret joy she had come to know in the last few days; she had conceived again. She knew it would be many days before she could speak of it to Deneys, for he was often abrupt and terse with her, Annetjie du Preez and Sarel's confrontation with Dominee Conradie still bitter in his mind.

She lay very still beside him, thinking of her aspirations, hopes which she could never share with him. Much had happened already in the women's movement. A group of black women in the Orange Free State had staged a successful demonstration against the enforcement of the Pass Laws in that province against women. Hundreds of them had refused to carry passes and had gone to gaol. The prison became so full that the authorities were forced to stop arresting pass offenders, and eventually the women were excluded from the Pass Laws. And not so long afterwards, a large group of Indian women had taken part in the passive resistance campaign organised by Mr Mohandas Ghandi, a well-to-do Indian barrister in Johannesburg, against the Immigration Act, which forbade Indians to enter the Transvaal. In so doing, these women had broken the usual constraints demanding submissiveness and passivity from the female sex.

At this point, there had been no attempt to link these groups with the white suffrage movement and there was still a vast gap between the women of different races ... but Arabella saw what was happening as a ray of hope for the future. The longing to play a more active role in these developments gripped her like a fever.

In those dry and savagely cold days of winter, her frustration increased tenfold. She decided that her freedom as Deneys' wife was only a false liberty. Her husband was, as she had feared all those years ago when she was still a single woman, her authoritarian keeper.

She thought of Ben and his grief. Unbeknownst to Deneys, she had begun a correspondence with him and with Bishop Sebastian, which gave her a strange comfort, a curious sense of belonging where she no longer felt it with Deneys. And she knew that Ben, in his mourning, welcomed the contact.

21

The short, severe, winter spent its strength at last and spring swiftly spread its coloured cloak over the countryside. Buzzard pairs climbed in lazy spirals on the rising warm air, and, as the sun rose higher every day, snakes stirred in the veld and basked on the warm-faced rocks and stones. Arabella's views and past actions had been widely condemned, and earned for Deneys, not only the unspoken sympathy of his male friends and acquaintances, but also that of many of the women. Between him and Arabella there was a silent rift; it was a time of loaded silences and defensive attitudes. Arabella consoled herself by writing to Rachel, who had given birth to her third child – a daughter, Hannah – and Ben, who was due in Pretoria on political business just before Christmas. At the beginning of November she gave birth to a son, Christian, named after Deneys' brother – a smiling, contented little child with his father's brown eyes.

It was peaceful sitting under the old apple tree in the back garden. Mending and darning, Arabella watched little Mimi toddling on the grass nearby, chuckling when Wasp ran sniffing at her small heels. Thor, whose large eyes gazed at her hopefully, lay at her feet, his head on his great paws while the small bantam cock scratched in the dirt surrounded by his hens. She sat on a wooden chair heaped with pillows where the hot December afternoon sunshine was blurred, greened and softened, and where the steady hum of bees buzzed around the riot of flowerbeds brightening the shadowed grass. It was steaming hot in the house; the teasing aroma of slowly cooking food floated from the kitchen, where Maisie polished the silver, and smoke rose in lazy blue coils from the chimney.

Arabella heard the screen-door open, then slap shut. Thor rose from the grass, growling, and stood stiffly to attention while Wasp began to bark excitedly. She looked up to see a tall dark-haired figure in a light grey suit hobbling forward on crutches.

'Ben!' she exclaimed, jumping up. 'What an unexpected surprise.'

'My political business is over,' he explained, smiling as he stopped before her, resting lightly on his crutches, 'so I thought a quick trip to Heideville would not go amiss. Besides, I wanted to see you again.'

He turned as Mimi toddled over and eyed him uncertainly from the refuge of her mother's skirt.

'My daughter, Mimi.' Arabella looked down with a sudden rush of tenderness, and patted Mimi's small golden head. She lifted the child into the crook of her arm, and smiled up at Ben from under the brim of her wide straw hat. She was thinner than he remembered. Her expressive face had a tired look in spite of the smile, but as always, there was that air of quiet alertness which had never ceased to fascinate him. Seeing the stranger accepted, Thor and Wasp immediately sat down and Thor flicked his right ear at an intrusive fly.

Arabella asked Samson to bring them coffee and cake, and called Maisie to take Mimi inside for bread and milk. Then she and Ben sat side by side on the wooden chairs at the table holding her mending-basket as the hens clucked in the coop and the tantalising smell of herbs rose from the kitchen.

Ben sat for a moment, his hat dangling from his hand, and all at once the silence between them was significant. It seemed that a long time passed, before he said, 'You have a lovely garden, Arabella – as successful as everything else you have attempted and brought to fruition.' His eyes were compelling, a strange mixture of smoky and clear grey, quick and clever, but there was a brooding quality in them. 'Where's your husband?'

'Deneys is at the office. He has two important clients today, both from the next village. He gets business from all over these days, because he's so exceptionally good.' She was smiling, but there was no pink in her cheeks or lips. 'How is Luke? I believe he's still in England.' The green eyes studied his face, a confusing mass of thoughts and feelings fighting beneath the surface.

Ben laid his hat and crutches carefully down beside him, and fondled Wasp's head, as the dog wagged his tail in ecstasy, his tongue lolling from his mouth. 'Luke has joined a small new flying school. There's great interest in the new flying machines – bi-planes, they're called. He's mad about flying. I only hope he doesn't get himself killed, in his enthusiasm. They are flimsy, dangerous things at the best of times – just wooden struts and canvas.'

She pondered over this, then abruptly changed the subject. 'There seem to be such confused rumblings coming out of Europe these days, Ben. Did you hear anything more about the Balkan War when you were in England last summer?'

Ben frowned thoughtfully. 'The Balkans have always been simmering and it seems to me that the world's out of equilibrium, lop-sided at the moment.' He swung one highly polished shoe out casually before him. 'While I was away I visited British friends in court circles in Berlin, and it would appear that the Balkans débâcle and the subsequent collapse of the Turkish Empire has brought deepening tensions into Austro-Hungary which, unfortunately, could not prevent the collapse of its neighbour.' He spoke carefully.

Her face was pale. 'Do you think it will affect the rest of Europe – that the conflicts will spread?'

'They could, though I doubt if any of the major countries would want to join in – they've too much to lose. My friends in Berlin call Kaiser Bill a Wagnerian imbecile, but for all that I must say that the continual expansion of his navy and Germany's world trade is testing British naval supremacy to the utmost.'

Arabella was listening intently, and nodding. 'Yes,' she said. 'And where do you think all this will lead?'

He shrugged. 'As a politician, I prefer to be cautious, dear girl, and watch how the wind is going to blow.'

She wrinkled her nose, smiling faintly. 'Well, talking to a politician then, I believe that the majority of the male Parliament once more threw out the Bill for women's rights.'

Ben's eyes were inscrutable now, lost in his own thoughts. A new silence fell between them. From where they sat they could see the heatwave in the bright blue sky, touching the rim of the long wooded slope of the nearest hill tumbling down to the river.

He sat there in his elegant clothing, his artificial leg extended stiffly in front of him, then he said: 'I did not come here to talk of politics, dear girl, I came to see you. Your letters of late have been disturbing, to say the least – especially the last one.'

She had never before realised how much she liked his well-modulated, almost drawling voice, and something strengthened in her. By the time Samson appeared with the coffee and orange cake, her tightness had somewhat relaxed. She poured the strong dark liquid into the cups, and offered one to Ben. As he sipped, she settled herself more easily on her chair, and sighed.

He studied her with careful candour. Her brows, the same colour as her hair, momentarily drew together. She did not look away from him, although his nearness suddenly disturbed her, made her acutely aware of him.

'If you've come to tell me I've made a mistake in my marriage, you can save yourself the trouble, Ben.' Her expression was sad but intent.

He frowned. 'No, that's not what I came to speak to you about. I doubt if it would do any good, anyway – you've always gone ahead and done what you wanted, ever since I've known you. But I do know you're unhappy.'

Arabella glanced at him. She had known Ben a long time. She might still be resentful of him deep down, but under this and their past torment was a deep tide of affection and understanding. 'I think it's pretty normal in marriage.' She put down her cup, picked up a pair of socks, and looked at them soberly. 'Just like socks – filled with holes. All they need is constant mending.'

'And now?' asked Ben, softly. 'You can't go on living in quiet desperation, which is what you are doing.'

There was such loneliness in her, such frustration. 'I'm not as happy as I should be, I suppose,' she admitted. 'I'm shunned by my husband and most of the community for one reason or another. I live a half-life, for want of a better word. But what of it? Millions of women exist in even worse conditions.'

He finished his coffee and cake and asked if she minded if he smoked. He opened his case, thoughtfully lit one of his gold-tipped cigarettes, then snapped it shut and looked her right in the eyes. 'I know that state well, Arabella, and I'm not a woman. At least I have my work to escape to – always did.'

Silence closed in again, isolating them. Out of the corner of her eye, Arabella could see the edge of his silver-grey trousers.

'It is difficult being a woman,' she mused, 'especially when there's conflict between what one must be, and half the time wants to be, and what one longs the other half of the time to do, but can't.'

Ben regarded the tip of his cigarette, then turned to her. 'You have me, Arabella. For the first time I'm free, and I'm going home to England again for a few months, soon. Why not come with me, and bring the children? It'll do you a lot of good to get away. Put everything back into perspective – and you can see Luke again.'

Arabella stiffened. At first she simply sat there, not answering, afraid and not afraid: in sudden and absolute confusion. She wanted to escape – to leave the garden. Not to hear. She felt nervous in a way she had not done for years, and her mouth was sticky and dry as she said, 'I couldn't do that, Ben. You may be free, but I'm not. It would never be right –'

'But we're relatives after a fashion, dear girl. I would only be escorting you back to your roots for a while – no harm in that. Why not bring a chaperone – your maid, anyone you like. I'll arrange for the best nannies, everything you want.' He watched a spiral of smoke rise as it left his lips.

She was stunned, unable to stay calm. She thought of England. Freedom. Culture. *A larger world.* Her misery and fear and frustration left her. Her weariness lifted. 'I'll have to think about it, Ben. It's all so confusing, and Deneys would never agree.'

335

Into a short reflective silence, Ben said: 'By all means think about it, dear girl, but don't take too long. I plan to leave in our autumn to catch the northern spring.' He brushed his good knee. 'I'd like to have you along – you and the children.' He leaned towards her, and her face suddenly brightened, so near his. 'You're a wonderful person, Arabella. You're the kind of woman who is an asset to a man in every way.'

She flushed. 'I hardly know what I am any more, what with this and that,' she said lamely, at last. 'Marriage, in a very strange way, seems to have drained my confidence.'

'If you ever left Deneys, I would marry you at once.' His voice, in spite of its quiet, held vehemence and certainty. 'I think I've always wanted to marry you.' He put his fingers over hers, and pressed them. She did not stir. The touch of his hand was suddenly almost unbearable in its comfort.

'I've made my bed, Ben, and now I must lie on it,' she said earnestly. 'I've never been one to run away, you know that.'

He nodded. 'Yes, and I respect you for it. But one day you'll come to me, I know it.'

She coloured again. 'Now, Ben, that sounds terribly extravagant.' She pressed his hand, laughed a little, then removed her hand and glanced at her watch; its enamelled cover caught the bright sunlight. 'It's nearly three-thirty. Will you stay to dinner?'

'No, thank you, dear girl. I came with the postcart and will be leaving with it in twenty minutes for the four-thirty train to Pretoria.'

With surprising agility, he sprang up, supporting himself against the table. Then he gave her his hand. She took it simply, and rose. They were standing close together. She began to smile. Then the smile left her face, and her eyes widened with a terrible suffering.

'Ben,' she said, and then could not go on. She thought; He knows I love him, and he loves me too. We never stopped loving each other, all these years, in spite of everything. But we must never speak of it.

'I'd better go,' he said finally. 'The cart will be arriving soon.'

She walked through the house, with Ben limping behind her, and they came out together on to the green shadow of the verandah. To Arabella their silence had a fullness, a richness, even if it was sad and confused. She was not alone; if she was desolate, it was a desolation that was finally shared. Suddenly she lowered her head, and stared at the plain gold wedding band on her left hand until a flash of pain made her close her eyes.

'Arabella?' Ben put a hand on her arm. 'Is it worse than I ever thought?'

She shook her head. 'No, it's just –' Her shoulders trembled and she began to weep before she could stop herself. 'It's just so god-damned lonely ...'

'My God!' With his crutches under his elbows, and supporting himself against the wall, he took her by the shoulders and stared down intently into the tear-wet pools of liquid green. 'I never guessed it was that bad.'

'But it's not only my marriage, it's the whole community," she whispered. 'You don't understand –'

'I think I do. In the past I was a fool about you, but I've finally come to my senses.' He brought her close against him, enfolding her in his arms as he brushed his lips against her temple. 'Listen to me, dearest girl. I will be in Pretoria for this week. Come to me there, and bring the children. We'll work something out.'

'I want to believe you, Ben.' As he lifted her up, she leaned her forehead against the side of his neck where she could feel the strong, slow drumming of his pulse. Security and closeness seemed an almost tangible substance in his arms and somewhere deep within her a yearning grew. 'But I'm doomed to remain where I am.'

'No, you're not – you deserve more than this limited kind of life. You're too talented, too clever to be buried here in the bush forever. I want to give you a chance at that other world, my dear. Think about what I've said. I'll wait for you until Friday.'

Then, with deliberate care he lowered his mouth to hers in a slowly stirring kiss. His lips moved on hers, parting and playing and, with subtle persistence, demanding a response. Excitement washed her body, until she heard Maisie with Mimi in the kitchen and baby Christian crying, and they drew apart.

He smiled, completely disarming her. 'I love you, Arabella, and I want to marry you. Come to me at this address, I'll be waiting. And don't worry about the legal side – I'll have it sewn up so neatly that not even the cleverness of Deneys du Rand will be able to unravel it.'

He held out a visiting card which she took, and it was a long painful moment before she regained enough control over her chaotic feelings to say, 'I'll think about it, Ben – but don't hold out too much hope.'

He took her hand, then let it go. 'Goodbye, my dear. I know you'll change your mind.'

She stood and watched him hobble away to the postcart, which drew up outside. As he closed the gate, he paused, standing very upright on his crutches, outlined against the lonely sky. She lifted her hand and waved to him, and he waved in return. Then she turned and walked back inside, to a deep silence and the old desolation.

22

Ten minutes later, Deneys arrived back and Arabella saw him bend down and lift little Mimi up, throwing her gently into the air with happy playfulness in the kitchen doorway. He threw back his golden head, chuckling infectiously, then set her down on her feet, and taking her hand, walked forward. He was preceded by the dogs, barking and jumping about with joyous and wet recognition, but when he saw Arabella, he came to an abrupt halt, brown eyes alert and veiled.

He stood before her as Maisie came to claim the little girl, and she was uneasily aware of the familiar strong fingers, full of power and decision, unbuttoning the light beige jacket of his suit.

'Deneys, you're home early,' she began, trying to still the heightening of her emotions.

'My last client cancelled his appointment for this afternoon,' he said, his eyes kindling as he looked at her. 'His gelding broke a leg this morning. I was talking to old Widow Hendricks when I passed the Post Office,' he paused in a deceptively casual fashion, 'and she said that your cousin, Lord Stradcombe, had just left in the postcart for the station. I didn't know he was visiting here.'

Arabella stiffened. 'He popped in unexpectedly for a short while. He had political business in Pretoria.'

The muscles tightened along Deneys' jaw as he began to pack his pipe bowl, poking the tobacco down with vicious fingers. 'If I ever get my hands on him, I'll kill him!' he said with low savagery, and clamped his pipe between his lips.

'Whatever do you mean by that?' Arabella bit back her rising anger.

Deneys took out his pipe and raked her over with his eyes. 'My meaning is quite clear. If that man ever darkens this doorstep again, he'll have a murder on his head.'

Arabella read the jealous fury in his eyes. 'Only over my dead body,' she challenged sharply.

'Then let it be so!' He bit his pipe-stem with rage, then strode out into the passage without a backward glance.

With a sinking heart she watched him, minutes later, lead his horse from the stable, and saddle him. He had changed into his cord riding breeches and as he led Kitchener round to the front, something tickled her right cheek. She flicked it with a forefinger and it came away wet. Mimi toddled into the kitchen, the fine bright golden hair framing her warmly rounded cheeks, and Arabella thought of baby Christian, so innocent and vulnerable as he lay in his cot in the nursery. These children deserved more than she could give them here, in this small isolated village. They needed a bigger world with more opportunities, more choices – more progress.

From that moment, she was translated into a world which held only herself and her children. There was no thought in her of Deneys, except in burning anger. She had to be free from this cramped life – she had to go with Ben on the four-thirty train.

Time and place lost their meaning as she raced from the kitchen, telling Samson to get the cart ready, and calling to Maisie to dress Mimi for travelling and put Christian, still in his cot, into the cart. She quickly packed a valise, running from room to room gathering up everything she would need for the journey. She would leave a note for Deneys on the dining-room table and by the time he read it, they would be far away, beyond his reach. Then it would be up to Ben to put the legal side into action to prevent Deneys from upsetting her plans.

It was still glaringly hot when she placed a pillow in the back of the cart for little Mimi who sat, sucking her thumb beside the cot where baby Christian gurgled happily, unaware of the great drama taking place in their lives. Maisie, who refused to leave the children, climbed up beside them, and soon Mimi was contentedly leaning against her.

They were off ... racing down the rise in small puffs of dust, past the larger houses on the outskirts of the village. Arabella felt the surge of the mare's muscles as she braked sharply at the drift crossing the river, low for this time of year, then, as the horse neighed and plunged forward, the hooves scoring great marks in the soft ground, she heard Mimi's gay little voice, prattling her baby-talk, and turned to see her mass of golden curls – the colour of her father's hair. The world suddenly stopped before her. Every moment of every day she would be reminded of Deneys when she looked at Mimi, at little Christian. Her heart contracted in a spasm of pain. Deneys would never leave her life, after all. Something of him would live, was living now. He was very much alive, in his children.

The moment of defeat came when the mare struggled up the other side of the drift and stopped suddenly, jerking the cart to a halt.

Arabella forgot the shouldering hills about her; she no longer heard the children as she remembered with vivid clarity the first time she had stepped off the train at the station rising before them, holding Deneys' hand, filled with the warm and expanding presence of his love. She had been so full of plans then, her mind overflowing with wild dreams and romantic notions ...

She could see him now, in her mind's eye – the exuberance and enthusiasm of his personality, the pride and love he could never manage to keep out of his eyes when he looked at his children ... She glanced back up the rise and thought of their small home which had sheltered their passions and their sorrows, their laughter and their tears. The hills on one side, the rearing mountains further away on the other, and the whole scene seemed gradually to transform itself around her. Everything that had become hostile and alien and cruel was changed now into something strong and challenging, and as she gazed about her, there slowly crept over her the black humiliation of knowing that she could never leave Deneys, she could never run away from herself – for that was what she was attempting to do. She suddenly felt physically wretched, emotionally pulverised, and drowning in guilt.

Distantly a rock pigeon called from the river; a large hare, moving out of the grass, saw the mare, leaped high and raced back into hiding. The sun began to sink lower, and a shaft of light warmed her face. A new pride flared in her, directed against Ben. Oh, he loved her, of that she had no doubt, but in his own selfish way, as he had loved her before. He had been quite callous in wanting her to go to him, for his pleasure, and leave her husband, without a thought of the consequences either to the children or herself. He had betrayed her once, with no feeling for her deepest hurt, only for his own jealous wounds. Rosamunde's death had merely put everything out of perspective. Grief and sorrow had blurred the truth. More than all Deneys' threatening attitude and his aggression, it was Ben's show of kindness towards her that had made her want to do as he suggested. It was so often kindness, she thought bitterly, not torture that broke a victim's spirit. Kindness crept around your back and stabbed you there, so that your will evaporated into gratitude. When had she changed? And how could it have happened without her noticing? She did not know. She just had the sense of having already travelled too far to turn back. Too far down a road where she did not want to go, and for once and all, she had to settle the score with him.

Flies buzzed incessantly as she lifted Mimi from the cart, telling Maisie to stay with Christian. She walked swiftly into the station, the hem of her dark-green skirt scuffing up the red dust. Only a few people stood on the cindery, wooden platform, and they were strangers to her. Her heart sank. Ben had gone ... there must have been an earlier train – but that could not be. She had not been mistaken about the time.

Then she saw him at the far end of the line, his back towards her, gazing out across the tracks in the direction from which the train was due. With Mimi in the crook of her arm, she walked quickly towards him, past the curious glances of the others waiting on the platform. The drive to the station had, in a strange way, soothed her nerves a bit. It had been an interlude when time had ceased to matter, and so had all the hundreds of trivial problems that had plagued her for weeks. There was no past any more – it lay behind the corrugated-iron-roofed station buildings and up the long, dusty road; and there was no future with Ben because he was leaving on the railway line which snaked away towards an unbroken horizon. The future with Deneys had not yet begun – and she had the power to change it.

'Ben!' The name burst from her lips and surprise showed on his lined, tanned face with its greying moustache for the briefest moment as, leaning on his crutches, he turned to face her. Her heart lurched for a second at the sight of him – of the smart town suit which accentuated his lean, elegant frame, the slow dazzling smile that lit his face as she drew nearer with the child in her arms.

'Ben, I must talk to you.'

Her tone was bright and controlled and she ignored the slight tremor of confusion that went through her as he gallantly doffed his hat. Then she flushed as she realised that they had the attention of the entire platform, but fortunately they were too far away for anyone to hear what they said.

'This is indeed a pleasure, my dear. I knew you'd see it my way, but not as soon as –' He was interrupted by her voice, steady and calm, but with an unfamiliar brittle quality.

'It's over, Ben.' She made her voice sound as calm and unprovoking as possible. 'It's over – the game between us,' she repeated, hugging a bewildered Mimi to her, and for that moment he was taken aback.

A measurable silence followed, then he said, 'What game, Arabella? Whatever are you talking about?'

'It's all been a game, Ben – the kind of game men and women play all their lives without knowing it, but now it's over. You've played with me ever since I can remember, from our very first meeting. Now I want you to go away and never contact me again. It's better if we never see each other again, do you understand?' It was ironic. She had not known she was going to say what she had. It had just forced its way out, like water through a new spring.

He stood very erect on his crutches, and gave her a lop-sided smile. 'Really, my dear, I haven't the faintest idea what you're talking about. I love you and I know you love me, and I also know that you want to return to England with me, so what's the argument?'

She stepped back gracefully, her head held high. 'Yes you do love me in your way, Ben – and I love you, but it's very different from the love I have for Deneys. I'll always love you, but it's not enough, and nothing you say will ever change that.'

He swung towards exasperation. 'You're deceiving yourself, my dear. What can that Boer offer you that I cannot? We're the same kind of people, you and I. We come from the same race, the same way of life. One day, you'll wake up to the truth, and regret it, I assure you, Arabella.' Ben's voice caressed her name as if it was his treasured possession, and in the brief glance he gave her, she felt herself almost branded.

With an effort, she composed herself. 'The only person who is deceiving himself is you, Ben, and it's no use you trying to manipulate me any more, for it just won't work.'

He eyed her enigmatically. 'If there's any manipulation going on, Arabella, it is coming from you. You women do it all the time. When you come to your senses, however, contact me in Pretoria and we'll work out something of benefit to us both.'

Beneath his stare she bridled, mentally regathering her scattered emotions. 'I meant what I said, Ben. This is goodbye. I shall stay with Deneys.'

She stood before him, small and straight, her face like marble, eternally shut to him, her mouth white and still, as the air between them burned with the suppressed emotions of years. Ben became older before her eyes, the glow that her presence had given him shrinking greyly back into the deepening lines in his face.

They could hear the train in the distance, its whistle sharp in the air, as it chugged towards the station. Mimi cried in fright at the noise, and clung to Arabella, and through the steam that invaded the platform soon afterwards, she saw the little face uplifted in sheer terror at the large, noisy engine rushing up to them like some great sooty monster. She stepped further away from Ben as she hugged Deneys' little girl to her, feeling a peculiar sensation as her eyes met his over the small golden head. He looked with a silent question into hers, and unable to meet his gaze any longer, she averted her face. Tears came, though some were caused by anger at his attempted manipulation of her. His face melted for a passing moment into an unguarded and revealing mixture of rage and disgust, and with a sense of surprise she saw the passion of his disappointment. He slammed

342

one crutch on the wooden floor of the platform with an unworded curse, as the few passengers alighted. The people waiting jostled and chatted as they climbed up into the waiting carriages, the engine belching steam and hissing violently.

She heard an accordian playing from somewhere in the train, that old familiar war song the British troops sang on their way up north behind Lord Roberts: *'We are marching to Pretoria ... Pretoria ... Pretoria ... We are marching to Pretoria ... Pretoria here we come.'* The deep poignancy of the moment suddenly overwhelmed Arabella. Her eyes were lit for a second with an uncrushable memory and she saw again so clearly the dashing khaki-clad Major of the Imperial Light Horse ... but she also saw a dusty, handsome young Boer who saved that Major's son on a hillside in Natal ...

She turned away before she could see Ben's devastated face, and walked from the train, even though she heard him call her name. The tears dried on her face as she stopped at the station entrance, hugging Mimi closely to her. Her heart almost broke as she watched the train start up again with a tremendous noise. She put her cheek on top of Mimi's small head, and stared dully before her, unable to think, able only to feel her intense sorrow, which seemed out of all proportion. The impatient train chugged away, and the rousing song went floating across the platform and was gone, vanishing with the train, and her last meeting with Benjamin Saville.

Arabella carried Mimi out to the cart and stood in the hot air waiting for her internal storm to abate. Gradually she felt an incredible sense of release. She had literally been freed, let off a life sentence of a different and more unbearable pain.

Quickly she climbed up on to the driver's seat and the cart rattled away and began the ascent of the long, dusty road to the village. The strain had gone from her face, which looked young, and even joyous. For the first time in many months, she felt elated. She had faced a great challenge, and now it lay behind her, while a new one waited ahead. It would take time to understand Deneys and his deep masculine pride, and she would need all the tact and delicacy at her command to do it. The day which was passing had taught her many things, and among them those which she knew she should have understood long ago.

The air was fresher now, as the cart wound past the outlying farms making yellow and brown patchworks here and there, where cattle grazed peacefully in the rocky, half-cleared pastures. Blinks of light lit the trees at the side of the road, and cloud shadows raced across the tawny lion-coloured pelts of dry veld grass. She could smell the dryness of it, and the pungency of dung, and high above she watched a black eagle swoop and heard the hiss of the scarred air as it came down to take a dassie which was scampering over some rocks. She saw its wings jigsaw on fragments of stone as it flew across the veld calling angrily as the dassie disappeared behind the rocks. Out of the periphery of her eye she noticed a large spotted genet cat resting in a runnel in the long grass alongside the road.

Her heart beat rapidly as they neared the house, the sweet-scented vine covering the verandah hanging heavy with ripening wine-coloured grapes, shot through with tiger stripes of dying golden sunlight. Seeing the house, she suddenly remembered the letter she had written Deneys waiting for his return on the dining-room table.

She had then a black sense of shame that she had ever meant to desert him, and anxiously she urged the mare towards the back gate. There she was met by Samson, waving his skinny arms in white shirt-sleeves, his blue waistcoat dangling open at the front.

'Aai, Missus – the Baas he read the letter the Missus she wrote – he very angry! The Baas he take Kitchener and he gone from this place!'

Arabella, the shame still clouding her, leaned forward. 'Did he say where he was going, Samson?' A cold film of sweat broke out on her face. She swallowed, waiting for his answer.

'The Baas, he say he gone after the Missus and the childing! Aai, Missus – there be terrible trouble when the Baas he comes back to this place!'

Frowning in consternation, Arabella said sharply, 'It's all right, Samson. The Master did not follow me to the station. Please take the cart around to the stable and water the horse. Maisie and I will carry the children back into the house. We'll wait there for the Master.'

The hopeful urgency she had felt all the way back from the station had left her completely, as she carried Mimi inside, followed by Maisie with Christian crying hungrily in the cot. It was very quiet and dark in the passage until the dogs ran up barking joyfully, and snapping at their heels. Glancing at the grandfather clock, she saw it was five – way past the time to bath Mimi and the baby, feed them and put them to bed, and now Christian was bellowing with a powerful pair of lungs.

She heard Maisie fill the zinc hip-bath in the kitchen for the children's baths, the sound of the dogs and the birds outside. None of this concerned her. That there was the sun and moon did not matter, for there would never again be any sun for her, or any peace, without Deneys.

After seeing the children to bed, she changed into one of her husband's favourite gowns – a striped blue silk with large leg-of-

344

mutton sleeves and pale-blue lace inset at the bodice, neck and wrists. An explosion might lie ahead, but she had to face it. Her reflection in the mirror reassured her somewhat. Although there were faint lines at the corners of her eyes nowadays, she still did not look her thirty-four years. Her hair was still thick and brown, her mouth as generously curved as ever. She went out on to the verandah once or twice to see if Deneys was in sight. Down the road the faraway whistle sounded of a train coming from the direction of the Mozambique border, but of Deneys there was no sign. She felt treacherous tears gathering in her eyes, and was suddenly afraid. Why was she standing here, desperately wanting him, and yet so full of questions about him, about his attitude to her, about her own place in his life, in her work ... that she was like a frightened child? But she found no answer.

23

Christmas 1913 was fast approaching. To arrest her feeling of almost suicidal depression, Arabella decided that this year, they would celebrate it in real English style, with all the traditional trimmings. Even though she felt she was dying inside, the way people died of broken hearts, the preparations so occupied her thoughts, taking them away from Deneys' absence, which had been a week now, that she slowly began to feel an almost joyful anticipation. Soon the house was filled with spicy fragrances from the kitchen, and a real pine tree stood in the sitting room, which was decorated with ivy, red and green paper flowers, and paper chains which she sat up all night creating.

On Christmas Eve she placed a rag doll under the tree for Mimi. She had made it herself, then painted on the face, which was very lifelike, with her best oil-paints. She had bought a second-hand wooden rocking horse from Paul Słowoski for Christian, even though she knew it would have to wait for him for a few years, and with Samson's help, had repainted it. Now it stood beside the doll, along with a shiny new red waistcoat she had sewn for Samson, a lace-edged muslin apron for Maisie, and a handsome gold watch on a chain for Deneys, which Paul Slowoski had ordered from Johannesburg. The children's stockings were already at the fireplace, and the tree was gay and twinkling with the glass baubles and tinsel Bishop Sebastian had sent from Durban.

After Samson and Maisie had gone to their rooms across the yard, she wandered into the kitchen which was filled with delicious odours. She thought about her life with Deneys, of giving up her suffrage work. She did not want to do it, but somewhere the frail seedling of acceptance was stretching its first leaf in the dark. Life changed; she herself was changing. She had not wanted it, but it was happening nevertheless. One cycle of their life was over. It had begun long ago on that hillside outside Suncrest, and it had ended when she had said goodbye to Ben at the station. But what lay ahead?

For a moment her despair lifted as she looked with pleasure at the food all ready in the pantry for the next day: a goose stuffed with sage and onion, mince pies, Christmas cake and plum pudding.

'That's the most wonderful smell in the world.'

Thoughts scattered and flew away and she thought she was dreaming, as she recognised the deep, musical voice behind her. Never, she thought, had she heard such a beautiful sound. A flush warmed her cheeks as she swung round to face him. Deneys was back!

The strain in him that was visible from the doorway was at close quarters overpowering. Gaunt-faced, vibrating, he stood and looked at her from sunken desperate eyes for an instant before he gazed at the goose and the pies with satisfaction. 'I can't remember when I last ate an English Christmas dinner – it must have been during my student days.' His tired face lit into a remembering smile.

'I thought – for a change,' she said, as they stood a shade awkwardly. 'Mimi won't remember much of it, of course, and Christian is not even aware of what's going on.'

She looked up at his strong, square, unshaven face, then stilled as she found something in his eyes that she understood only too well: the same longing she had experienced herself much too often lately.

There was a long pause. The house around them was very quiet: holding its breath, she thought, as she was holding hers.

Deneys was strangely abstracted, faintly frowning. 'I'm glad to see you came back. I read your letter.' He cleared his throat, taking refuge and time in picking up a mince pie, and examining it. She waited for what seemed a small age, not daring to break his train of thought.

'I still hate Saville and I'll never forgive him for trying to take you away from me.' His face clouded with recalled rage. 'But I was wrong about you. I was wrong in my attitude towards you and your cause. I never should have been so damned – dogmatic!' he whispered savagely into the quietness of the house.

She looked at him wonderingly, the tears glimmering in her eyes. Half-afraid to move, she searched his face, and the warmth, the directness, the steady values and basic goodness came across to her as something long and deeply known.

She bit her trembling lip. 'Deneys – I gave you cause to feel angry with me. I shamed you before the entire community, without a thought for your feelings or your work. I was selfish and self-centred at a time when you needed my support. I'm sorry, really I am.'

'I nearly lost you to that – that devil!' he said huskily, and she felt his strong, urgent fingers on her shoulders. 'You still give me a warm feeling in my gut, Arabella – you're still good to hold in my arms. You came into my life and challenged me and I missed it – I missed *you* – I didn't know what to do to get you back!'

'Oh Deneys, I love you with all my heart, and I'm so glad to be back.' She pulled him close to her in a whirl of muslin and shawl fringes. His arms curled around her, gathering her almost fiercely close.

'I have a gift for you, out on the verandah,' he said, gently pulling away from her for a second, as she met the warmth of his heavily lashed eyes, so like those of his small son. 'Wait, I'll fetch it.'

He came back carrying a gramophone, its wooden needle and large horn shining in the lamplight. He placed it on the kitchen table, and stood back to see her reaction.

'Deneys, where did you get it? It's wonderful – and there are records too!'

Deneys smiled with intense satisfaction as he put a record on the machine and wound it up. 'It's a Strauss waltz, one of the first ever recorded. The other is the voice of Enrico Caruso singing an aria from Puccini's *Girl from the Golden West*. Isaac got it for me and sent it by train a few days ago. I kept it at the office and then you left –'

Suddenly the sound from the gramophone seemed to jump all over the room and he held out his arms to her. For a while they danced together, then, when the record ground to a halt, Arabella's hair tumbled down her back as he pulled out the pins and it spilled free, filling the room with a heady perfume. She was quite dishevelled, and he regarded her with a deep and tender affection. Her heart was pounding, but she felt exhilarated. She had been so depressed by his absence, that now to have him here, his arms about her, made her feel extraordinarily light-headed. She had hardly dared to hope he would return in the way he had, and still less had she expected the incredible sense of adventure he aroused in her as he took her once more into his arms. She held him close, while her fingers caressed his back. He let out his breath in a long sigh as every nerve and fibre of her being cried out to him to take her, and it became an agony to think of being denied.

It was impossible to think of existing without him as he lifted her into his arms, and in two rapid strides was at the sitting-room couch beside the Christmas tree, where he laid her down.

'God, I must have been insane to treat you the way I did –' His voice was hardly audible in the darkened room, and his strong face was gentle and brooding as he confessed, 'You and my father were right. There was no love in the church, there was no love for Annetjie du Preez – and you both saw it. I must have been blind.'

Arabella made no effort to stop him undressing her. She caressed his naked chest, pulling him down until he lay full-length upon her and they enjoyed a turbulent reunion, an intense, private interlude that was as much to his liking as to hers.

Midnight was striking when he carried her to bed, the new gold watch on its chain wound mischievously around his forehead. He tiptoed past the nursery so as not to waken the children, and Arabella felt a sense of continuity, of belonging. She knew the place where she had been, and the woman she had known, and they seemed to lead inevitably towards Deneys. As she clung to him in the warm darkness of the passage, she was completely at peace, though with the knowledge that the years ahead would still be hard and interrupted. There was so much to do. But she and Deneys would do it together.

24

Against the unwelcome novelty of trade unionism in South Africa and the outbreak of serious labour strikes, the mounting tensions between the great powers of Europe were but a distant inconvenience. Months of conflict and contradictions followed as simmering antagonisms between the two sections of the Boer people finally broke to the surface. General Hertzog with his followers seceded from the South African Party of Botha and Smuts and formed the Nationalist Party to keep the Dutch apart as a separate entity.

It was at this time that General Smuts visited Deneys in an attempt to persuade him to come out in strong support of Louis Botha. They spent most of their time cloistered in the study, but during the short breaks when Arabella took them coffee and biscuits, the General, with his piercing blue eyes and precise way of speaking, explained to her that the differences between Hertzog's Nationalists and Botha's South African Party were developing into a bitter struggle, that many Dutch-speaking families were divided on the issue, and that he wanted Deneys to use his eloquence and brilliant mind to support his side.

Finally Deneys agreed, knowing that he now stood against the majority of villagers who had joined the Nationalist Party, and that in so doing, he had placed his law practice in jeopardy. As the days passed in Heideville, normally placid tempers were beginning to rise, and faces were growing longer. Everywhere there was the clamour of party rivalries, and personal animosities filled the atmosphere as those who before had been friendly towards Deneys now became silent and hostile. Many of them looked at him, their hero during the war, as some kind of traitor to their cause.

The whole country festered with passionate feelings: the Orange Free State was solidly behind General Hertzog, the Cape and the Transvaal were evenly and hotly divided, and Natal was for General Botha.

Arabella, now strongly supporting Deneys, was bitterly disappointed that the first Bill for women's rights to appear before the Union

Parliament was a racially exclusive one, for white women only. When the Bill was defeated, she thought about her work for the women's cause. She had fought to get where she was, and as always, longed to build on what she had done, but she also knew that Deneys needed her support as never before.

One summer's evening in October, she was sitting at the piano with him, playing *The Old Apple Tree* – a popular song from a few years back. They sang a few bars, and stopped laughing when there was a sharp rap on the front door.

Deneys strode out of the room to answer it, while Arabella slowly rose from the piano, annoyed at being so unexpectedly interrupted. There was a low murmur of men's voices, then Deneys led a tall, lean, vaguely familiar man into the room, and introduced him as Herman Muller.

Arabella looked at him in dismay. As if she could ever forget that sombre face with the light-blue eyes of the man who had suspected her of being an English spy on the hillside outside Suncrest during the war! Politely he acknowledged her presence, his light eyes searching and keen. Without his hat his straight dark hair was greying and receding slightly, and he wore a plain dark suit. He still had the close-guarded expression she remembered, but now there was overall a distinct air of satisfaction. Not a smile, just an atmosphere. He came towards her, his whole presence charged with potent energy and a tension she could not dismiss.

'Sit down, Herman,' Deneys said, coming to stand at her side. He took her hand and the pressure was reassuring, though she felt that he was bracing himself for this meeting.

'Thank you, Deneys.'

Herman sat down and Arabella went to make the coffee; all the time she could hear the low rumble of voices. While the water boiled on the stove she brought out an overflowing work-basket, and wondered why Herman was here. She knew he was a clever lawyer, that he had joined the Nationalist Party along with Deneys' father and eldest brother, Michiel, who, with his strikingly intelligent eyes and quick movements, had come only the last weekend to try to persuade Deneys not to oppose them. Michiel had made it clear that the Boers would triumph again. She trembled suddenly, her eyes clouding with apprehension. What did Herman Muller want with Deneys after so long?

The voices were growing more heated until she carried a tray into the sitting room, at which the men stopped talking. The tension in the room could have been cut with a knife, as she poured the coffee and offered around the new, delicately flowered gold-rimmed cups and saucers of English bone-china. She noticed that Herman was giving

351

Deneys a long, appraising look, and a sharp sense of fear caused a tingling in her hands and feet. In an uneasy silence she left the room and stood for a moment behind the door as the talk resumed, even more passionately than before.

'You can't win a war if you become extinct, Deneys – and that you should know only too well. How can you side with these people – you, who went into honourable exile because you did not want to live under their rule? How can you stand against us, when even your own father and brother strongly support us?'

There was a silence, then she heard Deneys' deep, determined voice. 'You know very well, Herman, that we are a fractious and stubborn race, but we are also strong-willed and determined – and with these qualities we can forge a new nation right here and now. We lost on our own, but with the support of the English we can build something even better.'

There was a silence that was almost deafening, then Herman replied bitterly, 'That is where you are wrong, Deneys. Don't you see that this union with the English is only a concession to their wishes? It can never compensate for the loss of our republics, of our liberty and our way of life. I tell you, we will be swamped by these people, so we must fight against extinction!'

Arabella moved away, settling into a kitchen chair, with her darning needle and a pile of socks at the table, wondering what would happen next in this divided country. She could hardly concentrate on the task in hand, as fear for her husband, who was making more enemies by the day, swept over her like a fresh torment.

Eventually, she heard Herman departing. His voice was angry and bitter. 'I reserve my deepest hatred for you, Deneys, because I regard you as the biggest traitor of all. You have betrayed our heritage! But I will fight you, Deneys. That is why I am here – to fight you every inch of the way!'

Arabella hurried from the kitchen to bid farewell to their unwelcome guest. In the small entrance hall Herman Muller looked down at her, his light eyes narrowed. 'Perhaps you can persuade your husband to change his course of action, mevrou, for he puts you and your children in danger, as well as himself. He will be the most hated man, not only in this dorp, but in the whole country, too.'

Arabella did not answer. She studied the man, knowing that Deneys must never underestimate Herman's real capabilities. He was bitter, but he was clever and he knew his business, and now he had become dangerous. All at once she experienced a hatred so overwhelming that she felt the lust to kill. She had often wondered how anyone could feel those murderous instincts; she understood now.

*

Deneys spoke at meeting after angry meeting against Herman Muller, who now lived on the outskirts of the village, next door to Ernst de Villiers, the magistrate, in one of the largest houses. Arabella watched in trepidation as Deneys was howled down at these meetings, while Herman was cheered. Both she and her husband were cut in the streets and ostracised from all social gatherings. Only Tienie and a small handful of friends were prepared to back the du Rands, and give Deneys assistance in the uphill struggle against the strong Muller faction.

Soon afterwards, a petty quarrel between a new manager and some miners on one of the gold mines spread until it brought the whole issue of the trade unions out into the open. The Government at first tried to stand aside but, alarmed at the growing signs of violence, intervened with Imperial troops, its own organised forces still in the process of formation, to try to prevent a mass meeting. They were too late. In the ensuing riots, the troops fired on the mob and victory lay with the strikers. Many of their grievances were very justifiable, and so the Government and the Chamber of Mines began to look into the problems, and there was a promise of peace ...

Then the situation worsened and a General Strike was called in Johannesburg. Louis Botha called out thirty thousand Boer horsemen to maintain order along the Reef and a civil war broke out between the two sections of embittered Boers. The Heideville Commando was called for service, but the men were suspicious of any commands from General Botha, and there was talk of mutiny on the way to Johannesburg. Deneys managed to talk most of them out of it, despite their suspicion of him, and only a minority returned home. Johannesburg was now in siege; the mines were idle and the railways at a standstill. The commandoes rounded up everyone who was a striker, including many innocents in the heat of the moment, which aroused deep ill-feeling against Botha who, in reality, had nothing to do with it.

Now there were thirty thousand Boers under arms, many of them Nationalists, and with political feelings running high, the atmosphere was inflammable. There was growing talk of using the commandoes to overthrow Botha's Government and proclaim a republic. The strike finally collapsed and at the end of January 1914, the commandoes were sent home. It was a very thoughtful Deneys du Rand who rode back with the men from his village.

In June, news reached the village that Archduke Franz Ferdinand of Austria had been murdered at Sarajevo. This did not mean much to most people in the country at the time, but then came the ultimatum to Serbia, followed by the mobilising of the nations, and finally, the outbreak of the Great War -- a war that was to change their lives forever.

The bombshell that shook Arabella's world was Louis Botha's announcement that the British Government had asked him to equip an expedition of South African troops to invade the German Territory lying on the borders in South West Africa: despite much opposition from the Nationalists, who feared the reaction of a victorious Germany, Deneys agreed to sign up. Arabella, her mind filled with thoughts of another war with more horrors and more wasted lives than the last one, realised sadly that there was nothing she could do to change his mind. The only respite came from the welcome news that Marietjie de Villiers was finally to leave the village to marry Marius Steenkamp, a young doctor from Middelburg.

As volunteers enrolled at various centres throughout the country, talk grew more heated in the village. Fear, confusion and doubt made strangers of most people, as the Boers asked themselves in heated debates how they would fare if Britain was defeated. Before anything more could be done about the matter, the Boer Rebellion within the country's own borders broke out, headed by General Beyers, General Christiaan de Wet, Captain Jopie Fourie and Captain Herman Muller.

Then Lieutenant-Colonel Maritz, a number of his officers and certain forces under his command went over to the Germans' side. They were now in open rebellion against the country, with the possible invasion of the Northern Cape. The whole country was placed under Martial Law, and the situation moved rapidly to a climax in Heideville.

While large German Zeppelins, like silver sausages, floated in the skies at night over a blacked-out London, dropping fire and death, Arabella now lived in a sense of unbelief. It was war again – nothing could prevent it, and she could only wait to hear when Deneys would leave.

25

The fluffy black cat sunning itself on the kitchen windowsill looked up intently, and the ears of Wasp, lying outside the fly-screen, lifted as Deneys walked into the room at eleven o'clock in the morning, where the October sunlight slanted across the floor. Arabella knew from his step, and from the fact that he never returned home before half-past five, that something was badly wrong. Her heart began to pound. She hurried towards him, and he heard the starched rustlings of her grey cotton dress.

'Deneys, what is it?' She was very pale and tense as she searched his face with growing alarm. 'I know something is wrong.'

He looked down at her, his mouth under the neat moustache, a pale line in his face, 'I did not mean to frighten you, darling, by coming home early, but something has come up that cannot be avoided.' There was a strange inflection in his voice that she found even more disturbing than the expression on his face. 'I have something to tell you of the utmost urgency.'

'What is it, Deneys? Please tell me! What has happened now?' She was suddenly bracing herself against disaster.

Taking her small capable hands in his, he said, 'Bella, listen to me very carefully. Herman Muller has just been made the District Commandant and I have received word from a well-wisher that he is coming tonight with a strong force to take the village on behalf of the rebels, and that I am to be shot in our backyard.'

Her eyes opened wide; her mouth gaped, and she could only look at him, shocked and desperate. She tried to speak, but her throat was too dry. Something was stirring in her, something rising with an awful pain.

'But he can't do that,' she stammered at last. 'He has no right!' When she saw the grey bitterness in his face, she fell silent. Such a rage and hatred came to her then, such an overpowering sorrow, that her hands clenched and tears ran down her face. 'He can't do this to you, Deneys! He can't!'

She became aware that Deneys was unclenching her hands, very firmly. He said: 'I have to escape, my dear. I have my doubts about being shot, for we Boers are not given to assassination, but one never knows in the heat of the moment. I have made many enemies, Bella, and the least that can happen would be arrest and indignities. I have to go, but I will come back for you and the children, never fear.'

He drew her to him and held her tightly, and she could hear his breath in her hair. 'I know that already, out of sight, there are rebel pickets on every road leading from the village, so a daylight attempt is out of the question. My only hope is to escape after dark.' He took her face in his hands, and kissed her gently on the mouth. 'You are not to get involved in this. I want you to stay here with Samson and Maisie until I send word, do you hear? They won't touch you, the children or the servants. I will send for you as soon as I reach my brother Johan in Pretoria. He and his wife Marie will put me up, I know that. He's on Botha's side.'

'I just can't believe this is happening – I just can't! It's all too horrible for words.' Her eyes were brilliant with repulsion.

'You must pretend to be ignorant of the whole matter – promise me, so as not alert anyone, anyone at all.' He released her, suddenly vigorous and decisive. 'I will now return to the office and carry on as usual. At five o'clock I will come back here. I will tell Samson to prepare secretly for the flight and get Kitchener ready.'

Arabella hid her own anguish as his eyes took on a remote expression. The pain was coming to her huge and monstrous as she said: 'You must eat a light lunch first – there won't be too much time this evening. I'll pack some biltong and rusks with a flask of coffee for the journey.'

She put her arms about him, then let him go. Swiftly she brought out cheese and cold venison pie, and buttered freshly baked wholewheat bread. The boiling water sizzled, passing through the kettle spout as she quickly prepared the coffee.

Later, she watched him go, and heard him shut the front door. It was all a dream, an ugly, dreadful nightmare. She would wake up soon, and it would all be over. But she knew it would not go away, and she hated the thought of him riding alone into a hostile, dangerous world.

After a few moments of intense soul-searching, she decided to go with Deneys. Frantically, she raced round to see Tienie, who, with her wonderful generosity, agreed to have the children and Maisie while she was away. But Arabella still had to face the problem of telling her small daughter.

'Mimi darling,' she said after the children's afternoon nap. 'Papa and Mama have to go away for a little while and you must go to Tant Tienie. We will be back soon, I promise.'

'No, no, no!' Mimi's fretful tones rose shrilly. 'Want to go with Mama!'

Arabella was utterly wretched and full of fear. How could she leave the children? Would she ever see them again? She wished to God that it had not happened. There were too many hating men in this world, she thought bitterly, who wanted vengeance. When would it end?

After a moment or two, she bent down, her face level with the small child's. 'Why now, you're a big girl, darling.' She drew her close. 'You are to look after little Christian at Tant Tienie's, you hear?'

Mimi's green eyes darkened and the small mouth opened to begin another protest, but Arabella hurried on, 'See, here's a rose for you to wear, just like Mama's. Now you can walk all the way to Tant Tienie's like a big lady.'

The game worked liked magic, but Arabella knew that it was going to take all her powers of strategy to hold this mood as Mimi looked at the tea rose she had unpinned from her lapel. As she fastened the bloom on the neck of her daughter's dress, Mimi cuddled close against her, winding her little arms about her neck. The fragrance of her small body was to Arabella just then, the most wonderful scent in the world. She felt a wave of tenderness reaching out to her, almost too sweet and powerful to be endured, and she prayed that she would be spared for her children. I can't bear it, she thought wildly. I can't bear to think that I may never see them again. But she knew that her restless, anxious thoughts already lived with Deneys, surrounded by vengeful and deadly enemies.

Her eyes filled with tears as little Christian, a month off two, toddled up to her, clapping his chubby hands, and soon he was lifted up to chuckle in his mother's arms. She hugged both children, then tousling Christian's soft brown hair, she stood up, towering over them with fiercely protective love, torn between her feelings for them and those for her husband. Then, with Maisie carrying the small bag of clothes, she led them outside into the strong sunlight between the jagged shadows of the trees, only too aware of the dangerous world beyond this house – a world which she had deliberately elected to enter.

By late afternoon, all was ready. The thoroughbreds, two of the finest and fastest horses in the district, were saddled and food was packed in the saddlebags. Samson announced with a wide smile that he, too, was coming, on his fast Basuto pony. As the sun began to fall behind the blue mountains, and long golden shadows lay in the garden under the trees, Arabella dressed in a pair of Deneys' riding breeches and a jacket which Tienie had temporarily altered earlier, and when her husband, with Thor at his heels, came into the darkening yard, she and Samson were waiting for him, holding the three horses.

There was a short, sharp altercation between Arabella and Deneys about her going along on the journey, but as the inky shadows fanned out into the yard, they saw rebel horsemen suddenly dotting the skyline along the nearest hill, and Deneys nodded abruptly. Not risking a noise, they walked the horses down the deserted street. It was then that a young farmer, Stefan Coetzee, came galloping up to them, urgently telling Deneys he was a Government man and had decided that the village was the best place for him.

Leaning forward on his pommel, he said with soft fierceness, 'The whole countryside has risen, Meneer, and mounted bands are patrolling in every direction. It was only by hard riding that I got through.'

Deneys nodded, his face grim. 'Stefan, the village is not safe any more. We must get away as quickly as we can, then it's every man for himself. The Government can't help us now – they have their hands full elsewhere.'

The muscles about Stefan's face tightened. 'Can I join you, Meneer du Rand? I have left my wife, my mother and my property to the mercy of the rebels, but I know for certain that they won't molest my womenfolk.'

'Yes, come with us, Stefan. We'll go by the gaol and the municipal pound as quietly as we can, and leave the village that way.'

Arabella found her stomach tightening as they mounted and her tense fingers clutched the reins. They left not a moment too soon. Within twenty minutes of their departure, every exit was blocked off by pickets who had been closing in silently as they left.

They rode cautiously at first, under the vast sky now sown with streamers of blazing stars and the darting flashes of orange from glowing fireflies. They reached the railway crossing four miles away without being challenged, and stopped in a hollow to discuss the next steps as they had no definite plans after leaving the village. The whole area and, it seemed, the entire country was in revolt, and wherever they went they would be among enemies. At last they decided to leave the horses in a paddock on the nearest deserted farm, and climb up the hillside for the night.

Arabella rubbed her weary eyes with a dusty hand. She was leaning against a rough outcrop of rocks, one of Deneys' rifles ready beside her. It was nearly dawn with a light ground mist rising knee-high over the countryside below, as they heard the smooth snick of cartridges in long guns nearby. Easing forward, Deneys kept to the shelter of the rocks so that no sudden movement of his body would give away his position. Inching towards him, Arabella eventually joined him at the edge of the rocks, and lay very still beside him as they looked down into the gorge below.

Thinking the coast was clear, Deneys beckoned to Samson, signalling him to fetch the horses from where they had left them. Then, as the little man groped his way down the hillside, they heard a movement, stealthy and slow. In growing horror, as the sky paled with light before the sun had shown itself along the eastern horizon, and touched the underbellies of the low clouds with gold and crimson wash, Arabella found herself looking down on at least seventy armed men, within a stone's throw of their position. Most were wearily sitting on the ground, their horses tethered further down the hillside, among the bushes.

'It's obviously one of Muller's contingents for intercepting me,' Deneys whispered. 'They appear to be watching the railway crossing and have spent the night here under our very noses.' He allowed a faint grin to lighten his tired features with a sudden flicker of irony. 'I recognise some of my best clients among them.'

He paused, his eyes narrowing as a covey of rock pigeons looped their way in dawn flight across the veld below. 'We must get away from here, Bella, as soon as possible as there appears to be another outpost on the kopje behind this one. But first, Stefan and I have a job to do.'

'What job?' Arabella was alarmed.

'There are rebels riding down the hill waving and shouting to others out of sight near the crossing,' Stefan muttered, crawling over to join them. 'And our man, Samson, is bringing back our horses.'

Deneys looked at him, assessing the situation. 'The station at Belmont is the nearest point of safety – but come, Stefan, we have work to do before we leave.'

As silently as Red Indians, the two men made their way down the hill, twisting through clusters of heavy bush as some large bird of prey called high up among the dense foliage, and lower down, a group of pale bushbabies rested in the undergrowth. Watching tensely, Arabella could see them crawling towards the rebels' tethered horses, unnoticed by the men below, who were breakfasting, still sitting on the ground, eating biltong and drinking from flasks of coffee. Kneeling, Deneys and Stefan undid the tether of first one horse, then another, and with a sharp slap on their flanks, sent them quietly on their way. Soon all the horses were free, and trotting off down the slopes, to the immediate consternation of the men, who jumped up, looked around wildly, and were soon running agitatedly down the hillside and out of sight.

As Deneys and Stefan crept back through the bush in the growing light, she saw Deneys, suddenly alive with an instinct of coming danger, swing round. A bullet, meant to take him in the heart, sped across the open space, its deadly sharpened point sinking deeply into the bark of a tree behind him. Gasping, Arabella saw the figure of a man emerge from a bush, and she recognised the long, lean shape of Herman Muller!

Before she had time to think, Deneys' rifle was pointing straight at Herman. A shot rang out, and the would-be assassin fell to the ground. Paralysed, she sat and watched Deneys walk over and examine the body, then rise quickly and beckon Stefan close behind him.

Her legs were weak with horror and disbelief and she could not move as Deneys clambered up the rocks while Stefan went down to join Samson bringing up the horses.

'It's safe now,' Deneys whispered, eyeing her anxiously. 'Herman's dead. I had to shoot him, there was no other way, though not one I would have chosen had I the choice. The rebels here have no horses to chase us, but we are not out of danger yet. Come, we haven't a moment to lose. Daylight is our greatest enemy.'

Arabella's head swam with passionate relief that Deneys was safe. She wanted to join him, but the rocks were wavering before her, and she had to sit down to save herself from fainting. Seeing her fright, he moved up to her, took her hand and held it tightly.

'If I could have prevented you from seeing it, my darling, I would have done so,' he said with enormous bitterness. 'But we must go now – it's extremely dangerous to stay. They know we are here now, so we must not delay any longer.' His hand was warm on hers. Then, he led her down the twisting trail, and it was not long before the small party rode out of the hollow, bearing west.

Suddenly, Samson motioned them to stop. They halted at once, but for a moment heard nothing except the breeze rustling in the bushes. Then, faintly, they detected the sound which had first reached the keen ears of the little black man, of footsteps sliding down a rock.

Hurriedly they guided their horses off the track and in among the thickets. There they waited, each with a reassuring hand on a bridle, fingers closing the horses' nostrils lest the animals should neigh and thus betray their presence. It was not long before a small party of horsemen rode past, in the exact spot they had been themselves only moments before. They waited until the rebels had gone, then with great relief, rode out in the opposite direction, making for the nearest railway station. Unfortunately, they were spotted by men there who, leaping on their horses, immediately gave chase.

Deneys turned to Arabella. 'Bella,' he breathed, 'please turn back now before it's too late. You have no experience in galloping at high speed over long distances. Listen to me – *go back*!'

Arabella's mouth went dry as she heard the rebels pounding up behind them. Her mind was working furiously. She did not want to hold the others up, she did not want to be a hindrance, but she was here now and she meant to stay at Deneys' side. His danger was now hers – a dreadful and enormous danger which she had chosen to share with him.

'I stay with you – and I'll keep up, never fear.'

Her voice sounded calmer than she felt, but as soon as Deneys saw her face, he shook his head. 'God, if anything happens to you, what will I do? Have you thought of that? Damn it, woman, you are the mother of my children!'

'I'll survive, my darling, don't worry. Now see to yourself, because I'm not leaving. Have you ever thought of what *we* would do without *you*? I'm here to see that you take no more risks. Herman Muller could have shot you, right before my eyes!'

He put his hand swiftly on her shoulder. 'You are one damned woman, my little wife. No wonder Saville wanted to take you from me! Now, stay close and try to keep your head down as much as possible.'

They thundered across the veld. Her horse raced with long neck outstretched under the low branches of a thorn tree. Laid low across his back, she pressed her face close into the horse smell of his flowing mane, and felt the slash of the sharp branches rake the cloth of Deneys' jacket on her back. She felt the great strong gathering and surge of his muscles as he jumped over a dry stream. Her body was bruised and battered, she was developing a saddle boil, her hands and thighs were raw and sore, but she knew she had to keep up with the men, now drawing away from her as they galloped towards a cluster of sheltering acacias forming natural bridges where the trees and bushes were bent and intertwined.

There she joined them, mortified that Deneys had been forced to stop to give her time to catch up. Hardly daring to breathe, she heard the rebels lessening their pace behind them, and they dropped, for a while, into an easier pace. They sheltered in the trees as Arabella stroked the muzzle of her gelding and ran her hand along the proud line of his neck.

Deneys took her reins, positioning his horse close to hers. 'Listen, Bella. Climb up behind me, and hang on tight. You'll never make it otherwise. Now do as you're told, or you'll be dead by nightfall. I can ride with both animals.'

He took her raw and calloused hand in his, then, brushing her hair from her face, he said gently, 'You look very appealing in that hat, did you know that?'

Her dry, cracked lips formed a quirky smile, as she nodded and allowed him to lift her up behind him, and take the reins of her horse. They left the shelter of the trees. It was a stiflingly hot day, the hills shimmering in a deep heat haze. They kept an eye on Samson, riding out in front. His courage and cool head had saved their lives several times already, and Arabella began to realise that he did not see the bush and the animals as they did – he sensed them through a unique combination of finely tuned intuition and experience. He was always alert to any danger ahead, and seemed to have an uncanny sense of which places the rebels were likely to hide, and could warn them in good time. Arabella did not know his age, but she knew that he was not a young man, and marvelled at the way he moved through the bush with the sinewy ease of a youth. For a vivid second she remembered her flight with Pendulu to Ladysmith so long ago, and she wondered what had happened to him, and to young Umfaan ...

Several cartloads of bonnetted women passed them, driving towards Heideville.

'The village has been taken by Commandant Muller's men,' one buxom young woman with rosy cheeks and flaxen hair called to them. For a moment, triumph unconcealed shone in the fresh face as they rode past.

'Though we have no more fear of being overtaken by the rebels,' Stefan said despondently, his eyes following the women, 'and my wife and mother are safe enough, it will go hard with my flocks and herds. I am a man of substance, Meneer, as you are.'

Arabella sat behind Deneys, as if turned to stone, picturing their small house and possessions back in the enemy-held village, and she thought of her children with a heavy, mourning heart.

A little way ahead, they were chased by another band of rebels but managed to outrun them. In the blazing heat of the afternoon, towards three o'clock, they finally approached the railway line which ran directly to Pretoria. By then most of the rebels had dropped away, but almost a dozen, more determined than the rest, tried to make a final pounce before the quartet reached the cover of the corrugated-iron station buildings, baking in the frightful heat. Arabella could hear the galloping hooves not far behind.

Deneys shouted back at her: 'I don't know if the station is rebel-held or not, but we'll have to take the chance. Listen – there's a train coming in from the east.'

He wheeled the two horses around, and they looked towards the train, chugging nearer every precious minute, enveloped in clouds of smoke. But as it came closer, so did the rebels. The few people talking quietly on the platform looked up in amazement as the fugitives burst panting on the scene, and passengers leaned out of the windows, waving as the train thundered to a stop with a screech of brakes and another explosion of steam.

26

Arabella lay beside Deneys in the guest room of his half-brother Johan's house in Pretoria. The trees outside moved their gentle shadows on the window shades as the moon poured a cataract of silver on the house and garden. She drowsed uneasily, for the shocks of the previous day invaded her restless sleep like vague forms of menace. Voices, events, violent movements, pushed against her eyelids. She thrashed from side to side, muttering. The lamplight outside flickered on the drawn shades over thick lace curtains, and she woke with a start, overwhelmed by a horrible terror. She heard the rumbling of the first milk-cart down the street, though it was still hardly dawn, and the clock in the passage strike four. Lying in the bed, she listened to Deneys' even breathing, the terror still crushing her, knowing that before daybreak he would be gone, back to the danger of Heideville, after picking up Stefan and Samson, who had taken the horses when they had barely escaped the rebels and boarded the train.

General de Wet had caused most of the Orange Free State to rise, the rebel Maritz was invading the Cape Province at the head of the German troops, while the Northern and Western Transvaal were up in arms against General Botha. The railway line to Johannesburg and the Transvaal was still open to the south, but beyond that there was much doubt and uncertainty. On their arrival at his house, Johan had taken Deneys to General Smuts at Defence Headquarters in Pretoria, where he was instantly promoted to Commandant, with orders to command the Heideville military district.

Now he woke, and met her troubled gaze as he lit the oil lamp beside the bed. Twisting round on to his side, he took her hand. 'Bella, my darling, I'll be back as soon as I can make it. I have good men – we can match any commando the rebels send to oppose us, man for man.' He laid a hand upon her thigh, gently caressing it. 'I'll see that the children are safe, and Tienie and her family – she's done us a great service. We'll bring back Maisie, the animals and the household goods as soon as we can put the rebels down.'

He gathered her close and her deepest feelings released themselves as she relaxed against him, needing his affection and the physical contact of his presence. Resting her hand on his chest she lifted her head and kissed him, moved by the intimacy of his touch, as the night marched towards dawn and the moment of his departure. As they drew apart, Deneys rose from the bed and Arabella lay back against the pillows, immune to the dull pain from her lanced and drained saddle boil, knowing that the moment had arrived to say goodbye.

'Johan is coming with me,' he said, buttoning up his shirt with quick, decisive fingers. 'Stay here with Marie and little Dirk until we return.'

She felt a prickle of tears, and then was helpless to stop them overflowing. A moment later she was in his arms once more, turning her face into his shoulder in the blind certainty that love and comfort would be found there.

Lifting her head at last, she smiled apologetically, her green eyes shining with unspeakable love. 'I'm sorry I broke down. It only makes it harder for you, darling, and now I've made you all damp.'

'Yes, but comforted with it,' he told her huskily. 'And I love you, you dearest stubborn little woman.'

Fierce battles were taking place all over the country, and after weeks of skirmishes, Heideville was finally freed. Deneys sent a message that the house had been pillaged, but there was no wanton destruction and the animals and poultry were safe. The children were in good hands, but missing her in their own small ways, and every shop and warehouse in the village had been looted by the rebels. Later, news came through that General Beyers, one of the leaders of the rebellion, had been chased and drowned in the Vaal River, General de Wet captured and imprisoned, and Captain Jopie Fourie executed.

By December 1914 the situation was under control and the distinctive South African commando system ended forever. General Botha was victorious but deeply saddened by the fact that he had been forced to quell his own countrymen. The days now of mounted men were over as, far away, the new machinery of war appeared on the battlefields of Belgium and France. Arabella braced herself as the war – a dim nightmare far away from South Africa – now loomed larger every day on the horizon of the country, as they were relentlessly pulled into it.

She thought of Luke, who had joined the newly formed Royal Flying Corps, and of Deneys, who would go to South West Africa after he had returned with the children. She knew that the war for her had just one face – and that was his face.

By early February 1915, everyone seemed to have settled down more peacefully, but the ill-feeling between the two sections of the Boer people had not been properly resolved, as Arabella and Deneys moved into an attractive house in Yeoville, a suburb to the north of Johannesburg.

Now it was Passover, and in the luxurious new home of Isaac and Rachel, a party of twelve sat around the table in the mahogany-panelled dining-room with its enormous fireplace and incandescent gas-chandeliers, the red velvet draperies drawn over thick, expensive lace. The room was vast, and filled with flowers. Of the Brandauer family, only Isaac's oldest sister, Miriam, her husband Solly and her daughter Tirzah were present. They had refused to go to the house of widowed Ruth Brandauer where everyone else was gathered, because Isaac had not been invited.

Five-year-old Louis, the youngest of the Brandauer children who could understand what was going on, stood up, his rich chestnut hair gleaming in the candlelight. His clear piping voice penetrated the room: 'Why is this night different from other nights?'

Arabella, her pale hands clasped in the lap of her violet lace gown, looked at the eager anticipation of the small children seated with their parents at the long table decked in gleaming white, where candles cast a warm, flickering glow on the graceful silver wine cups, drawing the ruby gleam of the wine in the crystal carafe and reflecting shafts of light from the jewelry worn by the other two stylishly dressed women. Then her gaze wandered to the special central Seder plate, bearing the foods that symbolised the sorrow and joys of the Passover, set beside the bowl of delicately perfumed pink roses and lilac Michaelmas daisies.

She watched the candlelight shine on Isaac's faintly lined face and the exquisitely embroidered yarmulke on his curly red hair, as he intoned the age-old prayer, 'Blessed art Thou, O Lord, our God, King of the Universe, who has sanctified us by His Commandments and commanded us to eat bitter herbs.'

She glanced across at Deneys in his neat, dark suit, his collar stiff and white, a borrowed black velvet skullcap on his head, sitting beside Mimi and Christian who watched in fascination as Isaac passed the maror – horseradish dipped in haroset – to those around the table. She knew that she had found her deepest comfort in her beloved husband, but there was still her work – the vocation she had been forced to sacrifice. Would she ever be able to take it up again, for all her love of him and her children?

'This haroset, which is a mixture of nuts, apples and wine, my dear Gentile friends, is quite, quite delicious, representing as it does the sweetness of God's kindness to us Jews, which made slavery in Egypt bearable,' Isaac said. Arabella remembered that he had shocked Rachel only days earlier by announcing that he was going with Deneys to German South West Africa as the war correspondent for his paper, which had grown large and powerful enough to compete with all the important newspapers in the country. His words were very poignant to Arabella now, as she reflected that bitterness was still present wherever tyranny flourished. She thought for a moment of the world, of its hunger and passion and greed and beauty, never escaping from underlying cruelty or uncertain pleasure.

Rachel smiled across at her, elegant in white foulard and a rope of oriental pearls dangling far below her waist, her face appearing and disappearing in the flicker of the candleflames as she sat beside Isaac and her two oldest children. She had been adamant that her two friends join them for Pesach, and Arabella was contentedly happy as the Passover meal itself began, ample, cheerful and noisy, between recountings of the Passover story from the Haggadah.

'Why do we eat so slowly, Papa? It takes forever and ever,' piped up little Louis sitting near his father, his mischievous freckled face gleaming with curiosity and childish impatience.

'Now, Louis, we eat very, very slowly at this meal because we are now a free people and no longer slaves who can be forced to hurry,' Isaac explained, bending his face to the small attractive boy, and drawing him in, over the kneidlach balls and chicken soup, and abruptly there was silence.

'Are the Germans making slaves of the British and the French in that big war so far away, Papa?' asked seven-year-old Mark, a tall, thin, earnest boy with dark hair and his mother's eyes, leaning forward beside his little sister Hannah. 'Rabbi Shifrin told us today that they want to take away the land of other people, like the Egyptians took away our land.'

Isaac wiped his lips on a napkin, his heavy-lidded eyes softening as they gazed at his clever eldest son. 'But we are going to fight them, Mark – and beat them at their own game.'

There was a horrified gasp from Rachel. 'Isaac, this is no place to speak of such things!' she said, looking at him with pain in the depths of her dark eyes. 'Here we rejoice in freedom and peace in a celebration centuries old.'

Isaac coloured, embarrassed. He smoothed his smart black string tie, and rapped on the table through the sudden babble of voices.'Quite so, my dear, quite so. Now it's time for the pieces of matzo hidden earlier to be found for afikomen, and the first little one who finds it gets a gift. Go, Mimi – go with the boys. Take Christian and Hannah with you.'

Holding the hands of the two smallest children, Mimi ran off with the boys, all chattering excitedly. Arabella's head was suddenly aching as she sipped the special home-made Passover wine; she could feel the wine spread a warm fire through her body, but the violence and misery of her thoughts were now almost too much for her. She thought of the battlefields – of shells, guns, fire and flame. Everything she had, including herself, was nothing while she had to think of losing Deneys. She began to sweat between her shoulder-blades, though the big room was cool, and stared with unseeing eyes at the colourful Picasso painting on the opposite wall, as the talk resumed around her.

Louis found the hidden piece of matzo, and a quarrel broke out when Miriam, Isaac's sister, suggested he give the prize, which was a shining gold sovereign, to Mimi as his guest. Clutching the precious coin, Louis planted his two sturdy little legs apart and defiantly refused, whereupon Deneys laughingly protested that he keep it. The remaining matzo was distributed and eaten. The door was ceremonially opened and passages read from the Psalms by everyone, with Deneys' rich baritone rising above the rest.

As the fourth cup of wine was filled and the room resounded with voices reciting Psalms from the prayer books, the flickering flames caught the large lamp of beaten bronze hanging from the wooden vault of the ceiling, and burnished it in mottled light and shade.

Arabella felt a powerful bond with all those about the table, where she could sense the past feeding into the present and then out into the future. Her eyes fell on her small daughter, resembling in that moment some small exotic princess from an old fairytale, in her blue velvet dress with the lace collar, her hair gleaming in a magic of burnished gold, then went on to little red-haired Hannah, with her small enchanting face, and to Miriam's nineteen-year-old daughter Tirzah, whose warm black eyes seemed almost too large for her heart-shaped face. Arabella could see in these young girls a modernism that was not yet revealed, and suddenly she knew that her work was not over. She and Rachel were the synthesisers between the women of their day and these young women of the future, and this sense of continuity would breathe through their lives always. Intuitively, she knew that when this phase of her life was over, she would again take an active part in the suffrage movement, for it would always burn in her soul. Something was beginning to pound in her body, triumphant and vital. Her face flushed; she started to smile. Her work was not over, it had only just begun . . .

The voices in the room lifted unanimously with the words, 'Next year in Jerusalem!' Cups of wine were raised and the last blessings and prayers said, followed by traditional songs and the final song for which the children had been waiting all evening, about the little goat that Father bought for two coins, which had a seemingly endless amount of verses.

The happy, boisterous young voices which had never known war and violence rang through the room and laughing and clapping broke out as everyone rose from the table, and the candles were pinched out. There was a swish of violet skirts as Arabella stood up, and the lights in the glass chandelier were turned on.

Then Deneys was there, firm and reassuring, and as she gazed up at him, a warm smile started to play about her lips, and finally reached her eyes.

27

Park Station, Johannesburg. The sun of the early autumn afternoon shone almost defiantly through the glass roof, lending confidence to Arabella's small erect figure as she walked with Deneys, Christian and Mimi along the crowded platform. Samson, who had been determined to accompany his master, had already gone ahead the day before. A hush of anticipation hung over them and the bustle of activity, preceding the imminent departure of the train to Durban now waiting on the line. It had come, then, at last. The time for wishing and dreading was over, and there was nothing Arabella could do to put it off.

There was the sound of hissing steam, the occasional *thump-thump-thump* as a train pulled away from a platform, and a band drawn from one of the regiments played *Tipperary* – a new British war song. A small crowd of khaki-clad soldiers stopped to listen, and some began to sing bashfully in time with the music.

Deneys turned to her, looking remarkably handsome in the strange khaki Colonel's uniform, and pressed her hand.

'Bella, I'll keep in touch. If you don't hear from me for some time, don't worry – it'll only be because we are away from communications. By the end of next week, we should be off the boat and in German South West Africa. Samson will be there though I wish he'd stayed safely at home. He's getting too old for this kind of thing.' He looked down at her soberly. 'You are everything to me, darling.' The brown eyes above her would not let her turn away. 'Everything that has been good and beautiful and desirable in this world –'

'Oh Deneys, please! I cannot let you go on, because every word you say only makes it more difficult.' Tears rose and filled her eyes behind the pale-grey veil matching her small hat. They blurred his loving face, but she felt his hand, warm and strong and urgent, on her own.

'I trust the children into your care, my dear, until we meet again, and I know you'll not fail me.'

She nodded numbly, then said, 'Your poor old father was so

distressed when he thought you'd be fighting for the British.' She tried to smile. 'But the British will be only too delighted to have you on their side this time.'

Deneys smiled broadly. 'I am fighting *with* them, not *for* them, as I told Pa – remember that!'

The sudden hiss of couplings and a burst of all-enveloping steam hit the platform, which was thronged with khaki-clad figures carrying packs and rifles, crowding the space around them. Deneys hugged Mimi and comforted Christian as he cried at the sudden noise and confusion. Arabella watched their small son cling to his father. For the second time in her life, she was saying goodbye to a soldier she loved, going to war ...

'There they are!' Deneys exclaimed, a buzz of voices drowning his next words, as a group of people weaved their way through the crowd towards them. It was Isaac in uniform, and Rachel, her oval face troubled under the brim of her wide straw hat, followed by Ada the nanny bringing up the rear with the children. Arabella looked from face to face. They were old friends, and yet today, they seemed unfamiliar.

'Ah, Mimi!' The words rose involuntarily to Isaac's lips at the child's unconscious beauty. 'What a sight!'

Mimi was so young, yet suddenly all the innocent perfection of childhood seemed centred in her. Arabella had never known Isaac so drawn to a child, and she looked at her daughter now in Deneys' arms. Under the golden curls covered by the little jade velvet bonnet, the green eyes were clear, the small features firmly cut for all their softness. Such innocence and such directness of gaze – Arabella trembled and could not look away from the lovely child.

The hum of noise surged around them, then the small fingers were loosened from the khaki sleeve they had been clutching and Mimi was put gently down on the platform. Holding little Christian in the crook of her arm, Arabella felt her heart contract as the small girl came to her, and put her tiny warm hand into her mother's. The group about them retreated in a blur. People jostled each other in an effort to reach the train; couples hugged and kissed as farewells were cried and shouted.

The blur cleared before her eyes as she lifted them again to Deneys' face. She could have sketched his strong, handsome firm features, so vividly were they to remain with her.

One had to adapt to the present, she thought; it was futile to cling to the past. Her lips formed a smile, curving the generous fullness of her mouth as he bent his head and kissed her. Then he was gone with Isaac in a catch of khaki as soldiers everywhere swung packs on their backs and surged forward.

As she held Christian and clung to Mimi's damp little hand, Arabella could feel the hot press of bodies behind her, crushing her skirts, knocking the small hat askew, in eagerness to see over her head. Sometimes she saw eyes move and lips smile, and in that moment all individuality was lost. Then there was the waving of the green flag, and more farewells were called to the last-minute slamming of heavy doors. The whistle blew, quickening the pulse of all, and the train, smoothly and confidently accelerating, moved out. She could see Deneys' fair head emerging from one of the open windows.

And as he lifted his hand in farewell, she found herself responding to the parting. With Christian in her arms, and pulling Mimi along with her, she pushed forward, waving.